ROCHELLE ALLISON

TANLINES

The Sweet Spot

dedicated to summer love

Under the boardwalk,
down by the sea
On a blanket with my baby
is where I'll be

Contents

Acknowledgement

Big thank you to all of the incredible women who worked on this with me. I write stories like this for girls like you.

Mel, your grammatical prowess and brainy commentary are awe-inspiring. I do not know what I'd do without you! So much gratitude.

To my beta readers and ladies who read early on: Veronica D, Alanna H, Katie H, Kassiah F, Cecilia M, Korrie, Julie K, Rae W, Rachel S, Denise LM, Lauren D, Fran W, Kelli M, and Colleen W - THANK YOU for your time, your perspectives and your all around help.

Thanks to my love, André, and my boys Isaiah and Israel for being loving and supportive and believing in me even when I didn't believe in me.

Thank you God, for giving me the ability to write.

And thanks, Santa Cruz…for being such a dreamy place.

Wren

Summer

We've found a match!

Message From: Arlo Janvier

Subject: Hello, daughter!

Everything—the brisk, salty breeze, the frantic call of gulls, the sugary aroma of fried dough— disappears as I read the notification that's just popped up on my phone. I read it so many times the words stop making sense.

Daughter?

Hello *daughter?*

"Um, hi? Do you guys have swirl cones?"

There's a pink-haired girl across the counter. She reminds me of an anime character I saw once. She elbows the tall, skinny guy at her side, who looks like he's one bong rip away from a comatose nap. "What are you having? Chocolate? Strawberry?" She narrows her glittered eyes at me. "Do you guys do dipped cones?"

So. Many. Questions. Shoving away my own personal crisis, I beam a practiced grin of sunshine her way. "We sure do. Would you like one?"

"Actually, can I just get a cherry Icee?" she asks, tilting her head.

"Icee machine is on the fritz. Sorry." Giving her an apologetic smile, I point down the boardwalk. "There are other places around here that have them, though."

"Oh." She pauses, gaze drifting back to the Sweet Spot's menu as she taps her teeth with a long, hot pink nail that matches her hair. "I'll just take a vanilla cone, then. Dipped."

"Sure thing." I glance at Skinny. "Anything for you?"

"Wren," Rodrigo yells from the back. "Why is the Icee machine dripping? I thought you said Ronnie fixed it!"

"I'll take a chocolate," says Skinny, eyes skittering lazily over the menu above my head. "Extra, extra big. No dip."

"Wren!" Rodrigo's tremulous voice is right behind me this time, accompanied by a dreamy wave of cologne. Sometimes I pass by extra close just to sniff him.

Smiling politely at our customers, I turn and snatch two waffle cones from the holder. "Ronnie did fix it," I murmur, sliding past my adorable, but neurotic, manager. "I have no idea why it's dripping."

"*Pero*, didn't you notice?" he asks, thumbs flying over his phone as he follows me back to the counter. "It's pretty hard to miss."

"It's early. I haven't sold any Icees yet." I hand the plain chocolate ice cream cone over and nod at Anime Girl. "Dipped cone coming right up."

Rodrigo disappears again, probably to eviscerate Ronnie-the-handyman via text, and I procure my first dipped cone—it's an art form—of the day. Today's weather forecast promised clouds and rain this afternoon, but for now, the boardwalk's as bright and chipper as ever. Behind us, the gem-like blue of the Pacific shimmers and sparkles as a handful of surfers ride mid-sized waves.

Anime Girl barely says thank you as I hand off her picture-perfect ice cream, then she and her buddy wander off, absorbed by the mid-morning crowd in seconds. It's the first Saturday of summer break, so the Santa Cruz boardwalk is the place to be. By the time I leave for the day, it'll be near impossible to get the sounds of the boardwalk—screams of glee, laughter, top 40 hits—out of my head.

You'd think I'd be able to hear the ocean, as close as we are to it, but sometimes the boardwalk is just too loud.

My thoughts return to the notifications from Kith&Kin. I didn't tell Mom I was submitting my DNA. She's already suspicious of genealogy tech in general, convinced the government is using our info for more nefarious purposes. I mean, maybe they are.

But also, I didn't want her thinking I was looking for my dad. Because I wasn't, not specifically—she's enough parent for me. Swabbing my cheek and mailing the result to some suspect company with a coupon was equal parts summertime boredom and curiosity. Who am I? I know only that I'm half Greek from her side of the family.

But now it's matched me to some dude named Arlo who just might *actually* be my father and there's no one I want more than my mother.

Before I can freak out any worse, my phone vibrates silently in my pocket. Rodrigo doesn't like when we keep our phones on us, but I loathe feeling disconnected. I need to be able to reach my people.

Sure enough, it's my best friend Saira texting a picture of the beach at sunrise. The caption reads **you should be here** followed by a sobbing emoji.

Where was I this morning at sunrise? Oh yeah, drooling on my pillow… probably dreaming of beaches at sunrise. I rub at my chest, trying to tamp down the envy as I respond.

Wren: Wish I was there, too.
　You have no idea how much.

Saira's in Encinitas with her older sister, Janya. They go down every summer to visit their aunt and uncle, who have an enormous beach house. I usually go with them, but this year I had to drop out so I could work at the last minute. I'm still bitter.

Saira: You have any days off? Auntie Bina wants to know if you can make it down next Wednesday and stay the wknd. We'll come back up together.

I peek at Rodrigo, who's standing in the open back door, talking on the phone. The ocean sparkles dreamily in the distance.

4

Wren: No days off. Asha still has bronchitis and needs another week.

Saira: She's full of shit.

Wren: Yep.

Saira: That sucks :/

Wren: No kidding.

The hair on the back of my neck prickles, and I look up to find a pair of frumpy tourists staring at me. Sliding my phone back into my pocket, I bulldoze their salty frowns with a chipper grin. "Hi ladies! Sorry about that—family emergency. What can I get for you?"

When my lunch break rolls around, I peel off my apron and slip out the back, leaving Rodrigo and the new guy, Sean, to handle the rush. They'll be okay—Sean's a pro. We recruited him from Carousel Cones.

Ordering a trio of street tacos—carne asada and extra guacamole, always—and chips from my favorite spot on the boardwalk, I hustle down to the sand to eat. This is my favorite time of day, when I get to relax, staring at the water while stuffing my face. Little kids and families pepper the beach, caught up in the wonder of summer. A group of girls lounges to my left, taking countless pictures and spritzing each other with tanning oil. Can't lie; I kind of envy them.

Yanking my sneakers off, then my socks, I bury my toes in the sand just to remind myself that there are worse places I could be working. And then, taking a deep, grateful breath, I tuck into my tacos. *So good.* I wonder if Arlo Janvier likes tacos…although, with a name like that, maybe he prefers escargot.

Maybe I'd know if I read his message. I can't, though. Not here in public, on the beach, and maybe not ever. What if he's a perv? A serial killer? A politician? I try to love on everybody, but my bleeding-heart liberal of a mother would die.

I'm halfway through my second taco when my phone bursts into Fleetwood Mac's "Dreams". Mom's ringtone. Wiping my mouth, I bring the phone to my ear.

"Hey, Mom. How'd you know I was on break?" I ask, though we all know she has a knack for 'knowing'. Fingers crossed she doesn't suddenly know about Arlo.

"Lucky guess," she says. "How's it going today? Anything interesting happen?"

"Not really. It's the same as every day," I lie, wondering if her spidey-mom senses are tingling.

Out on the waves, a surfer loses his balance and topples into the cold water. I shiver in empathy. Even during the summer, that water's frigid.

Mom pauses. "I know you're still upset about not being able to go with the girls, but I'll make it up to you. I really appreciate you helping out this summer."

It takes me a moment to respond, thanks to the sudden lump in my throat. "I know."

"I'm supposed to be taking care of you, little bird." Her voice is so pained that I'm simultaneously annoyed and filled with guilt I'm making her feel bad.

I drag a tortilla chip through my salsa. "Mom, it's fine." And it would be, if we could just stop talking about it. Life is real, not fair. "It's not your fault."

"Darius is coming to dinner tonight," she blurts. Soothing, instrumental music tinkles softly in the background. "Is that okay?"

"Of course, it's okay," I say. What she should really be concerned with is the fact she just invited her chef-boyfriend to dinner when she can't cook, but I keep that thought to myself.

"Good, good. I didn't want you to be caught off-guard. I saw him at the farmers' market earlier today and one thing led to another, so. You know."

"I do know." Mom and Darius have had a *thing* for each other ever since he brought his niece to the studio for Youth Yoga three years ago. You'd think they'd be past the tiptoeing by now, but she has a habit of holding guys at arm's length.

A gust of wind tosses a bunch of my chips onto the sand. Cursing inwardly, I scoop them onto a napkin. "Mom, I gotta go."

"Oh, okay. Love you, Wren."

"Love you, too." I disconnect and shove my phone back into the pocket of my shorts, allowing myself a short sulk.

This summer was supposed to be a fabulous, sun-soaked interlude between high school and college. Janya, Saira and I planned to start in Encinitas and work our way up the coast, stopping at a handful of chosen beach town Airbnbs. I'd been scrimping all school year, sticking to thrift shop clothes, saving the money I'd made from tutoring and my after-school job at the boardwalk, so we could have this summer.

But then May came. And the rent on my mother's yoga studio skyrocketed without warning, thanks to our shitty, new landlords. As if that wasn't enough, Mom's elderly Corolla decided it needed a new transmission and just like that, her savings—and mine—were gone. She hadn't wanted my money, but she'd needed it.

Who was I to argue with the universe when it was giving me such a big, flashing CANCELED sign?

Thankfully, classes start at UC Santa Cruz during the last week of August, and I've got a full ride. It's the one bright spot in this dark cloud of blah, and no one can take it away from me.

* * *

Back at the Sweet Spot, the line is about eight deep and poor Sean's up to his eyeballs in soft serve. Rodrigo's nowhere to be found, but Ronnie's back at the Icee machine, trying in vain to fix it.

"Thank God," Sean says when he sees me, his cheeks red with exertion. "I need three chocolate dips and one regular chocolate with sprinkles."

"Coming right up." I throw myself into the fray, going deep into the frozen zone. I can't say I enjoy slinging ice cream and churros, but time flies when it's this busy.

Finally, the family we're serving walks away with cones and smiles. Sean sinks against the counter. "I need a smoke."

I tilt my head toward the back. "Go ahead; I'm good."

"You're an angel," he mutters, pushing a hand through his curly, dark hair. He disappears out the back door and I turn to the counter, leaning on it.

A rogue breeze kicks up, sending napkins and straw wrappers flying down the boardwalk like confetti. My hand's inching toward my pocket to sneak-text Saira when four guys wander up to the Sweet Spot.

The one leading the charge, a red-headed freckle face in a tank top, leers up at the sign and then at me. "Sweet Spot, huh? Does that refer to this place or you?"

It's not the worst I've heard, but I won't dignify it with a response. Biting the inside of my cheek, I take a step back and wait for him and his friends to either order or keep on going.

"You're such a dick." A built, happy-go-lucky blond guy in boardshorts elbows his buddy aside, grinning as he slides a crinkled ten toward me. He looks just a little stoned, and I swallow a laugh. "Can I get a cotton candy, please, pretty please?"

"Of course, you can." Taking the money, I turn to make change at the register. "Can I get you guys anything else?"

"Yeah—your number, Sweet Spot," the redhead calls out.

"Shut the fuck up, Matty." This, coming from the tallest of the crew as he gazes impassively at the menu. He's got wavy, brown hair and light eyes, but it's the UCSC Banana Slugs t-shirt that catches my eye. That'll be me in a few months. "Can I get an Icee?"

Straightening, I glance back to where poor Ronnie is still fighting with the stupid Icee machine. Either he heard the question, or he feels my stare burning into him, because he looks back and shakes his head.

"Sorry, but our machine's been broken all day," I say to the tall one as his eyes flicker away. I suspect he may have been checking me out. He's good looking, albeit probably as high as his blond buddy, who's really going to town on that cotton candy. "There's a place down by the carousel that has them, though."

"Nah, just gimme a Sprite." He frowns, rustling through his wallet. "You want anything, Luca?"

I grab a cup and pause, waiting while the last of the foursome, another tall, dark, and handsome, stares down at his phone, thoroughly engrossed. He looks like the kind of guy that would spend an entire day on the waves.

"Luca," Tall Guy drawls, exhaling an impatient, drawn-out sigh.

"Hmm?" Luca looks up slowly, blinking at his friend and then at me.

I see hot, fit guys all the time around here, on the beach and on the boardwalk, but this one's something else. With his dark tan, light brown eyes, and a head full of silky, black hair pulled up into a bun, he's not just hot. He's just *wow*.

Then he smiles, just a little, and it's like the sun coming out to play on an already gorgeous day.

10

Luca

⁓⚬⚬⁓

I glance up from my phone just in time to dodge a family led by an older, rather rotund gentleman in a Hawaiian shirt and Burt Reynolds sunglasses. He glares at my phone and then me, scoffing as he tugs his wife along.

Grimacing, I slide my phone into the back pocket of my shorts. I get the attitude, but it's not like I'm some fourteen-year-old playing mobile video games—I'm waiting on an email from my father. He wants me to come to São Paulo, Brazil, for a summer internship. I'm already coming for fall semester, so summer's not really in my plans, but Pai's a hotshot in the software sector over there. If he wants me to head over a few months early, I owe it to him to at least consider it.

And then there's Brooke, the blonde I met in my econometrics class last semester. We've been flirting via text since classes ended, but when I asked her out last night, she left me on read. I'm not too worried—she's made her interest clear—but I'd like to see her, maybe tonight.

So, I have reasons for being glued to my phone. Still, I'm sure I look like half the adolescent douchebags stumbling blindly around the boardwalk, faces lit up by screens.

Inhaling deeply, I take in the smells, sights, and sounds of the Santa Cruz boardwalk. Funny thing is, I came here way more as a kid living in the Bay Area than I have as a college student attending UCSC. I have a treasure trove of pure childhood memories of days just like today, bright blue skies and puffy white clouds, that cool, sharp breeze whipping in off the water.

My heart tugs a little as one of the surfers out on the water catches a wave. It's been a long, hectic school year, and I haven't been surfing for a minute. I elbow Kellan, gazing longingly at the wide strip of blue expanse out beyond the sand. "Let's hit up Pleasure Point soon."

"Tomorrow," he agrees, flicking his blond hair from his face. Out of all my friends, he likes surfing the most, maybe because he grew up here.

Up ahead, Matt's pointedly checking out a petite brunette who's stopped to lick the ice cream dripping from her cone to her wrist. Her chest is as big as she is small—Matt's kryptonite—but she's with a couple of guys, so I yank homeboy along by the arm before he gets us into a fight. He hasn't even started drinking yet, and already he's in a mood.

"I'm thirsty as fuck," Logan says, dropping into step with me. "Kinda hungry, too."

"Thanks to your little wake n' bake." I shake my head, remembering his and Kellan's shenanigans this morning involving the bong. "You talk to your girl yet?"

"Nope." Logan narrows his eyes, scanning the never-ending parade of food stands. "I'd kill for a slushie or an Icee or something right now."

Kellan glances back over his shoulder, his eyes as glazed as Logan's. "Slushies and Icees are the same thing, man."

Logan yawns, stretching. "Whatever. I just know I need something before we go on the Giant Dipper. The cottonmouth struggle is real."

I grab compulsively for my phone, scrolling quickly to my email account. A promo for some new pizza place in Santa Cruz, an email from a classmate about summer study groups, a reminder from the dentist to schedule my next checkup…and, finally, the email about the internship from Pai.

Chewing my lip, I debate whether or not to open it. Admittedly, I was half hoping he'd just let it go, but I know better. He never lets anything go. *Shit.*

"Shut the fuck up, Matty," I hear Logan say, followed by snickering. Ignoring the guys, I open the email.

To: Luca Cardoso

From: Carlos Cardoso

Subject: Pereira Internship

Luca,
 Spoke to Pereira this morning; he'd like to have you start by mid-June.
 I'm holding a flight for you, leaves next week. You'll be staying at the apartment in Jardins.
 Will call you later to finalize plans.
 Pai

Attached are my flight reservations and a brief overview from Marcos Pereira's secretary, explaining the specifics of the internship.

My stomach knots up as I scan the flight details. I love Brazil, but if I leave now, I won't be home until Christmas.

"Luca," snaps Logan. He's frowning faintly, a wrinkle deepening between his eyebrows. Whoops. He's probably been trying to get my attention for a minute.

We're at the Sweet Spot, one of a zillion places on the boardwalk selling ice cream and whatever else people with the munchies are craving. The girl behind the counter stares up at me, a patient smile curving her lips. With her light eyes, long ponytail, and light gold tan, she's kind of beautiful.

I smile back, caught off guard.

Logan exhales, the very picture of longsuffering. "I asked you what you wanted."

"Um." I squint up at the menu. "I'll have an Icee."

"No can do." She wrinkles her nose, bringing my attention to the smattering of freckles sprinkled across it. "Machine's not working. Sorry."

"She literally just said that, dude," Matt says with a snort, tossing a smirk my way.

Her fingers go to a gold charm hanging from her necklace. Her eyes, though…she keeps those on me.

I smile at her, real direct. "I'll just have a churro, then. Thanks."

She nods, and I watch as she walks away, appreciating how nicely her ass fills out her shorts. Our eyes meet again as she hands the churro over. She's got a little dimple on one cheek that deepens reflexively when I smile at her. "How much do I owe you?"

"I got it," Logan says, slapping a twenty down.

I take a bite of warm, soft, sugary churro. It tastes like childhood, sweeping a powerful wave of nostalgia over me.

"Thanks," Logan's saying, sliding the change she gives him into his pocket. He gives her a five-dollar bill. "Here's a tip for dealing with these losers."

"You don't have to…"

"Please," says Logan, winking at her. I narrow my eyes, wondering what his angle is, but she laughs, shaking her head as she pockets the bill.

Logan turns to go, slurping contentedly at his soda, but I glance at the girl, my words flowing before I've consciously decided to release them. "Hey, can I get another one, please?"

I watch as she goes to get it, and this time, she catches me staring. Her cheeks flush, but she lifts her chin as she hands over the churros. "Here, I gave you two."

Yeah, the feeling's definitely mutual.

"What's your name?" I ask, handing over my debit card.

She mashes her lips together as she slides it through the card reader at the register. "Wren."

"Like the bird," I say stupidly, eyes falling to the little, gold bird on her necklace. I bet she hears that all the time.

"Like the bird," she echoes, a wry grin surfacing. She returns my card along with an extra napkin.

"You hear that about ten times a day, don't you," I guess, leaning on the counter.

Nodding, she tucks a loose curl behind her ear where she's got a row of tiny earrings, glittering gems of various colors. "Maybe like…five times a day."

"Well, I'm Luca," I say, offering my hand.

She accepts. "Hey, Luca."

"Hey." I rub my thumb over her hand, holding it lightly.

This close up, I can see that her upturned eyes aren't just green. They're ringed with gray, like the beach on a bright day that's hinting at rain, framed by long, dark lashes.

"Lucaaaaa," Matt yells, in an obnoxious, artificially high voice that carries well above the din of the crowd.

I swing my head around, annoyed. The guys are shuffling aimlessly, waiting for me to bring my ass over so we can start going on rides. *Come on.* Like they've never tried to holler at a cutie. I'll have to have a chat with them about their cockblocking ways.

"I guess I have to go." I release her hand, watching as she smiles. "See you around, Wren."

"Bye." She takes a step back, hitching her thumbs into her pockets. Thin, silver bangles and friendship bracelets of all colors line her wrists. She's

16

a fresh-faced beach girl through and through, and those shorts are sweet, but I'd love to see her in a bikini. Hopefully she goes to UCSC and not the local high school.

I'd ask for her number, but the timing feels off. I'll either be working at a firm in Berkeley this summer or heading to Brazil for summer *and* fall. There's just no time for hanging out at the boardwalk. Besides, should I be flirting with this girl when I'm still wondering about another?

"You got a sweet spot for Sweet Spot?" jokes Matt, eyeing my snacks as I join the group.

"Maybe." I offer him a churro, which he accepts and polishes off in two bites.

"Yeah, bro, she was cute," Kellan says approvingly, raising an eyebrow. "You thinkin' about it?"

"I don't know." Shrugging, I finish eating and chuck my napkin into a nearby trash can. "Pretty for sure, though."

"Hey, if you're not interested, I might just go back," Matt says, making like he's about to turn around.

Laughing, I hook my arm around his neck and keep him moving forward—away from the "Sweet Spot" and toward the Giant Dipper. "Never said I wasn't interested."

"Nah, asshole," he half-yells, earning a look of horror from a trio of elderly ladies passing by. "You know the rules. No lockin' it down if you're not gonna make the play."

"He's holding out for Brooke," Logan says dryly, cutting me a look.

"Brooke? Not that prissy bitch from Kappa Kappa whatever?" Matt squirms from my grip as he frowns at me.

I sigh, giving him the side-eye. "Watch your mouth, Matty."

"Watch your own mouth. Something about her feels shady." He shrugs. "She was at that pool party last week, all over some guy—"

That sucks, but I interrupt him anyway. "We're not together—she can do whatever she wants."

"Nah, bro, I'm telling you—she's a player." Matt sniffs. "She acted like she didn't even see me when I know she did."

My phone vibrates with a notification. I yank it out, but it's just my little brother Daniel, asking about the Xbox in my old room. Sighing, I text back that he can take it.

"Can't play a player," I continue, folding my arms as I lean against the wall.

"Player, huh? She know that?" Logan asks, arching an eyebrow as he slurps away at his soda.

"You focus on Olivia," I shoot back. That's the longtime girlfriend with whom he's been fighting nonstop, hence all the herb he smoked this morning. I poke Matt, too, not about to let him off the hook. "And you. You need to go ahead and get laid."

Matt perks up, a sly look glittering in his pale, blue eyes. "By who, Sweet Spot?"

"Her name's Wren," I say, shoving him ahead. "And no, not by her."

"Listen to you, being all possessive and shit!" he crows. "I knew you were feeling her!"

"Shut up, Matty."

But he's right. I am feeling her.

Wren

The sun's still pretty high in the sky when I clock out. Waving goodbye to Sean and Rodrigo, I slip out the back door and thread leisurely through the crowd. I've been working after school and summer jobs at Santa Cruz boardwalk since I was fifteen, but this moment—trading employee status for that of a tourist—always feels like heaven. I love this place.

Sliding my backpack on, I hoof it over to the main parking lot. It's packed as always, people coming and going. I find my little, green Civic hatchback, and getting in, text my mother.

Wren: *Do you need anything from the store?*

She rarely has her phone on her, so I probably have a few minutes before she replies. Choosing my latest favorite playlist, I get my daily parking ticket validated and head out onto Beach Street. Sure enough, I'm halfway to the apartment by the time Mom replies.

Mom: *I've got everything I need, little bird. Thx.*

20

Santa Cruz isn't just where I live, it's in my blood. My mother grew up here, and Gramma Kate still lives in the same Boulder Creek house she raised Mom in.

My father's the only outlier, I guess.

According to Mom, after years of unsatisfactory relationships dating losers and idiots, she drove down to Los Angeles on a whim and got artificially inseminated. She wouldn't call it a whim, by the way, but I suspect it was. She'd just turned thirty. It's not like she was getting old and running out of time, even if she felt that way.

"I didn't need some guy, Wren. I just wanted you," she said, when I asked once why she didn't just wait until she found The One. I don't know why I bothered. She's never found men particularly necessary. "Besides, 'The One' doesn't exist, and even if he did, I probably wouldn't have found him until my ovaries were shriveled."

When I was little, Mom and I lived in a tiny studio apartment within walking distance of the beach. I remember some things about it, like the tiny swing set out front and walking to the grocery store. Mom and I spent her days off at the beach, having picnics and looking for shells. Gramma Kate was still teaching over at UCSC in those days.

I pass our favorite farmers' market, the place I got my ears pierced when I was seven, the skate park where I broke my arm when I was nine. There's Mom's yoga studio, closed for the day, and the preschool she took me to when she finally opened that studio. The way she tells it, she cried more than I did—I was just psyched to see all the other kids and toys.

Pulling into the apartment complex we've lived in for the past decade, I bypass my usual spot—occupied by an inconsiderate doofus despite our apartment number stamped on it—and park beside a rusted-out beater that's been rotting there for months.

I'm hit by a blast of seasoning smells the second I walk in the door…mostly curry and cumin, Mom's favorites. I like them too, but I'm not sure how I feel about them together. Wrinkling my nose, I kick off my shoes and drop my bag on the couch. "I'm home!"

No response. Venturing into the kitchen, I take note of the sliced French bread, the chopping board full of vegetable scraps, and the pot on the stove, set at a low simmer. God knows what's in there. Woven placemats and fancy silverware decorate our table, a teal relic we rescued from a garage sale back in middle school. Mismatched, multicolored chairs surround it. This set-up kind of embarrassed me when I was younger and obsessed with what other people thought, but I love it now.

"Little bird's flown home," coos Mom, sweeping into the kitchen with cheek kisses and caresses. She's in faded, worn, bell bottom jeans and a flowy, purple blouse. Her dark, waist-length hair falls down her back in soft waves. Maybe it's the yoga, but I swear the woman doesn't age.

"Hey Mom." I tug at my necklace, wondering if I should tell her about Arlo Janvier now or later. *Definitely later.* I give her a quick hug instead. "I'm gonna go take a shower. What time is Darius coming over?"

"Not for a couple of hours." She waves me off, one silky sleeve of her blouse coming dangerously close to the contents of her simmering pot. "You have plenty of time—come, come. Tell me about your day."

Grimacing, I lean in the doorway, half in and half out of the kitchen. This conversation was a lot more satisfying when I was in elementary school and not perpetually feeling sorry for myself. "Same stuff, different day. You know how the boardwalk gets. People everywhere."

"Hmm." Nodding, she adds a generous sprinkling of what might be turmeric to her creation. "Anything stand out?" She glances at me, eyes narrowing. "Anyone?"

Luca and his caramel-colored eyes come to mind. He stood out, all right. "Not really."

"I don't believe you. There are so many stories out there—you just have to open your eyes."

"Okay, so there was this one guy," I hedge. "Luca."

"Luca!" She tosses a grin over her shoulder. "I love that name! It was on my short list had you been a boy!"

"Really? Weird."

She laughs, nodding. "Isn't it? The universe loves a good coincidence. Tell me about him."

"I mean, I don't know much. He came with some friends, and I sold him a couple of churros."

Setting the spoon down, she turns to face me, an expectant half-smile gracing her lips. "And?"

"And he was gorgeous." I shrug. "Like really, really gorgeous. That's it."

"You know his name, so obviously he asked for yours." She arches an eyebrow. "Right?"

My face warms, completely negating the nonchalant vibe I'm trying to put out.

"Of course, he did." She smirks, pointing at me. "He'll be back, mark my words."

I try to ignore the thrill of anticipation that zings through my body at her prophetic words, but it's near impossible. I would love to see Luca again, so I want to believe what she's saying. But also (and I really, really, try to ignore it so as not to encourage her), she's a tad clairvoyant and usually right about stuff like this.

"What is that?" I ask, nodding my chin at the pot.

"Stew mushrooms and cauliflower, from Trinidad. I got the recipe from Adrika," she says. "I just made a few modifications."

God help us. This isn't the first time she's attempted a recipe from Saira's mom.

Later, after a long, hot shower, I wrap my hair in a towel and flop onto my bed. Staring up at vintage concert posters half covering my turquoise ceiling, I allow visions of Luca's dreamy, bedroom eyes to float through my mind. I hope my mother's right.

I hope he does come back.

* * *

Darius, bless him, eats his bastardized Trinidadian dish with the enthusiasm of the smitten. Smitten with my mother, that is, not the stew. They've been friends for years, but I've always felt like my mother and Darius were going to end up together. Not just dating or fooling around or whatever they do that I don't want to think about, but *together*.

I wish my mom would just give him a chance. A real chance.

On first glance, you'd think they were opposites. He's so tall he practically has to duck when he comes in the door, his skin so dark it gleams like mahogany. Mom's petite—I certainly didn't inherit her size—and pale, her freckled, peachy skin prone to burning.

But they both love good wine and old jazz, farmers' markets, and daytrips along the coast. He's grounded and she's flighty and they just work.

"So, how's it going down at the boardwalk?" he asks, sipping the wine he brought for dinner.

"It's cool." I shrug, pushing the last of my food around my plate. "Easy money, I guess."

"Lily tells me you open most days." He leans back, flipping his long locs over one shoulder. "I used to prefer opening. Meant I had a couple of daylight hours to myself at the end of the day, something I can't do lately."

"Yeah, exactly." This is true; if I have to work a job like the Sweet Spot, at least I can get it over and done with as soon as possible every day. "Although, Holy Basil's not exactly slumming it."

He chuckles, nodding. Darius is head chef at one of the most popular—and expensive—boutique restaurants in Santa Cruz. He and his innovative fare have been featured in local and regional magazines alike. "No, not exactly. We all gotta pay our dues, though."

His gentle chastisement rings true, and as he and Mom share a gentle smile, I feel the knot of frustration in my chest dissolve. "You're right."

"You'll be all right," he adds. "Think of these as character building days, okay?"

* * *

On Friday, I'm wiping down the now operational Icee machine during the afternoon shift when a familiar, husky voice calls my name.

I turn to find a grinning Saira standing on the other side of the counter. "You're not supposed to be back!" I cry, dropping my rag.

"Guess I better leave again, then," she teases, sticking out her tongue. She got it pierced last spring break, so she's always doing that now. Her mother would kill her if she found out.

Laughing, I pull her closer. I can't believe she's here. "Seriously, what're you doing here?"

She grins, cocking her head. "I missed you, obviously."

Checking to make sure the coast is clear, I quickly duck out the back of the Sweet Spot and snatch my best friend into a hug. She gives me a hardcore squeeze, nearly lifting me off the ground. Saira's strong as hell, thanks to over a decade of softball.

"You have no idea how glad I am to see you." I swallow the melodramatic lump in my throat. "When did you guys get back?"

"Late last night." She pushes her long, glossy black braid back over her shoulder. "And it's just me. Janya's still in Encinitas."

"Did something happen?"

"Not really." She cocks her hip, sticking her hand onto it. Some of my earliest memories are of Saira Mangal, standing just like this on the playground at school…usually telling someone off. "I suggested we skip the whole coastal tour thing since you were stuck here. I was like, 'let's do it over spring break,' and she was like, 'totally' and then she hooked up with some white boy she met on the beach. Justin or Jason or something."

"For real?"

She rolls her eyes. "You know my parents will freak when they find out."

"I still can't believe you cut things short." I'm so glad she did, though. I'm seconds from weeping tears of gratitude. "You didn't have to do that."

"It just wasn't the same without you." She squeezes my hand. "Anyway, it all works out. Daddy's personal secretary had to go for emergency surgery, so he needs someone to take calls down at the car lot. I'll be riding into the office every morning with Anik."

"*You*, work?"

"You know Daddy; he thinks it's high time I learn the family business," she says. "He says I need marketable skills."

The Mangal family owns a luxury car dealership over on auto row. Saira's older brother Anik has been working there since he graduated from college and will take over one day. Janya's in pre-med at Berkeley and Saira's the little princess of the family. I never thought I'd see her actually working a summer job.

"He thinks you're a great example, by the way," she adds.

"Selling churros and ice cream?" I ask flatly.

"No!" She pokes my stomach. "Working hard, saving, and helping your family. He's so proud of you it's ridiculous."

"I love your dad." I lean back against the counter. "How'd you know I was here, anyway? You didn't text."

"Lucky guess," she says. "I mean, where else would you be?"

"True, true."

"When do you get off?"

"Never, if she doesn't get her lazy behind on the other side of this counter," snips Rodrigo, appearing from nowhere like an evil wraith.

Rolling my eyes, I follow him to the back door. "Four o'clock. You wanna come meet me?"

"Text me. I'll be running errands for the parents, but I'll come back. Maybe we can ride the Sky Glider."

Heart light, I return to my post. I'd been doing a pretty decent job of convincing myself I was okay, but having Saira back makes a huge difference.

Rodrigo leans on the counter beside me, eyeing me. "Asha quit."

"That sucks, but I'm not surprised," I admit. "Sorry."

"I was going to fire her, anyway. Ronnie said he saw her out with friends one of the days she called in sick," he says, massaging his temples. I swear,

28

Rodrigo is twenty-something going on fifty-something. "I'd offer your friend the job, but you two would never get any work done."

* * *

Saira groans, peeking through her fingers. "God, I hate this thing!"

"Don't look down, then," I say with a laugh. "It was your idea!"

We're on the Sky Glider, a ride reminiscent of a ski lift that brings people from one end of the boardwalk to the other. It's slow and scenic, but not the best option for people like Saira, who are afraid of heights.

Me? I love the Sky Glider. Always have. Gramma Kate and I used to buy huge clouds of cotton candy and then eat them while riding. The best was during sunset, when the water looked gold and lights began to twinkle around the park like neon stars.

I glance down at my dangling feet, remembering her voice in my ear. *"We're flying, aren't we, little bird?"*

"Is it almost done?" Saira whispers, squirming beside me.

"Yup." I link my arm through hers. "Just a few more seconds, and..." Our feet drift down to the platform, where an attendant quickly lifts the restraint and helps us off. "Why'd you even go on?" I laugh, tugging a lock of Saira's hair.

"Because you love that thing," she says. "And I bet you haven't been on since you started working this summer."

"You would be correct." Kissing her cheek, I tug her back down the boardwalk. "Let's go on the Giant Dipper. I know you love that one."

Everyone loves the Giant Dipper. It's one of the oldest, and most iconic, roller coasters in the country. The temperature's started dropping, so I pull my hoodie from my backpack and slide it on over my head. My shorts do nothing for warmth, but as long as my chest and arms are covered, I'm okay.

Saira and I ride twice in a row, then schlep on over to Fisherman's Galley for some of their legendary fish n' chips.

"So, remember that Kith&Kin thing I was thinking about doing? Where they run your DNA sample?" I dip a french fry into the dish of tartar sauce that came with my meal.

Saira nods, her mouth full.

"The results came back the other day," I say. "And...I think it found my father."

Her eyes widen, and she hurriedly swallows. "Are you serious? Why didn't you tell me?!"

"I just did!"

"Well, who is he? What did he say?"

I grimace, shrugging. "I—I don't know. I haven't read his message yet."

"What? Wren! This is what you wanted!" she scolds, reaching across the table to poke my hand. "Why haven't you read his message?"

30

"It's too weird, Saira! What if it's a mistake and I get my hopes up…or what if it is him and he's a total weirdo?" I moan, closing my eyes. "Mom is going to have a conniption fit."

"Chill, babe," she says, stroking my hand. "One step at a time. Let's look at the message together."

Taking a deep breath, I dig around my bag until I find my phone. I pull up the app, sign in, and navigate over to the communication corner, where a little red balloon announces that I have two unread messages. My heart starts pounding, and despite the fresh breeze, I feel shaky and hot.

Saira pulls her chair to my side of the table and presses the first message. It's from Kith&Kin itself, informing me that my sample's been processed and that the results are in if I want to examine my connections.

The next message is "Hello, daughter!" from Arlo Janvier.

Saira peers at me, finger poised and ready to click. "Ready?"

"Do it," I rasp.

Hi Wren,

I hope this letter finds you well, and I hope it's okay that I messaged you.

I started using this site at my friend's urging. He recently connected with a whole slew of Swedish cousins and aunts and uncles. He didn't even know he was Swedish.

Anyway, imagine my surprise when my results turned up a daughter… although I suppose I should have known there was a chance you existed.

I'd love to hear from you, and maybe meet you one day, but I understand if that makes you uncomfortable. I can only assume that since you are also using this site you were looking, too.

Yours,
  Arlo
  (Dad?)

P.S. I'm not Swedish. I'm French. (French American.)

* * *

"He seems normal," Saira muses as we stroll the shore, our bare feet covered in a wash of cold, foamy seawater. "Sweet, even."

I finger the sharp little wings on my wren necklace, thinking about Arlo's tentative words. "He does. Thanks for reading with me."

She cuts me a half-smile, leaning affectionately into me. "You gonna answer him?"

"I think so. I just need to chew on it for a while."

She nods. "You should. Think about it, I mean."

Shading my eyes against the sun, I squint down the beach to where a crowd is beginning to form. "Hey, do you want to hang around until the movie?" I ask, feeling nostalgic. It's Friday, and the boardwalk always shows free movies on the beach when the sun goes down. "They're showing *The Lost Boys* again."

The Lost Boys was filmed at the Santa Cruz boardwalk back in the 80's, so it's a crowd favorite that airs every summer here. I've lost track of how many times my friends and I have seen it right down on this very beach.

"We haven't done that in forever! I'm so down." Saira does a little leap, kicking up sprays of sand. "But only if we can watch the sunset first."

"Deal." Leaving the water behind, we head for an empty spot farther up. I procure a blanket from my bag, smirking when Saira does the same. We're beach girls, born and bred.

Saira lies beside me, sighing contentedly. "Remember when you had your eleventh birthday party out here?"

"When my mom made those wretched vegan cupcakes and forgot the sugar?" I cringe, remembering.

"Yes!" Saira cackles, slapping her thigh. "And then Missy Callahan's dad started making balloon animals until some lady shouted at us and said that balloons were bad for the environment and we should be ashamed of ourselves!"

"The one in the muumuu? I forgot all about that!" I cry, laughing until tears stream down my cheeks. "Whatever happened to—"

Something smacks my ankle, hard. Startled, I sit up on my elbows to see a bright, green soccer ball at my feet.

"Sorry, sorry!" a guy yells, jogging over. The sun is behind him, so I can't quite make out his face, but then he says, "Sweet Spot?" and I totally know.

* * *

"Sweet Spot?" Saira's expression hovers between fascination and disgust.

"Wren," I say crisply, eyeing the rowdy redheaded guy from the other day. "My name is Wren."

"Wren, huh? I'm Matt." His bright eyes light up as they travel down my bare legs. "Fancy seeing you here, although not really since you work, like, five feet away."

My heart flip-flops in my chest, but only because the rest of his crew have begun to roll up. And Luca's among them, looking like *such* a snack in a pair of low-slung gray sweatpants and a black t-shirt that shows off his muscles. I'd almost forgotten just how pretty he was. Three girls walk by, tripping over themselves as they pretend not to notice.

Luca tucks his hands into his pockets, smiling down at me contritely. I'll bet that smile's gotten him off the hook a million times. "Hey, Wren. Sorry about the ball."

"No worries." I'm just surprised he remembers my name.

"Don't let him off the hook so easy, Sweet Spot. He launched that damn thing like this was the World Cup," complains Matt. One of their friends, the blond from the other day, wraps an arm around his neck and pulls him away. I remember him, too—he had cotton candy. They shove each other around for a minute before resuming their game.

"He's right." Luca grimaces, sheepishly clasping his hands behind his head. His hair's in a bun again. I wonder how long it is. "I really am sorry."

"It barely hit me," I lie, my heart fluttering crazily. *For God's sake, Wren. He is just a guy. A really, really cute guy.*

Saira squirms beside me, nearly bursting with curiosity. Before I can eke out some sort of awkward introduction, Luca bends down, offering her his hand. "Hey, I'm Luca."

"Saira," she says slowly, giving his hand a hearty shake. She glances between us. "How do you guys know each other?"

I shade my eyes against the sun. "They came by the stand last week."

"I came back, you know, but you'd left." Luca tilts his chin at me. "They said you'd already clocked out."

"Oh really? Huh. Yeah, I usually just work the first shift." My casual voice does a pretty good job of hiding my soaring heart. He came back? Rodrigo and Sean didn't even tell me, those jerks.

He gazes steadily down at me, a little smile playing at his mouth, giving me a horrible case of butterflies. "What're you guys getting into later?"

I look at Saira, who smirks back at me. "We were thinking of catching the movie," she says, jerking her thumb toward the growing crowd over by the boardwalk. "Why?"

The slowly setting sun hovers just over the water, highlighting Luca's eyes in gold. A shiver works through me, and it's not just from the sharp breeze cutting across the sand. "Want company?" he asks.

I sneak a guilty peek Saira's way. "Do we?"

"Of course, we do." She stands, stretching. "But I'm gonna go to the bathroom, so watch my stuff."

Luca brazenly takes her place as she walks away, dropping onto her blanket and stretching out. He smells so good, like laundry detergent and something earthy and soft. Sandalwood, maybe.

"I have that hoodie," he says.

I smile a little, looking down at my black hoodie. It's the one with the iconic "classic dot" Santa Cruz logo emblazoned across the front. Every local has this hoodie. Shoot, most tourists have it, too. "Who doesn't?" I tease.

"Mine's old and falling apart." He chuckles.

"I've been through so many of these." I touch my fingers to the fabric. "I even went through a phase in middle school where I had it in pink and white."

"Of course, you did."

We share a smile. Matt jogs by, kicking up sand as he chases the ball.

"You go to UCSC?" asks Luca, balancing his forearms on his bent knees as he gazes out at the water.

Pride and excitement surge through me. "I will be. I start this August."

He raises his thick eyebrows. "You're a freshman?"

I nod, hoping that's not some sort of deal breaker, and tuck my knees in. "You?"

"Yeah, I'm at Santa Cruz," he says. "I'll be a junior."

My stomach tightens in anticipation of seeing him on campus. I can already imagine finagling ways to study with him.

"But I'm spending the fall semester abroad, in Brazil," he adds, almost as an afterthought.

I lean back to look at him. "Brazil? Are you serious?" Here I am, trying to get used to the idea of living in a dorm a few miles from my house, and this guy's moving halfway across the world.

He nods. "There's an architecture and urbanism program with the Federal University of Santa Catarina in Florianópolis."

"Are you majoring in that?"

"Architecture's my major." He cups his hand around the back of his neck. "I'm also minoring in software engineering."

"Whoa." I cock my head, intrigued. "Those two things sound quite different from one another."

"They are." He huffs softly. "What about you? What're you studying?"

"Cognitive science…with a focus on psychology." I feel like such a poseur saying this out loud, like a little girl playing make-believe. College has always been a far-off dream, and now it's right around the corner. "I think I want to be a therapist."

But Luca just grins. "Psych classes are fun. I took a couple my first year, too."

Out on the sand, the soccer game continues. The blond guy from the other day—cotton candy—volleys the soccer ball, deftly keeping it away from Matt.

"I guess so." Taking a deep breath, I shake my head. "I'm kind of nervous about it."

"I'd tell you not to be, but everyone's nervous at first." Luca smiles. "The campus is beautiful, at least. Lots of trees, trails...I'm sure you've been there, right?"

"I pretty much grew up there. My grandmother was a tenured professor in her day."

"Really?" Luca's eyes widen. "What did she teach?"

"Anthropology, which fascinates me, too." I twist so I'm facing him. "I think that's what freaks me out—what if I pick the wrong major and it takes me forever to realize it?"

"You have plenty of time. Half the people I know changed their major at some point, some twice. When I started, I wanted to major in tech."

"What changed?"

"I think I just grew out of it. When I was younger, I was really into gaming, coding, all that stuff. My dad's a software architect, so it's in my blood. It's always been our thing." He draws his finger through the sand. "Then, to celebrate graduating high school, I went to Tokyo with some friends. It was unbelievable—I'd never seen a city like that. I'd never seen *anything* like that."

"I can only imagine. It's huge, isn't it?"

"Massive. I was fascinated by the scale of it, the architecture." A small smile flickers over his mouth. "It was a work of art."

38

"You sound passionate," I venture, watching him closely.

He pauses, then nods. "I am."

"Why don't you just major in architecture, then?" I scratch my neck. "Why hang on to the minor? Are you even interested in coding anymore?"

"I enjoy it, but more as a hobby. Not a career."

I lean back on my hands, thinking about what he's just said. "Well, you have plenty of time. Half the people I know changed their major at some point," I mimic.

"Funny how that works." He laughs, recognizing his words.

Saira's shadow falls over us. "This looks cozy."

Luca stands, brushing sand from his pants. "Just keeping your spot warm."

The blond, cotton candy loving friend ambles over. "What's the plan tonight? We still going to that party out in Seabright? Matty wants to get beer first."

"Maybe later." Luca's light brown eyes flicker to me for just a second before returning to his friend. "You guys wanna catch the movie first? They're playing *The Lost Boys*."

* * *

The sun finally dips below the horizon, turning the boardwalk into a glittering playland against a violet sky.

The boys—Luca, Matt, the blond—Kellan, and another guy named Logan—accompany us over to the movie screen. There's no seating, just blankets and beach chairs sprawled all over, so it's hard to find a spot. Normally we'd have come over earlier and secured something better, but we were a little distracted by the antics of Luca and his friends.

"What d'you fools want from the liquor store?" Logan seems bored, tossing his keys from one hand to another. He's not the friendliest person, but he seems tight with his friends. It's obvious the four of them are a unit.

"You're going now?" asks Kellan. "You'll miss half the movie."

Logan scoffs. "Like I haven't seen *The Lost Boys* a dozen fucking times."

"Whatever," says Luca, shifting so he can tug his wallet from his back pocket. He slaps a bill onto Logan's hand. "Sierra Nevada. Get what you want."

"Yes, sir," intones Logan, following Matt to the boardwalk.

We're sitting on the edge of the crowd, waiting for the movie to start. It's Santa Cruz-summertime-chilly, crisp and perfect. I'd have worn jeans if I'd known we were staying for the movie, but it's nothing I haven't done a million times before.

Still, I shiver a bit when the wind picks up, and Luca notices, cocking his head. "Cold?"

"I'll be all right." I lean into Saira. We're squeezed together on top of my blanket, hers spread over our laps.

Luca scoots over, bringing his warmth into contact with my body. My heart begins to race, making me, ironically, even more shivery. He is by far the best-looking guy I have *ever* seen in real life and trust me, between UCSC, the beaches and downtown, there are scores of pretty boys in Santa Cruz.

"Better?" His voice is lower now. Huskier.

"Much." I clear my throat. "Thanks."

I wonder if he has a girlfriend. There's no way someone this attractive is single. Then again, maybe he likes playing the field. Yes, that's definitely it. I'm probably one of many dishes on his flirty, little smorgasbord. *Not that I'd mind him eating me.*

Good thing it's dark because my face just went up in flames.

"Do you live on campus?" I blurt, scratching my cheek. "During the school year?"

"Used to, not anymore." He checks his phone briefly before tossing it onto the blanket and leaning back on his hands. "We share a house close to it, though."

"Oh, okay. I figured you probably roomed with one of these guys."

Luca's eyebrows shoot up. "I room with all of 'em. Logan and I grew up together, and we met Matty and Kellan freshman year."

I pretend to think. "Let me guess—Matt's always been the one securing the beer kegs and six packs."

"That obvious, huh?" He narrows his eyes. "What about me? What's my persona?"

41

Saira chuckles under breath. She's chatting with Kellan, who's sitting on her other side, but I suspect she's got one ear in our conversation. I link my right arm beneath her left for support because Luca's question was rather loaded.

"The only things I know about you are that you like churros and soccer," I say, shrugging one shoulder. "And that you're going to be an engineer."

"Sounds like you know a lot." From the corner of my eye, I see those full lips of his curve into a sly smile. "What else?"

We're so close to each other that if I look straight at him, our faces would be only inches apart. "Why don't you tell me? Are you the Nice Guy or the Heartbreaker?"

"Maybe I'm a little of both."

* * *

I lean back into the cradle of Luca's legs, enveloped by his warmth and scent. Every time he says something, his whisper tickles my ears…and I love it.

When the boys got back from their beer run earlier, the crowd had thickened around us, leaving barely any room. It had made sense for Luca to sit behind me, gathering me between his legs, leaning his chin on my shoulder. At least, that's what I tell myself. I'm sure it's what he told himself, too, although he seems totally casual about all of this.

Then again, boys like Luca live in the realm of the upper hand. He knows

42

I'm attracted to him.

Meanwhile, I can't tell if Saira is into Kellan, but it's obvious that he's into her. I don't blame him. My best friend is tall and slender and gorgeous, her skin the color of a new penny, her huge, dark eyes and long eyelashes and sassy attitude a turn on for a lot of the guys we meet.

Needless to say, it's a little hard to concentrate on the movie now that we have our own lost boys to contend with. Flirty and funny and generous with beer, they rib each other and sometimes us. Kellan knows nearly all the lines of the whole movie, and he keeps reciting them right on cue.

"One thing about living in Santa Carla I never could stomach: all the damn vampires," he croaks, earning a giggle from two girls sitting a towel over.

"You want another beer?" Luca asks, the warmth of his breath and vibration of his voice sending signals deep into my core. If he can do that with just a question, what could he do if we got physical?

Tickled, I cringe away, but he just blows on my ear again. Swallowing a giggle, I glance over my shoulder. "Are you having one?"

The movie screen's reflection dances against his dark eyes, making them sparkle. "Yep."

"Sure, then."

"Matty," he whispers loudly, punching his friend's arm.

"What's your deal?" Matt whispers back, not taking his eyes off the screen as he rubs his arm.

"We need two more beers, stat."

"Get 'em yourself, Doc," Matt says, but he rummages around, pulling two more cans from a box beneath a towel.

I accept mine, tapping it gently against Matt's. "Thanks."

"Anytime, Sweet Spot." He glances at me, winking. "Anytime you're ready to move on from this loser, let me know."

"Thanks, Matty," Luca says loudly.

"Shhh!" several people around us hush, as if it's not already ridiculously loud down here.

"Oh, like you can hear anyway," I snark, emboldened by the beer.

"Ridiculous, right?" Saira huffs, scrunching up her face. "Like they haven't already seen this movie a million times!"

Luca's quiet laughter rumbles through his chest, transferring to me.

And then I know: No matter what happens this summer, I'll always remember how good tonight felt.

We goof off for a while after the movie finishes, waiting for the crowd to thin out a little before heading back up to the boardwalk. Luca helps me shake out my blanket, even folding it for me so I can tuck it into my backpack.

"That was fun," Saira whispers, tangling her fingers briefly with mine. Her eyes are bright and happy, her light brown cheeks flushed rose gold.

I run a hand self-consciously over my hair, wondering if it looks as wild as it feels. "Kellan's cute. I think he likes you."

She peeks at him, then looks back at me, smirking. "Maybe."

I lean closer. "Did he ask for your number?"

But Luca joins us before she can answer. "So, what's the plan? You two staying here or heading out?"

"I don't know. Are you guys still going to that party?" That might sound forward, but hey—they invited themselves to the movie.

"Probably. You wanna come?"

"Maybe?" I nod, feeling like I'm still in high school as I adjust my backpack. "Where is it, exactly?"

"Over in Seabright, some kid Kellan knows from way back. He grew up down here."

"Where'd you grow up?"

"East Bay."

I nod, glancing at the time on my phone. "Berkeley?"

"Walnut Creek, but we ran the streets of Berkeley all the time."

"And you're still hanging out down here in the summer?"

"Maybe on the weekends, but I have a job starting in Berkeley soon, so it makes more sense to stay in the Bay during the week."

My hearts sinks the way it did earlier when he told me about his semester abroad. He sounds busy. And noncommittal. "That's cool."

"Hey, let's go ride something," he says, scanning the scene. "What's your favorite?"

"She works here, dude. She's probably sick of all this shit," Logan says dryly, sweeping past as we make our way up the steps. The movie crowd has been bottlenecked, so it's slow going.

"I'm not," I tell Luca, irritated by his friend's assumption. I keep getting the impression Logan doesn't like me, or like he doesn't approve of his friends hanging out with Saira and me. Maybe we're too young. Or maybe he's one of those rich, preppy types. "I love these rides. I have different favorites depending on my mood, but the Sky Glider's close to my heart."

"Awww," coos Matt, and Luca gives him a light shove. "Of course, it is, Sweet Spot."

"I'll watch from down here. I don't think I can handle the Sky Glider again," says Saira. "But I'll do the Giant Dipper later if you want."

We finally empty out onto the wooden, sand-gritted planks of the board-walk. It's a technicolor world at night, all lit up and glowing neon. "We can do the Giant Dipper now," I say, feeling a little guilty that I've been all over Luca when just a few hours ago, we were bitching about Janya doing the same thing.

"The Sky Glider's right there, silly," Saira says, giving me a little push. "You two should go." She peeks at Kellan. "Right?"

"Sure." He shrugs. "We'll meet you guys at the other side."

Luca

I haven't ridden this thing since I was a kid, but I remember it now. Below our dangling feet, people walk along the crowded boardwalk, growing smaller the higher we climb. Rollercoaster cars crest over the Giant Dipper's highest hill, dipping and appearing again seconds later on a brutal curve. Out on the beach, one couple walks along the water's edge while another rolls around a blanket, getting busy. Smiling, I let my eyes wander farther out, over the dark water, waves crowned with a frothy glow. There's a lot of light pollution, but I can see a few stars.

Wren's nervous, I can tell.

I don't know if she's afraid of heights or afraid of me, but she's shivering again. Kind of like she was down on the beach. Granted, the temperature has dropped a lot since the sun went down, so maybe she's just cold.

Regardless, the second the attendant lowers the bar, I wrap my arm around her. She doesn't look at me, but she smiles.

"You looked cold," I explain, but I don't think she minds at all.

She squints out at the water. "Maybe a little."

Way earlier, when the guys and I had been deciding what to do, I'd suggested the boardwalk. Matty had busted my balls, teasing me about Sweet Spot, but I'd couched it in a desire to kill time before the party by grabbing a couple of burgers and kicking the ball around the beach. I won't be seeing Santa Cruz for a few months, so why not?

I pretended not to care when we passed by the Sweet Spot—the stand—and there were two guys behind the counter instead of the cute girl with the green eyes and long, wavy ponytail. But Matty was right, and we all knew it.

But then I did find her. And now that we're here, after having spent the past few hours together, I'm wondering what my end game is. Like I told Wren, I probably won't be coming back down here for a while.

I guess I'm just curious to see where this goes. There's something about her that keeps me interested, and it's not just the way she looks, although I like that a lot, too.

"How long've you been working here?" I ask, once the silence between us has stretched a little too long. Maybe I'm a little nervous, too.

She looks up at me. "Every summer since I was fifteen."

"A real Santa Cruz girl, huh?"

She wrinkles her nose. "I guess. It's kind of a tourist trap."

"What's your favorite ride?"

"This one." Color rises in her cheeks.

48

I pause, grinning at that. "Favorite thing to eat?"

"Here? The taco stand over by the bumper cars." She tilts her head. "And I have a thing for cotton candy. My grandma and I used to eat it on this ride all the time."

"Used to?" I echo, hoping it's not what it sounds like.

"Yeah, way back when she actually left the house." She huffs softly. "Gramma Kate's still around; she's just old."

"My stepfather likes to say he'd rather be old than dead."

"Exactly! We should be so lucky." Wren shrugs, picking at a loose string on her shorts. "Anyway, Gramma Kate's still got it—she kicks my ass whenever we play gin rummy."

"She sounds like my vovó Ana. She'll kill you before she'll let you win at a game of buraco."

"Vovó?" She cocks her head. "Is that your grandma?"

I nod, tapping her thigh with my fingertip. "And buraco's a card game, like rummy."

Her eyes twinkle. "I see."

"What about your parents?" I ask.

She averts her eyes then, scanning the lit-up park laid out before us. "They split when I was pretty young."

Maybe it's a sensitive topic. It is for a lot of people. "Mine, too." A lock of her hair blows free, and we reach for it at the same time. She lets me tuck it behind her ear as her cheeks go pink, and I know I'm going to kiss her. "I take it you grew up here, then?"

"Yeah, my whole life. I've been to the Bay plenty, though. Walnut Creek's pretty."

"It's all right. My mother and stepfather still live there with my little brother. We came to the boardwalk all the time when I was a kid, though." I peek down at the glittering scenario below, which is still just as crowded as it was at midday. "Lots of memories here."

"So many memories." She sighs. "Your friend said I was probably sick of this place, and maybe I should be, but I'm not."

"Don't listen to Logan. He's a grump."

She waves off my words, shaking her head. "I like that this place doesn't change. There's something safe and nostalgic about it, a happy place you can dip in or out of whenever you want."

I gaze into her eyes, imagining the boardwalk the very way she's describing. It's a romantic notion, for sure, and an appealing one.

But then she snorts, rolling her eyes. "Or maybe I'm full of shit. To be completely honest, I have a love/hate relationship with this place. I mean, I go to bed at night with the sounds of clanging and creaking and screaming and all of this"—she gestures to the scene around us—"banging around my head. So, there's that."

"No, I get you. The boardwalk's great but visiting is different than working here. Every job has its pros and cons," I say. "I worked at my stepfather's cushy real estate office a couple summers ago and that *really* sucked ass."

"Why?"

"I was just bored...I wanted to hang out with my friends. I finally got fired because he found me on a gaming website when I was supposed to be electronically filing liens."

She smiles ruefully. "And what about the job you mentioned earlier? Is it less boring?"

I laugh quietly. "It's a part-time job for a research architect."

"That's right up your alley, isn't it? Why don't you sound more excited?"

She doesn't miss a thing. I drum my fingers over the safety bar. "Things aren't as simple as I'd like them to be. My dad wants me to fly out to São Paulo for a software internship in about ten days." I look out at where the glittering sea meets the dark sky, the stars sparkling above. "It's a good opportunity, and it would look nice on my transcripts."

"But you don't really want to go."

"I'd be gone for half the year instead of one semester." I shrug, shaking my head. "I've done summer internships every year since I was a junior in high school—even the time I went to Tokyo. I kind of want to take this summer off."

"Can't you just tell him that?"

I scratch my chin, surprised I'm telling her this when the only other person who knows how I feel is Mãe. "My dad really, really wants me to go. He's always hoped I'd follow in his footsteps and all that."

She wrinkles her nose. "I guess I've never experienced that. My mom doesn't care what I do, as long as I'm happy."

51

"My mother's the same way. But my dad thinks I'd be squandering a once-in-a-lifetime opportunity. Life wasn't easy for him growing up, so he can be hardcore."

She cocks her head. "Are you guys close?"

"About as close as we can be with him living in São Paulo."

"Is that why you're going to school there in the fall?"

"Not exactly. São Paulo is nowhere near Florianópolis."

"Closer than it is to Santa Cruz," she counters, raising an eyebrow.

"For sure. I'll visit him a couple weekends a month, but I chose UFSC because it's a great school in a country I love. I'm American, but I'm Brazilian too, you know?" I glance down at her. "If my father had his way, my brother and I would've done all our schooling over there. He thinks we're too Americanized."

"You and your little brother?"

"My older brother, Nico." Who won't ever go, mainly to spite Pai.

"How often do you get to see your dad?"

Her questions dig into my chest, between my ribs. My father's lived overseas for half my life. "A couple times a year."

We fall silent, rocking gently as the ocean breeze jostles our car.

"I get wanting to chill this summer, but I think you're lucky," she says after a moment, leaning back. The move tucks her more deeply into the crook of my arm, and I take the opportunity to pull her closer. Her cheeks dimple with a smile. "I'd do anything to get out of here."

"You will. You've got time."

"I know. I just get tired of seeing the same stuff over and over—it's hard not to feel stuck." She peeks up at me. "I probably sound like an ungrateful brat. It's not like I'm slaving away in a factory somewhere."

"Everything you're saying is valid, Wren. But you won't be doing this forever, just like I didn't work for my stepdad forever. You'll work hard, study hard, and eventually what you *have* to do will line up with what you *want* to." The words resonate in my brain, advice I should be taking myself.

The Sky Glider pauses. We're close to the middle now, approaching the highest point. I squint down to the crowd near the end, wondering if our friends are there, but it's impossible to make out faces.

"Have you started packing for your trip?" asks Wren.

"I usually wait until the last minute." I run my hand over my hair. "I probably shouldn't. Once I almost didn't get my passport in time, so you'd think I know not to procrastinate."

"International travel seems pretty intense."

"Have you ever been outside of the U.S.?" I ask.

"No, but I will one day." She peeks up at me. "My bucket list is about a mile long."

"Where would you go first?"

"Oh, man. Santorini, Greece. Japan, the Maldives, definitely Brazil—so you'd better send me a postcard. I want to see Christ the Redeemer." She pauses, and I chuckle. I'll totally do it. "Marrakesh, Morocco. And I have to see the Northern Lights before I die. Doesn't matter where—I hear you can even catch them in Northern Ireland."

"Really? I did not know that."

"I read about it in an article once and knew I had to see it."

"That's a pretty epic list," I say. "I've been to Brazil a million times, but only because my dad lives there. Also, Mãe. She's from there."

"Is Mãe your mom?"

I nod. "Mãe is Portuguese for mom."

"Ah." She cocks her head, her eyes wandering over my face. "Is your dad from there, too? Sorry I'm being so nosy."

"It's fine." I laugh, cuddling her closer. "My grandparents moved here before Pai was born, but he spent his summers back in Brazil and even went to college there. He's always loved the old country, so no one was really surprised when he finally packed his shit and left for good."

"How old were you?"

"When my parents split? Nine."

She nods, biting that full bottom lip. I'd like to bite it for her. "That must've been hard."

I shrug. "It was, but he was gone all the time by that point anyway."

"Is Pai, dad?"

"You're catching on."

She's quiet for a moment. "Do you speak fluent Portuguese?"

"I'm a little sloppy. I'll be fluent by the time I get back from Brazil."

Silence falls again, but it's comfortable this time. Someone squeals as they pass going the other way on the Sky Glider, and Wren laughs, her hand landing on my thigh. I don't think she means for it to, but once it lands there, I cover it with mine. "Is that all?"

A tiny smile dances at her mouth. "I must admit I'm very curious about you."

"The feeling's mutual."

"I'd ask your favorite food, but I seem to remember you having a thing for churros."

I squeeze her hand. "Good memory."

"Nope," she murmurs, those jade-colored eyes shifting down to my mouth. "You're just hard to forget."

Sliding my hand around the back of her neck, I bring her closer. Her eyes close as the space between us dissolves. Our lips touch. She's soft, just like I knew she'd be. I want inside, so I ask for it by running my tongue lightly over the seam of her lips. She opens for me, and I lick my way in, tasting her sweet, little mouth. She tastes like bubblegum and beer, and fuck, I'm stiffer than a surfboard right about now.

There's a subtle jolt as the car we're in crosses the top of the line and begins its slow descent to the end of the ride. I back off, opening my eyes as I subtly adjust myself.

It's hard to keep it innocent when Wren licks her lips, like she's still tasting that kiss. Her eyes drift open as she stares up at me.

"You're really fucking pretty, Wren," I say. I can't help it. "You know that, right?"

Her face blooms into a smile, and she shrugs. "So are you."

"I'm pretty?" I bat my eyelashes, expecting a laugh.

"Pretty hot," she clarifies, and the suddenly serious look she shoots me goes straight to my dick.

Yeah, I've got plans for this girl. Maybe not tonight, but soon.

We come to a stop. I take her hand when we get off the glider, pulling her down the stairs to where everyone else is waiting. I took Wren on that ride to get her alone, but also to give Kellan a chance to talk to Saira. They're chatting it up, so maybe the plan worked.

Meanwhile, Logan's being sulky. He didn't want to come to the boardwalk today at all. He wanted to do bong rips and go eat at some hipster sushi joint in downtown Santa Cruz before heading over to the party. He was outvoted partly because no one felt like sushi and partly because I wanted to try and find Wren.

Also—and he'd never admit this—he's annoyed the cute girl chose me. I've known Logan my whole life, and he's always been a competitive little shit. Not that it matters, because while Logan might be fighting with his girl, they're not broken up. He's not even single.

So, fuck him.

Saira grins when she sees us, breaking away from the cozy little conversation she's got going with Kellan. "Thanks for taking her, because I sure as hell couldn't do it again."

"Nah," I say, squeezing Wren's hand. "It was fun."

* * *

We ride the Giant Dipper—all of us. The Shockwave. The Cliff Hanger—twice. The Fireball. We buy massive bags of cotton candy and share it with the girls, resulting in a sticky mess.

"Wait, the photo booth!" cries Wren, pointing. "C'mon!"

"It's tradition," Saira explains as they disappear into the booth.

"I'm ready when you are, bro," Logan says, yawning and stretching. He's a little mellower, now that he and Kellan went and smoked in the parking lot, but he's still being a dick. "To get out of here that is, not take pictures."

Matt belches, throwing his now empty beer cup into a nearby bin. "Let's party, bitches."

Kellan leans against a post, texting. "Hold on, I'm checking the address. I think they moved again...and I really don't want to show up at the wrong house."

I'm wondering if Wren and Saira would actually come to the party when they finally emerge from the booth. "Do you wanna..." Wren swallows, seeming shy. "Go in with me? My phone's dead, so I don't have any pics from tonight."

She's so cute—how could I say no? "Let's do it." Ignoring Matt, Logan and Kellan, I squeeze into the booth and pull Wren onto my lap.

Squeaking in surprise, Wren yanks the curtain closed and shifts so that we can both see the screen. We smile for the first one, and then she sticks out her tongue, so I do too. Pretty typical. But then, because it's dark and hidden and I want to, I turn her chin toward me and kiss her. Despite the cotton candy clinging to her lips, there's nothing sweet about this kiss. I want her, and I've hung out with her enough over the past few hours to know the chemistry between us is real.

And man, does she respond. She moans quietly, a small, soft sound that flips a switch in me. Yanking her body closer, I squeeze her thigh and lick deeply into her mouth, running my tongue along her tongue, tasting and discovering her. I'm distantly aware that the camera must be finished taking pictures, but I don't stop kissing Wren. I don't want to.

But Wren pulls away eventually, her chest rising and falling like we just did a hell of a lot more than kiss. Her hair's a mess, her lips wet and swollen from me sucking and biting on them. Bending toward me, she kisses me again, taking control this time, sweeping her tongue through my mouth like she's taking what she needs. It makes me think of other things, other scenarios where she's on her back, her legs wrapped around me. I can imagine how warm she'd be.

The sound of snickering floats into the booth. Wren shifts on my lap as we allow the kiss to fade. She feels my erection; I know she does. I see it in her wild eyes, the way they widen when I hold her still, so she'll stop squirming.

Logan cuts his eyes away as we tumble out of the booth. I feel drunker than I did before we went in, light-headed and ridiculous over this girl as she reaches for the photo strips coming out of the dispenser. I can't help but smile when I see them. They go from cute to low-key pornographic pretty quick.

Saira covers her mouth, giggling as she peeks at the photo strip over Wren's shoulder.

I'm staring at Wren, wondering what the next move is, when she looks up at me. Her sparkling eyes flicker to something behind me, and then the color drains from her face.

The sounds of scuffling tear through the loudness. I spin around right as Kellan plows into me, as if he was shoved.

"You wanna go, motherfucker?" Matt snarls, launching his fist into some dude's face.

Shit.

The crowd parts. There are three of them to our four, but they're mean, ugly and drunk as hell. Why am I not surprised? Matt is always starting shit. Doesn't matter, though. He's my boy. Pulling up beside Kellan, I sock the tallest one in the face before he can advance on anyone. We tussle for a second before a couple of other guys jump into the fray to separate our group from theirs.

Everyone's yelling and pushing. Adrenaline courses violently through my veins, making me shake, and my heart's pounding so fast I can barely see straight. I can't remember the last time I fought, not like this.

Wren.

I look back to find her and Saira still standing over by the photo booth, terrified. Saira's phone is in her trembling hands.

"Do—do you want me to call the cops or something?" she stammers.

"No." I shake my head, rushing over to them. "We'll get busted for drinking—and fighting."

Logan appears beside me, clamping his arm down on my shoulder. "Gotta go, bro. Cops are coming."

Sure enough, the distant wail of approaching sirens pierces the air.

"Shit." Scrubbing my hand over my face, I look down at Wren. "I gotta go."

"Go," she urges, giving me a quick hug. "Come back and find me sometime." She gives me one photo strip and pockets the other and then I'm gone, pulling Matt through the crowd of onlookers, trying desperately to disappear before the cops show up.

"What the fuck, Matt?" I grumble as we squeeze out of the nearest exit.

"Wasn't me, not this time," he says, looking both ways as we cross the busy street.

"It wasn't," Kellan says, hurrying alongside as Logan leads the charge. "Dude in the black shirt bumped Matt first."

It doesn't matter who started the fight. Matt turns twenty-one in a couple of days, but he's still underaged. We all are. Plus, he's gotten in trouble for fighting before.

Red and blue lights pull up to the other end of the boardwalk. We slink quickly through the parking lot, where Logan uses the fob to find his car.

"Hey, did you get Saira's number?" I ask Kellan, turning to look at him as Logan eases out of the parking lot.

"Nope." He looks at me, his eyes searching mine in the dark. "You get Wren's?"

I turn back around with a heavy sigh, shaking my head. "No."

Matt reaches forward, squeezing my shoulder. "Sorry, bro."

Wren

⁂

Nothing like a fistfight to ruin a perfectly good evening.

Soon after the boys disappear Saira and I head toward the exit in unspoken agreement. Time to get the hell out of dodge.

"I'm still shaking," Saira mutters, rubbing her arms as we approach the gate.

"Me too." I slide my arm through hers, keeping her close. "Everything happened so quickly."

"Do you think they got out of here okay?"

"I don't know." I glance around as we step out onto the sidewalk. The hour is later than I realized, but the boardwalk is still crazy-busy, which is typical for this time of year. There are three cop cars parked along the curb in front of the other entrance, lights flashing silently. "I'm pretty sure they left from this side, so I hope so."

A car stops to let us go, and Saira tugs me over the crosswalk. "Sleepover?"

"Definitely. Although, I'm not sure how much I'll actually sleep."

She hums in agreement. "My house or yours?"

"Yours. I'm sick of my house," I gripe. "I've been looking at it every day and every night all summer."

"All right, all right." Saira swings our hands. "I'll follow you home so you can get your stuff and then we'll go back to my place. Mom must've really missed me because she made dhal puri *and* roti for dinner."

"And you honestly thought I'd pick my place over yours?" I ask dryly.

Mom and Darius look up from the TV in surprise when we burst through the door. It never occurred to me he'd be here. I'm beyond relieved I didn't catch them having sex on the couch or something.

"Oh. Hey, guys." I pause just inside the door, toeing my sneakers off.

"Wren?" My mother's already halfway across the room, probably attuned to whatever vibe Saira and I are bringing in. She might try to smudge us with sage if I don't proceed with caution. "Saira! I thought you were in Encinitas!"

"Hey, Lily." Saira grins, giving my mother a hug. "I came back last night. Missed Wren too much."

"Aww, my girl." Mom hugs Saira, stroking her long, dark hair. "You two have always been so close."

I take Saira's place, suddenly grateful for the familiarity of my mother's arms. Guess seeing Luca dragged into a fight shook me up more than I realized. I'm just glad it was over quickly.

"You look a little pale. What's going on?" Mom asks, frowning as she holds me at arm's length. "Bad day?"

"Just super tired," I lie, loosening my ponytail. "But I'm going to sleep over at Saira's if it's okay."

"Of course, it is," she says. "Just be home by noon—remember, we're going to Gram's for dinner."

Shoot, that's right. It's Gramma Kate's 70th birthday. "No worries."

"I'll have her back by eleven," Saira adds. "We're just gonna hang out."

Mom entreats her to join us for the birthday party as I turn to Darius and offer a belated hug. "Sorry we interrupted your movie."

"Nothing to be sorry about, baby girl," he says in his deep, raspy voice. "How was the boardwalk?"

"Ah, the boardwalk." I shrug, flinging my arm dramatically. "Same yesterday, today and forever."

"That's real." He laughs, nodding. "That's what we like about it, though, right?"

* * *

Forty minutes later, we're in Saira's bedroom, cuddled in the aromatic comfort of curry and spices. Mrs. Mangal is from Trinidad and, unlike my beloved mother, can cook like nobody's business.

64

"Stop eating all the dhal puri," Saira says, smacking my hand. "We're supposed to be sharing."

"It's past my dinnertime, and I'm only eating my share," I retort, scooting back on the carpet so that she can't reach me.

"I'd better not find ground chickpeas all over the ground," she warns, shooting me a look.

"You sound just like your mother."

She snorts. "Remember the time Anik got cake crumbs and frosting all over the stupid white carpet in the living room, trying to impress you?"

"Your mom was like, *'we don't eat in front of the TV, Anik!'*" We crack up at the memory. Poor Anik. He had a mad crush on me for a minute when we were kids.

"Wonder what he's up to tonight?" I muse, licking my fingers.

"Who Anik? Pfft. He's dating some girl," says Saira, taking an enormous bite of roti. "Anyway, forget him. Let's discuss Arlo."

I look up at her, tilting my head. "What about him?"

She wipes her mouth delicately. "I don't know. Have you thought any more about responding to him?"

"When would I have had time to think about him?" I set my food down. "We've been hanging out with those guys all day. We'd probably still be with them if they hadn't started fighting."

"Yeah, that sucked. I was feeling Kellan and I know for a fact he was feeling me."

"They all go to UCSC, you know." I feel all wistful now, extra sad that Luca and I didn't exchange numbers. Did our kisses affect him the way they did me?

"Yeah, I know." Saira turns back to her food, scooping a chunk of curry up with her roti. "Don't worry. We'll see them around campus."

"Maybe you will." I frown, shaking my head. "Not me, though, not for a while; Luca's studying in Brazil this fall."

"Aww, really?" She wrinkles her nose. "Well, at least you have the summer."

"I think he's going to Brazil at some point, if he's not working in the Bay," I say. "Either way, he won't be around here for a while."

"Well, he obviously likes you, babe. Maybe you two can pick up where you left off whenever he does make it back."

As good as that sounds, there's a sinking feeling deep inside that has me thinking things might not be so easy. If Luca's based in the Bay Area this summer, he has no real reason to come back down.

No reason besides me, anyway, and I don't know if that's enough.

* * *

Two days later, I'm back at the Sweet Spot, much to Rodrigo's relief.

It's a drizzly, gray Monday morning and not much is going on. Sighing, I lean on the counter, eyes glazing over as I watch the wooden planks of the boardwalk darken with moisture.

I had a great weekend with Saira and my family, but now that it's over and I'm back on the grind, it's hard for me to think about anything other than Luca. I thought about him over the weekend too, obviously, even though I tried like hell not to. I wanted to be present with my family, not a distracted, lovelorn idiot obsessing over a pretty boy.

It wasn't easy.

I keep wondering if he's thinking about me, if I made enough of an impression. Grabbing my phone, I scroll to my photos and open the one I took of our photo strip. The original is safely enshrined in a spot by my desk at home—this is just for convenience.

We had such a perfect night up until the moment those nasty guys started shit. I keep seeing Luca's face, hearing his voice. The way he teased me with his playful words and flirty gaze. His touch. I've had boyfriends, but guys like Luca feel next level. Even with the photographic evidence, it's hard to believe it happened at all.

There's a photobooth a little way down the boardwalk, and while it's not the one that Luca and I went into, it's a steady visual of the heated moments we shared inside. I'd never been kissed like that before. I'm no virgin, but the way he took my mouth? I felt it *everywhere*. I still do.

I'm still kicking myself for not getting his phone number. Saira didn't get Kellan's either—unlike me, though, she's okay with that.

"Kellan was cute and all," she'd said with a nonchalant shrug. "But it's not like there aren't a hundred guys just like him."

Casting a furtive glance around to make sure the zone is Rodrigo-free, I shoot her a text.

Wren: I really wish Luca would pop up again :(

She answers back so fast I just know she's sitting on her phone. She started working at her dad's office today, and the texts have been coming in fast and furious.

Saira: Aww. I know u do. Have u looked for him on the socials?

Wren: I looked, but I couldn't find him. Idk his last name.

Saira: Whaatttt?

Wren: It never came up! What's Kellan's last name?

Saira: Idk, but I didn't spend half the night sucking his face.

A cute mom with three tiny, exuberant children veers over. Internally rolling my eyes at Saira's comment, I return my phone to my back pocket. She's right, obviously, but still.

Once I've given the little angels their sprinkle-covered ice creams, I return to Saira.

Wren: I told him to look for me if/when he comes back down.

Saira: fingers crossed

Dear Arlo

⸙

Dear Arlo,

I never considered the possibility of finding you or of you finding me. Don't take this the wrong way but based on how I ended up with your DNA, it never occurred to me you'd be interested in pursuing a relationship.

I joined this site for the same reasons as you and your friend, to find out more about myself. I know that, through my mom, I'm mostly Greek with some Irish thrown in. That's what they say, but I wanted more info, like did I have any African or Native American roots? (No African, but I'm 22% Cree through my maternal grandmother.)

All I know of you is what my mom told me, and that's all she knows, too: you are tall, with green eyes and blond hair. My mom has brown eyes, so maybe I got mine from you.

I'm still trying to wrap my mind around all of this, but thanks for reaching out. I think I'd like to stay in touch. My email address is: angelwren@sweetmail.com

Sincerely,
  Wren

Luca

"Your father called this morning," Mãe says, raising a perfectly manicured eyebrow at me. "Again."

Swallowing my irritation, I brush past my mother and open the fridge. I'm unofficially back at my childhood home in Walnut Creek for the summer because commuting from Santa Cruz makes zero sense while I'm working in Berkeley. Only problem is the lack of privacy and Mãe's borderline smothering-mothering.

And then there's dear old dad, harassing me all the way from São Paulo. I still haven't decided whether or not I want to go.

"What else are you going to do this summer?" he keeps saying. "Sleep? Surf? Get laid? Don't be lazy."

Don't be lazy. He's been saying that to me my entire life. I'm far from lazy. I'm just not the workaholic he is.

Mãe's spoon clicks rhythmically as she stirs her coffee. "You need to stop avoiding him, baby."

"I'm not avoiding him. I'm just busy." I shove a bagel into the toaster and check my watch; I have barely a half hour before I need to be on the road.

"He's a pain in the ass. I know," she laments. "But he's your dad and he loves you. He just wants you to be successful."

I know she's right. So, why does taking this internship feel like forcing a square peg through a round hole?

"Luca," Mãe presses, warning lining her voice. She's about respect just as much as she is about love, and she won't hesitate to swat me if she thinks I'm ignoring her. It doesn't matter that I'm almost twenty-one and have over a foot on her.

"I hear you, Mãe. I'll call him while I'm driving in."

"Hey." Coming up beside me, she reaches up and strokes my cheek. "You don't have to let him bully you into going if you don't want to go. Just let him say his piece, okay?"

Forty minutes later, I'm heading through the tunnel on my way to Berkeley. The phone rings twice before Pai picks up, his voice as clear as if he was in the car beside me and not halfway across the planet.

"Luca. Hard man to catch."

"Sorry, Pai." I pause to take a sip of coffee. "Been a little busy."

He chuckles. "Listen, it's time to make a decision. Pereira's a busy man. He has another prospect he can bring on board if you don't accept, but I doubt they'd be as qualified."

"I don't know that *I* am qualified," I hedge. "I've been focusing on architecture and civil engineering for a while now."

"I wouldn't worry about it—you've always been a natural with software," he says smoothly. When I fail to respond, he sighs. "Is this about being in São Paulo for the summer? I don't understand why this is a problem—you love it here."

"Yes, but I already have a job *here*."

"A part-time job. As a secretary," he says, the cordiality evaporating from his deep, mildly accented voice.

Gritting my teeth, I wait a beat before responding. This isn't the first time we've had this discussion, and I don't know what grates more: my father's intentional obtuseness or my tendency to react to it. "As a paid intern for a research architect. I'll be shadowing people who do what I might want to do."

"*Might* want to do. When you get to be my age, you start to see that a career is a career. A dollar is a dollar. You're good at coding, Luca. Get great at it. Make the money. Then you can do whatever the hell you want."

"I'm good at coding, but architecture is my passion. You know that." My fingers are clenched around the steering wheel so tightly they've turned white. I try to loosen them. "I owe it to myself to at least try."

"You are one of the brightest young men I know," Pai says. "You are being offered an excellent opportunity and a host of connections, things that could change the trajectory of your life. Do this for me, Luca. Trust me. And if you don't feel differently by the end of your time in Brazil, I'll back off."

73

"Can I ask you something?"

"Claro." *Of course.*

"Is this about my career or yours?"

"It's about both." He laughs. "But let me make it easy for you. Come now, or don't come at all."

I catch a glimpse of my confusion in the rearview mirror. "What?"

"There's no point spending the fall in Florianópolis if you don't want to establish connections here, meu filho. Let me know what you want to do, okay? I have to go."

"Pai."

"I have a meeting, Luca. We'll talk later." And with that, he hangs up.

The sun glints off the cars in front of me, the air conditioning blows past my cheeks. Stunned, I touch my finger to the radio dial, shutting off the music that came on when the phone call ended. Maybe I'm crazy, but it feels like I was just verbally strong-armed by my own father. He knows how much I want to take the urban architecture courses at UFSC, but he's always paid for my education. If he wants to pull funding to make a point, he can.

Mãe always said my father was a ruthless man. She says this almost affectionately, like it's harmless, no different than being clumsy or impractical, but I'm starting to wonder if Nico had it right all along. He never forgave Pai for choosing his career over his family.

What Mãe calls ruthless, and Nico calls unforgivable, I always called

74

ambitious. Growing up, people—family—told me I was a lot like him, so I thought I understood him. Successful, passionate, and hard-working, Carlos Cardoso built his software firm from the ground up and I admired him for it. I loved him for it.

But he'll do what it takes to get what he wants, and right now, he wants me at his side in São Paulo. I graduate in two years. He wants me to meet his associates now, to get a feel for the software industry. The family business, I guess.

Maybe I should be proud he believes in me as much as he does. I just never thought he'd threaten my plans because I wouldn't submit to one of his.

Wren

Fall

The alarm on my phone goes off, vibrating silently on the tabletop. Rubbing my eyes, I check the time. It's nearly ten, but the library is still pretty busy. That's the way it is around here. But I'm exhausted. Between my full course load and work study on the side, I have to get some sleep.

Yawning, I close my books and slide my laptop into my backpack. My phone lights up with a text. It's my roommate.

Leighton: Mojito Monday?

I groan inwardly, because experience has taught me that there's no stopping this girl once she's in bartending mode. So much for sleep.

Wren: Can't. Anthro final tomorrow.

Leighton: So just have one ;)

I don't bother responding. Knowing Leighton, she's already cajoled our suitemate, Skye, into having said mojitos. Resistance is usually futile with her.

Ten minutes later, I walk through the glass doors of my residence hall, Angela Davis House. As usual, I'm met by loud music, weed and incense—tonight, it's technical/instrumental guitar shredding and Nag Champa. I'm not sure about the weed. I don't really smoke.

Letting myself into our first-floor suite, I find Leighton, Skye, and Leighton's kind-of-boyfriend Noah sipping on mojitos in elaborate, pink glasses.

"Hey, girl, hey," Leighton says, raising hers in greeting. "The studious student has returned. Come have a drink."

Noah smirks and drinks, the same dainty, pink glass looking ridiculous in his big, meaty paws. He and Leighton are smooshed into giant, yellow inflatable chairs on the floor. They barely fit in our triple, so we only pull them out for company.

I cock an eyebrow, dropping my backpack on the floor. "You do realize it's Monday, right?"

"And way past five o'clock, so don't be a killjoy, darlin'," she drawls, climbing to her feet. Blonde-haired, blue-eyed Leighton grew up in Nashville and her accent ripens when she drinks. Picking up an empty pink glass, she gestures toward the impromptu bar on her desk. "What'll it be? Classic? Muddled? I have grapefruit…"

"Classic, I suppose." I allow a small smile. It's hard to say no to her. "And small. Thanks."

"No worries, girl," she says, nodding her head toward Skye, who's curled up on her bed. "We all need a little something today."

Rather than scrambling up to my bunk with my drink, I sit with Skye, who sleeps below me. "Hey. You doing okay?""

"I don't know." She lets out a slow, shaky breath. "They've been talking about hospice."

My heart squeezes painfully, and I reach out to take her hand. Skye's dad was recently diagnosed with pancreatic cancer, and she's been in the thick of family phone calls all week.

"You gonna have to defer next semester for sure?" I ask quietly.

Skye nods, looking down at her lap. "Pops might not have a lot of time. I need to be there with him...and for my mom."

I take another sip, absorbing this. It's been one blow after another for Skye. First, she found out her dad was terminally ill, and now she's realizing she may not be coming back after Christmas break. Maybe not ever. She told me once that Santa Cruz was her dream school growing up, that she'd fallen in love with the city after visiting family here as a kid.

Skye was valedictorian of her senior class and won all sorts of grants and scholarships to UCSC. She's one of the smartest people I've ever met, and probably one of the prettiest. Leighton told her, during our first drunken bonding session, that she looked like a black Barbie with her smooth, brown skin, catty hazel eyes and symmetrical features...to which Skye replied, "but with natural hair, thank you very much."

Now, just months after starting freshman year, she's returning to St. Croix, the small, Caribbean island she's from.

"I'm sorry. I'm so sorry." I squeeze her hand. "Let me know when you're heading over to admissions, okay? I'll go with you."

"Okay." She squeezes back, reaching for her drink. "It'll probably be soon. Tomorrow, maybe."

Silence falls, and the whispery flirting between Leighton and Noah dies down. I glance over at them just in time to see a little kiss. I look away, but Leighton sees anyway, shooting a rubber band at me. "How'd it go at the library?" she asks. "You finish that paper?"

"I did, thank God." I take a small sip of mojito. "You study for your final yet?"

"Yes, ma'am. I had a free period around lunch, so I took advantage." She closes her eyes, resting against Noah. "I'll study a little more in the morning…I don't have class until eleven."

"Sterling's been asking about you," Noah says, petting Leighton's hair. Their socked feet are entwined.

"Oh, yeah?" I swallow a sigh. Noah's roommate Sterling is into me, has been since orientation week. He's handsome, in a trust fund kind of way, and he's intelligent, in a book smart kind of way, but there is not one iota of chemistry between us.

"Yeah. He wanted to come over tonight, but he has a major Econ paper due that he's been putting off." Noah angles his phone toward a pair of mini speakers on Leighton's desk, filling our space with mellow, lo-fi beats.

Well, good. Had I come back to the room to find Sterling hanging around waiting for me, I would've been annoyed as hell because I've made it clear I'm not interested.

"You good?" Skye whispers, snickering.

I cut her a look. She knows what's up, even if Noah over there is Mr. Oblivious. "Right as rain."

My phone comes to life, glowing from within the bedsheets. It's my mom.

Mom: I got something from Rodrigo in the mail today, addressed to you. Want me to hold on to it or send to the dorm?

Rodrigo, my old boss from the Sweet Spot? Frowning, I think back to my last, measly little paycheck. Maybe it was miscalculated, and I'm owed more—that would be freaking fantastic.

Wren: Hold on to it. I'll stop by the studio Friday.

* * *

Snuggling into my favorite fleece hoodie, I walk briskly up the sidewalk and in the front door of Mom's yoga studio. Maybe today will be the day I tell Mom about Arlo Janvier.

We've been emailing back and forth for months now. I know more about him than he does about me, like that he was born in France but lives in Manhattan. No wife, no kids. Except for me, that is. (And whatever other kids might have resulted from his sperm donations. It's too weird to think about, so I try not to.) He has a rescue dog named Melvin and a kitten named Pamplemousse.

I told him I took French for two years in high school, but that's about it.

I've always known that Arlo has green eyes and blond hair because my mother told me when I was younger (she chose her donor's features) but we haven't exchanged pictures yet. I feel like if I see myself in his face, it'll make it all too real. I'm more comfortable here in the in-between, where Arlo is my dad only in theory.

Mizuki, one of Mom's favorite instructors, smiles brightly from the counter. She's been teaching at the studio for eons, but her pregnancy has progressed to the point where it's easier for her to work the reception desk. "Wren! How're you doing? How's UCSC?"

"Hey, Mizuki." Grinning, I walk over and clasp her hands. "It's everything I hoped it would be. How've you been? How's the baby?" Standing on tiptoe, I peer over the counter and down to her very round, pregnant belly.

"I feel good! I actually taught a prenatal yoga class this morning." Her cheeks flush with pleasure. She and her girlfriend have wanted this baby for years, enduring one miscarriage after another. Seeing her at this stage feels like such a victory. "And the baby's doing great. Kicking a lot, especially when I lie down. We took a video last night if you want to see it?"

"Yes! Send it to me." I squeeze her hands. "Is Mom in the office? I told her I'd be stopping by."

"She mentioned that," she says, inclining her head toward the closed door across the small foyer. "Go ahead—she's expecting you."

Mom opened Lotus Studios fifteen years ago, when I was three. I can't count how many late nights I found her poring over bills and receipts at our kitchen table, trying to work the numbers in her favor. The recent rent increase wasn't the only time we worried we'd lose the studio, but we've always pulled through thanks to Mom's tenacity and her very loyal following amongst Santa Cruz's locals.

She sits now behind an intricately detailed cherry wood desk, a cherished antique from my great-grandparents. A watercolor with the words *Follow Your Bliss* hangs on the wall behind her. "Little bird," she says with a pleased smile, raising her arms to me.

"Maternal goddess." Rounding the desk, I bend to give her a hug and a kiss.

"How are things? How's school?" she asks. "Want some kombucha? That batch I've been brewing is ready."

I wrinkle my nose, remembering the large, glass container of dark, floaty muck in the kitchen. "Eh, I'm good. Thanks, though."

"You sure? You know it's great for the microbiome, and it's essential we nourish our immune systems, especially during winter."

I smile fondly at her, sinking onto the purple corduroy couch across Mom's office. "I'll be okay."

"How's Saira doing? I saw her Mama at the store last week." Mom rests her chin on her palm, a small smile playing at her lips.

"She's good—I just Facetimed her. She'll be back for Thanksgiving." Saira's over at Berkeley, although she's been talking about coming home and transferring to UCSC. I steal a ginger candy from the crystal bowl on Mom's desk, popping it into my mouth. "So, what did Rodrigo send? The suspense is killing me."

"Oh, yes!" Mom reaches into her desk, pulling open in a drawer. "Here you go."

It's a large envelope, a little bulkier and heavier than the average letter. I rip it open, hoping it's a couple of paychecks because I'm broke as a joke these days.

But it's not. Instead, there are three slightly battered postcards from Brazil. My heart gives a surprised lurch in my chest as I flip one over and read the back.

Wren,

I hope these postcards are getting to you.
This is the São Paulo Cathedral. As an architecture nerd,
it's one of my favorite places in the city.
Hope freshman year's everything you
hoped it would be.
Luca

Swallowing, I flip the card over and examine the cathedral in the picture for a moment. The next card features Christ the Redeemer against a bright blue sky. My heart skips a beat—he remembered. The postmark on this card, and the message, tell me it was sent first.

Hey Wren,

Greetings from São Paulo.
Sorry we couldn't hang out again.
Didn't know where to send this,
so I sent it to the Sweet Spot. Hope you get it.
You said Brazil, and this was on your bucket list...
Here you go.
Luca

The last one is of a calm, quiet beach, palm trees studding the curvy coastline: *Lagoinha.*

Wren,

Just started fall semester at Universidade Federal de Santa Catarina

in Florianópolis. It's beautiful here. Killer beaches.
I surf all the time but I miss home.
Luca

I read the words over and over, trying to imagine the boy I met in such a far-away place. His handwriting's more of a rushed and messy scrawl than the other two, and I imagine he may've been a bit homesick when he wrote it.

"What are those?" Mom asks after a moment, peering over curiously.

I hand the postcards over, warmed from the inside out. "Postcards. From Luca. Remember that guy I met on the boardwalk?"

She examines the postcards for a long time, eventually looking up at me with a satisfied gleam in her eyes. "Those pictures in your room—this is the guy you were with, isn't it?"

I give her a serious side-eye, wondering just how much she's seen. Before college started, even though I'd displayed the photo strip in my room, I'd kept the ones of Luca and I kissing hidden in a drawer. I mean, come on—they were *way* too intimate. Still, I wouldn't put it past my mother to have discovered them during one of her cleaning frenzies. She always says she's not being nosy, but I have my doubts.

"Oh, come on, Wren. You had those pictures up for months," she says, folding her arms. "And they're gone now, which leads me to believe you took them with you to your dorm."

"Yes, yes, Detective. You're right."

"So, he did come back for you, didn't he? I knew it!"

Chuckling, I lean forward and pluck the postcards back into my possession. "This isn't the movies, Mom—he didn't come back *for me*. He and his friends just happened to be at the boardwalk again and we ran into each other. It was right when Saira came back from Encinitas."

"Come on, little bird. I need more than that."

"Saira and I were hanging out on the beach, waiting for the movie to start. The boys were playing soccer and we ran into each other. It was a total coincidence. We ended up spending the whole evening together—we even went on the Sky Glider." I pause, and Mom smiles knowingly.

I narrow my eyes. She totally saw the kissing pictures. "And into the photobooth."

But she just scoffs, leaning back in her chair. "Why didn't you two just exchange numbers? Is that too old-fashioned for this generation?"

"No, I think we would have." I sigh, staring at the slants and loops of Luca's handwriting. "But there was a fight on the boardwalk that night and things got derailed. He and his friends left pretty abruptly."

Her eyes narrow. "Was he fighting?"

"More like defending his friend. It was over really fast, but cops showed up and needless to say no one was feeling very romantic at that point." My chest tightens as I remember Luca, glancing back over his shoulder at me as he and his friends melted into the crowd. "Anyway, apparently he left soon after for this internship in São Paulo." I hold a postcard up. "I thought for a long time he'd forgotten about me. Guess not."

"He couldn't forget you," Mom says, standing. She wanders over to the window overlooking the street. "You're special. One of a kind."

"You have to say that. You're my mother."

"Doesn't make it any less true," she says sagely. "Regardless, there must be a reason fate allowed Rodrigo to sit on these all damn summer, right? There must be a reason you're only now seeing them."

Yeah, well, maybe if Rodrigo had sent me these earlier, I could have written back—the first postcard has a return address. I wonder if Luca's back in the States now.

"Anyway." I stand, sliding my bag over my arm. "How've you been?"

"I'm okay." She smiles a little. "Busy, busy. Getting ready for Mizuki's maternity leave."

"Oh, that's right—who's gonna man the front desk?" I unwrap another ginger candy. "Or rather, woman the front desk."

She tosses her hands up.

"Maybe I can do it, part-time," I muse, considering my work study as one of UCSC's library assistants.

"Maybe." She nods thoughtfully. "We can talk about it."

"How's Darius?"

She blinks really quickly and looks down at the desk.

Alarmed, I go to her side of the desk and squeeze her shoulder. "Mom?"

"We decided to cool it." Her voice is even, steady, but her shoulders sag.

"What? Why?" I ask quietly, lowering to a squat so I can look up into her face.

"Holy Basil is opening up another location in San Clemente, and he's been offered head chef there." She sniffles, giving me a brave smile. "He asked me to go down there with him, but I told him I couldn't go."

Mixed emotions swirl through me. I'd miss my mom so much if she left, but I'm old enough to be on my own. San Clemente isn't that far away, and I tell her that. "You should follow your bliss," I say, linking our fingers together.

"Oh, Wren. This is my bliss. My entire life is here—you, the studio, Gramma Kate. These streets, these beaches." She shakes her head. "I care about Darius, but I don't need Darius. The universe obviously has different plans for us."

When I talk about the universe, it's tongue in cheek, but when my mother does, she's serious. "If you say so," I say dubiously, straightening up. "I just want you to be happy."

"I am happy." But her eyes shine with tears as she stands, and she drags me into a fierce hug. "I'll be fine. This is grown folks stuff."

"I'm grown," I remind her, my voice muffled by the fabric of her pashmina. "You can always talk to me about this kind of stuff, you know. Always."

She squeezes me a little tighter.

"I really like Darius," I whisper. "And I know you do, too. Maybe…"

"It's done, little bird." Setting me at arm's length, she inclines her head toward the clock on the opposite wall. "Listen, I have a class in ten…I'd love to have you stay. It would be like old times."

"I guess I could do that. You have an extra pair of leggings I can wear?"

Looks like the Arlo conversation will have to wait.

Dear Arlo

T o: Arlo Janvier

Subject: re: stuff

Dear Arlo,

I'm finally done with exams. Thank God! If I never see another test again, it'll be too soon. Where did you go to college? Did you always know you wanted to be a photojournalist? What was your most exciting assignment? The scariest? Do you have a favorite?

At first, I was more interested in the science of the mind. I wanted to help people, to counsel them—my friends always said I was the best listener. But lately, I've really been feeling my sociology classes. I think I want to study family and community and the impact 'nurture' has on us, not just 'nature.' How who we are impacts who we become. Still pretty broad right now, but I can feel it coming together.

By the way, I haven't told my mom about you yet, but I will soon.

Wren

From: Arlo Janvier

To: Wren Angelos

Subject: re: re: stuff

Dear Wren,

I went to NYU. It was my dream school. Interestingly, I too started off majoring in sociology, but I realized pretty soon I wanted to study people groups by photographing them. It was a major shift for me, leaving science for the arts. Thankfully, my parents are artists and they supported me.

My scariest job was a couple of years ago, photographing a series of violent protests in Southeast Asia. Some of my best photos came from that assignment, but there were times I thought I wouldn't make it home. Most of my assignments are exciting...one that comes to mind is last year's Winter Olympics. Similarly, I have too many favorites to pick just one, but last year's Holi festival in Udaipur is high on the list. I'd love to share my photos with you one day.

I hope your mom doesn't feel blindsided when you tell her. That was never my intention.

Yours,
  Arlo

Luca

Surreal. Being back here is surreal.

Carried by the crowd, I float through SFO airport, bleary eyed and blinking. Christmas music plays quietly from the overhead speakers, frequently interrupted by announcements. Except for a very brief trip back home in early August, which I paid for myself, I haven't been on American soil in ages.

My phone buzzes. Stepping aside so the couple behind me can rush ahead, I slide my phone from my pocket and glance at the screen. It's my brother, Nico. I texted him a few minutes ago, upon landing.

Nico: In the cell phone waiting area. Text me when you get your bags.

Luca: Will do.

I yawn, widely. Not only is Brazil five hours ahead of San Francisco, but our already-long flight was delayed thanks to shitty weather. Following the overhead signs, I weave my way through the late-night airport crowd and head toward baggage claim.

The carousel finally appears. Bags go around and around, slowly being picked up by people who look as exhausted as me. I spy one of my battered, black suitcases, followed closely by two more. Usually I travel light, but I was living abroad for six months. Dragging my bags off the carousel, I send Nico another text and drag myself outside.

He pulls up about ten minutes later, grinning as I lug my oversize bags over.

"Hey, bud," he says, enveloping me in a tight hug. "Welcome home."

"Thanks, Nic." I return the hug, clapping him on the back gratefully. "And thanks for coming. Sorry it's so late." It's nearly two a.m. Nico has work in the morning, and small children, so I appreciate the sacrifice.

"Don't even worry about it," he says, popping the trunk. "It's not every day your little brother returns home from the motherland after having been gone for so long."

Chuckling at his extra dramatic choice of words, I load my bags and shut the trunk. We jump into his minivan and pull away from the curb right as one of the airport officers begins to wander over.

Yawning again, I close my eyes and sink against the headrest. I spent the second half of the flight sleeping, but my system is going haywire with the time zone change. It feels good to relax.

"How was the flight?" asks Nico.

"Longer than ever. I fell asleep during both my movies."

"Damn, I haven't been back there for...eight years," Nico muses. "How's Pai? You two patch things up?"

I rub my hand over my beard. I haven't shaved in days. "We're not actively fighting anymore, if that's what you're asking."

Nico glances at me, squeezing my shoulder. We kept in touch all right during my time away, but I kept things positive, focusing on my job, and then later, my studies. Most of what he knows about what went down is from Mãe, who can't keep a secret to save her life...not that our dad's shitty behavior's a secret.

Pai grew up in LA, a third-generation Brazilian kid with an aggressive desire to outperform everyone else. We have a lot of family in Brazil, so he went to the University of São Paulo on full scholarship, returning to the US only to attend grad school at Stanford. That's where he met Mãe. They fell in love, got married and had Nico and me, but after a while Pai's desire to return to Brazil to advance his career in software development drove a wedge between them.

That, and the other woman he'd started seeing over there.

Somehow, despite all of that, the divorce was probably as amicable as it could be. Mãe says they'd grown apart long before they split, but I've always marveled at how well they seem to get along.

Until recently, anyway. Mãe was furious when Pai pulled his stunt last spring, his refusal to finance my semester abroad if I wasn't going to take the internship as well. I don't think they've spoken more than a couple times. It took me a little longer to get angry, somewhere between August and September.

Because my father had been right—I was fucking great at software engineering, even software architecture. I was Marcos Pereira's wunderkind all summer, his protegé, his favorite and I made more money than I thought I would. But while the prestige and money were addictive, the work wasn't, only confirming what I'd known all along: coding was all right, but it was not ultimately what I wanted to do with my life.

The city lights sparkle by, reminding me of São Paulo's immense skyline. I wonder if Wren ever got my postcards. I included a return address once, when I was staying at Pai's place in the Jardins district, but I didn't expect to hear back. We'd had one night together. One fun, relatively innocent night—we didn't even sleep together. We hadn't made promises or plans.

But it was Wren I thought about while I was in Brazil, no one else, and I thought about her a lot more than I'd expected to. I'd thought about her sweet smile, her kisses, her questions. I thought about how she wanted to travel, and here I was doing it.

"Have you ever been outside of the U.S.?"

"No, but I will one day." She peeks up at me. "My bucket list is about a mile long."

"Where would you go first?" I ask.

"Oh, man. Santorini, Greece. Brazil—so you'd better send me a postcard..."

She was on my mind when I visited Rio de Janeiro and saw Christ the Redeemer late in the summer, as I gawked at the awe-inspiring architecture of several famed cathedrals, when I traversed the frenetic, glittering chaos of São Paulo at night. I'd told her she'd do these things one day and I'd meant it.

And yet, for the first time, I fully understood my privilege in having traveled as much as I had. The postcards seemed like a good way to acknowledge that. To let her know I hadn't forgotten her or our conversation on the Sky Glider.

I close my eyes and see hers, shining like stars beneath the lights of the boardwalk. How much has she changed since then? That was a lifetime ago. She's gotta be with somebody by now. Six months is a long time to be alone.

Mostly, I just hope college is what she hoped it would be.

* * *

Logan clinks his beer bottle to mine, just hard enough that the foam starts to rise. "Welcome back to the good ol' US of A, man. Good to have you home."

"It's good to be home." Taking a long pull of the crisp, cold brew, I settle back in my chair to people-watch. We're having lunch at one of our favorite old haunts in Berkeley, a couple blocks east of campus. "What've you been up to?"

In some ways, I probably already know—Logan and I kept in touch regularly while I was gone. I know he and Olivia finally went their separate ways, that his little brother transferred from Santa Clara to San Francisco State, and that Logan's making his way through Gabriel García Márquez's books. Partly because he's pretentious as fuck, but also because he's considering writing a paper on the author for his Spanish Lit course.

"Not a damn thing," he says, scrubbing his hands over his face. "Just work and school. Hey, Ben gave me your keys before leaving."

Ben's the kid who subleased my room while I was overseas. "Yeah, he emailed me. Thanks."

Our server, a cute, willowy brunette, comes over to get our lunch order. I can tell by Logan's half-smiles and hooded stare he's hungry for more than just burgers.

"Something tells me you'll have her number by the time we leave," I say once she's gone.

"Maybe," he says cryptically. He might just be high. He and Kellan often have wake n' bakes on the days they don't have class.

"How have you been doing without Olivia?" They were together for a long time, and even though they bickered more than not in the end, calling it quits must have been tough. "She handling this okay?"

"I talked to her this morning." He shrugs, turning his attention to his clasped hands. "She's having a hard time. Keeps asking if I ever cheated on her."

I watch him carefully. "Did you?"

Logan's pale blue eyes shoot up to mine. "What? No. You know I was faithful."

"You've always had wandering eyes, Lo. Maybe Olivia noticed."

"Fuck you, man," he says lightly, draining the rest of his beer. "Looking is not touching."

"No, but the intention's there regardless of whether it's ever carried out." Logan's always been free with his appreciation. Usually he does just look, but where there's smoke there's fire and Olivia's no fool.

96

"Where's all this coming from?" He narrows his eyes in suspicion, his eyes darting between mine. "Sounds like you got it all figured out."

"Just talking, Lo." I lean over and punch his shoulder, nixing the fight before it can start. I just endured months of strained relations with my dad. I don't need it here with my friends.

We go on to other things, but the mood's been tainted. Logan's been my best friend since we were kids, but he can be selfish and entitled, unwilling to concede. I learned a long time ago to choose my battles, and when it comes to him and his ways with women? I have no dog in that fight.

Afterward, when we're standing on the sidewalk outside, huddled in jackets against the sharp, winter wind, he hands me my keys. "You coming back tonight?"

I shake my head. I've been staying at the Walnut Creek house since I got back from Brazil. "Mãe and Dominic are having Nico, Phoebe, and the kids over for dinner so I'm gonna stay up there one more night. I'll be back tomorrow."

"Living the good life, huh?" He pats his belly. "Bring your boy back a plate."

"Done deal." We do our secret handshake, a silly but timeless relic from our teen years.

Logan laughs, eyes crinkling at the edges, and something in me warms. *This* is the kid I grew up with.

Sliding my hands into the pockets of my jacket, I head in the opposite direction, toward the side street I parked on. Berkeley's sea of diversity, funky stores and familiar murals feel like home, and I slow down some, enjoying the vibe.

Remembering a rare vinyl Nico mentioned wanting for Christmas, I duck into Rasputin. He's a hipster of the worst kind, but I love him, and if his precious record even exists, this place will have it. Logan and I used to come on the weekends back in the day, taking BART to the station on Shattuck and then riding our skateboards through the streets.

Smiling at the memory, I wander over to the appropriate bins and start flipping through them. It takes nearly twenty minutes, but I find it. Cheering inwardly, I pull the record out and examine the playlist on the back, wanting to make sure it's what Nico talked about.

A husky, feminine giggle floats above the Led Zeppelin playing throughout the store, and I pause, looking up. I could be crazy, but it sounded like Wren. She laughs again and I look around, trying to match it to one of the people wandering about the store.

"Luca Cardoso, as I live and breathe. I heard you were back."

Another familiar voice, but a different one. Turning around, I come face to face with Brooke Henley. This isn't so shocking—she's from around here, if I remember correctly. "Brooke, hey."

She smiles coyly, reaching up to pull me into a light hug. Her expensive perfume is just as heady as it's always been. "Hey, yourself. What're you doing in Berkeley?" Her eyes run over the records I was just searching through.

"Just had lunch with a friend. You remember Logan, right?"

She nods. "I think so."

"Anyway, I'm doing a little Christmas shopping now." I hold the record up. "I was close by, so I figured I might as well."

"Nice! I did all my ordering online this year. Less hassle." Brooke tilts her head. "Are you sticking around or heading back to Santa Cruz? My friend's throwing a chill little party later on. You should come."

I'm still tired from my travels and the rigorous semester that preceded them, but her expectant smile has me considering. "I'm actually staying with my family out in Walnut Creek tonight, but I'll think about it."

Brooke tosses her hair back, keeping her eyes locked on mine. "Well, let me know. I'll text you the address." She's sending some pretty strong signals today, making me wonder if she's one of those girls who enjoys chasing more than being chased.

"Will do. Good to see you, Brooke."

She tiptoes to kiss my cheek. "You too."

I don't watch her go, instead heading over to the cashier to pay for Nico's record.

My feelings toward Brooke have shifted since last summer. We were supposed to hang out the night before I left but she and her friends never showed. I found out later they went to a house party a few blocks away instead. Matty had once called her a player, and while I wouldn't go that far, I know I'm not the only guy she's interested in. Which is cool; she's not the only girl I'm into, either.

But a low-key party sounds fun. I shoot Logan, Matty and Kellan a group text before I can overthink things. Why not? Jetlag or not, I could use a night out.

Wren

~⚬⚬⚬~

"Just one more stop and then we can go home." Janya Mangal aims her fob at the trunk of her car, popping it open so she can toss her bags in.

I'm a little more careful with my new-to-me vintage concert posters. Cradling them to my body, I slide into the backseat.

"I can't believe you actually found those," Saira says. "That was nothing short of luck."

"I know!" I sigh happily, gazing out the window as Janya pulls onto the street. I've collected artsy concert posters since middle school, but Mom's the one who really loves them. She'll freak when she sees the Fleetwood Mac Tusk Tour poster, circa '79. "Thanks for taking us, Janya."

I'm spending the weekend with Saira and we're staying in her sister's Berkeley apartment. Unbeknownst to Mr. and Mrs. Mangal, Janya basically lives with her boyfriend, Justin in his apartment. He's the boy Janya fell for Encinitas, the one we figured she'd cycle through and forget about in a few weeks.

But she's as head over heels now as she was then, and apparently, so is he. The PDA is nonstop, so Saira and I keep to Janya's real apartment while they stay at his.

Anyway, when Justin mentioned that Rasputin Music in Berkeley was having a special sale on original concert posters, I knew I had to go.

"No worries." Janya twists in her seat as she reverses out of our parking spot. "I'm just glad you finally made it up for a visit, Wren. My apartment's been going to waste."

I reach up to squeeze her shoulder. "I'm glad I could come, too."

"And whose fault is that?" Saira teases, rolling her eyes at me in the side mirror. "Seeing as you're living with Justin? Such a tawdry situation."

"Oh, shut up." Janya laughs, shoving Saira. "You sound just like Auntie Aditi with that mess."

Saira shoots her a suspicious glance. "She knows?"

"No, but that's what she'd say if she did." Janya's lustrous black ponytail swings as we round a corner. "Seriously, though. You guys came all the time when you were younger."

"That's because we were in high school and had nothing else to do," says Saira.

"Such a little bitch." Janya laughs.

I laugh too, but I squeeze Saira's hand. She's been terribly homesick, and lately, really depressed. Something's going on with her and that's the real reason I came to Berkeley.

"And anyway, I'm like, right down the street," continues Saira. "You could come see me, too, you know."

"When are you coming home for Christmas?" I ask Janya.

"Two weeks. Justin's going home to San Diego, but he promised he'd come to Santa Cruz to ride the holiday train with me."

"Ahh, the holiday train! I can't wait!" cries Saira, bouncing in her seat. She peeks back at me. "We're gonna do it, right?"

"Are you kidding? It's not even a question." We've been riding the Santa Cruz Holiday Lights Train every December since elementary school. It's tradition.

Janya's phone bursts into a gooey, popular love song. She never texts and drives, so she tosses it onto Saira's lap. "That's Justin, see what he wants."

"Something about a party in the weeds? And do we want to go?" Saira looks up, wrinkling her nose. "What?"

"The Weeds," Janya says with a chuckle, drumming her fingers on the steering wheel as we pause at a stop sign. "Is what they call their friend's place. He lives on the top floor of this building in downtown Berkeley that has a rooftop with a garden. A very overgrown garden."

"Of weeds?"

"Of weeds and weed." She snickers. "Among other types of flora."

I clear my throat. "Sounds very Berkeley."

Janya glances at me in the rearview mirror. "You want to go? We don't have to; we can always order takeout and stay in, too. I know you two want to head back home in the morning."

"Nah, sounds fun," says Saira, glancing at me. "Right?"

"Sure." I nod. "Let's do it."

"Hey, whatever happened with Arlo?" Janya asks suddenly. "You guys still in touch?"

"We've been emailing, yeah."

"Have you told your mom yet?"

"No, not yet." Guilt prickles through me. Keeping this from my mother is killing me.

"You should tell her. The longer you wait, the bigger this gets."

"She'll probably freak the hell out, Janya," Saira says, placing her sister's phone in the console.

"I don't know about that." We stop at a light, where the elder Mangal girl casts me a thoughtful glance. "Maybe she's always known this day would come. She has to have considered you might want to meet the other side of your family, you know?"

"He was a sperm sample, Janya. The whole point was for her to keep it simple and do this solo." I turn my gaze out the window, watching a group of younger teenagers messing around at a bus stop. "This is not doing it solo. This is messy and complicated."

"I don't know, but the longer you keep it a secret the messier it's gonna get."

* * *

I exit the bathroom, wiping my hands on my pants since there was no towel with which to dry them. Justin's friends are quirky, to say the least, their loft decorations of reclaimed materials and random art even more eclectic than my mother's apartment. She'd probably love this place.

It's obvious why so many people hang out at The Weeds. There's food and drink, music and people in abundance. The rooftop itself is funky and aesthetically pleasing, populated by a sundry assortment of succulents, aloes, ferns, wildflowers, bluebells, and yes, weeds. It's like being in the Garden of Eden. I rejoin Saira, who's sitting with Janya, Justin and their friends around a rustic firepit in the rooftop's center.

Janya hands me a fresh beer and pats the cushion beside her. "Are you cold? Posey brought out blankets."

I don't know who Posey is, but I accept a blanket gratefully, snuggling beneath it with Saira.

Taking a long drink of my beer, I turn my attention to the stars. Peter Tosh's guitar shifts into random EDC before fading into someone's questionable recording of a Phish concert. Swatches of sound from the street below float up between songs: honking cars, laughter, voices. Berkeley on a Saturday night.

New people come and go, people I don't know and whose names I won't remember. Joints are passed, beers are cracked open. Posey's brownies do the rounds. Janya warns us to just have one.

"Like we've never had weed brownies," Saira says with a scoff. "Wren goes to UCSC, for God's sake."

"You've never had Posey's brownies." Janya pops half of one into her mouth. "But please, go on with your bad selves."

Saira and I decided to share one. I break a piece of brownie off and eat it slowly, enjoying the chocolate melting on my tongue. It tastes better than most I've had—apparently Posey works for a vegan bakery.

I've just finished my half when Justin pokes my arm. "Wren! You go to Santa Cruz."

"I sure do."

"Dallas goes to Santa Cruz." He tilts his head toward one of the guys standing next him, a tall, blond kid with big, brown eyes and freckles. They must have just walked in, because I didn't notice them before. "He's just visiting, too."

"Hey." Dallas shoots me a cute half-grin I'm fairly sure gets the girls. "What year are you?"

"Freshman."

"Yeah, me too." His grin grows. There's something familiar about him, but I doubt we've ever met. "I stay in Amnesty."

I stand up so he doesn't have to bend to hear me. "I'm over in Angela Davis."

He nods, pushing his hand through his longish, blond hair. "I know a couple of kids who live there."

We share the awkward smile of people who've just met but have bizarrely intimate knowledge of one another's living situations. Saira walks by, giving me googly eyes over Dallas' shoulder.

"So, what's your major?" And then I roll my eyes at myself. "That was lame. You don't have to answer."

He laughs, eyes sparkly and gleeful. Maybe he had a brownie, too. "You gotta ask, right? I'm studying sports medicine, but sailing's my thing. I've been doing it competitively for years."

"Nice! Are you on UCSC's sailing team?"

"Yup."

"Maybe I'll have to come to a meet or whatever sometime."

"It's just a race. Or a regatta." He cocks his head as he gazes down at me, settling into a quieter, flirtier mode. "You definitely should. What—"

"Dallyyy…" A skinny kid stumbles over, handing Dallas a pipe fragrant with greenery. "D'you wanna hit this?"

"Already did, so I'm good right now." Dallas chuckles as his friend disappears. "Sorry about that. He's gets goofy when he's yicked."

That slang feels like home. "You grow up in Santa Cruz?"

"Born and raised."

"Me too. Santa Cruz High."

"Cardinals, huh?" He smirks. "I went to Kirby."

"Private school, huh?" I say, mimicking his tone. A thought occurs to me and I perk up, pointing. "I bet you were on their sailing team too, weren't you?"

"Every year."

"I may have seen you guys at some point." During certain times of year, the water around Santa Cruz is filled with cheery, bright sails. I wonder how many times Dallas was one of them.

"Yeah, we were pretty hard to miss," he agrees. "Anyway, what're you studying?"

"Psychology."

"Messing with people's minds, I see how it is." He looks down at his phone suddenly, face illuminated by the glow. "Shit, my brother's looking for me. We gotta go."

Bubble, popped. I take a step back, startled by the abrupt shift. "Your brother?"

"Yeah. He's at another party around the corner."

"How'd you end up here?"

"My friend knows somebody here. A girl." Dallas whips out his phone, typing something into it before refocusing his attention on me. "Would it be weird if I asked for your number?"

My heart skips a little. Dallas has that irresistibly chill appeal I thought I got over in high school. "Not weird at all."

I put my info into his phone and hand it back, glad it's dark. Posey's brownie has me feeling pretty silly, and I don't want to imagine what my face must look like.

"When're you headed back?" he asks, taking a couple steps back.

"Tomorrow."

"Sweet. I'll see you around then, Wren."

Luca

I fight another yawn, trying to concentrate on Logan's rambling story. He's drunk, and he's not the only one. I can barely sit up, thanks to a winning combo of vodka and jetlag. That could be a drink.

I'll have a vodka jetlag, please.

Kellan pockets his phone, glancing over at me. "Dally's on his way back now."

"Where was he?" I ask, finishing my drink. It's mostly melted ice by this point. A vodka jetlag, on the rocks.

"Up the street, at a friend of a friend of a friend's house or something. I don't know. I told him to get back so we could go."

The girl Kellan's been chatting up whispers in his ear. Whatever it was, it must've been dirty, because he bites his lip and hauls her onto his lap.

Yawning, I glance at my watch. Just past two in the morning. There was a time that would be of little consequence, but I'm still on Florianópolis time and all I want is bed. Too bad I have to Uber all the way back to Walnut Creek tonight.

But it's worth it. I'll take advantage of the quiet house tomorrow, sleep a little extra.

"I'm think I'm gonna try one of those White Russians." Brooke leans in, tapping her long, pale pink nails over my hand. "You in?"

"Not unless I want to pass out in my Uber." Rubbing my face, I get to my feet and stretch.

"You look like you might pass out right now," Brooke says with a pout.

"I might." I give her an apologetic smile, squeezing her shoulder. "Sorry. I just haven't gotten over this jet lag yet."

"I understand." She leans close, her breath awash in Kahlua or whatever she's been drinking. "When I went to London last year for spring break, it took me nearly two weeks to recover."

"Let's go," Kellan says, holding up his phone. "They're outside."

Kellan's little brother, Dallas, came up with some friends from Santa Cruz. They hung out for a while before wandering off to check out another party nearby, but now the hour's late and it's time to go. Everyone but me, Logan, Kellan, Brooke and her friend—the one currently sucking Kellan's earlobe—has left.

Kellan's gonna get laid, that much is obvious, but I'm surprised Logan stuck around. The girl he was talking to left earlier. We say our goodbyes and leave, joining another after-hours crowd milling around on the sidewalk.

"You wanna share an Uber home with me?" Brooke asks, biting her lip. Her aquamarine eyes are shiny, her cheeks red from drinking.

Damn. I want to, I really, really do, but I can't. Not tonight, not when I'm dead on my feet. It wouldn't be the experience either of us are hoping for.

"I'm actually going to head back to my mom's to try and recover." I yawn yet again, pulling her into a hug. "But let's talk soon."

"Ugh, what a killjoy," she teases. I know she's disappointed. I am, too, but my dick doesn't work when I'm this tired. "Go home, old man. Call me tomorrow."

"I will."

"You guys coming?" Brooke's friend calls, climbing into the back of a huge SUV with Kellan and the boys. "There's plenty of room!"

"Might as well," Brooke says, shaking her head as she walks away. "Later, Luca. Don't be a stranger."

"You good, brother?" Logan claps my back and steps off the curb. "You could just crash at Kellan's Airbnb instead of trekking out to Walnut Creek. His money ass got a place in the Berkeley Hills."

I shake my head with a tired laugh, imagining how loud that scenario would be. Normally that would be appealing, but tonight I need sleep. "Not tonight, bro. I'm going home. Where it's quiet."

Logan peers at me in drunken concern. "You good?"

"Yeah, I'll be fine." A car matching my ride's description pulls up, and I start toward it. "See you tomorrow, Lo."

But before I can get in, Brooke jogs back over, grabs my face, and kisses me square on the mouth. We don't deepen it much, but it's nice. Something to think about.

And then she wipes her thumb across my bottom lip and leaves, lobbing one last sultry look over her shoulder.

Wren

It's late, and the clear, cold air feels fantastic against my hot cheeks.

Janya giggles, more giddy than usual. "We have to get boba! Have to." She squeezes between Saira and me, linking her arms through ours.

"They're open late," adds Saira. "The best you'll ever have, promise."

It's about one in the morning, and we just left the Weeds. Justin forgot his phone upstairs, so we're waiting for him on the sidewalk.

"You want boba tea, don't you, Wren?" presses Janya.

I pat her arm. "Of course, I do."

Across the street and down a little, a group of people pours out from the front door of another apartment building. I watch them with a detached sort of interest, wondering what their evening's been like. Berkeley isn't that far from Santa Cruz, but the vibe here is so different.

"You're thinking about that blond kid, aren't you?" Saira reaches around her sister to poke my shoulder. "What was his name? Dallas?"

"Dallas?" Janya gasps. "What's his brother's name, Ponyboy?"

She and Saira dissolve into giggles.

"Bet you never thought you'd come all the way up here just to meet someone from Santa Cruz," continues Saira.

"Do you two even need me for this conversation?" I tease.

Janya hugs me closer. "I'm just saying, he was so cute. You should definitely sample that."

"Not all of us are big, sampling sluts," says Saira.

"Contrarily, I'm in a monogamous relationship," Janya says. "Unlike some people. But whatever…"

Their bickering fades into a soft, lilting ramble—fighting is their love language.

A giddy hoot from the group across the street rekindles my attention. They're all drunken hugs and flirting and laughter, but then one figure swims into sharp relief against the others. A face that shoves my heart into a rapid staccato.

Luca?

I mentally review all that I know about him, which isn't much. He's from around here, from the Bay Area, though he told me Walnut Creek. Still, this is close enough I suppose, and the semester's over, so maybe he's back

114

from Brazil. I think of the postcards he sent me, tucked safely into my journal alongside the photo strip of our night together.

My stomach quivers as I scan the rest of his crowd, now recognizing Kellan and that other guy, the not-so-nice friend. Luca pauses to talk to one of them, clasping his hands behind his neck, and the move is so familiar that it sends a flutter up my spine.

Memories wash over me: watching *The Lost Boys* under the stars, talking on the Sky Glider, the way Luca's dark eyes shone beneath the lights of the boardwalk. His mouth, fitted over mine…his tongue, dancing with mine.

And then a pretty girl with long, blonde hair rushes over and kisses him, thoroughly power washing any lingering memories from my mind. It's like being smacked by a rogue wave at the beach, and I flinch into Janya's embrace.

"Aww I love you, too," she says with a sigh, rubbing my back. "Come on, Justin's back. Let's go get some boba."

* * *

After a teary goodbye with Saira, I leave early in the morning. I grab a coffee from a local coffee place, enjoying how the fog from the bay enshrouds the roads with mist. It looks like I'm driving through a dream.

It doesn't feel like it, though.

For one thing, Saira finally told me what was going on with her. A couple weeks ago, after a party, a guy she thought was a friend had sex with her when she was passed out. She couldn't bring herself to call it what it was, and I was the only person she'd told. I asked why she hadn't told Janya, and she said she couldn't deal with her family just yet. Which says a lot, because they're tight.

She's already submitted the paperwork to transfer from Berkeley to UCSC. I'm glad she's coming home; I just hate that this is why. We talked and cried until we fell asleep, but it was on my mind the second I woke up. My heart has never felt so heavy.

And then there's Luca. I've thought lots over the months about what it would be like to see him again. Usually, in my fantasies, he's all over me, asking me out, kissing me. Sometimes, we end up rolling nakedly around my bed.

Not once did I imagine it going down the way it did, with someone else's lips on his. Seeing Luca so unexpectedly and then not being able to make contact hurt. Like, really hurt. I woke up thinking about him, and hours later he's still on my mind. Not even my favorite true crime podcast is enough to yank me back to reality.

Sighing, I merge onto I-880. God, that girl. Did they spend the night together? Probably. I knew from the first moment I saw him—boys like Luca are never single, and even if they are, they're never alone. Why'd I have to see him at all last night? Why couldn't I have just had my fun, flirting with Dallas and goofing around with the girls?

Because really, Luca is firmly in the past. The more I think about it, the harder it is to convince myself that our interludes on the boardwalk were anything more than summer fun. Not even a summer fling—we may've exchanged spit, but we never exchanged numbers.

He did send the postcards. So, maybe he tried. It's not my fault I didn't get them until it was too late, but it wasn't his, either. Still, he could've at least given me his phone number or an email address. He didn't even write his last name.

Fleetwood Mac comes blaring over the Bluetooth. Pausing my podcast, I switch over to my mother's call.

"Hey Mom."

"Good morning, little bird," she says. "Are you on your way back already?"

"Yep. You at the studio?"

"Yes, we had sunrise yoga. Oh!" she cries. "Mizuki went into labor this morning! She's at the hospital now."

"Aw, really?" Something warm and good opens up in my chest. Something real. "That's so exciting! Keep me updated on that—I'll be back in Santa Cruz in about an hour."

"Take your time," she pleads. "There's no rush."

"Traffic's light. But I'll be careful."

"All right. I'll let you go, then. I love—"

And then it happens. The feeling I've been waiting for, that it's time to tell her everything. "Wait! I have to tell you something."

She pauses for a beat, probably waiting for me to go on. "Okay, what?"

I let out a long breath, my brain all scrambled the way it gets whenever I think about Arlo. "I think I found my father."

Mom sets an ornate tray with two steaming mugs of tea, two spoons, and a dish of sugar cubes onto the coffee table. "Here you go. It's cinnamon."

"Thanks." Leaning forward, I take one of the mugs.

"I hope you like sugar cubes," she says, eyes closed as she sips her tea. "I found them at the farmers' market. Couldn't resist."

Wrapping my cold hands against the warmth of the mug, I take a small sip and lean back into the couch. We sit quietly for a minute. A long minute. When I told Mom about Arlo earlier on the phone, she told me, very calmly, to save it until I got home. I couldn't tell if she was livid or just really zen.

But now I feel the weight of her stare, and when I peek over, she's watching me. "Go on," she says, as if moments, and not hours, have passed since I dropped my bomb.

So, I do. I tell her all about sending my sample into Kith&Kin.com and about Arlo Janvier's first message. I tell her about the moment we decided to leave the platform and move to personal emails, and all of the things that we've learned about each other over the past few months. When I get to Melvin and Pamplemousse, her calm exterior crumples and she puts her tea down.

"Mom?"

"Months, Wren? Really? You've been doing this behind my back for months?"

"You make it sound like we're having an illicit affair," I mutter, chewing on my bottom lip.

"You might as well be!" she cries, holding a jeweled throw pillow to her middle.

"That's not fair," I say, although maybe it is. "I didn't tell you because I knew you'd react like this."

"Can you blame me? I never, ever thought I'd have to deal with this," she says. "It's not like it was an open adoption, where there was always a possibility you'd one day connect with your birth parents, Wren. I did it this way for a reason. Kith and Kin? Really?"

"I'm sorry," I whisper, tears filling my eyes. I don't know what else to say. "I didn't join to find a dad; I just wanted to know who I was."

"You know who you are," she says, squeezing my knee. "You're mine. Gramma Kate's. You're an Angelos."

She's right, of course. But she's wrong, too. "I'm not just an Angelos, Mom. There are things about me that are different from you and Gramma Kate. Maybe they're from Arlo, maybe not, but it's my right to know."

"I guess I just... I didn't realize you wanted to know."

"I didn't either. Not until he contacted me." But a tiny voice deep inside wonders if this is true. What was I expecting, submitting my DNA to a site like that? Every sort of family member but a father? Maybe.

"I guess meeting up is the next step," she murmurs, drawing her finger around the rim of her cup. "Right?"

"He'd like to meet me, yes." He wants to meet the both of us, but I'll tell her that later.

"Not for Christmas, I hope. Too soon." She takes a huge gulp of tea and winces. "Sorry; that sounds awful. I know this is important to you."

"And I know it's weird for you." I drop another sugar cube into my tea, watching as it dissolves. "I get it."

"I love you, little bird. And I'm glad you told me." My mother sits up, tucking me into her side. "I just don't want you to get hurt."

And I realize I'm not the only one who could get hurt here. Having Arlo in the picture opens her up to the possibility of pain and disappointment, too. But I push that aside. Ignore it. I close my eyes and lean in, luxuriating in the familiarity of her mom smell, and whisper, "I think it'll be okay."

Dear Arlo

From: Wren Angelos

To: Arlo Janvier

Subject: I told her!

Hey Arlo,

I told Mom. She freaked out a little, but she's warming to the idea.
   I have to run to class, but I wanted to let you know.
   Wren

P.S. I've been listening to the podcast you suggested, where they read letters as if they were written by historical figures.
   My faves so far:
   Briseis' letter to Achilles after she's taken from him,
   and Esther, from the Bible. She was a real badass.

From: Arlo Janvier

To: Wren Angelos

Subject: re: I told her!

Dear Wren,

I'm not surprised your mother was upset, as she's probably feeling a little protective over you. Let me know if she'd like to talk, hopefully I can put her at ease.

I've been listening to your podcasts, too. Didn't think I'd have the stomach for true crime, but it's an addictive genre...

talk soon,
  Arlo

Wren

Spring

Emails with Arlo finally turn into phone calls. The first time he calls me, one evening when my classes are over, I'm so nervous I almost let it go to voicemail. But I don't. His voice is deep, his accent not as French. Obviously. I mean, it's not French at all because despite his name—Arlo Janvier—he's pretty American. He was born in New York City!

For Christmas, he sends me a gorgeous photography book about Paris and NYC hoodie, promising to one day bring me to both places. The thought of going anywhere with him is a little weird, but I appreciate the sentiment.

Mom knows we're in close contact, even though she's not thrilled about it. I try to give her space. I don't want my enthusiasm to overwhelm her, just as much as I don't want her reticence dampening my enthusiasm.

And then, right before spring break, I get another email.

From: Arlo Janvier

To: Wren Angelos

Subject: Guess what?

Heya Wren,

How are classes? How's creative writing going? Did you finish your short story on time?

Anyway, I have good news. I have about a week between assignments, so it would be a great time for me to shoot down to Santa Cruz and finally meet you. This coincides with your spring break, so I think it's meant to be. What do you think?

I've emailed your mother, too. (I figured you wouldn't mind, since you gave me her email address.) I think it's important she stays in the loop, don't you?

Talk soon,
  Arlo

My heart lurches. Wow. This is it—after nearly a year of communicating, I'm finally going to meet my dad. As much as I want to meet him, I don't know if I'm ready to. But I can't exactly tell him that, can I? More importantly, should I? No, no absolutely not. I respond before I can psych myself out any further.

From: Wren Angelos

To: Arlo Janvier

Subject: re: Guess what?

Hi Arlo,
*   All is well here in the sunshine. The weather is beautiful, even when nippy.*
*   Classes are fine...I totally nailed the short story! Math, not so much. I'll be glad when I'm done with that, yuck.*
*   I'll talk to Mom, but I think a visit would be great! Let me know the exact dates so I can keep the calendar clear.*
*   Xoxo,*
*   Wren*

Gnawing on my lip, I hit send. All of the fears I've had since we started talking, the ones that had started diminishing as we got to know each other, are bubbling to the surface again. What if the ease with which we communicate via the written word deteriorates into awkwardness in person? What if what I see as cultured and articulate online is actually snobby and insufferable in real life?

Worse, what if I'm the issue? Maybe it doesn't matter whether or not he impresses me.

What if I don't impress him?

* * *

Dallas and I leave the movie theater, still munching on the enormous tub of popcorn we bought.

"Ugh, take it," I say, shoving it back to him. "There was no reason to get a refill of this."

"I got the refill because it was free, and obviously that was a good idea because you're still eating it." Grinning, he tosses a kernel up and catches it in his mouth without breaking a stride.

"Because I have the munchies!" I moan, rubbing my belly. "No more for me."

"No more weed or popcorn? Because I still have a nice, fat nug waiting in the car..."

"No more popcorn! Also, you're a bad influence," I tease, linking my arm through his.

He laughs, pulling me along. "I'll take that as a 'yes.'"

Dallas and I started hanging out a couple of weeks after we got back to campus after winter break. He'd crossed my mind once or twice after our little meet up in Berkeley, but between class, work, and spending quality time with Saira, who was now officially a UCSC student, guys weren't taking up too much mental real estate.

And then we ran into each other one Friday, at a coffee shop on campus.

"Wren?" he asked, all excited.

"Dallas," I said, as surprised to see him as he was to see me. "Hey!"

"Swear to God, I was gonna text you, but it's been so crazy…our roommate got kicked out—"

I listened to him ramble until it was my turn to order, when he insisted on paying for me. I had class, but we agreed to talk later. We've been hanging out ever since.

We're attracted to each other, and we've kissed a few times, but Dallas doesn't seem interested in *actually* dating. And honestly, neither am I. For one thing, seeing Luca that night in Berkeley a few months ago made me realize how much I liked him, even if it'd been months and months since we'd hung out at the boardwalk. Until that fades maybe it's better that I take Dally up on his offers of harmless, no-strings-attached shenanigans. We have fun together. It's easy. And while Saira thinks our friends-with-benefits arrangement is a bad idea, we're keeping things light. That's what the college years are for, right?

"So, I think my dad's going to try and visit during break," I say, watching Dallas pack a bright green nugget of weed into his favorite bowl. We're in his dorm now, lounging on his bunk.

"Really? That's cool," he says, his bright blue eyes lighting up. Dallas doesn't know all the details, just that I've never met Arlo. "You excited?"

"Nervous," I admit. "But excited, yeah."

"Ah, it's gonna be great, you'll see." He winks, slipping a lighter from his pants. "He's lucky to have you for a kid. Here, you hit it first. To celebrate."

Arlo texts later that night. I'm fresh out of the shower, still a little stoned from my smoke session with Dallas, when my phone beeps with a message.

Arlo: I'll be there from 3/20 to 3/26.
 Staying at the Surf City Beach Hotel.

Wren: Awesome choice! (thumbs up emoji)

Arlo: can't wait!

I swallow, my heart skipping a beat.

Wren: me neither

* * *

Of course, because I'm not ready for this, the next two weeks speed by. Mom and I meet a couple of times to hash out Arlo's visit—she tends to neurotically over-plan when she's anxious and so do I—deciding we'll invite him over to the apartment for dinner on his second night in Santa Cruz.

"That'll give the two of you some time before he has to deal with me. And to, you know, recover from jet lag," she says, whirling around the kitchen as she attempts a vegan shepherd's pie. "Give him a chance to settle in."

"Whatever you think is best." Jumping up from my chair, I wrap my arms around her from behind and give her a good squeeze, startling a yelp from her. "Everything's going to be fine. In fact…"

Letting go of her, I pluck up my phone, navigate to my music app, and put on one of our jams: Bob Marley's "Three Little Birds". Mom sang it to me so much when I was little that I thought it was actually my song.

She laughs, pressing her hands to her flushed cheeks. "You're right, little bird, you're right."

We dance around the kitchen, Mom busting out her signature hippy-dippy moves, until the song ends. Nothing calms the soul like Bob, so I turn down the volume a bit and let the playlist run.

But after a while I start to feel like a phony, pretending I'm all hakuna matata when really, I've been battling feelings of uncertainty all week. I lean against the counter, watching my mother work as I look for the words to say what I'm feeling.

"Okay, I'm full of shit," I blurt. "Totally and completely full of it."

Mom glances back, furrowing her brow.

"I know you're nervous about meeting Arlo. I am too, but for different reasons." I suck in a deep breath, only to whoosh it all back out again. "He seems so interested in me now, but what if it turns out he liked me as a concept, this long, lost daughter deal, more than actual me? From what he's told us, he doesn't have any other kids. None that he's raised. What if he's romanticized things? What if having an actual relationship with me is underwhelming?"

My mother is silent for a while, carefully measuring spices and stirring her pot. When she does finally meet my eye, it's with thoughtful determination. "I'm going to try really hard to be a friend right now and not your overprotective mother. Because as your mom, I would kick that man's ass if he made you feel like anything less than what you are."

Tears spring to my eyes. Damn, I love my mom, even when—maybe especially when—she's channeling Mama Bear.

"But as your friend," she says, taking my hands in hers, "I'd ask you to remember that he was the one who contacted you first. He didn't have to do that. He's a human being, and he was looking for connection, just like you are. The universe has brought the two of you together for a reason. I really believe that." She pulls me into a hug. "You have much to offer, Wren. He is going to adore you."

Wren

A cute, chubby hostess with winged eyeliner to die for meets me at the podium with a smile. I've always kinda envied girls who really knew how to do their makeup. "Hi! Welcome to Loni's. Just one today?"

I glance around the diner, nervously fingering my necklace. "Actually, I'm meeting someone. I don't know if he's here yet."

"No worries, I can check! What's the last name?"

"Um, Janvier?"

Pursing her lips, she scans the small screen attached to the podium. "Yes, he's here. I'll bring you right over."

"Thanks," I say, nodding like a bobblehead. "I love your eyeliner, by the way."

"Thank you!" A delighted smile sparkles across her face. "It took me forever to learn, but I love playing with makeup."

"Well, you're good at it. I'm clueless."

She laughs, waving her hand. "It just takes practice. All right, here we are. Your server will be right with you!"

She disappears, leaving me alone with a strange man who is apparently my father. He's blonde and green-eyed, like I knew, but much more handsome than I'd anticipated. Younger looking, too, although I know he's actually forty-two.

"Arlo?" I say at the exact same time he stands, saying, "Wren!"

We share a dorky, uncomfortable laugh. I lurch forward, not sure if I should hug him or not, but he meets me halfway. "Wren," he says again, smiling warmly. "May I hug you?"

"Oh, yes, of course!" I'm still nodding as he wraps his arms around me. He's lanky, yet solid. I hug him back, my heart racing. He smells like Altoids and cologne.

We sit on either side of the booth, staring at each other and smiling. I chose Loni's diner because it was familiar and cozy, but the food's great, too. I figured if things went to shit, at least we'd have had a good meal—and on my turf.

"Thanks for meeting me today," he says, bowing his head slightly. He definitely sounds like a New Yorker. I think. "And for taking time out of your spring break—you probably had plans, didn't you? I always had plans at your age."

He's nervous, I realize. Endeared by his rambling and slightly pink

132

cheeks—that must be where I get my proclivity for blushing—I shake my head. "No, I knew you were going to try and come down. I think the timing is perfect, actually."

"Oh, okay. Good," he says, smoothing his napkin. He's got nice hands, clean nails.

Our server, a brawny, short guy in the Loni's trademark '50's hipster dress shirt and bowtie, walks over. He smiles, using his pencil to push his Buddy Holly glasses up. "Heya, folks. I'm Carlos, and I'll be serving you today. What can I get you to drink?"

"Hi, Carlos, how ya doing?" Arlo says, tossing him a friendly smile before ducking his head to scan the menu. I let out a silent, relieved breath. Mom always taught me that the way people treat those in customer service is a good indicator of who they are. "I'll have a cherry coke, please."

"And I'll have a Shirley Temple, please." I peek up at Carlos. "Extra cherries, if you can."

"Of course—what's a Shirley Temple without extra cherries?" he says with a wink. "Coming right up!"

"You're in for a treat," I tell Arlo. "All the sodas here are top notch—they make them by hand. My mom and I have been coming here since I was little."

"Been getting Shirley Temples since you were little too, I bet."

"Yeah." I laugh. Mom even has a picture of me slurping one down. It's on her desk at the studio, in a frame the same color as the drink.

He nods, sitting back. "My mother and I had a place like that when I was a little kid, a pâtisserie in the city. We'd get macarons...croissants. She said it reminded her of home."

I lean closer, imagining this younger version of Arlo. He told me once that his parents emigrated from Paris to Brooklyn a couple of years before he was born in the 1970's.

"What kind of croissants?" I ask tentatively.

His eyes crinkle as he smiles. "She liked plain, but I liked chocolate."

My heart skips. "Me, too. In fact, there's a French bakery in town that has the *best* chocolate croissants. They've got macarons, too—my mom splurges once a year and orders a bunch for her birthday."

"Not cake?"

"Nope." I shake my head. "Macarons. She loves 'em."

"Interesting."

I chew my inner cheek, staring unseeingly at the menu. "So, is that place still around? The patisserie?"

"Nah, it's something else now, a specialty grocer or something." He smirks. "As if we don't have enough of those in New York City."

"That's kind of a bummer. I'd hate it if they shut this place down," I say, imagining how I'd feel to see a lifetime of memories bulldozed or transformed into a fancy-pants grocery store.

Arlo nods. "It was a bummer. I went maybe a year after Ma passed away, just sort of a nostalgic thing. You know." He shrugs, drumming his fingers on the table. "And it was gone. Everything changes, I suppose."

"Yes, that's true. My grandmother always says that change is the only constant."

"She's a wise woman."

I smile. "She's got sayings for everything, I swear. I always tell her I need to start writing them down, make a coffee table book out of them or something."

I'm being a bit facetious, but Arlo raises his eyebrows. "You should. You absolutely should. Start now, don't waste time. Older generations are such a resource, such a wealth of wisdom and information…and you never know how long someone has."

The faint ache that visits my heart whenever I think about my grandmother dying comes now, and I nod. "You're right. I should. Maybe…maybe you could meet her before you head back to New York."

"I'd like that." He cocks his head. "I want to know who you are, the people who made you. I know I had a hand in the physical process, but that's such a small part of who we are."

"Sounds like what I'm studying at school," I say. "Nature versus nurture. Either, both."

Carlos returns with our drinks. After taking our order—I get a bacon cheeseburger, which my mother would loathe if she was here—while Arlo gets an omelet with home fries.

"Anytime I can get breakfast food, I do," he confides, those emerald eyes twinkling. "That's another favorite."

✳ ✳ ✳

"You're sure this is a good idea?" Mom smooths her hands over her jeans as she surveys the room. "You don't think we should've just gone out, after all? Someplace neutral?"

"This is fine," I assure her, laying out the cutlery. We're eating out on the balcony. It's a nice night, and there's actually more room out here than in the cramped kitchen.

"I just don't want things to get weird. You know."

"I told you; he's really nice. Things aren't going to get weird." But I get it. The way she and Arlo get along—or don't—matters. They have a bond whether they want to or not. Me.

"Maybe not for you, no, but I've had this man's sperm inside me despite the fact we've never met."

Grimacing at the unnecessary visual, I straighten up. "Gross, Mom."

"Well, it's true," she says petulantly, hands on her hips.

"You were the one who wanted to have dinner on your own turf," I remind her. "You said you felt most comfortable here."

"I know what I said," she says, disappearing into the kitchen. "I'm opening the wine. Want something?"

"I'm good for now."

136

I fiddle with the flowers I arranged earlier, making sure the garden roses and peonies are evenly distributed in the fringe bush foliage. As crazy as my mother makes me, I get why she's apprehensive. I felt the same way before meeting Arlo. But now we've hung out twice, and it's been as easy as breathing. I'd worried that someone as accomplished as him, this city dwelling, world traveling photojournalist, would be difficult to entertain let alone impress. But Arlo's surprisingly low-key. A good listener who seems as curious about me as I am about him.

"Pictures are just stories," he'd said during our first lunch together. "When I take people's pictures, I capture little bits of their stories and then, if I'm lucky, they tell me the rest."

Then he took a picture of me in the booth at Loni's.

I smile now, remembering. My smile had been a little goofy, and I was clutching my napkin like it was a security blanket, but it was good. Real.

Mom strolls over, sighing. "Sorry, little bird. I'll be fine. I just can't believe we're finally meeting this guy."

"I know." I tug her close for an affectionate side-squeeze. "But tonight's gonna be great."

"Better be. I spent all day cleaning, and you know how much I hate cleaning."

My phone lights up with a text.

"Arlo wants to know if he can bring anything."

"Just himself," says Mom, sipping her wine.

I pass on the message. "He says he'll be here in fifteen minutes."

Mom's just put on her favorite Ella Fitzgerald album when the doorbell rings. I hurry over to the door, peering through the peephole as I open it.

I can barely see Arlo because of the enormous white bakery box in his arms.

"Hi, Arlo! Is that from Elodie's?" I ask, squinting at the lavender scrawl across the top of the box.

"Sure is." He leans around the box and kisses each of my cheeks; Arlo is very French in that way. "I know you said you were all set, but I couldn't resist getting a little something."

"More like a big something." I shut the door and glance around, wondering at my mother's disappearing act. I thought she was right behind me, but I guess not. "Here, let me take that."

Arlo hands off the box, jerking his chin at the row of shoes near the door. "Should I take off my shoes?"

"If you want. We usually do."

"Good thing I wore clean socks," he says, winking as he bends to untie his boots.

Mom's in the kitchen, tossing a nervous smile our way as she fusses with the fruit and cheese board. "Oh, hi!"

I set the bakery box on the counter. "Mom, this is Arlo. Arlo, my mother, Lily."

"Welcome, Arlo." She puts down the cluster of grapes she'd been using as a prop and wipes her hands on her skirt. "I'm glad you could come."

"Hi, Lily," Arlo says, giving Mom's hand a gentle shake. "Thanks so much for having me. It's an honor to meet you."

"Oh! Well." Mom swallows visibly as their hands connect. "Sure. You, too."

"I mean it. You've raised a remarkable young woman."

Her eyes widen, and she nods. "Thank you."

And there it is: my parents, in the same room, in the same frame, shaking hands. It's awkward and there's a lot of thanking going on, but it's happening.

Eventually my mother extricates herself from the situation and folds her arms, looking at the box on the counter. "So, ah, what've you got, there?"

Arlo grins and flips open the box, revealing a rainbow-colored assortment of macarons. "I know you said you didn't need anything, but I couldn't come empty handed."

"No way." I dart forward to look closer. Macarons aren't cheap, and there have to be about thirty or forty here. Not to mention, they're Mom's favorite. I can't believe he remembered what I said.

Mom gasps softly, her cheeks patched with pink. "You must've cleaned Elodie's out."

"Almost." Arlo shrugs, a faint smile etched across his face as he watches her. "I wasn't sure what kind you liked, so…"

Mom tucks her hair behind her ear, laughing softly. "So, you got them all."

Swallowing a smile, I turn to the cabinet and procure another wine glass. "Arlo, would you like a glass of wine?"

"A little young to be serving alcohol, aren't you?" he teases, eyes sparkling in amusement.

"Well, we have lemonade, too." I open the refrigerator with a flourish.

"Wren thinks she's older than she is," Mom says, bumping me aside with her hip. "Arlo, what can I get you? We have red and we have white."

"I'd love a glass of..." Arlo peers at one of the bottles. "Shiraz."

* * *

"So, Lily. Wren told me all about your yoga studio. How did you get started? Is that something you've always wanted to do?"

Good call. There are few things Lily Angelos loves talking about more than yoga and her beloved Lotus Studios.

Nodding, she passes him a bowl of hummus. "Well, I started practicing back when I was in high school. My mother had a friend who'd started doing classes on the UCSC campus and she told me I was welcome to come for free..."

So far, so good. The conversation is flowing, and dinner is delicious, thanks to Darius.

Yes, Darius.

Despite the hurt feelings and disappointment, they've kept in touch since he left and when Mom mentioned that my father was going to be in town, and that we were having him over for dinner, Darius offered to have one of his chef buddies in Santa Cruz cater it.

She'd just had it delivered to the apartment when I showed up earlier. I found her in the kitchen, gazing wistfully at an impressive array of take-out containers.

"What's wrong?" I'd asked, purse slipping from my shoulder. "Did they forget the—"

"Darius footed the bill. When I got there, and I tried to pay, they told me it was taken care of."

I scratched my head, surprised but not really. "That was nice of him."

"Nice, and a little inappropriate. He's seeing someone down there in San Clemente."

"You miss him, don't you?"

She'd just scoffed.

But now, eating the heavenly vegetarian meal that Darius provided, she doesn't seem sad or nostalgic or even thinking about her ex. No, she's a little tipsy and, dare I say, flustered by Arlo's charm and golden boy looks. I can tell by the way she keeps stealing peeks.

Which is funny, because he's not her normal type. She likes bohemian men, jazzy men, artists. Dudes with locs or ponytails. Sometimes even stoners.

Arlo's an artist, yes, but he's more clean-cut, with his trimmed blond beard, carefully combed hair, almost-skinny jeans, and plain, long-sleeved shirt.

I get it, though. He's cute for a dad.

The notion almost has me choking on a cherry tomato. Not because he's cute, but because he's a dad. *My* dad.

But Arlo's also a good conversationalist. He asks lots of questions. Most people enjoy talking about themselves; he mentioned that to me once, in one of his emails. He told me then that it's been his secret weapon for getting access to people when he wants to photograph them or the things they do. Make the connection, show interest—and people will do almost anything you want.

I hide my smile as he does it now, content to gorge myself on roasted cauliflower.

Meanwhile, Mom's been polite, answering all of Arlo's questions, but I can tell she's wary despite her curiosity. Like she doesn't trust him. Or maybe it's herself she doesn't trust. I doubt she expected him to be so appealing. Polishing off another glass of wine, she leans back and folds her arms. I keep an eye on her as they delve into local politics, wondering what she's thinking. She gets ornery when she over-imbibes.

"What do you think, Wren?" asks Arlo, cocking his head. "About that zoning law?"

"No, no, Arlo—what about you?" Mom interjects. "All of this talk, and we hardly know anything about you."

Vaguely alarmed, I glance at her, but Arlo's already leaning forward, hands clasped atop the table. "Sure, what do you want to know?"

She peppers him with a few questions, things I could've told her. Where he grew up. What his parents did. Where he went to college—NYU. I half wonder if these are things she already knows, things she learned from the agency when choosing the man that would father her child all those years ago.

"Wren tells me you got your start as a military photographer?"

Stiffening, I stare at her, wondering where she's going with this. My mother is a militant pacifist (oxymoronic, yes), and she eschews war of any kind. For any reason.

Arlo nods. "That's right. I served in the Army for four years, documenting everything from civilian life on base to combat in Afghanistan."

"That must've been rough," I say.

"It was." Arlo frowns. "It's...not an easy life. But someone's gotta do it."

"Do they?" Mom asks.

Arlo's eyes slide back to her. "Yes," he says simply. "War is shitty, but freedom isn't free."

She purses her lips. "Hm."

"I'd like to see some of your work from those days," I break in, giving my mother a look. She averts her eyes, face flushed from wine and, hopefully, embarrassment. "If you'd ever share it, I mean."

"Of course." Arlo gives me a small smile before returning his attention to my mother. "In fact, I brought some of my work to show Wren. I can share it with you, too, if you're interested."

My heart skips as I look at them. I can't help it; I want these two to like each other. It would make my life a hell of a lot easier.

She nods slowly, raising her eyes to his. "I'm sure we can figure something out."

Luca

Winter

I'm sitting in my car at midnight, checking the console for a book I told Brooke I'd lend her, when she and Logan get out of a car across the street and disappear inside her apartment building. He emerges moments later, hands in his pockets, face is set low against the wind.

I wish I could say I couldn't believe what I was seeing, but that would be a lie. There have been signs—inconsistencies in Brooke's stories, her phone going to voicemail at random times…once there was a UCSC sweatshirt. She said it was her friend's and that she'd borrowed it one night because she was cold, but something about it didn't sit right.

"What the actual fuck."

I'm tempted to leave and not come back, but instead I get out of the car with the book and cross the street. Brooke's not expecting me. It's pretty late, so my initial plan was to shoot her a text and let her know I was leaving the book downstairs, by the mailboxes, but now I think I'd prefer to give it to her directly.

I ring her from the call box downstairs like I've done a hundred times over the past year.

Her voice crackles through a moment later. "Hello?"

"Hey, it's me. Luca." You know, in case she thinks it's the *other* guy she's been seeing.

"Hey, you! Come on up!" The door buzzes, unlocking.

I tuck the book beneath my arm, wondering at the false note in her voice. Has it always been like that, or am I just hearing it differently tonight?

Ignoring the elevator, I jog up to the second floor, where Brooke's apartment sits midway down the hall. She opens her door almost immediately, face flushed and eyes bright. She's in jeans and a sweatshirt, her hair pulled back in a messy ponytail. "Hey, handsome."

Matty's words from way, way back haunt me. I shudder to think of how easily this girl played me, and had I been five minutes later I never would've known for sure. I never would have seen them together.

"I brought that book." I pat her back lightly when she comes in for her usual hug, handing over the book.

She blinks, eyes wide. "Aw, I know it's late, honey. You didn't have to do that."

My brain's going a mile a minute. I check my watch without actually looking at the time. "I was in the neighborhood."

146

"Come in, come in," she says, standing aside. I can't tell if she suspects she's been caught, but either way she's careful enough not to say anything.

Going into her apartment is the last thing I feel like doing. Shaking my head, I take a step back. "I gotta go. Enjoy the book."

"What?" She shakes her head, the picture of confusion. "What's going on?"

I'm too angry, and too tired, to get into it with her so I just go, ignoring her when she calls my name.

* * *

It's not that I thought Brooke Henley was the one, but we'd been good together. I thought, anyway.

We never talked about it, but we were exclusive. The sex was great, and we never fought. Granted, neither of us was ready to settle down, despite her parents' antiquated interest in Brooke acquiring a husband along with a degree and Mãe's giddiness over how 'cute' we looked together the few times I brought her to Walnut Creek for family dinners.

I thought it was good that our relationship was so low maintenance—she didn't even mind when I returned to São Paulo for another fall semester abroad. I thought the phone calls and Facetime sessions were enough, and that she was as busy as I was. But in truth, she had Logan to keep her company while I was gone.

The stunned quiet I've been abiding in starts to devolve into rage—but not just at Brooke.

147

No, I'm angry at myself because I didn't listen to Matt. He always saw right through Brooke's beauty, her cultured bullshit. He told me what he saw, what he sensed, but for some reason I still let her in.

As for Logan—what the fuck? There's a superabundance of hot, single girls in Santa Cruz; why the hell would he go after the one I was seeing? He'd acted like he couldn't stand her when apparently, the opposite was true.

We've been friends for most of our lives, but now I feel like I don't even know who he is.

My mind wanders back to the times we all hung out together. Brooke and her friends became friendly with us after I got back from São Paulo the first time, right before Christmas. When exactly did this start?

But thinking about this bullshit is useless. New Year's is around the corner, and then, the final semester of my senior year. I'll have to find another place to live, because I can't trust Logan anymore, but I'll cross that bridge when I get to it.

* * *

Brooke: Hey, call me.
We need to talk about the party tomorrow...
What's the theme this year?

She signs off with her usual pair of pink hearts. I don't reply to her text. I haven't replied to any of the messages she's sent lately. We've never been a particularly lovey-dovey couple, but we usually talk at least once a day, so I know she notices.

While she doesn't know for sure that I know, her guilty conscience is most likely eating at her…it's the sole reason she isn't more pissed off by my lack of a response right now.

Logan doesn't know I know, either. I make a point to ignore the shit-eating grin he's giving his phone. For all I know, he's texting Brooke right now.

"Heads up, Luca."

I look up just in time to catch the can of beer Matty tosses at me.

"Really, man?" I give him a look, placing the can on the table so it can settle before I open it.

"What? You said you wanted one."

I ignore him, turning my attention to Kellan. Every year, his very rich parents throw a very fancy New Year's Eve party in their very swanky home down in Aptos. There's always a theme, we're always invited, and it's always a good time.

"So, what's the theme again?" asks Logan, kicking his dirty, sneakered feet up on the coffee table. "The 50's?"

"The Fabulous Fifties, specifically," Kellan says, offering me the bong. I decline, so he passes it on to Logan. "Formal like always, but with a twist."

Cracking open my beer, I take a long pull. It's a little fizzy, but it's calmed down enough to not make a mess.

"Are you bringing anyone?" I ask Kellan. I'm looking forward to staying at his childhood home for a few days, even if Logan's stupid ass is coming along, too.

"Besides you jokers?" He grins. "Maybe. I ran into this girl I knew in high school and we've been texting."

"When you say you knew her, do you mean casually?" Matt asks, flipping through channels on television. "Or biblically?"

Kellan smirks, lowering his lips to the bong.

"Nice!" Matt rips his eyes from the screen long enough to stretch back and bump Kellan's fist in approval. "You got any other old friends coming? What about that one girl from last year, the blonde in the pink dress with the nice—"

"She's engaged, bro," wheezes Kellan.

Matt makes a face, returning his attention to the TV.

Setting the bong aside, Kellan turns to me. "Do you want to ride together or are you riding solo with Brooke again?"

Leaning back against the couch cushions, I shrug. She came with us last year, but we'd been new then, lighthearted and flirty. "Nah, I thought maybe Logan could bring her."

Matt glances back with a confused frown, but no one says a word. Not that I'd expect them to—I didn't know I was going to say what I said until I said it. The words just wouldn't stay put.

Kellan's eyes bounce back and forth between Logan and me like we're playing tennis. Logan's frozen, staring at his hands. Any lingering doubts I had dissipate as I realize that he's not going to deny it. What an asshole.

Matt turns off the TV and comes to stand right in front of the couch, watching expectantly.

"You know, since he's fucking her," I add casually, draining the rest of my beer.

This stirs Logan, and he drags his red-rimmed gaze to mine. "It's not like that, Luca."

"Then what's it like?"

He runs his hands through his hair, mouth opening and closing like a dying fish.

Getting to my feet, I look over at Kellan. "Well, I won't be going with Brooke, so let me know if you want to just ride together. I'm gonna go pack."

I stalk out of the room, Matty on my heels. He follows me right into my bedroom and closes the door, eyes wide as planets. "All right, man, spill. What is even happening right now?"

"I stopped by her place the other night to bring her a book and saw her and Logan getting out of his car. It was late, almost midnight." My phone beeps with another text from Brooke. I ignore it, silencing the ringer and turning it face down. "And you heard him just now. Motherfucker isn't even denying it."

For once Matt's serious. He leans against my door with a huff. "I don't believe it. He doesn't even like her."

We've talked about the possibility of Brooke's infidelity before, usually when I needed a sounding board or someone to talk me off the edge when my suspicions over her behavior reared up, but we never knew for sure.

"Apparently, he does." Exhaling loudly, I flop back onto the bed. "I should've listened to you."

"Shut up. This is next level." He scratched his head. "Brooke, I mean…yeah. Bad vibes. But Logan? I never thought he'd go this low."

"Me neither." For the first time since this shitstorm began, a bolt of sadness pierces my chest.

How do you do this to one of your oldest friends?

Wren

I smack Dallas' arm as he glances over at me yet again. "Focus on the road, silly."

"But you look so hot in that," he says with a sly grin, gaze snagging on the hem of my dress.

"Thanks. You look pretty hot, yourself."

We're en route to a party at his parents' house, a fancy New Year's Eve affair they throw every year. When Dallas told me that this year's theme was the 1950's, I went straight to the internet and found a belted, pink wiggle dress with soft, red vintage roses and a sweetheart neckline. It conforms to my every curve, making me look like a real vixen.

"Not as hot as you, sweet thing."

Dallas has become one of my closest friends, even though we tend to straddle the line between platonic and...not. There's a refreshing lack of expectations when it comes to our relationship. I never saw myself settling into this kind of scenario, but it's easy with Dallas.

Because we have fun together. A lot of it. Sometimes that fun ends in an orgasm, but mostly it's days out on his sailboat and late-night study sessions and silly adventures around the forests and mountains of Santa Cruz. It was a no-brainer to say yes when he asked me to go with him to this party. Apparently, it's kind of a big deal among the upper crust of Aptos, but I'd go even if it was a barbecue at the beach.

Laughing, I gaze at the scenery as it blurs by. It's been cool and overcast all day, the bright silver sky slowly darkening into a gunmetal gray as the sun goes down. "It's not every day I get to dress up, you know? I'm excited."

"Good, because we're gonna have fun tonight." He glances at me as he turns into a swanky residential area. "They go overboard, Wren. Like, in the best way."

He's not kidding.

Walking into the Morgans' New Year's Eve party on Dallas' arm is like something out of a movie.

Waiters in tuxedos meet us at the door, offering petit fours and hors d'oeuvres. Others float by with champagne, but Dallas pulls me along, promising we'll get some later.

"Trust me, I've tried," he laments. "But they know we're not twenty-one. My mom has them trained."

A live band plays music in the solarium—they burst into "Rock Around the Clock" as we pass by. Everyone is dressed for the occasion, and it feels as if we've been transported back to a sock hop.

154

Dallas grins at me, nodding toward the back of the bright, spacious house. "C'mon. I want you to meet my parents."

Mr. and Mrs. Morgan, who look suspiciously like Danny and Sandy from *Grease*, are holding court on the back deck, surrounded by their friends. The deck is enormous, emptying out into an endless backyard. It's surprisingly balmy despite the sharp temperatures tonight, and when I look, I see several outdoor space heaters. Christmas lights and fancy lanterns line the perimeter, creating a cozy glow.

"Mom, Dad, this is my friend Wren. Wren, these are my parents," Dallas says, his hand resting on the small of my back.

"Welcome, sweetie!" Mrs. Morgan says, clasping my hands. She's a beautiful, lithe blonde. I see where Dallas gets his looks. "Do enjoy the party. There's plenty of food and drink, and oh! Make sure you visit *la chocolaterie!*"

"Thank you! It's so nice to—"

"Yes, yes, we're glad you could come," Mr. Morgan's booming voice interrupts. He has an infectious grin, red cheeks, and a dark mustache, curled at the edges. I wonder if it's always like that. He claps Dallas on the back. "Keep out of the wine cellar this time, eh, boyo?"

They laugh uproariously as Dallas leads me away, chuckling. "Looks like they've been hitting up the wine cellar, themselves."

"Aw, they're having fun." I poke his belly. "And what's the *chocolaterie?* Because I'm all over anything involving chocolate."

"Then you're in for a treat. Literally." He throws his arm around me. "Come on, I'll show you."

We step off of the deck and into the backyard. Opulent, white tents surround a swimming pool, where white flowers float serenely across the glowing, blue water. Like the deck, each tent is lit with fairy lights and lanterns. Some feature sitting areas with low couches and chaise lounges, while others boast charcuterie boards of every possible combination. I've never seen so much food in my life.

"This is why I told you to come hungry," Dallas jokes. "Anyway, there's your chocolate."

"Holy shit."

In front of me is a bona fide celebration of chocolate—truffles, brownies, cookies...there's even a chocolate fountain. A pair of bow-tied bartenders stand at a smaller table nearby, serving chocolate cocktails. "Do those have alcohol? You have to get me one," I whisper, grabbing Dallas' arm. Everything is so over the top, and I love it.

"I will." He gives me a small push. "Go ahead and go nuts...I'll be right back, promise. I just saw someone I know."

Nodding, I wander over to the table, unsure of where to start. My mother would love something like this, the creativity, the whimsy. I'm tempted to sneak my phone and take a few pictures so that I can show her later, but I don't. Heaven forbid I come off as gauche in a crowd like this.

Instead, I pick up a delicate, porcelain plate and begin filling it with treats. I'm reaching for a plump, juicy chocolate strawberry when someone quickly plucks it up. I turn to chastise Dallas for his mischief, but it's not him.

It's Luca.

My heart pangs sharply in my chest, letting me know it missed him far more than I gave it credit for.

The thing is, Luca is friends with Kellan…and Kellan is Dallas' older brother. I realized this when I started following him on social media and saw the two of them together in pictures. Dallas had mentioned his brother several times, had even told me his name, but I didn't put two and two together until then.

I couldn't believe it. Santa Cruz is small, but it's not that small.

And yet, despite the fact that Kellan and Luca both attend UCSC, our paths never crossed. When Dallas did finally introduce me to Kellan, I didn't ask about Luca and Kellan didn't offer any info. Maybe it was guy code, or maybe it seemed irrelevant seeing we'd only met a couple of times way back when. Kellan remembered me, though. I wonder if Dallas told him he was bringing me tonight.

"I thought that was you." Luca's light brown eyes twinkle as he puts the strawberry on my plate. "But I wasn't sure."

Laughing softly, I glance down at my dress. "I guess I look a little different."

"You look incredible," he says, his gaze drifting down the length of me. "Just like Ava Gardner."

"Ava Gardner?" I echo, distracted by the sight of Luca in a tux. It's been a long time since I've seen him, enough time that the sharpness of his beauty had begun to fade in my mind. But now we're inches from one another and it's slamming into me with the force of a hurricane.

"Actress from the 50's?"

"Oh, right!" I duck my head, pleased and embarrassed. "You really think so?"

He nods, grinning as he leans over and plucks a shell shaped truffle from the table.

"Well, thank you. I don't know much about the fashion of yester-year, but I do love this dress." My appetite seems to have fled with the arrival of all the butterflies in my stomach, but I take a little nibble of brownie. "You clean up really well too."

"I got this suit off the internet. Very last minute." A brief shadow seems to cross his face.

"Well, how've you been? Update me. How was Brazil?" I skewer a piece of pineapple, passing it beneath the chocolate cascading from the fountain.

"It was all right," he says. "I've actually gone back since then."

"Really?" This surprises me, as he'd seemed so ambivalent before.

His eyes search mine. "Did you ever get the postcards?"

"I did, eventually." My face warms, but I can't escape his gaze. Is he thinking about that summer the way I am? I can't think of anything else. "They were a pleasant surprise. Thank you."

"You're welcome." He pauses, a tiny smile playing at his lips. "So, how do you know the Morgan family?"

"I'm friends with Dallas." I bring a piece of fruit to my mouth, reluctant to go into detail. The chemistry between Luca and me is as intense as it was the last time we were together, and I'm not quite ready for this feeling to end.

158

Which it will, when he realizes what sort of friends Dallas Morgan and I are.

"No shit?" He raises his eyebrows. "Small world."

"Small campus," I counter, only partly joking. Nearly 20,000 students attend UCSC. Despite that, connections like the ones we're making tonight are not rare. It's only strange we didn't run into each other sooner.

"Where is Dallas, anyway?" he asks, frowning slightly.

"I'm not sure. He said he saw someone he knew," I say, looking around for the first time since we started chatting. It feels as though we're in a bubble.

"He just left you here?" Luca wrinkles his brow and laughs. "Oh, Dallas."

"Well, to be fair, he knew I wanted to gorge myself on chocolate, so…"

"Fair enough." He pauses as if he's considering something. "Can I get you a drink, then?"

"Actually, I'd kill for one of those," I whisper, pointing with my skewer. "I think they've got chocolate martinis."

"Coming right up."

I can't wait to tell Saira about this little serendipity. Dallas invited her tonight, too, but she already had plans. Something tells me she'll be kicking herself when she hears that Kellan was here. She might not have been as sprung for him as I was for Luca, but she'd liked him.

My purse lets out a little bleat. Snickering, I pull my phone from it. It's Leighton. She programmed a sheep ringtone to play whenever she texted me. I text back, letting her know where I am and promising I'll message her again when the clock strikes midnight.

When I look up again, Luca's handing me my martini. "Your drink, miss."

"Thank you, sir." We bring our glasses together in a graceful touch. "Cheers."

"To the New Year," he says, his eyes locked on mine as we each take a sip.

"Oh." I close my eyes. "That might be the best thing I've ever tasted."

"Better than cotton candy?" he teases.

My eyes pop open and I smile like a total goof, because everything about this moment feels magic. "Better than churros, even."

He runs his thumb gently over the corner of my lips. "You've got a little…"

"Back off my date, Cardoso."

I spin guiltily at Dallas' voice, but he's got a big old grin splitting his face. His cheeks are red, a sure sign he's started drinking and for a second I'm kind of annoyed he ran off and got started without me.

Then again, I've been here doing the same thing with Luca.

They meet in a classic handshake-man-hug, smacking each other's backs, and then Luca jerks his chin at Dallas. "Where ya been, man? I wouldn't have had to keep your *date*," –he glances at me–"company if you hadn't left her to fend for herself." He's teasing, but there's an edge to his voice.

To my surprise, Dallas submits, throwing me an apologetic glance. "Sorry, Wren. I didn't think I'd be gone so long. I saw some kids I went to high

160

school with—we used to sail together."

"No worries." I squeeze his arm, not wanting him to feel too bad. Dallas is like a puppy—adorable, easily distracted, impossible to stay mad at.

"I was actually gonna get you a drink, but it looks like you already have one," he says, eyeing my martini.

"Yeah, Luca hooked me up."

Dallas cocks his head, looking from my drink to Luca's. "Whatta gentleman," he drawls. Wrapping his arm around my shoulder, he brings his lips to my ear. "Let's go find some fun."

I nod breathlessly, staring at Luca.

But I don't know who I'm saying yes to.

*   *   *

The next few hours are a giddy, alcohol-soaked blur. After supplying me with a second, and then a third chocolate martini—I suspect this is his way of upping Luca—Dallas insists on giving me the grand tour of his parents' home. We start in the wine cellar and then ascend to his childhood bedroom on the second floor. We finish in the attic, where there are plush, old couches and an enormous telescope for dedicated stargazing.

By ten o'clock we've joined the dancing crowd in the solarium, cutting a rug with a spirited rendition of the Jitterbug. Dallas is suspiciously good at this, going and going until I'm laughing so hard I can hardly stand. I beg out, escaping to the side of the room where I take pictures of him in all his glory.

Once we've returned to the backyard, we hit up each tent to sample their numerous and sundry delicacies. Several of Dallas' friends catch up with us near an elaborate firepit tucked away in the farthest corner of the yard. There's a marshmallow roasting station set up beside it, naturally, but at this point I couldn't eat another thing if I tried.

Luca, Kellan and Matt are here with their friends, too. Luca's tawny eyes glimmer at me from across the fire. He's loosened his tie, and several strands of slicked-back hair have fallen free, giving him a rather rakish rich-boy look. We've run into each other more than a few times over the course of the evening, and every gaze he shoots my way grabs my heart and wrings it violently. What is it about Luca Cardoso? Is it just his ridiculously fine face? Is it pheromones?

Or is it something else? Some sort of supernatural chemistry, an auspicious connection that keeps us gravitating toward one another like orbiting stars?

I don't know, but there's a hunger in those eyes, one he must see reflected in mine because after a while he puts his drink down and makes his way over.

Luca

I've been watching Wren and Dallas all night, and I'm not sure what to make of their relationship. She said they were friends, but I'm a guy so I know how to read guys. Dallas knows how to read guys, too, and the second he saw that there was something brewing between Wren and me, he started marking his territory.

Still, it seems casual. Fun. If they're just flirting, I might make a move. But if they're sleeping together, I'm hands off. I've never been the kind of guy to steal someone else's girl, and after what went down with Logan and Brooke the thought turns my stomach even more. It doesn't matter that I'm not as close to Dallas as I was to Logan, or that their relationship might not be what mine was with Brooke. Point is, that's not me.

Maybe there's a reason Wren and I never seem to be available for one another. Maybe our paths are destined to always cross but never align.

But then why do we keep running into each other like this? And why does it always feel like it's impossible to look at anything but her whenever she's around?

She can't keep her eyes off me, either. Even now, she sits there across the fire, her phone in one hand and a flute of champagne in the other. There's a sparkling world of people and chatter and music and lights, but she's staring right back at me like she can't look away.

I've never had problems getting women. When I was little, Vovo Ana—my grandmother— predicted I'd be a ladies' man one day, and while Mãe bucked against that prophecy, I can't say it's untrue—I definitely went through a wild phase in high school. Still, I know what it's like to be wanted *only* for my looks, and it's something I've grown more discerning about as I've gotten older.

Sometimes I think that was the heart of the issue with Brooke. Maybe our relationship was destined to end because we never really took the time to go deep enough—too much of our relationship was superficial, surface level. I can blame Brooke for a lot of things, but I can't blame her for that.

Wren is a little harder to read, but I remember our conversation on the boardwalk. There was something about the questions she asked that suggested her interest went beyond the way I look. I'm glad she likes the way I look, though. I like her everything. If she caught my eye as a fresh-faced cutie in cut-offs, how can I resist her looking like a 1950's pinup dream with that glossy, red pout, and tight little dress. It's nearly impossible to keep my gaze from drifting down her long, crossed legs.

"You gonna stare at Sweet Spot all night or you gonna talk to her?" whispers Matty, his hot breath too close to my ear for comfort. "You're being creepy as fuck."

Swallowing, I set down my drink and stand. I love Dallas, but he's young and clueless. And drunk, judging by the bottle of champagne at his feet. He's been yammering away with his buddies for the past fifteen minutes, leaving the pretty girl at his side to languish. I won't be an interloper, but

I'm okay with teaching little Dally a lesson.

Wren's lips part as I approach. She seems to sit up a little straighter, never once looking away.

"Want to dance?" I ask, stopping just in front of her.

She gives me a surprised, but pleased, smile. "Yes, I would." Setting the champagne flute on a small table nearby, she gets to her feet. The movement jostles Dallas, who does a double take when he sees me.

"I'm borrowing your girl," I say, wanting to see if he'll bite. I want to know where they stand.

He opens his mouth and closes it, looking between the two of us. Then, shrugging, he waves his hand. "Have fun, I guess. Come back and find me when he becomes insufferable, Wren."

She gives his hair a playfully sharp tug, prompting him to reach back and pinch her thigh. I step back, pulling her away before their little game goes any further. Dallas' eyes meet mine with a dark twinkle—*game on, motherfucker*—as we leave the fire.

"I'll have you back before midnight," I tease, offering my arm.

Eyes shining, she slips her arm through as we thread through the crowd. "This party is like a fairytale, isn't it?"

"It is," I agree. "This is my fourth New Year's Eve being invited to this event, and I swear every time, it's more over the top than the one before."

"I've never been to anything like it," she says with a sigh, gazing around. "I'm so glad I came."

165

"I am glad you did, too."

Her eyes dart back to me, and she smirks. "Are you flirting with me, Luca?"

"Do you want me to be?"

Roses bloom on Wren's cheeks. "I don't know. Maybe."

"Those postcards…you said you got them eventually?" I tighten my grip on her as we leave the grass for the steps of the deck. "Did they get lost or something? I found the Sweet Spot's address online, maybe they got rerouted or something."

"I think they made it all right. My boss just misplaced them." Now she's the one tightening her grip. "He sent them to my mother once he found them."

I nod, leading her around a cluster of people.

"I would've written you back had I gotten that first one on time." She offers a shy smile. "I didn't think you remembered me."

"Come on. That night was pretty memorable."

"Then why didn't you come back?" she asks, looking ahead as we breeze through the open French doors. "Before you left the country, I mean."

I pause, thinking back to that summer. There are a few reasons I didn't go back to the boardwalk, but they'll all sound lame, like our time together didn't mean anything to me. Instead of going on to the solarium, where everyone's dancing, I maneuver Wren into the Morgans' library. It's a real old-money type room, filled with books and art and ornate armchairs. It's also quiet and devoid of guests, although by the discarded champagne flutes, hasn't been for long.

166

Closing the door, I cross the room to put some space between us. "I had a lot going on that summer. Things were rocky with my dad, and I wasn't in the best headspace. I had to leave sooner than expected, and with all the shit I needed to get done I didn't want to get caught up."

Her eyes fly to mine. "Caught up?"

I chuff softly, charmed by her complete lack of artifice. "In you."

Blinking, she looks at the floor. "What would've been so bad about that?"

"Nothing. Nothing was wrong with it except for the timing."

"We could have kept in touch on social media or something." She fingers the beads on her purse. They're the same shade of red as the roses on her dress. "But I guess you thought we'd never see each other again."

"Yeah. Didn't you?"

Shrugging, she turns to look at a painting on the wall, a watercolor of two horses racing down a sun-bleached beach. "I don't know."

I take the opportunity to look at her, the delicate lines of her bare shoulders, the way her slender waist flares out into the luscious curve of her hips. It's hard not to touch her, knowing how soft her skin is.

Fuck it. "What's the deal with you and Dallas?"

I can sense her smile even before she turns around. It's a sheepish smile, though, and it only gets worse as she comes closer. "We really are good friends." She stops a breath away from me, looking up. "It gets physical sometimes."

Despite having figured this out, I'd hoped for a different answer. "Friends with benefits?"

She averts her eyes, faint spots of color blooming on her cheeks. "Yeah."

I still want to touch her, but what I'm about to say helps me keep my distance. "I've known Dallas for a long time, Wren. I'm not trying to mess up what you two have."

She swallows visibly. "We don't have much. But I understand."

"I can't be that guy." We're so close I can see the goosebumps on her shoulders. Closing my eyes, I take a breath of her and step back. "No matter how much I wish I was."

"You're right." Exhaling slowly, she looks at me with wet eyes. "You're better than I am, Luca."

"I'm not," I promise her. If she knew the thoughts racing through my head right now, the urge I have to turn her around, flip that dress up, and find the hottest part of her, she might feel differently. "Come on, let's go dance before Dallas comes looking for you."

Chest tight, I follow Wren back out of the library. A jovial group emerges from the room across the hall, loud and drunk. I glance inside, spying a tricked-out photo booth in the corner.

Wren peeks past me and laughs. "Of course, they have one of these. What's next, pony rides?"

Memories of another photo booth, another night. This girl. It hits me like a sucker punch, how badly I want Wren. All of her. "You want to?"

"I don't know," she says, gliding a tube of glossy stuff onto her lips. My dick twitches. "You gonna behave yourself in there?"

"I'll do my best."

Her perfectly red lips curve into a sly smile. "Then it would be a shame not to."

A bored looking guy in a loose, rumpled tux sits beside the booth, fiddling with his laptop. He glances up, giving us a small wave as we approach. There's a table covered with props just outside the booth—sunglasses, fake cigars, hats, masks—but we bypass all of that and slip inside.

"Just look at the screen," the assistant says, his voice floating through the curtain. "I'll give you guys a heads up when I'm about to start."

Unlike the booths on the boardwalk, there's nowhere to sit. Wren fixes her hair while I fiddle with my tie, and even though the guy mumbles that he's starting, we're both unprepared for the first shot.

"Whoops." Wren snorts, which makes her laugh. "That one's gonna be bad."

The shutter goes off again, catching her in mid-sentence. Squealing, she throws her hands out. "Hold on, hold on! We're messing it up!"

"Did you want a formal set?" I tease.

Tears of mirth glimmer at her eyes. Dabbing elegantly at them, she takes a deep breath. "No, actually. These will be perfect."

Grinning mischievously, I shake my head. "I think you want to do it again."

"Luca, no." Giggling, Wren tries to pull me back as I pop my head out and look at the assistant.

"We're going to have to do it again."

"Sure, buddy." He winks, cracking an amused grin of his own. I'd love to see the collection of images he's amassed over the evening—some of the people outside are pretty sauced. "Let me know when you're ready."

Turning to Wren, I run my hands over my hair. "You ready?"

To my surprise, she's once again serious, although her flushed cheeks bear witness to the hysterics she just recovered from. "Your hair…"

"What's wrong with it?" I ask, frowning.

She clasps her hands demurely. "Take it down."

"Why?"

"Because I've never seen it before, and I'd like to." Her cheeks go full red. It's adorable, how nervous this makes her. "For the pictures."

"For the pictures. Yes, ma'am." Giving the elastic a gentle yank, I loosen my hair. It's not that long, as I had it cut a couple of weeks ago, but it still hits my shoulders. Turning to face the screen, I give my hair a good ruffle, freeing it from the stuff I used earlier to tame it.

Wren's behind me, staring at me like she's never seen a guy with long hair. Chuckling, I face her. "What? Too wild for you?"

"No, I love it," she whispers, biting her lip.

Fuck.

170

"I love it when it's back, too, in the man-bun—"

"God, I hate that term." I groan, tipping my head back.

"Well, that's what it is." She sticks her hand on her hips, staring at me with so much heat in her eyes that it's contagious.

"Do you need more time?" the assistant asks, probably watching as this unfolds on his laptop.

"No, we're ready!" Wren arches her eyebrow. "Let's act it out. Like we're greasers."

"Yeah?" I nod, warming to the idea. Why not? "Okay."

The assistant opens the curtain, passing me a black bowler hat and Wren a pair of cat's eye glasses. I knew he was listening.

Wren gasps with delight. "Thank you! This is perfect."

"All right, on three…two…one…"

The first shot captures the two of us, arms folded and back-to-back, looking directly at the camera. No smiles, just manufactured sobriety. We change up the poses a little, but the mood stays the same. When the screen flashes for the last time, Wren sighs. "These are going to be epic; you'll see."

We exit the booth, returning the props to their table. After a moment, the photos slide out of booth, and they're just as ridiculous as I expected. "Do you still have the photos from last time?" she asks, grinning at the set I hand her.

Nodding, I try to remember where in my room they might be. Brooke found them once. It was one of the few times we fought. She wanted me to toss them, so I put them in a more discreet location. By the bed, maybe, in a drawer. "Do you?"

She nods, smiling. "Yeah."

Wren

Luca looks completely different with his hair down. I didn't expect it to affect me the way that it does, but oh my goodness. All I want to do is sink my fingers into those dark, messy depths and tug as he takes me to a shadowy corner somewhere. Or his car, to play a little "backseat bingo," as they said back in the 50's.

The band starts its rendition of Elvis' sultry "Blue Christmas" right as we step into the solarium, one of my all-time favorites. The universe must be having a marvelous time at my expense. I rest my purse on a decorative table and follow Luca to the dance floor, fingertips aching with the desire to touch him again.

Taking one of my hands into his, Luca wraps his arm around my waist and starts to sway.

I'm not much of a dancer, but I have good rhythm. Besides, it's not hard to follow a man who leads this well. "You're good at this," I accuse, peeking up at him.

His lips quirk up, and he nods. "My father wasn't a dancer, so my mother made me and Nico dance with her at parties. Still does. She loves to dance."

Oh, jeez. The image of Luca Cardoso dancing with his mom melts me. I duck my face, not wanting him to see evidence of my infatuation. Because yes, over the course of this night, it's back and better than ever—or worse, depending on how you look at it. I don't think my heart rate has come back to normal since he approached me at the firepit.

Actually, I've been spun since he stole my strawberry. *'Stole my strawberry.' Sounds kind of like 'popped my cherry'.*

My mind wanders to the girl I saw him with all those months ago in Berkeley. How many girls like that have there been for him? Am I just another one? Luca slows before twirling me around, startling a laugh from me. He grins, and my stomach flips as he pulls me back a little closer than before.

We're so close I'd have to lean back to look into his eyes, so I focus on his bowtie instead, the feel of his body, solid and tall, pressing against mine. Moving together like this, intoxicated by all of this longing, feels more intimate than I thought it would. Maybe he feels it too because he brushes his thumb between my shoulder blades.

Oh, God.

Desire washes over me like a warm wave, leaving goosebumps in its wake. I slide my hands up his chest and around his neck, clasping them there. After a moment, one of his hands drops to my waist, and he holds me close.

It feels like I'm telling him how I feel without ever having to say a word. Maybe he's letting me know, too. We turn in slow circles, my cheek pressed to his chest, until the song fades.

I'm getting ready to ask him for the next dance when the DJ comes on, clearing his throat.

"All right, ladies and gents—it's about that time. We have ten minutes until the New Year, so we're going to take a break and let you find your way outside for the countdown…" He continues talking, but the spell is broken. Why do I always feel like I'm being hurried away from this man before I'm ready?

Luca's eyes burn into mine as he takes a step back. "Come on, I'll take you back."

I grab my purse and slip my arm through his as we follow the crowd out onto the deck. Waiters stationed at the French doors are serving champagne, so Luca takes one for each of us.

"Thanks," I say. My buzz from earlier is gone, but I'm still high from spending the past hour with Luca.

Dallas, Kellan, and the rest of their friends intercept us as we cross the deck. "There she is," says Dallas, winking at me. "Have fun?"

"Yeah." I smile, hoping my warm cheeks aren't too obvious. "We tried the photo booth and the dance floor…"

"Oh, Sweet Spot loves photo booths." Matt chortles, waggling his eyebrows like an imp.

I stick my tongue out at him and turn around, hoping Dallas ignores him.

"You do?" asks Dallas, cocking his head. "We should hit it up later, then." He clinks his glass to mine and points to the sky. "Ready for a show?"

"A show? You mean something even more elaborate than all of this?" I tease. "Sure." I look at Luca, but he's already drifted back to Kellan and Matt.

"You ain't seen nothing yet," says Dallas, leading me back down the steps and onto the grass. The entire party has moved to the backyard, so it's more crowded now than it has been all evening.

We've only just gotten situated when someone yells, "Ten!"

We quickly catch up, the collective voice of the crowd growing in urgency and intensity as we count down. "...two! One! Happy New Year!"

Dallas takes me by the shoulders, planting a sweet, chaste kiss on my lips as the first fireworks explode in the sable sky. The crowd gasps and cheers at the explosion of color. "Happy New Year!" Dallas yells, beaming. He downs his champagne in one go, pumping his fist into the air.

"Happy New Year!" I laugh, following suit. It's been a crazy, unpredictable night, but every bit of it has been fantastic. I'm so glad Dallas invited me. I gaze up at the fireworks, lost in the giddy euphoria of the crowd.

When I finally can't take it anymore, I look around, finding Luca and his friends a few feet away, laughing and shouting. Maybe he senses the weight of my stare, because suddenly he looks over, eyes shining with happiness and fireworks. "Happy New Year," he mouths.

I feel it down to my very core. "Happy New Year," I mouth back.

* * *

At five minutes past two, Dallas pulls up to my dorm. Cutting the engine, he jogs around to my side of the car and escorts me out, keeping his hand on the small of my back as we walk.

"So chivalrous," I say around a yawn. My shoes, which became unbearable about an hour ago, dangle from my fingertips.

"It's the dress," he jokes.

We pause outside my door while I search for my keys. "I had the best time tonight, Dallas. Seriously. Thank you for inviting me."

"Thanks for coming," he says, slipping his hands into his pockets. His hair is still slicked back like a greaser's, but the bowtie is gone, and he left his jacket in the car. "I'm glad you had fun."

Finding my keys, I slide them into the lock and open the door. I turn to give Dallas a hug, gently kissing his cheek. "Talk tomorrow?"

In one swift move, he slides his arms around my waist and angles his face to kiss me. It feels good, like always, but it feels wrong, too. Turning my face, I break away and hug him again instead.

"Hey, how do you know Luca Cardoso?" he asks quietly, running his hands over my bare arms.

I probably should've seen this coming. We've been messing around for far too long—of course he's noticed the shift. Giving him one last squeeze, I step away. "Come in for a sec. It's cold out here."

Inside, I drop my shoes and purse on the ground and lean against the door. "I met him at the boardwalk a long time ago. Saira and I hung out with him and your brother and their friends."

"I knew you'd met Kellan, but I just didn't realize…" He pauses, wrinkling his brow. "I wonder why Kell never mentioned it?"

"Like I said, it was ages ago." I shrug. "And we only met a couple times."

"I don't know. It felt like there was something between you two tonight."

My heart skips, and I hesitate, not wanting to say the wrong thing. "If there is, it's not much. I haven't seen him in over a year."

"Safe to say Luca's interested, Wren," he says, lifting his eyebrows. "He spent half the night with you and the other half trying to be."

"That's not true." I laugh, shaking my head. "I spent most the night with you, dumbass."

"Hey, if you want to hook up with him, go for it. I'm not gonna stop you." His words are lighthearted, but there's an antagonistic gleam in his eye I've never seen before.

"What, you're giving me permission now?" I narrow my eyes at him. "Gee thanks, Dallas."

"I'm saying I get it if you wanna stop fucking around." He exhales roughly, yanking his hands through his hair. "I'll do anything for you, Wren, you know that, but I don't do relationships. I'm not trying to hold you down."

I fold my arms, stomach in knots. Nothing he's saying is a surprise except for how shitty it feels to hear it. It's hard keeping emotions completely out of fooling around. "You're right. You've always been clear about what you want. And don't want."

Dallas squints at me. "But what do you want?"

I look down at my bare feet. The cheap nail polish I put on this afternoon is already chipping.

"I don't know what I want."

"Be honest with me."

"Fine." I take a long, slow breath. "I am attracted to Luca, okay? Is that what you want to hear?"

"Not really, but I get it." He nods slowly. "So, I guess that's it."

"Not *it*. I still want you in my life, just…I don't know. I'd feel weird being into two people."

"Aw, babe." He pooches his lips into an exaggerated pout. "You're into me?"

I punch his arm. "Shut up, Dallas."

"I'm being serious," he says, laughing.

"I wouldn't have fooled around with you if I wasn't into you, doofus," I say, rolling my eyes.

That sobers him up, and he nods, clearing his throat. "Yeah, I hear you. I'm into you, too. You and this tight body," he says, squeezing my hips.

It's hard to tell if he's being his usual irreverent self or if he's just trying to soften the blow, but I don't bite. "You know I adore you, right? We'll still hang out?"

"Ugh, God, please…not the *I still want to be friends* speech."

"I do still want to be friends." I ruffle his hair. "Don't you?"

Dallas kisses my forehead. "Of course, I do. We were friends first."

"Good, because I don't want things to be weird."

"They won't be weird if we don't make them weird." He turns, pausing with his hand on the doorknob. "Listen, don't take this wrong, but you might want to take it easy with Luca. He *just* broke up with his girl."

My heart drops. I'm sure my face does, too. "What?"

"Yeah, apparently she was getting down with his best friend." He shakes his head, opening the door. "Kellan said things went to shit a couple of days ago. That's why Logan didn't show." He frowns. "Do you know Logan?"

A memory of the moody, blue-eyed boy in the Banana Slugs t-shirt comes to mind, and I nod. "I think so."

"Shady as fuck." Dallas shrugs, walking out. "Anyway. Talk soon, cutie. You know where to find me."

"Bye, Dallas." I close the door and let out a shaky breath. That was abrupt. And while the conversation itself went about as well as it could have, I can't help but feel like we might have ruined a good thing.

Then I remind myself that continuing to fool around with someone who only wanted a friends-with-benefits arrangement would've eventually hurt me. We've always been drama-free, but sometimes I would worry that he'd find someone else, and I'd have to suck it up.

Guess I was the one who found someone else.

180

Luca

R eaching blindly across the bed, I fumble around the nightstand for my phone.

It's eleven-oh-six. Bright stripes of sunlight bracket the hastily closed drapes.

There's a text from Brooke, but I ignore it—I don't need anything sullying this morning's good vibes. Instead, I close my eyes again and pull the blankets up a little higher. I never sleep this late, but then, I don't really go to bed at 4 o'clock anymore, either. After the party ended last night, Kellan, Matt and I wandered down to the Morgans' dock and finished off another bottle of champagne. It was the perfect end to a great night.

Actually, the perfect ending would have been Wren beneath me, but I rectified that the best I could by beating one out in the shower before bed. Just thinking about that, and her, gives me morning wood all over again. Groaning, I roll onto my side and attempt to think about something else. There's nothing I can do about it anyway—I'm in the Morgans' well-appointed guest room.

But now that thoughts of Wren have infiltrated my mind, it's hard to get rid of them.

The way her ass filled out that dress. The way she smelled, like vanilla and perfume and coconut. The way she looked at me when she thought I didn't notice, and the way she blushed when she realized that I did.

I love Kellan like a brother, and I would never do anything to jeopardize my friendship with him by stealing his little brother's girl from underneath his nose. But the truth is, Dallas is still a kid. I know he and Wren are around the same age, but it's not about that. There's a gravity to Wren. Depth.

"Listen to you, trying to justify this," I mumble into my pillow, yawning.

Nah, Dallas is all right. He acted exactly the way I would've in a situation like that, although based on what Wren said, they're not that serious. Maybe that's why he let her go with me, and why she allowed me to get so close.

And yet, in the end, it doesn't matter. Wren's off limits for now. If she makes a clean break from doing whatever the hell they're doing, we can talk. Until then, I'd do well to focus on my own shit, like the upcoming spring semester and my senior thesis. Continuing the application process for grad school. And figuring out where I'm going to live, because there's no way I'm rooming with Logan when we get back.

* * *

"I'll drive," I offer, holding my hand out for Kellan's key. "You look a little hungover."

182

"How are you *not* hungover?" Scowling, Kellan tosses me the keys and shuts the trunk of his car.

"Water. Lots and lots of water."

It's four p.m. The last of the cleanup crew is just pulling out, having transformed the Morgans' house back into the pristine specimen it once was.

Matt and I say our goodbyes to Kellan's parents and get in the car, where Matt proceeds to roll up a pillow and fall asleep. Kellan joins us moments later, still waving to his parents, who have their arms around each other as they watch us leave.

Kellan rolls up the window as I turn around in the driveway. "Even after all this time, she gets teary-eyed when I leave."

"Good thing you're right down the street," I say, thinking of how emotional Mãe gets every time I go to Brazil. "You think you're going to stick around for law school?"

Kellan is majoring in environmental law. He'd always talked about going down south to continue his studies, like UCLA, but lately he's been thinking about staying in the area.

"She'd love that for sure, but I don't know." He adjusts his chair, pushing it back so he can recline. "I'm definitely doing a gap year first, though. I need a break."

"Don't blame you," I murmur. It's been intense for all of us, but I won't be doing a gap year. My father would never fund something so frivolous, and I can't do it on my own. Not at this point.

We're quiet for a while, listening to some mellow indie band croon about lost love and betrayal. I'm about to broach the subject of moving out when Kellan turns the volume down.

"Crazy Wren was there last night, huh?"

I'd wondered if this would come up. Cutting him a half-smile, I shrug. "Yeah. I wasn't expecting that at all. How come you never told me about her and Dallas?"

"Didn't think it mattered, I guess," he says. "Didn't think you guys even talked again after that one night."

"I sent her a few postcards from Brazil that first summer." I glance at him. "Sent them to her job, I mean. But that was it."

"Huh."

"She been seeing Dallas long?" I ask, turning it around.

A smile creeps over his face. "I wouldn't call it 'seeing.' You know Dally's a little player."

I nod, keeping my eyes on the road, but I don't like that shit. I used to play around, but I guess I'm more sensitive to it lately.

"I think he likes Wren," he continues, "but after last night, it'll be interesting to see what happens."

I glance at him. "What do you mean?"

"Oh, come the fuck on," Matt pipes up from the backseat, awake after all. "You know exactly what he means. You and Sweet Spot, making eyes at

184

each other all night long. I'm surprised Dallas didn't try and deck you."

Kellan and I burst into laughter. "Dally's a lover, not a fighter," Kellan says, shaking his head. "And he's nothing if not confident. He must not have thought Luca was a threat. Oh man, that's funny."

I grin, remembering the hard glint in Dallas' eyes when I took Wren from the firepit. "Nah, he definitely knew the deal. I think it came down to Wren doing what she wanted to do."

"Truth," Matt says. "Sweet Spot's always been sweet on you."

"Lucky for Dallas, stealing isn't my style."

The mood shifts, like a passing rain cloud casting a shadow.

Kellan clears his throat. "Listen, it's your call, but Matt and I have talked about it, and we think Logan should move out."

Surprised, I look at him and then at Matt in the rearview mirror. "What?"

"He really screwed up, bro. And like, not just once," Matt says, his face hard. "I know you mentioned the possibility of moving out, but you didn't do anything wrong. If there's anyone who should go, it's him."

"When did you two discuss this?" I ask, legitimately shocked they'd thought it out this much.

Shocked and warmed.

"Yesterday." Kellan waves his hand dismissively. "Anyway, we're all on the lease, so we all have a say. We can't legally force Logan out, but I'm hoping he'll have the decency to bow out gracefully."

"You know—what he should've done with Brooke," mutters Matt. "Bow out gracefully."

Their loyalty means a lot to me—loyalty I didn't realize I missed until now.

Brooke's behavior stings, but it's Logan's betrayal that hurts the most. Part of me still misses him, misses the kid I grew up with. Most of my elementary school memories include him—skating, homework, trick-or-treating, sleepovers. And a lot of our firsts—smoking weed, getting drunk, jobs, getting grounded, driver's licenses—saw us at each other's sides.

There's a deep sense of loss when I think about Logan. Even if I could forgive him, things can never go back to the way they were—I've lost my trust in him. I don't hate him, and I don't have it out for him, but the guys are right: if anyone should move, the onus is on Logan.

* * *

We haven't been home a day when Brooke shows up at the door. Dressed in jeans and a t-shirt, her hair's pulled into a messy bun, her face free of makeup. I almost like her better this way.

"Why are you avoiding me?" she asks, hands balled at her sides.

"Why do you think?" I turn to go back into the house.

Brooke follows, as I knew she would. She picked a good a time as any to have this conversation, because no one else is home. I wonder if she knew that.

"I don't know what to think, Luca." She's quiet, her eyes wide, and this is how I know she's full of shit. Brooke's no pushover, and if she felt like I was doing her wrong, she'd be loud and indignant right now. "You went to the Morgans' party without me on New Year's Eve…God, you've barely spoken to me since the night you dropped that book off."

"You mean the night I saw Logan coming out of your building?" I lean against the counter, arms folded.

Her cheeks go colorless. Sagging into a stool at the counter, she shakes her head. "It's not like that, Luca. Please—"

"Funny, that's exactly what he said when I accused him of fucking you," I say, keeping my eyes on hers. "How long has it been going on, Brooke? Was it when I left last fall?"

Tears fill her eyes, and she shakes her head, looking down.

"Before? After?" I prod.

"Before," she whispers, pressing her fingers to her eyes. "I don't…I don't know why it happened. It just did."

"Original. You should've told me you wanted to call it quits." I shake my head, disgusted. "We're not in love with each other. You wouldn't have broken my heart."

"Maybe I am in love with you!" she cries. "That's what hurts—that you don't love me and never have. You never let me in. You never saw this going anywhere."

"You never saw it going anywhere, either." I almost laugh, though nothing about this is funny. "And how could you possibly love me and then sleep with someone else? With my *best friend?*"

"We were so drunk the first time," she wails. "I didn't think you wanted me. Not really."

Drunk? Well, that makes sense, now doesn't it. "When?"

"The night…" She pauses, taking a slow, uneven breath. "The night we went to that party in Berkeley."

"What party?"

"That holiday party. At my friend's house."

Hazy memories begin flickering through my head. Party in Berkeley? That was in the very beginning, when Brooke and I reconnected. I'd just gotten back from São Paulo the first time, and I had wicked jet lag, so I went back to Walnut Creek to sleep it off. I frown at the floor, remembering. Brooke left with her friend, Kellan and Dallas…and Logan.

"Wait. That was before we even started dating—you've been sleeping with Logan even longer than you've been sleeping with me?" I push my hair back, blown away. "Are you serious right now, Brooke?"

A sob rips from her throat, and she nods. "I'm sorry, Luca. I'm so sorry."

I stare at her incredulously. "Why did you even start up with me?"

"Because I liked you. A lot," she says. "I'd liked you for a long time."

"Come on." That's news to me. Before we got together, Brooke was notoriously hard to pin down.

Her eyes brim with fresh tears. "You know, it only happened with Logan a few times."

"Like whenever I was away, or too busy, or what the fuck ever." My stomach turns, and I push off from the counter. I can't look at her anymore. "You're unbelievable."

"Luca," she cries, her face contorted with pain.

Yeah, this fucking hurts me, too, but once I'm done with someone, I'm done. "Get out."

"Will you just—"

"No, really. Get out. This is bullshit." Returning to the front door, I swing it open and point. "You and Logan can have each other."

Tears streaming down her face, Brooke rushes by. I slam the door, not bothering to watch her go. I was done before, but now I'm really done.

I'd rather be alone than waste my time.

Luca

~~~~~~~~~~~~~~~

S lipping a blue and gold hoodie over my head, I pocket my keys and head out to the pool. It's a chilly February morning, making me want to stay in and be lazy, but I know I'll feel better getting in an hour of laps before class.

It's been about two months since things ended with Brooke. Two months since Logan moved out. Rent was tight for a minute without a fourth roommate, but we figured shit out fast. All it took was spreading the word around our circle of friends and we had offers within days.

Faruq's been with us since. He's Nigerian and spends most of his time studying—when he's not bickering with Matty over soccer. Most of his immediate family is in Alameda, so I bring him with me to the Bay a lot.

Jumping in my car, I head over to East Field House Pool. Swimming's been essential for me lately. I swam competitively in high school, and I always loved how it cleared my head. Some days, when Kellan, Matt and I have the afternoon free, we go hiking around Big Basin. Sometimes we smoke. Weed's a nice respite, but I'll never be as into it as the guys.

Life feels both simpler and more complicated.

My phone rings as I pull into the parking lot at the pool. Grabbing my backpack from the passenger seat, I root around until I find it at the very bottom. It's my mother. She's been on me a lot lately, but only because she's worried.

Mãe: Good morning, meu querido! Have you been checking your Instagram?

Chuckling, I shake my head. Since she discovered Instagram, I get texts like this all the time from her.

Luca: No.

Mãe: Well check it! I posted a picture of my manzanitas this morning. They're covering the hill out back and they're GLORIOUS.

Luca: I'll check it, promise.

Mãe: OK. You have plans tonight?

Luca: Not sure. Why?

Mãe: Dom is making picanha tonight. You want to bring your friends? Free beer!

Kellan and Matt, that is. Logan's high on her shitlist these days.

Luca: haha, you're shameless. We'll be by around 7. Want us to bring anything?

Mãe: No, silly, just yourselves. Love you xoxoxoxoxoxoxo

Luca: *Love you, too.*

I pause, half in and half out of the car. I'm almost never on Instagram lately, but I should probably look at Mãe's picture because she'll harass me until I do. Opening the app, I navigate to her page and dutifully 'like' her latest pictures. They're mostly of her garden, Dom and my little brother, and the sunsets they see from their house in Walnut Creek. The aforementioned picture of today's pale pink manzanitas gets an extra heart. With the morning sun beaming gently over the blooms, it really is stunning.

I'm about to get going when I notice my other notifications.

wren<3angel likes your photo

A smile spreads over my face. I guess she found me. I'd wondered when our paths would cross again, had wondered what was up with her and Dallas. I glance at the picture she liked, me surfing two summers ago. She had to do a pretty deep dive to find that one. The thought of Wren, scrolling through my pictures, does something funny to my chest.

Her account is public, allowing me to get a feel for the last few months of her life. The beach. The hiking trails up behind UCSC. Her mom, her friends…there are a couple of Dallas, older photos. Nothing suggesting they're together.

I get stuck on a photo she took on New Year's Eve, drinking in the sight of her in those heels, that dress. Her long, wavy hair, her glossy pout…*damn.* I follow her account.

Then I slide into her DMs.

LucaCardoso: *Hey, you ;)*

Wren

I'm in my Writing and Research Methods class, scribbling notes, when my screen lights up with a notification. Pausing my notes, I allow my eyes to drift down to the phone in my lap. It's from Instagram:

LucaCardoso followed you

My heart breaks into a gallop. *Jeez, chill out, Wren!*

But it's so hard to chill out when it comes to Luca. Using every ounce of willpower I can muster, I ignore the notification. People texting during class is one of my pet peeves, and besides, I need this class. I need to take notes—if I can concentrate long enough to actually take them, that is.

After New Year's Eve, I tried to wait and see if the universe would bring Luca and me together again. I needed to focus on school, and besides, I didn't need a guy to make me happy—even if that guy was Luca Cardoso.

Plus, he'd just gotten out of a relationship, and I didn't want to be a rebound—even if the sparks between us were flying hotter than ever.

But it was a conversation with my mother of all people that changed things.

"The universe?" she'd said, pulling out of downward dog to sit on her mat and stare at me. "Wren, what do you mean?"

"What do you mean, what do I mean?" I looked at her askance. I'd been attempting to do yoga with her but talking about my feelings was distracting. "You're the one who's always talking about letting things happen as they may…how the universe will arrange things. You know."

She sighed, shaking her head. "If that's the way I've described it, little bird, I've done you a disservice. When I talk about the universe, it's a matter of acceptance, knowing that ultimately it has our best in mind. Remember Gramma Kate's serenity prayer?"

I nodded.

"It's having the serenity to accept what you can't change and the courage to change what you can. What you're talking about is going into neutral. That doesn't work. You still have to make decisions, to go for what you want."

She was right, of course. I guess I was just afraid—it felt like no matter how many times fate brought Luca and me together, there was always something to keep us apart. And while he seemed to like me the times we'd hung out, what if ultimately, he didn't like me *enough*? The fantasy of Luca had been so sweet; could I handle reality if he rejected me?

But that was just dumb. Maybe, like Mom said, I needed to go for what I wanted. Better to try, at least, so I could move on—whatever that looked like for me. Luca was no longer living abroad, so I knew he was around. Somewhere.

I still didn't have his contact info at the time, but I had gleaned one important piece of information at the party: Luca's last name. So, I looked him up on social media and lo and behold, there he was: hiking the Berkeley fire trails and around Big Basin. Cheesing with Kellan and Matt on New Year's Eve. Horsing around with friends in someone's apartment. Having dinner with his mother. There were tons of pictures of him in São Paulo and all over Brazil.

The pictures of him surfing over on Four Mile and Pleasure Point were my favorite, for obvious reasons. That boy could wear the hell out of a pair of boardshorts. I hearted one before yanking myself out of the thirsty haze I'd floated off into. *Whoops.*

I didn't see any questionable photos of girls on his page, so he was probably single, right? And so was I. Maybe this was the confirmation I'd been looking for.

But that'd been a while ago.

I'm jostled from my thoughts by the rustling of papers and a general sense of commotion. Class is over. So much for my notes. Picking up my phone, I open Instagram and accept Luca's request. Then I notice that I have a DM. My stomach knots up in anticipation.

Luca Cardoso: Hey, you ;)

Luca Cardoso and I are finally, officially, in touch.

* * *

We message back and forth for a while, dipping in and out of each other's DMs throughout the day. I get butterflies every time I see that he's responded.

wren<3angel: *hey yourself ;)*

LucaCardoso: *getting in touch prob shouldn't have taken so long.*

wren<3angel: *Prob not*

LucaCardoso: *Why did it take so long?*

wren<3angel: *You're asking me?*

LucaCardoso: *I'm asking hypothetically*

wren<3angel: *last names, for one thing. I know yours now tho.*

LucaCardoso: *What's your last name?*

wren<3angel: *Angelos*

LucaCardoso: *I see what you did there. wren<3angel = Wren Angelos*

wren<3angel: **applause gif**

LucaCardoso: *;)*

When it becomes apparent that communicating through the app is too cumbersome, DMs turn to texts. My heart flips when he asks for my number, and I hold my breath until he uses it.

Luca: *Hey.*

Wren: Hey

That brilliant exchange dangles there for a minute. I yank nervously at my chain, tempted to wax poetic about cloud formations or the epic veggie burger I had for lunch, but then decide to be brave and go for the kill. I'm tired of being tentative.

Wren: Are we ever going to hang out again?

It takes a minute, but the dots appear, the ones that tell me he's responding.

Luca: I don't know. Are you available?

He doesn't ask when, and it takes me a moment, but I think maybe what he's really asking is if I'm single. Well, I'm single and my schedule's wide open, so the answer's the same.

Wren: yes

Luca: What are you doing Friday?

The butterflies return with a vengeance. Mentally reviewing my weekend schedule won't work—I forget things—so I open my phone calendar to check Friday.

Wren: Last class is at 2. Other than that, not much.

Luca: Text me your address. I'll pick you up at 7.

* * *

The tea kettle whistles shrilly, pulling Mom from her laptop. She pours herself a cup of tea, clearing her throat. "Arlo wants to visit for your birthday."

I select my favorite teacup from the cabinet and turn to look at her. "Oh, yeah? What did he say?"

"He was just asking about the hotels in the area. I guess he has a little bit of time between assignments," she says, shrugging.

Arlo knows he has my "permission" to come to Santa Cruz, but I appreciate the effort he's putting into making sure my mother is comfortable, as well. "What did you tell him?"

"I asked if he wanted beachfront or just some little motel in town. He said beachfront, of course." She drops a sugar cube into her tea. "I think he thinks he's going to entertain us while he's here."

I lean against the counter, stirring my tea. "Why wouldn't he?"

She sighs, smiling the tiniest smile ever.

Outside, a tall spindly palm tree sways in the chilly January breeze. The cloudless sky is marvelously bright. "Thanks for being cool with this. For giving Arlo a chance."

"Yes, well, thanks for being patient with me while I got used to the idea," she says, sitting back in her chair. "It wasn't fair of me to keep you from having a relationship with your father just because mine left when I was little."

I nod, blowing on the steam curling up from my cup. I understand why she was reticent at first—her dad's absence growing up wounded her, created

198

a void. She raised me to feel whole despite my own fatherlessness, but it's not easy for her to keep the two situations separated.

But she's trying, and that's enough for me.

* * *

Luca texts the next day around noon. I'm walking from one class to another, trying to stay in the sun, when I hear the silvery chime I've assigned to his contact. Stepping out of the flow of foot traffic, I read his text.

It took us so long to get to this point that sometimes I'm still half-afraid it isn't real. But it is.

Luca: So what's up with you and Dallas?

Wren: Idk. Haven't talked much since NYE.

Which is true, and kind of a bummer because Dallas and I were close for a while. I think his pride was wounded more than he wanted to admit. I don't know.

Anyway, let's see if Luca puts two and two together. A kid skateboards past alarmingly close, almost wiping out when he tries to squeeze between two groups of people.

My phone chimes again.

Luca: Why'd it take you so long to find me, then?

199

I sense he's teasing, but I'm not sure. It's hard to tell with text. Still, I decide to be completely vulnerable.

Wren: Dallas told me you'd just broken up with your girlfriend. I wasn't sure if you were still hurting from that.

I take a deep, fortifying breath.

Wren: I didn't want to be a rebound.

The three dots appear, disappear, appear, disappear. Right when my anxiety starts to ratchet up, he responds.

Luca: I get it. We can talk about it later. Too much to type.

I bite my lip. Does he mean that, or did I poke at a sore spot?

Luca

"Y ou can bring her back here after dinner, you know," says Kellan. He's standing in my doorway, eating popcorn as he watches me make my bed. "I feel bad kicking you out."

"You're not kicking me out. I just want a quiet spot to chill with Wren." I shrug. "You need the space for your project, anyway."

"He means he wants *an alone* spot to chill with Wren," Matt yells from the living room.

"My parents are still in Maui…I could give you the keys to the house," Kellan presses. "They wouldn't mind. And don't worry about Dallas kicking your ass…I doubt he'll even be around." He chuckles, then proceeds to choke on a piece of popcorn.

"That's what you get for talking shit." Snorting, I yank my sheets into submission. "Instant karma."

Kellan seizes a bottle of water—my bottle—from the dresser and drinks half of it, finally getting it together. "Seriously though, he and his boys have been spending a lot of time at the marina."

"Oh, yeah?" Our eyes meet in the mirror. "What's at the marina?"

"There's a big sailing club down there—I think our high school used to compete with one of theirs way back. He's been working a lot...and there might be a girl." Kellan shrugs, tossing up a kernel and catching it with his mouth. You'd think he'd have learned his lesson, but no. "Told you things were super casual between him and Wren."

I stop fiddling with my bed, straightening up. "Okay?"

"I'm just saying I would've said something if I thought you going after her was fucked up."

I nod, folding my arms. "I stayed away from her until things ended with your brother for a reason. You know that, right?"

"Yeah. Good man."

"Even though, technically, I saw her first."

He laughs then, backing out of the room. "Did more than just see her, bro."

Meanwhile, the flurry of texts between Wren and me tapered off once tonight's plans got nailed down. She's probably nervous; I know I am. Which is funny, because I can't remember the last time a girl made me nervous. Maybe a little bit with Brooke, when we first met for coffee, but it's different with Wren. I feel like we're getting another chance and I don't want anything to mess it up.

"Give Sweet Spot my love," Matt calls from the couch, where he, Faruq and some kid I don't know very well are engaged in a PlayStation battle.

"Will do," I say, shutting the door. I will, too. Matt's obnoxious, but he genuinely likes Wren. Always has.

And I've learned to trust his instincts.

* * *

Dusk falls as I pull up to Wren's building. Checking her dorm and room number one more time, I get out of the car and glance around. I lived here my freshman and sophomore years, but that was a lifetime ago. I'd almost forgotten what a pretty campus it was, with Redwoods and Douglas firs crowding the sidewalks and pathways.

Wren's room is on the first floor. I text her to let her know I'm outside, and then step back, waiting.

The glass door opens seconds later. "Hey, you," she says, rosy cheeked and smiling. She's wearing a soft, pink sweater that's falling off one shoulder and dark gray jeans that looked like they were painted on.

She looks incredible.

"Hey, Wren." I smile back, feeling my stomach tighten in anticipation as she hugs me. Wrapping my arms around her, I reciprocate with a brief, but very necessary, squeeze. Her hair smells exquisite, mildly floral. She feels even better. It's going to be hard keeping my hands off of her.

"Come on in; I'm almost ready," she adds, pulling me through the lobby and down the hall. "And I think Saira wants to say hi."

"Hi, Luca!" Saira jumps off the couch as we walk through the door while Wren disappears into a closet. Their dorm reminds me of the first one I shared with the guys: a cramped bedroom replete with bookshelves and minifridges and posters. "Long time, no see. How've you been?"

Grinning, I slide my hands into my pockets. "I've been good, Saira. You?"

"Oh, you know. Study, study, study. I've been taking extra classes each semester so I can graduate early."

"Impressive. Why?"

"I'm pre-law. I have about a zillion years of school left, so I might as well!" she says with a sigh. Her sassy grin tells me she's probably in her element, though. My brother Nico was like that—an overachiever in love with school.

"How'd I not know that?" I muse. "You know, Kellan's pre-law, too."

She nods, a small smile teasing at her lips. "I think I remember him telling me that."

"Saira, have you seen my boots?" Wren calls from the closet.

Saira goes to her, and for the next moments their quiet chatter rises and falls. Wren comes out, a purse slung over her shoulder. "Okay. Ready."

"Have fun, guys," Saira says, flopping back onto her bed with a pink laptop.

Wren blows her an air kiss and then we're outside, alone. Together. Finally.

A nervous silence descends between us…probably because we are, in fact, alone and together. For the first time.

"I know you're the true local," I begin, unlocking the car with my fob. "But there's a restaurant I thought you'd like. I don't know, maybe you've already been there—Bobby O'Shea?"

She smiles. "I've heard great things about it, but I've actually never been."

"Perfect. I think you'll like it." I open her door for her, waiting until she's tucked her feet in to close it, but she touches my wrist, stopping me.

"I'm glad we're finally going out." Her eyes are stormy seas today, green and blue and gold. "I've really been looking forward to it."

"Me too." Every part of me strains toward her, and by the way she's looking up at me, I know she feels the same way. I want to slide my hands into her long, wavy hair and mess it up, capture her pretty mouth in a kiss.

But we've waited this long, so I just take her hand into mine and give it a squeeze.

Bobby O'Shea's is one of our favorite spots to eat in Santa Cruz. We usually go for birthdays and celebrations, but this'll be the first time I'm bringing someone on a date. Situated on the water, with killer views—it's a shame we missed the sunset—it's got an upscale surf type atmosphere. Massive windows look out at the water while surfboards hang from the ceiling.

It's Friday night, so it's busy. I give the statuesque hostess my name, and after verifying our reservation, she leads us to a cozy, circular booth right against the windows. We slide in on opposite sides, scooting over until we are so close we're almost touching.

"How's this?" the hostess asks, smiling knowingly as she clasps her hands. She knows this is prime real estate; I asked specifically for this table.

"Perfect," Wren practically croons, twisting to peer out the window.

"Excellent. Your server, Katya, will be right with you."

"Cool, right?" I ask, stretching my arm around the back of the booth as I settle in.

Wren beams. "Very cool. You get major brownie points for picking this place."

Our server appears, smiling cheerily as she hands us our menus. Once she's given us the specials and left to get our drinks, I turn to Wren.

"So, talk to me. Fill me in. How's school been?" I ask. "Are you still feeling good about psychology?"

"Psych's cool." She shrugs. "I'm just glad exams are over. My brain's fried."

"Burnout, huh?" I tug on a curly lock of hair that's fallen over her shoulder.

She smiles the tiniest bit. "A little. My class schedule isn't as insane as Saira's, but I have work-study at the library, so it evens out."

We look up as Katya returns with our drinks: lemonade for me, a Shirley Temple for Wren. "Thank you."

"My pleasure." Katya smiles, cocking her head. "Have you had a moment to look over the menu, or do you need more time?"

On one hand I'm starving, and I know ordering would rectify that situation.

On the other, I might be even hungrier for Wren. I'd almost rather our server just left us alone.

But Wren pipes up, grabbing her menu. "Oh! We haven't even looked at these. What's your favorite thing here?"

Katya raises her eyebrows, surprised. "Mine? Um, well, the Tsunami Prawns are fantastic. They're a little spicy, but nothing too intense." She pauses, thinking. "Are you a seafood kinda gal, or do you prefer steak?"

"Mm, I can do either, but I'm in the mood for seafood tonight."

"Okay, then I'd recommend the Lost Boys Bouillabaisse. It's pretty classic."

Wren cuts me a smirk before nodding at Katya. "I'll have that. Definitely."

"Yeah? You wanna check it out to be sure?" Katya asks, pointing to a meal on the menu.

"Nope; that's what I want," Wren says with a decisive nod.

"Great. I think you'll be pleased." Katya looks at me. "And what can I get for you?"

"The blackened mahi, please. And a large order of the prawns; we'll share."

"Great! I'll be back in a bit." Katya picks up the menus and leaves.

Wren pops the cherry from her drink into her mouth, waggling her eyebrows.

Amused at her glee, I nod my chin. "What?"

"Oh, come on—Lost Boys bouillabaisse?" Wren grins. "I had to."

"Hey, that's right!" *The Lost Boys*—the movie we watched the night we hung at the boardwalk. "How could I forget?"

"It's too perfect—a sign from the universe."

"Definitely too good a coincidence to pass up." Chuckling, I take a sip of lemonade. "I liked your strategy of asking her what her favorites were, by the way."

"Oh, I do that all the time. You wouldn't believe the goodies I've discovered that way."

"Any duds?"

She frowns, thinking. "Maybe a couple, but no. Not really."

"You're adventurous. I like it." *I like you.* "Brave."

"Ha! Sometimes." She glances down at the table, tracing her fingers over the white cloth. "I almost didn't look for you on Instagram."

"You needed bravery for that?" I tease.

She nods. "I didn't want to seem pushy."

"You're the opposite of pushy, trust me," I assure her, rubbing my thumb over her thigh. There's denim between us, but I can feel the heat anyway.

"Well, and then there was the fact you had just broken up with someone. That kind of put New Year's Eve into a whole new perspective for me." Our eyes meet, and she drops her hand to mine. "I get why you didn't want to step on Dallas' toes."

"Honestly, stealing another guy's girl has never been my style, no matter how much I like her." I keep our gaze locked. "My dad messed around on my mom before they got divorced, and even though they weren't that close anymore I saw how it affected her."

"Wow. That…sucks."

"Yeah. Anyway, things were especially fresh the weekend I saw you again."

Wren cocks her head. "What happened, if you don't mind me asking?"

Katya pops up with the tsunami shrimp and two plates. "Enjoy!"

"Thanks," I say, waiting until she's gone before focusing on Wren. "I was dating this girl, Brooke, for about a year. Year and a half. We were exclusive, but I wouldn't say it was love or anything. I mean, we hung out a lot and we'd met each other's parents and she was always my plus one, stuff like that. We had a lot in common, but at the end of the day, I knew she wasn't *the* one."

Wren stirs her drink with the bright pink metal straw they stuck into it. "You believe in that?"

"What, 'the one'?"

She nods.

"I don't know. Maybe we all have a few potentials." Exhaling roughly, I tear my gaze from Wren's and look at the table. "The thing is, even though it seemed good with Brooke for a long time, I had suspicions. Like, I could never put my finger on it, but I wondered sometimes if there was someone else."

She sighs softly. "My mom always tells me to listen to my instincts, but that's hard to do when you're in a relationship. I think we see what we want to see."

"We absolutely do." I nod. "My boy Matt didn't trust Brooke from the very beginning. He even told me, but I ignored him… until the night I caught my best friend coming out of her apartment."

Wren's eyes widen. "That's so shitty."

"Yup."

She shakes her head, looking away. "I don't know what's worse…that she cheated or that it was with your best friend."

"That's what's so fucked up." I squeeze her hand. "Brooke didn't break my heart. But Logan kind of did."

"I'm so sorry, Luca," Wren says, holding my hand with both of hers now. "No one deserves that. No one."

"Yeah, so that's the whole, sordid story." Shrugging, I pick up a prawn and bite into it. "But enough of that. This shrimp, right here? This is amazing."

"Don't hog it! Let me try." She lets go of me, allowing us to move on. "I love shrimp."

Wren

There's something really arousing about a delicious meal shared with one's paramour.

Well, maybe Luca's not my paramour, per se, but I'd like him to be.

It's a complete feast of the senses: exquisite tastes and heavenly smells, shared smiles and laughs, a steady stream of conversation that peels back layer after layer of who he is. Of who I am. It feels like foreplay. Especially when our eyes meet and hold, like they're having another conversation all on their own.

It's always felt like foreplay with him.

"This is going to sound really douchey," Luca begins, as we walk out to his car after dinner. "But you have gorgeous eyes."

"That's not douchey." I peek up at him. "And thanks. I think maybe I got them from my dad."

"Maybe?" He huffs softly. "What do his look like?"

"They're green." I swallow, my heart thumping oddly. "I…haven't known him very long. I just met him for the first time."

Luca slides his arm around me, holding me close as we walk. He smells so good, like musk and spice and fresh laundry, reminding me of the day we talked on the beach. "Sorry. I didn't know."

"It's okay. He's uh, coming back for my birthday."

We stop at Luca's car. "Yeah? You excited, or nervous, or…?"

"Both. All of it."

His eyes search mine. He's curious.

"It's kind of a long story. I'll tell you all about it, but not here." I can't quite see his face because of the brightness of the streetlamp behind him, but he runs his hand down my arm and nods.

"For sure." Closing my door, he crosses to his side and slides in. Moments later, the heat is on and we're pulling out of the lot. "You want to come back to the house? Kellan just texted, said they finished early."

"Aww, did he do that just for you?" I ask. Luca had mentioned Kellan's group project earlier, promising he'd bring me to the house another time.

"Probably." Luca nods, running his hand over the stubble on his chin. He's not as scruffy as he was the day we met or as clean cut as he was on New Year's. I'm not sure which I prefer—he wears it all pretty well. "Kellan's good people."

"That, he is," I say, thinking of how highly Dallas always spoke of his older brother. "I'd love to come over."

"We can get a six pack on the way." His gaze smolders devilishly. "Since we had to keep it PG at dinner."

We stop at a little hole in the wall that specializes in local beers, then head over to his place. It's in an older neighborhood where most of the homes are original Victorians.

"Beach Hill?" I whistle, long and low. "Nice."

"Kellan's loaded." He shrugs. "He wanted to stay here when we left campus, and his parents didn't mind paying the lion's share of the rent."

"So lucky! I love this neighborhood." I look wistfully out the window, my gaze snagging on several dreamy houses I grew up admiring. "It's like being in another time."

"I never thought about it like that, but you're right," he agrees, pulling into a driveway. It's hard to see in the dark, but I think the house might be light purple. "My mother loves the Victorians in San Francisco…she took a thousand pictures when we moved into this place."

"Mine would, too." I try to recall the Instagram photos I saw of Luca's mom. Maybe I should ask to see another picture.

Walking quietly along the alley between two houses, we let ourselves in through a small, creaky gate and into a tiny, lush backyard. Lights glow from the first floor, but Luca leads me to an outdoor staircase leading up. "You can get to my room through the front door, but this is more private," he explains, hand on the small of my back as he ushers me ahead.

"This is nice," I say, admiring the deck as Luca unlocks the door. "Do you hang out here a lot?"

"For sure, especially when it's sunny."

Inside, his room is simple and cozy, two surfboards hanging along one wall. Taking a pair of bottles off the six pack, he stows the rest in the fridge.

"Did you grow up surfing, or was it something you got into when you moved here?"

"I've loved it since I was a kid. We hit up the beach as much as we could when I was younger, but I definitely surfed more when I got to Santa Cruz." He kicks his shoes off. "It was great for the first couple years, but these days I'm just too busy. I don't get out as much as I'd like to."

Leaving my purse and boots by the door, I wander around the room, admiring the black and white photographs of historical Santa Cruz. "These are great," I breathe, superimposing what I know of these locations over the images in the photographs. "It's trippy to watch a city evolve like this."

"Santa Cruz is a rad little town," Luca says, coming to stand next to me. He hands me a beer, clinking his against it. "Cheers. To reconnecting."

"Cheers." Smiling, I take a nice, long pull of the cool, crisp ale.

"Do you want to sit inside or outside?" he asks, ambling over to the door and peering out the window. "It's kind of chilly, I guess, but I have blankets."

"I think I'm in the mood for this couch." I sit, patting the seat beside me. "It's comfy."

He joins me, running his fingers through his hair. "Couch it is."

I hide a smile at the sudden awkwardness between us. Luca and I have been in each other's orbits for such a long time, but there's still a lot we don't know about each other.

"What does your mom do?" I ask, starting at ground zero.

"She works at an interior design firm in San Francisco." He leans back, balancing his bottle on his thigh. "They specialize in hotels. She's been there for nearly a decade."

"I can honestly say I've never met someone who does that." I scratch my head. "What exactly does she do?"

He pauses, thinking. "Basically, her team works with other companies, helping them to build cohesive brands. They create brand strategy, brand identity, stuff like that."

"Like logos and signs?"

"Exactly." He nods. "It goes even deeper, but that's the gist of it."

"That's really, really cool. And what about your dad?" I ask. "He lives in Brazil, right? São Paulo?"

"Right. He's in software, pretty high level."

"But that's not what you want to do," I say, remembering our conversation about this very thing way back when.

"Ultimately, no." A small smile crosses his lips, and he takes a sip of beer. "I want to focus on architecture."

"So, design, like your mom. Just a different manifestation."

Luca's smile widens. "I never thought about it like that, but yeah."

"You said ultimately. Does that mean you're still dabbling in software?"

"Nothing gets by you," he says, titling his head. "I've spent two summers and two semesters now, working in São Paulo."

"For your dad?"

"For him, for his associates."

"And how's it been going?"

Luca shrugs. "I make good money."

"But..."

"The kind of money that can be hard to walk away from." He sinks back into the couch, drawing deeply from his beer. "What about your mom? What does she do?"

"She's been a yoga instructor for nearly twenty years." I trace my finger through the condensation on my bottle, wondering why, after all this time, Luca is still so uncertain about his future. About following in his dad's footsteps. "She owns Lotus Studios in downtown Santa Cruz."

"That's hella cool," he says, nodding. "Business ownership is where it's at."

I nod, thinking of my mother's gusto, her independent spirit. "It's a good thing. Having her own studio was always her dream, so I'm proud of her for doing it. She loves helping people and loves being her own boss, so it's a win/win."

Luca raises an eyebrow. "But?"

Guess I'm not the only astute listener here. I like that. "But it hasn't always been easy. Take the expenses, for example. She almost lost the studio the summer you and I met, all because the building was under this new management that hiked the rent way up. Most of the money I made that summer helped my mom through the transition."

"Wow," he says softly, setting his beer down on a coaster from a local bar. "That's incredible. That you'd do that for your mom."

"She's my mom." I shrug. "Wouldn't you?"

"I would." He nods. "But I doubt everyone would."

"I was pretty salty about it at the time." I chuckle. "I had to cancel all of the big summer plans I'd made with my girlfriends. It was our last hurrah before college, so you know." Of course, being stuck in Santa Cruz that summer was how I'd met Luca, but I keep that to myself.

"Probably made you stronger," he muses.

"My mom's friend called it a 'character building time,'" I say, remembering Darius. "And my grandmother loves to say that said difficulties are requirements for growth." I sigh, realizing I miss Gramma Kate. I saw her all the time before I went to college, but now it hasn't been since Christmas.

I bet she'd love Luca. She's always been a sucker for a pretty face.

"Are you close to your grandparents?" I ask.

"Ironically, I'm closer to my dad's than my mom's," he says. "Ironic, because they live in Brazil. My mom's parents live in the Bay, but I haven't seen them in years."

"Why?"

"Mom's not too close to them. They weren't too crazy about the idea of her marrying some poor guy she met in college, even if he was Brazilian."

"It's mind-boggling to me that people still think that way." I wrinkle my nose, disgusted. "I'm glad your mom followed her heart. She made you."

"And my brother, Nico."

"Does he live around here?"

Luca cracks a smile. "Yeah, up in the Bay with his wife and kids."

"Tell me about your dad," he says suddenly. "You said earlier that you'd just met him. Did he leave your mom before you were born?"

I probably should have seen the conversation coming to this, but I was so caught up in Luca's world I didn't even see it coming. "I..."

A small wrinkle forms between his eyebrows, and he leans forward. "Look, if it's a sensitive topic—"

"My mom was artificially inseminated," I blurt, staring at the beer sweating between my palms. "She didn't even know my dad, so we kinda met him around the same time. We're all still getting to know each other, I guess."

"Oh, okay."

I look up. To Luca's credit, he stays neutral-looking. I can only imagine what's going on in that gorgeous head of his.

"It's nuts, I know." Butterflies—the icky, anxious kind, not the fluttery, fun kind—surge around my gut. I gulp down half my beer in an effort to drown them. "You've got a great poker face, by the way."

Luca smiles a little, cocking his head as he watches me.

"What?"

"It's not as big a deal as you think it is." Closing his eyes, he shakes his head. "That's not what I mean. Meeting your father is going to be one of the biggest moments of your life, for sure. But the way you came to be?" He aims his laser gaze straight at me. "Not a big deal. You're not the only person whose mom had you like that, and you're not the only one who's never met their dad. Doesn't make you different or weird."

A startled, borderline hysterical laugh bursts from my lips. "You really get to the point."

He raises his eyebrows. "I've been told."

"You're right. Of course, you're right." Relief that he accepts this for what it is washes over me. "It's just, I'm the only person *I know* whose mom had them like this. It can be hard to relate to."

"I get it."

"It sets me apart, you know?"

"Is that a bad thing?"

"I guess not." I finger my necklace, smiling. "I usually don't tell people because of all the questions that inevitably follow, you know?"

"But you told me." Luca grins smugly, squeezing my knee. Every time he touches me, my stomach shoots to my feet.

"You're hard to resist."

We look at each other, something passing between us. Lust, probably. "How'd you even find him?"

"He found me. I submitted my DNA to one of those ancestry sites online in an effort to, like, discover more about myself." I rub my forehead with a humorless laugh. "The more I think about it, the more I'm convinced my subconscious was leading the way. I mean, of course I'd find my real dad! How on earth could I find distant family members or whatever without finding him?" It's the first time I've actually said this out loud, but the notion's been percolating in my head ever since Arlo messaged me for the first time.

It was never about my bloodlines. It was about finding my dad.

"Anyway, the site matched my DNA with whatever was in the database. It linked me to a bunch of people, him included," I explain. "His name's Arlo. He's French. Like, born in France, moved to the US when he was really little."

His eyes widen. "And he reached out to you?"

"He did. It was the craziest, most unexpected thing ever." I stretch my legs, resting my socked feet on the coffee table. "We've been emailing ever since. My mom was a little freaked out at first, but she's warmed to the idea."

"That's incredible." Luca nods, gazing off into the distance. "I've always wanted to try one of those sites."

"Just let me know, I can give you my referral code for a discount," I joke.

"Maybe I will." Winking, he tips his head back and polishes off what's left of his beer.

"You want another one?" I jump to my feet, collecting both of our bottles. "I do."

I skim past him, a little jolt of excitement zapping through my entire body at the fact that Luca and I are together. At his place. Retrieving two more beers from the fridge, I open them with Luca's keys.

His hand slides up my thigh as I pause to hand him his beer. "Thanks," he murmurs, but he doesn't take it.

I look down at him, stomach flip-flopping at the golden glimmer in his light brown eyes. "You know, you're the one with the killer eyes, Luca."

I leave the bottles on the table and face him, enjoying the weight of his hand. This is what I've been thinking about for the past year and a half. Luca's touch. His intentional, intimate touch.

His other hand slides up my thigh, squeezing my hip. The heat between us builds. "Hey."

Moving sinuously, slowly, I ease onto his lap, resting my knees on either side of his hips. It's a risky move, launching us from maybe to definitely, but I don't care. I feel like we've been holding back forever and I'm over that.

Smiling slyly, Luca bites his lip. His heated gaze drops to my mouth as his hands round themselves over my ass. He squeezes, dragging me closer. "Don't stop now, Wren," he teases.

"I've thought about that night at the boardwalk so many times," I confess, ghosting my fingertips over his sharp cheekbones. *Jeez, what a face.*

"So have I."

My breath hitches. Resting my hands over Luca's broad, muscled shoulders, I lean closer and meet his mouth in a gentle kiss. I do this over and over, closing my lips over his bottom one, then his top, enjoying the feel of him. After a moment, he nudges my lips open, darting his warm, wet tongue into my mouth. It feels so good that I moan quietly, tightening my grip on him, pulling myself even closer. The movement pulls a muffled groan from him, too, and he stiffens beneath me.

It's like pouring gasoline on a bed of embers. Squeezing my ass, Luca sweeps his tongue into my mouth, chasing mine in a slick, sexy push and pull that has me panting and writhing in his lap. Glimmers of our other kisses shoot through my memory like comets, sweet and gentle on the Sky Glider, passionate and forbidden in the photo booth. This is a supernova of the hottest kind.

Luca's relentless, kissing me and kissing me, nibbling my mouth and sucking my tongue. His hands roam up under my sweater, running restlessly over the bare skin of my back, and his rough, sandpaper chin rubs deliciously against mine, making me think of other places I'd love to feel it. I grind my hips instinctively against his, the fabric of his jeans doing little to hide how hard he's become.

"Wren," he grits out, his head falling on the back of the couch. "If we don't chill out…"

"I don't want to chill out," I murmur, dropping kisses down the column of his neck. I lick and suck the tender skin there, chasing his pulse with my teeth, gratified when his fingers tighten almost painfully around my waist.

He laughs, groaning, and moves his neck from my mouth. "That's why you love *The Lost Boys*—you're a little vampire yourself."

"That's right." I wiggle my eyebrows. "And you fell right into my trap."

We share a smile, allowing the moment to mellow despite his massive erection. Frankly, I'm seconds away from going old school and riding him until we're both satisfied—even with our clothes on. It's all I can do to just leave it alone.

The longer I look at him, the more I feel like I'm falling into his eyes. It's a feeling I don't want to escape. Maybe he feels the same way because he caresses my face with aching softness. And, wrapping his fingers around the back of my neck, he pulls me in for another dizzying kiss.

Luca

I wake up in increments: the feel of fleece against my feet, the sound of soft breathing, muted, morning sunlight glowing through the curtains. Wren's asleep beside me, curled up beneath the blankets we passed out under last night.

Just the sight of her makes my dick throb like a freaking fourteen-year-old pervert.

I can't remember the last time I made out with someone until falling asleep. I drink in the sight of her, taking advantage of the fact she's not awake. Her delicate, almost-upturned nose and the faint constellation of freckles sprinkled across it. That dimple I've always liked, even more apparent when she laughed last night. The dainty gold necklace she always wears. She touches the small bird hanging from it all the time, a nervous tic maybe. I peer at it now, realizing it's probably a wren.

Fascinating, but not as fascinating as her breasts. I glance at the shape of them, tempted to slide her sweater up so I can suck one of those soft, pink nipples into my mouth. Last night they'd hardened beneath my hands before yielding like ripe berries beneath my tongue.

This isn't helping the situation in my boxers. Yawning, I sit up and run my hands through my hair. I spy our jeans, tangled in a heap in the corner of the room, next to one of my socks. Shaking my head in amusement, I slide carefully out of bed and pad to the bathroom.

When I come back, she's stirring, her wild nest of waves glinting copper in the morning light. "Hey, you," she says, her voice husky with sleep. Sexy.

Returning to bed, I run my hand down her soft belly and between her legs, which she clamps shut.

"I have to pee." She giggles, pulling me closer and pushing me away at the same time. "Why are you all minty? Did you brush your teeth?" She scoots from underneath me, her sweater barely covering that cute little ass as she escapes. "I'll be right back!"

Grinning, I watch her scamper off. That's how you know a girl's the real deal—when she's just as appealing in the morning. Wren's long, messy hair and smudged eye makeup just make me want to take her down and keep her in bed all damn day.

She comes back moments later, smiling shyly, and climbs back into bed with me. "I used your mouthwash."

"That's what I used, too. I didn't brush."

"I couldn't have you all minty and fresh while I was gross," she chides, side-eyeing me.

"There is nothing gross about you," I say, pulling her onto me so she's straddling me. I know she feels my erection. She shifts, her lips parting as her eyes gloss over. "Trust me."

"Good to know." She smiles slowly, anchoring her hands on my chest. "I guess we slept together without sleeping together, huh?"

"Guess so." Reaching up, I brush her hair from her eyes. "What should we do now?"

"I don't know." She glances over at the door that leads to the hallway. "Is anybody else home? Want me to make breakfast?"

"Not really hungry right now." As endearing as it is that she wants to make me breakfast in my own house, my stomach isn't calling the shots right now. Sitting up, I gather her closer and kiss her properly, filling her sweet little mouth with my tongue.

She murmurs her approval, wrapping her arms around my neck. Dancing my tongue around hers, I lower my hands to her ass and squeeze it, pulling her down hard on to my dick. It's a horny move, but I'm a horny guy, and I feel like coming. Even if we're not going to fuck.

We kissed last night until we were delirious, shedding pants and socks so we could be closer, but it never quite came to this. Between talking and the novelty of kissing, and knowing we'd just been on our first date, it just never went there. But things feel different this morning. Maybe it's my morning wood, or the fact I'm rested. Maybe it's Wren's barely awake, highly suggestible state. Whatever it is, it's turning me on, feeling the heat build between this perfect girl's thighs, imagining how wet she's getting as she squirms and moans.

Her breathing quickens. Reaching a hand up under her sweater, I close my hand around one of her soft, firm tits and squeeze. I rub my thumb over her nipple, rolling it between my fingers until she moans, tossing her head

226

back. More than happy to give her a dose of last night's vamp medicine, I clamp down on her neck and suck.

She squeals, fighting to extricate herself from my grip, but I hold tight. Acquiescing slightly, I lick the dark spot I've just made. "I haven't done that since high school," I whisper, grinning.

"Me neither." She grins, working my elastic free. My hair falls loose, and she runs her fingers through it.

Few things feel better than having someone run their fingers through your hair, and when Wren scratches her nails against my scalp, my eyes nearly roll to the back of my head. Pulling her chin down, I kiss her again, moving her over me until she starts to ride on her own. I want her to find her pleasure on my dick, even if I can't be inside her.

And I can't, not yet. Not like this. The setting might seem right, but the timing isn't, and Wren's the kind of girl I need to take my time with. We've only just crossed this line. I need to know I'm not taking anything from her. She needs to give herself to me.

But then she moans, palming my cheeks as she kisses me back. "Luca..." She's getting sloppy, a probable sign she's close to coming.

"You're so warm," I murmur against her mouth, feeling the friction build for me, too. "You feel...so good."

"I just..." She tilts her head back again and I take the opportunity to lift her sweater, revealing her pretty, pretty breasts. Leaning down, I take one into my mouth and swirl my tongue against her nipple.

"I...I..." She cries out, bouncing up and down on my lap so hard she shoves me right along into an orgasm of my own.

It happens so suddenly that I see colors behind my eyes. Wave after wave of hot, liquid pleasure thrums through my groin, leaving me sticky and satisfied. "Holy shit," I groan against her skin, stilling her with my hands. "I haven't done that since high school, either."

Panting, she gazes down at me. Her pupils are dilated, giving her light eyes a dark, feral appearance. "Wow."

"Wow." I lower her sweater and kiss her before moving her gingerly from my lap. "I think I'm gonna go take a shower. You don't mind, do you?"

She blushes hotly. "Go right ahead."

"You wanna come?" I ask, winking on the double entendre. "Again?"

Laughing, she flops down onto the bed. "I better not."

Nodding, I give her one last, smug smile and head toward the bathroom.

* * *

When I emerge from the bathroom in a cloud of steam, Wren's dressed and scrolling through her phone. She tosses it into her purse and rises from the couch. "Now do you want breakfast? Do you have anything in your fridge?"

"I should be cooking you breakfast." Crossing the room, I slide my hands over her ass and pull her gently into me. "But I think I'd rather go out. It's too nice out to stay inside, and anyway, you can show me your Santa Cruz."

"My Santa Cruz? As opposed to yours?"

"Yeah, hometown girl. You've lived here your whole life."

"Okay." She slides her hands in her back pocket, eyes shining. "Let's do it. We'll have to stop by my dorm so I can get some clean clothes though."

It really is a stunner of a day. The sun is bright, and fat, cheerful clouds drift lazily by a peaceful, blue sky. The temperature's mellowed out a lot too; it can't be less than 60 degrees. In the car, I put the music up and the windows down, listening as Wren shows me her Santa Cruz. There's one of her mom's favorite houses, a cozy craftsman bungalow. A couple of neighborhoods over we see Wren's favorite—a pale, mint green Victorian with whimsical, multicolored turrets. Food trucks. Thrift shops. Friends' neighborhoods. Places where she trick-or-treated as a kid. Her favorite beaches. Cafes with the best mochas. Bakeries with the best chocolate croissants.

"I'm sensing a theme here. You really do like chocolate," I note, squeezing her thigh.

"It's my favorite," she affirms, her hair flying in the wind like streamers of joy, so we stop off for mochas and chocolate croissants.

The next stop is UCSC, where Wren takes a shower and changes while I sit at her desk and talk to Saira. We've just gotten done catching one another up on all things dull and academic when she leans forward, a sly look entering her dark eyes.

"How's your boy, Kellan?"

I smirk, wondering how long she's wanted to ask. Saira doesn't strike me as anything but direct, so holding back must've taken some effort. "He's great.

Working on a major group project at the moment. Coastal environmental studies."

She blinks, surprised. "Oh, that's cool. He's from around here, right?"

"Grew up in Aptos." Clasping my hands behind my head, I lean back in Wren's chair. "He's considering leaving for grad school, but I doubt he's going anywhere. He loves it too much here."

"Huh." Saira raises an eyebrow and turns to something on her bed, but not before I catch the interest on her face.

"I'll let him know you were asking," I tease, chuckling when she narrows her eyes at me.

Wren returns in distractingly short shorts and a t-shirt, toweling her wet hair. "Wanna come with us, Saira? We're going to hike through campus, hit up all the hidden good spots."

"No, you two go ahead. I'm meeting Skye for lunch in a bit." Saira stretches as she rises. "Have fun, though! It was good seeing you, Luca."

She leaves, and Wren smirks down at me as she weaves her hair expertly into a side braid. "I think she was hoping Kellan would come with you," she whispers.

The shared tenor of our thoughts startles me a bit, but I go with it. "I was just thinking the same thing."

We spend the next couple of hours exploring UCSC's heavily forested campus as Wren shows me her favorite spots, some of which are my favorites, too. There are the Porter Caves and the Tree House—which has a swing—the Buddha Shrine and the Pogonip Koi Pond. Conversation ebbs and flows and meanders as we stop to examine roots and mushrooms and places where the sun shines through the canopy overhead. I've always loved the idyllic, woodsy charm of this campus—the low-key appeal is undeniable.

"I used to come here all the time to mellow out." I squat beside the square pond, tracking the vivid, orange koi that swim just beneath the surface. They dart and shift, scales glinting like flashes of light. "Freshman year, mostly. I was a little homesick."

"Aww, I bet. I still come here all the time." She lingers across the pond, gazing at it. "I don't think I'll ever stop."

"Yeah, I don't know why I did." I straighten up, sliding my hands into my pockets. "Too busy, I guess."

"We'll have to remedy that."

I look up right as Wren snaps a series of pictures of me beside the pond. "Really?" I laugh.

Her cheeks darken, but she grins. "The only pictures I have of you are from random photo booths."

"Fair enough." Walking over to her, I take the phone and snap one of us together.

We finish our tour by visiting the Wishing Tree, where Wren rips two pieces of paper from a notebook in her bag and hands me one. "Make a wish."

"Got a pen?"

Pausing for a moment, I flatten the paper against my thigh and wish for clear direction after graduating. Pai's been asking if I want to come to São Paulo, semi-permanently this time, but I just don't know. On one hand, the time I've spent in Brazil has been beneficial; I've learned a lot, made more money than I expected to. I have friends and business associates. Connections.

My father.

But it's not my only option. I'll be graduating soon, with honors, and with that comes a whole new host of opportunities. Despite all the time and effort I've invested in learning Pai's software industry, my heart still beats for buildings. I want to explore architecture and Berkeley's a solid option for grad school. So is Santa Cruz.

Wren hides her paper when I try to peek, flicking my arm. "No reading other people's wishes, Luca." She sweetens the admonishment with a kiss on my cheek and darts off to pin her wish to a branch.

I follow suit, amused at how into this she is—there's something infinitely appealing about the purity of her wonder. It definitely fits what I know of her.

We're winding our way back to civilization when the first hunger pang hits. Grimacing, I rub my stomach. "I'm gonna have to eat soon—I'm starving. You coming with?"

"Yeah, I'm hungry, too." Wren ducks beneath a low hanging branch. "You in the mood for tacos?"

"I'm always in the mood for tacos."

She nods. "Let's grab some and we can hang at my place for a while. My

232

mom's place, actually, since I live on campus now. But you know what I mean."

"The house you grew up in will always be yours." I hold my hand out to steady her as we step over an enormous, felled tree. "You want to call her, let her know we're coming?"

"I'll text her to let her know, but she went to Napa for the weekend with her girlfriends," she says. "We'll have the apartment to ourselves."

"You're sure she won't mind?"

"Positive. She's probably the chillest mom you'll ever meet."

Wren

After stopping at a taqueria in Santa Cruz, I take Luca to my old apartment building.

In some ways, it does feel more like Mom's place than mine nowadays. I don't sleep here, and my favorite foods are no longer in the fridge. My laundry doesn't litter my bedroom floor, and while the yellow stripe I painted on the wall over my desk remains speckled with old photos and memorabilia, there's nothing current.

But my bed, the same one I got in junior high, will probably always be here, made and ready for me should I choose to crash for the night. There are pictures of me all over the living room, the hallways, and the fridge. And I still have a key. These stairs, this crappy lock, that sagging couch all feel like home. Luca's right. It'll always be mine, too.

We park in my old spot and then Luca follows me upstairs, carefully sidestepping a potted fern someone left halfway up. The apartment smells the same as always, a combination of incense, essential oils and whatever she's been cooking with lately. Oregano, I think, and maybe rosemary? I peel off my boots and plug in Mom's turquoise and pink Christmas lights. She has a tiny tree in the corner, decorated with seashells.

"You can put the beers in the fridge," I call to Luca, who disappeared into the kitchen. Pulling open the heavy, teal drapes that cover the sliding glass doors, I take a peek outside. The front of our apartment faces the parking lot, but the back looks out over a wooded courtyard, complete with wrought iron benches and a little green space that Mrs. Martinez on the first floor recently resurrected into a succulent garden. It's probably one of my favorite things about this place. I spent hours down there as a kid in middle and high school, journaling, texting my friends, and being angsty.

Joining Luca in the kitchen, I rummage around the odds and ends drawer only to see he's already opened a couple of beers. "You beat me to it."

He holds up his keychain, from which an opener dangles. "Always ready."

We sit at the table and tuck into lunch, a sundry feast of tacos, burritos and freshly made chips and guacamole. Luca moans in pleasure, pointing at his food. "This was a good idea."

"See? Told you it was the best."

He nods, washing down his bite with a gulp of Tecate. "I thought I knew Santa Cruz, but you might be right."

"Might be?" Scoffing, I point a chip at him. "I dare you to show me tacos better than these."

"Challenge accepted." His arches an eyebrow. "Come to the Bay, and it's on. There's a food truck in Fruitvale I've been going to since I was a kid...you haven't had tacos like that. Ever."

"Lucky for you, I like challenges. Especially when they involve food." And cute boys.

"Then you'll love this." His eyes soften to a smolder. "It's more of an invitation than a challenge, anyway."

Biting back a smile, I shrug. "Maybe I'll take you up on that soon."

"You should."

Our gaze holds. I'm burning up, from the salsa detonating on my tongue to the wicked flare of heat building much further below. Bringing my beer to my lips, I attempt to douse at least one flame.

Luca's eyes twinkle, like he knows exactly how I'm feeling.

"Here." I shove half a taco across the table. "Try the carnitas."

He does, scanning the kitchen as he chews. "I like this. It reminds me of my mother's kitchen."

"How so?" I ask, curious as to how this might be. I don't know if Luca comes from money, but Walnut Creek is a really nice neighborhood in the Bay area.

"It's cozy, bright." He fingers the yellow cloud-shaped napkin holder on the table. "Colorful."

I look around, trying to see the familiar space through a new lens. "That it is."

"Makes me feel like I know your mom, just from being here."

236

"She'd love that you just said that." Smiling, I cross my legs under the table. "It is very her. When I was a kid, she was forever going to flea markets and thrift shops and garage sales...I have so many memories of her stopping on the side of the road to pick up things people had put out for the trash. It used to really embarrass me." I shrug, popping a chip into my mouth. "Then I got over myself. Besides, it became trendy and eco-conscious to get everything secondhand."

"Mãe's into that too," Luca says, nodding.

I cast him a dubious glance. "Really?"

"Oh, yeah. She loves estate sales and all that." Luca winks, stealing the beef burrito we're supposed to split. "Maybe you'll see when you come for a visit. Shit, these jalapeños are hot."

After lunch, I show Luca my old room. It's indulgent, but it's an interesting insight to who I once was—a museum of Wren. My childhood self, my teenage self; it's a time capsule of the posters left on the walls, the books stuffed onto the crowded shelves, the souvenirs and keepsakes.

Self-consciousness prickles through me as Luca examines the old movie tickets, dried flowers, family photos and fangirl fodder stuck to my bulletin board.

"Aiden Winchester, huh?" He grins, pointing to a picture of the singing, dancing movie star I'd crushed on in ninth grade.

"Ha-ha." I roll my eyes, yanking him away from there. Little does he know our boardwalk photo strips used to cover that very picture. "I'd like to see what sort of secrets your old room holds."

"You'd probably have to hunt through the attic for the good stuff." He snickers. "Or the dump. Mãe made me and Nico's old rooms into guest rooms."

"Nico's your older brother, right?"

"Right. Daniel's the youngest; he's in junior high now."

"Are you guys close?" I ask.

"Nico and I are." He walks over to my bed and sits. "Daniel is Mãe and Dominic's. By the time they had him, Nico was twelve and I was ten, so the age difference is pretty major. He's a cool kid, though. We hang out whenever we can."

"That's cool. Sometimes I wonder what it would've been like to have siblings." I frown, plopping down beside him. "Maybe I do. That's so weird."

Luca cocks his head. "Having siblings you don't know about?"

"Yes, especially when you consider how they all came to be. God knows how many of us are floating around the world."

"Have you asked Arlo?"

"No way." Snorting, I lie back and stare at the buttercup-yellow ceiling. "I'm still trying to get used to the fact I'm his kid."

"Can't say I blame you." Luca reclines on his side, resting his head in his hand as he looks at me. "It's a big adjustment."

"I think it'll feel more real as we spend more time together."

We fall silent. I wonder if he's noticed the tiny quotes I started penciling onto the walls back when this room was my haven.

I glance over at him, nervous all of a sudden. "Do you have anything going on later?"

"Not really." He looks at me. "Why?"

"I don't know."

"Why, you want me to go?" he asks, tickling my thigh.

"No way." Sitting up, I roll onto his lap and hold him down. "You're not going anywhere, Mr. Cardoso."

"Mr. Cardoso, huh? That's kinda freaky." He wraps his hands over my ass and squeezes, jostling me back and forth the way he did this morning. "Not complaining, though."

Flattening myself over him, I kiss each of his cheeks, ghosting my lips over his stubble and his mouth. When I get there, he's waiting for me. Holding my face between his hands, he licks his way into my mouth.

Our tongues tangle and play, chasing and retreating until Luca flips me on to my back. Flushed and turned on, I slide my hands up into his hair, high off the way he feels and smells and tastes. He overwhelms me in the best way.

His hips buck against me, and I wrap my legs around him, grinding myself against his hardness.

"You're trouble," he whispers, unzipping my hoodie. Dragging his warm, wet mouth across my neck, he sucks my earlobe into his mouth.

"I don't mean to be," I breathe, dizzy, trying to keep my eyes open in the onslaught.

"Yes, you do. But I like it. You're the good kind of trouble." His breath is hot against my ear. He slides his hand between my legs, pinching gently at the insides of my thighs. It tickles, but it turns me on, too. "I've been thinking about watching you come."

My breath catches. Hearing him say that, *like that*, makes me wet. "Because of this morning?"

"Like this morning, yeah." He rubs the seam of my shorts as his tongue trails down my throat and over my clavicle. "But I've been thinking about it even longer."

"Since New Year's?" I ask, remembering the heat in his eyes that night.

"Since I saw you on that boardwalk." I'm not wearing a bra, so when he pushes the soft material of my shirt up, he hums in approval, sucking my nipple into his mouth.

"Luca," I moan, holding him to my breast. My legs shake as his fingers slip beneath the hem of my shorts.

"That's me," he says, those clever fingers sneaking into my panties.

Our eyes meet. The last thing I see before my eyes drift shut is Luca, smiling devilishly around my breast. It's only been a few hours since our playtime in his bed, but I'm already primed and ready for his touch. And boy, is he delivering.

Luca takes turns with my nipples, sucking one before releasing it with a wet pop and going for the other. He rubs his long fingers rhythmically between my slickest flesh, up and down and up and down before sliding one inside me, wrenching a gasp of pleasure from my throat.

I tighten around him, pulling his hair when he adds another finger. "That's so good," I whisper, feeling myself tumble a little closer to coming.

"Yeah?" He doubles down, pumping his fingers deeper, faster, his thumb rubbing circles around my clit. The combination of sensations—his mouth, his hands—swirl into a vortex of pure bliss. My orgasm cascades over me, rippling from my center all the way to my fingers and toes.

I cry out as I come, trembling and inarticulate. It seems to go on and on, finally fading as he pulls his fingers out of my shorts and sucks them into his mouth.

I watch, panting, as his eyes gleam. He wants me. I can see it; I can feel it, and as ready as my body is ready for his, my heart is still uncertain. We're so new. Maybe he senses it, because he rises, coming up to kiss me. "You okay?"

"More than okay." My face warms, and I hold him tightly.

Huffing softly, he kisses my neck and pulls back. "I'm not trying to do anything you don't want to do."

"I do want to. I just…"

"It's okay." Lying down beside me, he takes me into his arms. "I respect that."

"But aren't you painfully hard right now?"

"Mhm." Grinning, he puts my hand on his dick. "But I'd rather take it slow.

I think you want to, right?"

I nod, my chest near bursting with a deep sense of intense like for Luca. My throat closes and I swallow back the salt of tears, not wanting to ruin this with a weird, emotional breakdown. *That was some orgasm.*

"You sure you're okay?" he murmurs, thumbing my chin.

I gaze into his pretty eyes, ensnared. "Perfect."

* * *

Saira perches on the futon, popping pretzels into her mouth as she squints suspiciously at me. Our three-bunk bedroom with Leighton came with a lounge this year, so we have a little more space than before.

"Why're you looking at me like that?" I ask, chuckling as I sort laundry into 'wash' and 'wait.'

She raises a sculpted, freshly-tweezed-looking eyebrow. "You know damn well why, *bestie.*"

"My eyebrows, right? Yeah, it's been a while. You can tweeze me between laundry loads."

A pretzel comes sailing my way. "You didn't come home last night!"

"I texted you!"

"I know you did." She flips her long, black hair over her shoulder. "But tell me you didn't spend all night underneath that boy letting him give you some good, good d—"

"I didn't!" I laugh, sending her pretzel back.

"Why not? You've wanted him foreverrr."

"Because we just started seeing each other for real." I shrug, squashing the urge to sniff last night's hoodie. It smells like Luca. "I don't want to rush and ruin it."

"Yeah, I get that. Sometimes they take off once they get a taste," she says sagely, nodding. "The ol' fuck n' flee."

I cackle out loud at that one.

"Also known as the hump n' dump," she adds with a saucy grin.

"Well. I don't think Luca's like that," I say, still laughing. But I don't know this for sure—I wouldn't be the first girl who's had her pants charmed off. "But I really, really like him and I need to take my time."

"I get it." Saira smiles gently, nodding. "Remember Ben?"

"Of course, I do. He was a sweetheart." Ben was Saira's first serious boyfriend. They were together for all of junior year of high school, when his family moved to Portland. She's over him now, obviously, but she still holds him up as kind of a standard for what to do right with relationships.

She nibbles the salt off another pretzel. "I know good things take time."

"Exactly." I toss a dirty sock into the wash pile and pause, leaning against the wall. "I want it to mean something when we do it."

243

"Well, good. I sure hope Luca's worthy."

"Me too."

"I mean it. You deserve a good guy." Saira had always disapproved of me and Dallas. She felt like it was opportunistic on Dallas' part, even if we had both agreed to keep things casual. "When are you seeing him again?"

"I don't know." Despite our night together, we left things pretty open-ended when he dropped me back to campus. "Soon. He might come by Tuesday after class." Picking a loose thread from the comforter, I wrap it around my finger.

Leighton and Skye come in, each holding an enormous pizza box. "We're starving. Y'all want some?"

"I could go for pizza," murmurs Saira, putting her pretzels away.

"Hey, babe," I say to Skye, touching her arm. "How's the roommate situation going?"

"Better." She puts the pizza down on our coffee table. "I told her if she kept bringing her man over at all hours, I'd start bringing mine. She didn't want that."

Snorting, I give her a fist bump. "Nice."

"The Golden Rule," Leigh says. "Who would've thought?"

"Just seems like common courtesy to me," Skye says, wrinkling her nose.

"I must admit, I would've loved to see her face if she showed up while you and Xavy were getting it on," Saira says with a snicker.

Skye scoffs, plopping down beside Saira. They didn't know each other before, but their shared Caribbean heritage—Skye's from St. Croix and Saira's mom is Trinidadian—became an instant point of connection when Skye returned to UCSC.

Eating a piece of pepperoni mushroom, I navigate to the UCSC laundry app to see if any washing machines are available downstairs. There are, so I wipe my hands on my jeans and heave my laundry into my arms.

"Hey, I'm gonna go and get these clothes started. A couple of machines just freed up."

"You better hurry," Leigh says through a mouthful. "There might not be much left by the time you get back."

Luca

꧁꧂

"So, Luca," Mãe begins, pausing expectantly. I can barely hear her with the music and family chatter on her end—a typical weeknight evening at the Walnut Creek house. "When do I get to meet this girl?"

Huffing softly, I balance the phone between my ear and shoulder so I can grab groceries from the trunk of my car. "Soon, Mãe, soon. We just started seeing each other."

"But you said you've liked her for a long time," she argues. Dominic, my stepdad, pipes up in the background, and Mãe promptly tells him to hush. Maybe she switches rooms, because suddenly it's quiet. "Listen, baby. That's how it was with your stepdad and me. You know this. We were friends for a long time before he finally made his move. We were engaged within months."

"I know, and that's great," I say, and I mean it, "but I'm in no rush to get engaged."

"I know that, smartass," she says crisply. "My point is that I don't want you to sit around and procrastinate because of what happened with Brooke."

Here we go again. Once you're on Mãe's shitlist it's hard to get off—and lately my ex tops that list. My mother knows how it feels to be cheated on, and she was devastated to see it happen to me. To make things worse, she'd liked Brooke. When things blew up, I think she felt almost as duped as me.

But I'm too distracted by Wren to think about Brooke these days, and when I do it's to wonder why I stayed with Brooke for so long. Our relationship wasn't *bad*, but it wasn't this. There wasn't a near constant urge to text, or long, rambling, late night phone calls. It wasn't a mutual fascination that bordered on infatuation. In fact, I think about Wren way more than I'm comfortable admitting and sometimes that makes me want to pull back. Ironically.

"This is nothing like that," I say after a long moment. "Although now that you mention it, yeah—I don't want to screw things up. Again."

"You weren't the one who screwed up last time," she says, getting fired up all over again, "but I understand."

"I'm taking my time with Wren. We're taking our time." And we are, although making Wren come every time we're together after dark *might* not be the best definition of taking things slow. "She's worth it."

"You're right." She sighs. "There's no rush. I just want you to be happy… because you're worth it, too."

"I know, Mãe."

"Wren is welcome anytime."

"I know that, too." Setting the grocery bags down, I wrestle my keys from my pocket and open the front door.

"Just don't take too long."

I laugh. "Mãe!"

"I'm just saying, baby."

"I hear you, but listen, I just got home. I'll talk to you soon, yeah?"

"Yeah, okay," she says. "Danny says hi, by the way."

"Tell him I said hi. Love you."

"Not as much as I love you."

Inside, Matty's eating a bowl of cereal at the counter. "Thank God you went shopping. I'm dying, over here."

"You could just buy your own food, ya schmuck," I tease, sidestepping his grabby hands.

He points his spoon at me. "Please tell me you got real milk."

"As opposed to imaginary?" Propping open the fridge, I begin unloading the food. "I did."

"Thank God. I can't handle that nasty almond shit Kellan buys."

"Well, seeing that Kellan buys it for Kellan because Kellan is lactose intolerant..."

248

"Kellan what?" Kellan says, scratching his belly as he emerges from his room. "I know you two love me, but damn." He narrows his eyes at Matty, who's returned to his cereal. "You better not have finished off the almond milk."

"Wouldn't dream of it," belches Matty, slurping as he tips his bowl back.

"I got you more, anyway," I say, shaking the carton of almond milk before sliding it into the fridge.

Kellan yawns. "Anybody up for a hike? I just finished my paper and I feel like celebrating."

"I'll go," I say. "I'm not smoking, though. Unlike you, I still have a shitload of stuff to get done."

Kellan nods thoughtfully. "We can pass this time."

"Fine, fine. We'll leave Maryjane at home, just this once." Matty drops his bowl and spoon into the sink with a clatter. "I swear, I don't know what the world is coming to."

An hour later, we're standing in the lush greenery surrounding Berry Creek Falls. Late afternoon sunlight blazes hazily through the redwoods, creating misty rainbows where the water splashes. The temperature's dropped since we started hiking, but it feels good.

Wren and I have taken a few hikes, but we have yet to come up this way. I snap a couple of pictures and send them to her with a text.

Luca: Berry Creek Falls with Kellan and Matty.

Her reply comes a couple minutes later.

Wren: I haven't been since I was a kid. It's beautiful up there.

Luca: It's a good hike, we should do it.

Wren: I was just thinking about you, btw.

Luca: Good things I hope

Wren: you could say that... ;)

"Ten bucks Luca's texting Sweet Spot," Matt calls, jumping down from a rock. "I can tell by the shit-eating grin on his face."

Kellan snorts, glancing over at me. "At least he's smiling."

I send Wren a selfie, with the falls and my friends in the background.

Luca: How've things been going with your pops?

Wren: they're good <3
 Crazy how different things are since last spring break.
 We barely knew each other back then.

Luca: glad to hear it

Wren: Would you want to do dinner
 w/us one of these days?

The same hesitance that's kept me from bringing Wren to my parents' house hits now. I want to be there for Wren, and I'm definitely curious about her dad, but things get exponentially more complicated when families and friends are introduced.

Kellan shoulders me as he passes. "Do we need to confiscate your phone, young man?"

I elbow him and turn away, focused on Wren's invitation. I used to not care about shit like this—parents were just people and meeting them was no big deal. But Wren's not just a girl, and the situation with her father feels fragile. Even if things are going well between them, meeting him feels significant.

The speech bubbles pop up on Wren's side of the conversation before disappearing again. I reply before she starts feeling weird, which she might be because it's taking me forever to give her an answer.

Luca: You sure? I know you don't get a lot of time with your pops.

Wren: No pressure.
Only if you want to.

Yeah, she's backtracking.

Luca: Definitely.
Just give me a time and place.

Wren: Okay.
Great picture, btw.

* * *

Kellan's parents took Dallas and a friend to Maui for spring break, so Kell's housesitting. Matt and I drive over with him on Saturday, pulling into the Morgans' long, winding driveway just before noon.

Matt pops his head into my guest room as I respond to a text from Wren, waggling his eyebrows. "That kitchen is hooked up, bro."

I follow him back downstairs, pausing at a group of family pictures on the landing. There's a classy black and white series of Dallas racing in a regatta. Spoiled little fucker. I wonder if Wren would've been his plus one for Hawaii had the two of them still been fooling around.

Eh, maybe I don't want to wonder.

Kellan's tinkering around in the kitchen, popping open beers and hauling burgers from the deep freezer. Matt wasn't lying—the fridge, pantry and countertops are loaded down with fruit, bread loaves, chips, dips and salsas, cookies and every drink imaginable.

My eyes fall on a note stuck to the fridge, held in place by a sailboat magnet:

Kellan,
  We made sure to leave the kitchen well stocked
  for you and the boys. Eat well and have fun!
  Don't burn down the house.
  Xo,
  Mom

"What's the plan for tonight?" asks Kellan, sliding me a Coors Light.

I give the beer a serious side-eye. Coors Light? *Really?* With the abundance of local craft breweries crowding the entire West Coast?

Kellan notices, sighing. "I know man. My dad loves this shit…I told him he was a sorry excuse for Irishmen everywhere."

"Hey now, don't hate on Pops!" Matt drinks his beer in one long gulp, belching long and hard. "He might have questionable taste in beer, but the man knows his whiskey."

"That's true," I agree, pointing my bottle at Kellan. "Remember that stuff he brought out last time? After dinner?"

Kellan nods. "The eighteen-year-old Jameson's. He has another bottle down in the cellar, I think."

"That's okay." I snort, opening an enormous bag of salt n' vinegar potato chips. "I don't have the $150 to replace it."

"Me neither," Matt says. "Let's stick to the cheap stuff. But not this cheap." He holds up his Coors.

"He doesn't have anything cheap down there," says Kellan. "But he has a good selection. Seriously, he doesn't care if we drink some of it."

"Twist my arm, why dontcha?" Matt's voice fades as he disappears down the hall, probably already heading to the wine cellar, affectionately known around here as the drunk tank.

"Anyway, you didn't answer me," says Kellan. "What's up for tonight? You seeing Wren later?"

"Yeah, we're having dinner with her parents."

"Both of them? At the same time?"

I nod, sipping my beer. Kellan knows the basics—that Wren's only met her father a couple of times—but I've kept the details private. Wren might not be the only one whose mom chose the path she did, and it's nothing to feel weird about, but I respect that it's hers to share.

Kellan pushes his hair from his eyes. "Have fun with that."

"When're you gonna cut that?" I tease, jerking my chin at him. "You going for the SoCal surfer look?"

"Yeah, I'm takin' it back to my parents' generation," he says, giving his hair a flamboyant flip. "And look who's talking, Mr. ManBun LaDouche."

I laugh long and hard at that one. "Girls love it, and my dad hates it. I'll never cut this shit."

Snickering, he returns to the burgers he's started defrosting. "What time are you meeting the parentals?"

"I'm picking Wren up at six, and then we'll head over to Marvel to meet her parents for dinner."

"Good choice," he says, tapping the counter. "Their pizza is on another level."

"That's what I hear." I stroll over to the windows overlooking the pool. I'm definitely a little nervous. Wren, who I'm starting to see has somewhat rose-colored leanings, seems confident that we'll all just love each other, but that's what worries me. Connections. Complications.

I don't want to hurt Wren, but what if I take Pai up on his offer to join him in São Paulo? The last thing I need is a spot on *her* mom's shitlist. Or her dad's.

"Hey, you doing okay?" asks Kellan.

I turn, guilty I haven't been listening. "Yeah. Just thinking about Wren. This is important to her, you know?"

Understanding washes over his face, and he nods. "She seems like a sweetheart."

"She is." But I don't feel like getting into it, so I redirect things. "What are you and Matt getting into tonight? You guys gonna go out?

"We'll probably hang out here," says Kellan. "Relax, grill out by the pool or something. Get some girls over here. Haven't had the house to myself for a while, you know?"

Visions of all the wild parties Kellan and Dallas probably threw in high school flash through my mind. "I bet."

A shrewd expression narrows his eyes. "See if Wren's friend wants to come over."

"Who, Saira?" I chuckle, shaking my head. "By herself?"

"She won't be by herself—Matty'll be here," he jokes. "Nah, I'm calling a couple of other friends up, too. Saira can bring whoever she wants. It'll be a party."

"Want me to ask Wren?"

Kellan leers at me. "For what, permission?"

"For Saira's number, jackass."

"Tell her I can pick Saira up." Kellan rubs his hands together, warming to the idea. "I'm definitely turning on the hot tub."

My fingers fly across the screen. "Want me to tell her that, too?"

"Naw, bro, have some chill."

Wren

Adjusting the top of my blue wrap dress, I swing open the door right as Luca's about to knock. His eyes widen, and he laughs a little. I should probably at least pretend to not be this enthusiastic at his presence, but...oh, well. I've never been very good at playing games.

"Hi," I say, drinking in the sight of him. In jeans, a black bomber jacket and a black t-shirt, he's a whole meal.

One side of Luca's mouth crooks up as his eyes travel slowly over me. "Hi." He smiles a little, slowly pulling me into a hug. "How's it going?"

"It's going great." I squeeze him tight, giving him a good sniff.

"Did you just smell me?" He huffs softly, running his hand lightly over my hair.

"Yep." My cheeks warm, as much with affection as embarrassment. "You always smell good."

His eyes dance as he slides his hands into his pockets. "I try."

"You succeed." Grabbing my purse and keys, I take one last look around before ushering him back out.

"You smell pretty good, yourself," he murmurs, sliding his nose along my neck as we walk to the car.

I shiver, catching his hand. The next stop is my mother's apartment. She's riding with us tonight so Luca can get acquainted with her one-on-one before heading to Marvel. I feel good about this meetup; Mom's been curious about Luca for quite some time.

She greets us with a megawatt smile at the door. "Luca, Luca. My daughter has been talking about you for *ages*—I'm so glad to finally meet you!"

"Likewise, Ms. Angelos." He chuckles, offering his hand. "Thanks for letting me tag along tonight."

Scoffing, she bypasses the handshake and wraps him in a patchouli-scented hug. "Hope you don't mind hugs, Luca," she sings. "We're big huggers around here."

"It's cool," Luca mumbles into a cloud of her scarves. "I come from a family of huggers."

"Can we come in, or do you just want to hang out here?" I tease, watching the commotion from outside.

"Shush, you," Mom says, pulling us inside. "I'm ready to go; I just have to get my bag."

She flits from the room, skirt swishing, bangles jangling.

258

"She's just like you described," Luca says, examining a picture of us hanging on the wall. "But younger."

"I know. She eats well and does yoga a million times a week." I shrug, looking around the apartment. It's the same as always, except for a new piece of art hanging over the sofa.

I touch Luca's elbow. "I'll be right back."

Mom's in her bedroom, sitting on her bed as she buckles a fancy sandal. She smiles up at me. "God, Wren, he's beautiful. Really beautiful."

I clap my mouth shut, caught off guard by her gushing.

"You said he swims, right? I can tell by those nice, broad shoulders." She shudders dramatically, getting to her feet. "You're still on the pill, right?"

"Oh my God, Mom."

"Even if you are, use condoms. Always."

"Stop. Just stop." I'd tell her we're not even having sex yet, but it's none of her business. Besides, I'm not sure how long that's going to be true.

"I'm just saying—"

"Well don't," I snap. "Yes, Luca's hot, but not so hot that it makes me a total idiot, okay?"

"Sheesh, okay!"

"Anyway, I came back here to say that I really want tonight to go well, okay? Please, just…"

She freezes, looking stricken. "Please just what?"

Taking a deep breath, I say what's been on my mind since Arlo's visit last year. It's not usually in my nature to keep things in, but this whole situation has always felt delicate. "I'm sorry if I've put you in a position where you have to deal with Arlo when you never thought you would, but he's a part of my life now—"

"Wren, I know that," she interrupts, shaking her head. "Where is this coming from?"

"I don't know, I just remember when he came over for dinner the last time. You can be a little…passive aggressive." I start to chew my thumbnail, but then I remember I painted my nails. "When it comes to him."

Mom looks like she wants to argue, but then her shoulders sink. She glances at her watch. "I'll be on my best behavior, okay? We should go."

That will have to do, I guess. We head downstairs to Luca's car, where my mother insists on riding in the back.

"Mom, come on," I say, standing outside of the car. "Just ride shotgun. It's fine."

"No; you should sit with your beau," she says. "But hurry it up—or we'll be late."

* * *

Arlo is waiting outside the doors as we walk up. His eyes dart to Mom and

Luca, brightening when they land on me. He grins, reaching his arm out for a quick hug.

"Hey, Wren."

"Hey, Arlo." It's amazing how quickly we fell into this, as if I've known him all my life. "This is my uh…" I falter, realizing Luca and I never discussed our status. *Ugh.* "Luca."

Arlo turns to the man at my side, again extending his hand for a shake. "Arlo Janvier." They're opposites in many ways—he's light-eyed and blond whereas Luca's dark-haired with deep, golden-brown skin—but they're about the same height. "Glad you joined us tonight."

"For sure—thanks for having me." Luca's eyes crinkle as he smiles. I would pay a hundred bucks to hear what his first impression is so far. Guess I'll have to wait.

"Hi, Lily," Arlo says. "How've you been?" There's an easy smile on his face as he looks at my mother, and I wonder how he sees her, if it's different than last spring. He's traveled a lot of miles over the decades, encountered lots of different types of personalities. It must give him perspective.

She smiles a bit, dipping her head. "Hi, Arlo. I've been all right."

Marvel Pies is a Santa Cruz hotspot, thanks to its sublime pizza and live music on the weekends. We weave our way through the loud, lively restaurant, following the hostess to our reserved table in the very middle.

"Luca, Wren tells me you have a bit of a second life over in São Paulo," says Arlo, cocking his head as he leans forward. "I've spent some time out that way. It's a beautiful city."

Luca nods, also leaning forward. "My father lives there, so I've spent the past few years bouncing back and forth. Internships, that kind of thing."

"Are you thinking of heading out that way after graduating?"

I look at Luca. He pauses, glancing my way before shaking his head. "Actually, I'm not sure. Things are up in the air right now."

"You want to go to grad school, right?" I ask. I'd always assumed he'd be sticking around over the next few years, but now I realize that might not be the case.

He nods. "Maybe in a year or so. I've been either studying or working non-stop since I started college, so I need a break, even if that's just for one summer."

"That's smart," Mom says, nodding slowly. She's mellow tonight, having stuck to club soda. "You're young; you have time to figure these things out."

"Yeah, that's what my mom says." Luca stirs his straw around his drink, shrugging. "I guess we'll see."

Conversation flows easily after that as we tuck into our pizza. Arlo and Luca chat like long lost friends, flitting from one topic (public transportation, airline mileage clubs, local weather patterns) to another (being bilingual, Manhattan in the spring, Luca's surfing) with ease. Mom and I make eye contact at one point, and I can see she's as amused by the burgeoning bromance as I am.

Afterward, in the parking lot, we pause to say our goodbyes. Mom's still inside, catching up with someone she knows.

"Are we still on for tomorrow?" Arlo asks me, checking his phone.

"One o'clock sharp. I'll be there, so be ready."

"What're you guys getting into?" Luca asks.

The wind picks up, tossing ribbons of my hair around my face. "I'm giving him the good old campus tour."

He raises his eyebrows. "You're in for a treat, Arlo—Wren knows all the good spots."

"Excellent." Arlo grins, raising his fist to Luca's. "I really enjoyed getting to know you, Luca. Hopefully we'll meet again."

"Feeling's mutual." Luca shrugs. "Come down during the summer, we'll show you how to surf."

"I know how to surf," Arlo says, eyes twinkling. "I spent a winter on Australia's Gold Coast when I was in my late twenties. Fell in love with it. I surf whenever, and wherever, I can."

"All right, my man." Luca grins, warm with approval. "We'll head out next time you're down for sure, then."

Arlo smacks his back. "Consider it done."

Luca touches my hand as he passes. "I'll be in the car, Wren. Take your time."

Arlo watches him walk away, a faint smile on his face. "Now that is a kid who's comfortable in his own skin. I like him."

"So do I."

He chuckles, his eyes crinkling the way mine do sometimes. They're a different green than mine, deeper and more vivid. Mine have some gray. "I can see that."

I continue, ignoring the warmth on my cheeks. "I'm glad you got to know each other a little bit."

"Me too."

Marvel's door opens and Mom appears. She looks around, and then, spotting us, makes her way over. "Thanks for picking up the bill, by the way. You didn't have to do that."

"Don't mention it." He smiles, tugging my side braid. "It's not every day I get to meet my daughter's boyfriend."

My heart squeezes every time he says something like that. Giving him a quick hug, I take a step back. "See you tomorrow."

"Actually, Wren, I have to talk to your mom for a second."

My mother slows as he approaches, taking a couple of steps back before freezing in place. I settle into the car with Luca to watch their subdued, stilted conversation, wishing I knew what they were saying.

"What's that about?" asks Luca, fiddling with the music on his phone.

"I have no idea." I lean back against the headrest. "Maybe her bullshit at the end of dinner last time?"

He squeezes my knee. We talked about this at length the other night, so he knows how I feel.

"People don't always do what we want them to." Luca's eyes catch mine. "Just give her time."

But I don't want to give her time. Arlo leaves in a few days…Mom doesn't need to be his best friend forever, but I'd appreciate her playing nice.

"She looks like she's listening," Luca says, setting his phone down.

Arlo's standing close now, talking steadily, gesturing as she looks up at him.

The surreal quality of the scene hits me square between the eyes all over again. "I can't believe those are my parents. Both of them."

"Arlo's a cool guy. You look like him."

"I do, right?" I turn in the seat, facing him. "Kind of crazy."

His eyes soften as we look at one another in the glow of his dashboard. "I like how you look tonight. I like…this." He rubs the edge of my dress between his fingertips.

I smile, my stomach in freefall. I'm really feeling his bomber jacket, too, and I'm about to tell him when he says, "It's been hard, keeping my hands to myself."

"You don't have to keep your hands to yourself."

The corner of his mouth tugs up as his eyes drift down. Just as he slides his hand over my thigh, fingertips skimming the sensitive skin, Mom gets back in the car.

"Sorry, guys." She rustles loudly as she settles in and buckles her seatbelt. "Arlo just wanted to know when it would be a good time to stop by the studio. I don't know what your plans are for the rest of the week, so I told him to just come on over whenever the mood hits."

I twist around, looking at her while Luca puts the car in drive, easing out of our parking spot.

"We don't have too many concrete plans from here on out."

Up ahead, Arlo's rental pulls out of the lot.

"I know, but he's here to see *you*."

"Yes, but I like the idea of you getting to know each other," I say quietly. Maybe that's not fair, but it's how I feel.

Mom pushes her hair back, nodding, and for a moment, she looks even younger than usual. Vulnerable.

Luca hands me his phone, telling me to play what I want, so I play Fleetwood Mac for Mom. A peace offering, of sorts. A thank you for behaving. An apology for asking her to behave. When we turn into the parking lot, I unbuckle my seatbelt so I can walk her upstairs. Luca slides out, too, opening Mom's door.

"Thank you, Luca." She pauses, slowly sliding her purse to the crook of her arm. "Feel free to come by with Wren again. I'd love to get to know you in a more..." She gestures briefly. "Casual setting."

He dips his chin, smiling. "I will."

"I'm not usually like this," she says suddenly. "I don't know what I'm doing, here."

266

My heart flip flops at her bluntness. "Mom…"

"I think you're doing all right, considering the circumstances," Luca says.

She smiles a real smile, her blue eyes fluttering my way before refocusing on him. "You say all the right things, don't you?"

His eyes sparkle as he grins down at her. "I never say anything I don't mean."

Laughing quietly, Mom gathers him into a light hug. "Thank you, Luca. Take good care of my girl, all right?"

"Yes, ma'am."

She rolls her eyes, swatting his arm with her purse. "Just call me Lily. 'Ma'am' makes me feel old."

Gratitude washes over me as I accompany her upstairs. "Just tell me what you think about him. Be honest."

"Who, Luca?" Her eyes gleam mischievously as we walk up the steps.

"Arlo." I side-eye her. "I can already tell you like Luca, you cougar."

"Luca is perfect." She swallows, shrugging. "Arlo…" She sighs. "Arlo's great. Also perfect, it seems."

We turn on the landing. "But?"

"I don't know, little bird. I'm happy the two of you have this special relationship, but maybe a tiny piece of me is jealous, who knows." We stop outside her door. Slipping her arm from mine, she roots around her purse for her keys. "And I guess...I never wanted you to feel like you needed a man to be complete, Wren. Not even some guy who's supposed to be your dad."

"It's not about needing a man." I swallow the lump in my throat. "It's about wanting to know the other half of who I am. Not just where I got green eyes, but all that stuff. And you don't have to be jealous, because nothing and no one compares to you."

"I know." Gemlike tears glitter at the corners of her eyes. Taking a deep breath, she leans close and kisses each of my cheeks. "I love you. Have fun tonight."

"I love you, too." I wait until I hear the door lock before turning to go. At the bottom of the steps, my phone emits a silvery chime.

It's a text from my mother.

Mom: I meant what I said earlier. Wrap it up.
I'm way too young to be a grandma.

Wren

I relax into the front seat, enjoying the mild breeze tickling through the open windows. The weather's been so sweet lately. "I can't get over how warm it is."

"I know. I might head out to Steamer Lane tomorrow, see what's happening."

"Did you start surfing when you came to UCSC?"

"Nah, I've always loved it."

"Really? Where'd you go in the Bay?"

Luca shrugs, glancing at me as we sail through an orange light. "Wherever we could. Sometimes we came down here, other times we'd head up to Humboldt or Sonoma. I mean, Logan and I got into it pretty young—we used to tag along with his older brothers when they headed over to Ocean Beach and shit."

"Ocean Beach?" I cringe. "Aren't the waves pretty brutal out there?"

"Yup." He nods, eyebrows raised. "Ricky and Liam were badass, though. Liam's in Hawaii now—he went pro."

"Wow." I let my gaze linger on Luca for a second, thinking of a picture he had on Instagram, surfing in a wetsuit. Damn, he'd looked good. Gives me the tingles just thinking about it.

"You ever go out?"

"I mean, I've tried a couple times. I suck."

"Maybe you haven't found the right teacher yet," he says, waggling his eyebrows.

"Oh, my God." I punch his shoulder, giggling. "That was so cheesy."

Laughing, he nods. "Hell yeah; you're coming with me and Kell before class starts up again. Bring your pops."

Grinning, I settle back into my seat. "Sounds like a plan. Speaking of Kellan, I'm almost afraid of what we're gonna find when we get to his parents' house."

"It's getting crazy, no doubt. Saira's in good hands, though."

I smirk. "I'm sure she is."

Luca cuts a sly glance my way, giving me a little smirk of his own. "I was surprised she went over there by herself."

"What?" Vaguely alarmed, I look over at him. I still feel protective over

Saira after what happened to her freshman year. "Why?"

"Nothing bad," he says quickly, touching my arm. "Kellan's the best guy I know—I vouch for him a hundred percent. I'm just saying…she and Kellan don't really know each other yet."

"She probably wouldn't have normally, but…he made an impression," I say, remembering the blatant interest glittering in my best friend's eyes when I'd mentioned Kellan's invitation earlier. It was the first time in a long time she'd seemed like her old self when it came to guys. "She won't chase a guy, but she won't play coy, either."

Friday night traffic slows us down, but I don't mind. I like the extra time with Luca. Every glance, word and laugh shoves my heart into a new rhythm.

"So, you mentioned taking a break from school," I begin, tucking my leg beneath me as I twist to face him. "Does that mean hanging out all summer, or getting a job or what?"

"A job," he says. "Even if it's just a part-time position. I have some money saved up, but there's rent to pay, groceries to buy."

"Oh, that's true. I don't know why I thought you'd go back home for the summer."

"Nah." Luca laughs. "Mãe's not the hardass that my dad is, but she wouldn't be okay with me camping out in her house all summer long."

"Any ideas of where you might work?"

"There's an architecture firm in Berkeley I interned at one summer a couple years ago. I was supposed to work there last summer, paid, but my dad convinced me to join him in São Paulo."

It's a scenario he's mentioned to me more than once, this far-away father who continually lures him away to work in the family business despite Luca's dwindling interest in it. I mean, part of me gets it. If Arlo wanted me to travel around the world as his photo assistant, I would. In a heartbeat.

But not forever. At some point, you have to do what you want to do and not what's expected or desired of you.

By the time we turn onto the Morgans' long, winding driveway, it's nearly nine o'clock. A restless breeze blows, sending wisps of clouds racing across a fat, round moon. Luca bypasses the crowded circular drive and goes for the garage, where he parks beside a black SUV.

Loud music, punctuated by shrieks of laughter, voices and splashing, meets us as we walk up to the front door. Opening an unlocked side door, Luca reaches back to take my hand as we make our way through the house. It's strange being here again, but with him this time.

I peek at the solarium as we pass by, remembering being pressed close to this boy as "Blue Christmas" played.

Luca lets go of me in the kitchen and makes a beeline for the fridge. "You want something to drink? They've got everything except for decent beer."

I peer over his shoulder into the cavernous refrigerator. There's a big, rounded bottle full of what looks like wine with fruit floating around in it. "Is that sangria?"

"Yeah, Kellan's mom made it. You want some?"

"Please."

Drinks in hand, we go out onto the deck. I don't recognize too many of the people mingling around, but I do hear a familiar laugh. Saira's sitting on the steps of the pool, Kellan in the water below, cozied up between her legs as they share a smoke. A joint, probably. Saira would sooner chew off her arm than smoke a cigarette.

Sliding his hand into mine, Luca ambles down the steps and out into the yard. We maneuver between a rowdy game of cornhole and a semi-circle of lawn chairs filled with people. My eyes meet Matt's, and he grins, pointing at me.

"Hey, Sweet Spot."

"Hi, Matt."

Luca looks down at me, a lazy smile tugging at his mouth. "He thinks you're the best thing since PlayStation."

Warmth unspools in my chest at the unexpected compliment. "Aw, really?"

"Good vibes, I guess." Squeezing my hand, he adds, "And he's rarely wrong."

Up ahead, the pool glows invitingly. Steam rises faintly from the rippling turquoise water, where Saira and Kellan send up matching glassy-eyed grins as we approach.

"Was wondering when you two would grace us with your presence," says Kellan, blowing a fat stream of smoke in our direction. "Presences?"

Saira grins, scratching her fingers through his wet hair as he closes his eyes and snuggles against her like a puppy.

Luca stops to talk to someone, but I ease in beside Saira, raising my eyebrows. "Looks like you two are getting along *swimmingly.*"

"Looks like," Saira drawls, biting her lip. "How was dinner?"

"Good, good. Mom behaved this time—"

"Thank God for small favors."

"And Luca and Arlo hit it off. It was kinda cute."

"Parents love Luca," Kellan says. He pauses, peeking back at me. "Not that there have been, like, a lot of parents."

Saira snorts, turning his head back around.

But I don't care what Luca did before. It's what he does now that matters, and right now he's right beside me, his arm warm and solid as it snakes around my waist.

* * *

Matt's voice rises triumphantly above the din. "Oh no, you're not!"

Someone squeals as Luca's eyes widen. Gripping my arms, he tucks me into his chest and turns us around seconds before a giant wall of water comes splashing at us with the force of a tsunami.

Giggling, I peek over his shoulder to see what all the commotion's about. Matt and the tiny blonde he's been chatting up all evening are bobbing in the middle of the pool, sputtering and laughing.

"I take it he pulled her in," I say as Luca lets go of me.

"You'd be correct." He wipes a hand over his sleek, wet hair. "Matt still flirts like we did in the seventh grade."

"I think it's kinda cute," I admit, watching in amusement as Matt attempts to dunk his date. Okay, maybe not *that* cute.

Luca laughs. "Don't let him hear you say that; he'll think he has a chance."

"How do you know he doesn't?" I stick out my tongue.

A devilish grin steals across his lips. Keeping his eyes on mine, he cups his hands around his mouth and stands up straight in the water. "Hey, Ma—"

Pressing down on his head, I attempt to do a little dunking of my own. I manage to get about half of him under water before he wraps his arms around my middle and dunks me first. I emerge laughing, shoving him.

"I take it back. Maybe you and Matt are perfect for each other," he teases, pulling me closer.

"Haha." I rest my hands on his shoulders, enjoying the feel of his hands spanning my waist.

"At least you're smiling."

"That tends to happen a lot around you."

His eyes crinkle, and then he smiles too. "Does it?"

I nod, my heartbeat picking up a little.

"Hope that doesn't change," he says, giving my waist a squeeze.

"Why would it change?"

"It might not, but everything changes. People change."

"Yeah, but…" I shrug, forcing myself to keep on looking him in the eye. "Sometimes things, people, change for the better. Or they change together. That's a good thing."

"Sometimes." He scans the pool, quiet for a beat. I'm about to ask him what he's thinking about when he brings his gaze back to me. "You make me smile, too."

Warmth. Trust. I never want to do anything to change that look, not after what he's been through. Rising to my toes, I press a kiss to his cheek. "Good."

Two girls float by on a giant, inflatable pizza slice, their loud, tipsy conversation popping our bubble. There aren't as many people at Kellan's as there were when we first arrived, but the pool's gotten more crowded. Luca slides his hands away as we lean against the wall.

"My mom texted me a little while ago."

He takes a sip of his drink. "About tonight?"

"About everything, but I'm not in the mood to hash things out with her." I huff softly. "It's not like I'm mad at her, you know? I mean, I was, but I'm past that. I think I'm just disappointed. I wish she'd give Arlo a chance. He's really trying."

"Expectations make things difficult," he says sagely, propping his elbows on the lip of the pool. "Mãe loves to say the biggest gift we can give someone is letting them be themselves."

"She's right." I look beyond him, focusing on a light that just came on over the deck. "But that's easier said than done."

"I know it is." Luca's eyes soften. "Speaking of Mãe, she's been after me to bring you out to Walnut Creek for dinner."

"Really?" I grin up at him, everything else forgotten. "I'd love that."

"They do family dinners every Sunday," he says. "You want to try next weekend? We can drive up around noon and come back that night."

"I'll check my schedule," I fib, knowing damn well it's clear.

"Let me know."

* * *

A tentative breeze picks up, rustling the persimmon trees around the pool. Yawning, I drag my fingertips across the water's surface as I float from one side of the pool to another. The water's so warm I could fall asleep out here.

Saira and Kellan are playing a sloppy game of Giant Jenga in the corner of the yard. Matt's passed out in his lawn chair, the tiny blonde sprawled across his lap. Everyone else has left.

Luca descends the steps leading from the house as I float into the shallow end, two water bottles dangling from his fingertips. I stare shamelessly as he crosses the yard, appreciating how the outdoor lighting flickers across his beautiful skin. His muscles, cast in sharp relief by the lambent light, flex as he moves.

A wave of desire ripples through me. We've been drinking, so maybe my inhibitions are down, but I'm not drunk. No, I've wanted Luca since the moment our eyes met across the counter at the Sweet Spot, and seeing him in those low-slung, black boardshorts doesn't help. I'd love to just run my tongue across his stomach, down his razor-sharp obliques.

Wading through the water, he hands me a water bottle, his gaze so heated I slide down into the water just to put out the flames.

"Thanks."

"You're welcome." He opens his water bottle and drinks, Adam's apple bobbing as he swallows.

I follow suit, drinking until my thirst is slaked. Setting the bottle on the side of the pool, I turn to find Luca in my space, a breath away from kissing me. "Hey," I say, a breathless laugh escaping.

Quirking a smile, he reaches down and squeezes my thighs, hoisting me up. Our skin glides wetly as I wrap my legs around his hips and my arms around his neck. He trails his lips over my throat, kissing the space below my ear. "Wren." His voice is hushed, barely audible over the wind in the trees. "Do you remember when we danced? At the party here?"

"Of course, I do…I was thinking about it earlier, when we walked by the solarium." I shiver against the breeze, images of that night playing behind my eyelids. "We danced to 'Blue Christmas.'"

"I wanted you that night." His hands slide down to my bottom where he lingers, his fingertips playing at the edge of my bikini. "I wanted you, and that was as close as I could get."

"I wanted you, too. But I respected the line you'd drawn. It was the right thing to do." I kiss his temple, running my nose over his damp skin. "Even if it did just make me want you more."

"Yeah." He chuffs softly. "Same."

"You know, I saw you once. In Berkeley."

"Really?" He draws back to look at me. "When was that?"

"It was during winter break, one or two years ago." I brush my knuckles over his cheek. "I'd just come out from a party, and I looked up and you were right across the street. I hadn't seen you since that night on the boardwalk, but I knew right away it was you. I wanted to talk to you...I'd thought about you a lot."

"Why didn't you?"

"Some pretty girl kissed you before I could." I chew my inner cheek, recalling the spear of disappointment that had pierced my heart that night.

"Downtown Berkeley or near campus?"

"Downtown, I think."

"Was she blonde?"

I nod.

"I remember that night. Too bad you didn't get to me first." Luca's dark eyes glint with a fire like the one I feel burning in me. "Who knows where we'd be now?" He brings me in for another kiss, and I open to him, sliding my tongue against his in a dance of barely controlled need.

My back hits the wall. Luca tightens his grip on my thighs, kissing me so deeply my head dips back. He drags his mouth to my neck, devouring the skin above my collar bone. Even with closed eyes and all senses taken over by Luca, I feel when the space around us goes dark. He goes still, pulling away to look around. Every light in the pool and backyard has been turned off. Everyone's gone.

Luca looks back to me, smirking in the moonlight. "I don't know if that's a request to get us to leave or an attempt to give us more privacy."

I laugh quietly, slicking back my hair. "I don't know what they think we're gonna do out here."

"I have a couple of guesses." Taking a step back, he eases me to my feet. "We can go in, if you want."

"Yeah, it's starting to get cold." I follow him out of the pool and into the spring chill, grabbing the still-damp towel I'd used earlier.

Luca tucks his towel around his waist. "So, what do you feel like doing? We can hang out here for a while, or I can drop you home if you're ready to go."

Pausing, I squeeze water from my hair. As much as I'd like to keep hanging out with Luca, the thought of fooling around in one of the Morgans' guest rooms isn't too appealing...especially considering what's probably going on right now in the other rooms.

"Or we can go to my place." He tips my chin up and kisses me again, letting his teeth catch my bottom lip before pulling away.

I shiver, and not because of the night air. If I go over to Luca's, we're going to do a hell of a lot more than kiss. "Okay," I whisper.

"Okay, what?"

"Let's go to your place."

Luca searches my eyes, and then, with a slow nod, presses a chaste kiss to my lips. We head back across the yard, up the stairs and into the kitchen. The lights are on, but other than the faint bass thumping rhythmically from somewhere, no one's around.

My teeth are chattering. The air conditioning must be set to glacial.

Luca huffs quietly, smirking as he grabs a blue and gold UCSC duffel bag from the kitchen table. "Guess they decided to take the party upstairs."

I send Saira a text, letting her know my plans. When she doesn't respond right away, I glance over at Luca, who's pulling a t-shirt on. "I feel bad leaving Saira. I don't want her to think I abandoned her."

"I don't know; she and Kell looked pretty cozy earlier." He leans against the counter. "You texted her, right?"

Nodding, I slide into my sandals. "Yeah, but…"

"But she's busy." He points up. "We can stay here, if you want."

"I don't."

"…watch a movie or something…"

"I don't!" I laugh, giving him a light shove.

"Then I'm pretty sure Kellan can drive her home."

Luca's right. Saira's my girl but she's also a big girl who chose to hang here all day and then go upstairs with Kellan. She wasn't drunk or impaired, and Kellan's good people. If it was any other guy, any other situation, I'd insist on checking with her, but I think in this case she'll be okay.

I send one more text before dropping my phone into my bag. "Okay, let's go."

* * *

This time we enter Luca's house through the front door downstairs.

"Don't you guys have another roommate?" I ask, following him through the quiet dark. "The one I haven't met?"

"Faruq. He's in Lagos with his girl."

Leaving the lights off, he drops his keys on the counter and takes my hand, leading me up the stairs and into his bedroom. It's just as I remember, maybe a little messier.

"Did you want to take a shower?" he asks, pausing in the doorway of his bathroom. He flicks on a small light there, just enough so we can see.

282

Slipping out of my shoes, I leave my bag on the floor and go to him. My hair's almost dry, but I smell like chlorine. "Are you taking one?"

"Maybe later." Giving my towel a tug, Luca drops it on the floor and pulls me against his warm, solid body. His calloused hands smooth down my back and over my ass, giving it a soft squeeze.

I close my eyes, nodding. "Later's good."

Cradling my face between his hands, he kisses me deeply, explicitly, his tongue chasing mine around my mouth, filling me with his taste. It's my favorite kind of kiss, the kind we share when we're truly alone, the kind that makes my stomach tight and my nipples hard. The kind that gets me wet.

I wrap my arms around him, holding him close as we move onto the bed. Luca fits himself into the cradle of my thighs, and I welcome him, eager to relieve the ache building there. It feels so good to be with him like this, body to body. No distractions, no interruptions. No people, no plans. Nothing to stop us.

Pulling me up, Luca unties my bikini top and tosses it aside before laying me back down. His eyes roam hungrily over my body in the soft, warm light. As much as I like the way he's looking at me, I love feeling his body more, so I urge him down, wrapping myself around him. Our tongues slide in a hot, wet dance, our bodies moving together like he's already inside me.

"Your mouth is so fucking sweet," Luca whispers, dragging his lips down my throat and to my chest. "I bet you're sweet all over." He twirls his tongue around my nipple, sucking it deeply into his mouth as he rolls the other between his fingertips. After a moment, he switches, his dark eyes meeting mine when I exhale a moan.

He climbs back up and kisses me again, and this time it's sloppy, wet, desperate. I can't wait anymore—I start to shove his shorts down with my feet.

With an amused smile, he backs onto his knees and tugs my bikini bottoms down my legs. My eyes fall to the bulge in his shorts as I lift my hips. *Mmm.* I didn't think there could be anything better than Luca's face, but he's impressive all over.

He runs his hands over my naked body, down between my breasts and over my belly button, tickling my hips. Our eyes meet. Breathing shakily, I bend my legs and open them, showing him all of me, wanting him to want me the way I want him. He looks down again, caressing me, using his thumb to part me, and then he lowers down and kisses my clit. I exhale, shaky. Spreading my thighs wider with his hands, he licks an incendiary trail deep between my folds.

His fingers search and explore as he nibbles and licks, like he doesn't know what he wants more: to play with his food or eat it. Panting, drowning in pleasure, I watch helplessly as he makes a feast of me, alternating between sucking my clit and licking me with the flat of his tongue. He slides a finger into me, and I cry his name, feeling the first hint of orgasm.

"Sweet all over," he murmurs. Sliding another finger inside, he draws circles with his tongue until I come, crying out, my back arched as swells of hot, liquid bliss undulate through me. When I've had more than I can handle, I push at his head, begging him to stop. He finally relents, biting gently at my inner thigh before wiping his mouth on it and climbing off.

Lightheaded, I open my eyes to find him standing beside the bed, sliding his boardshorts off. I climb to my knees, loving how his hooded eyes drop to my breasts. I know how he feels. I can't take my eyes off of his long, hard length, either. Yeah, he's beautiful all over. Every inch.

I wrestle him back to bed and push him onto his back, not wasting any time moving down his perfect body. His chuckle turns into a choked gasp when I take his cock into my mouth. "That's...so...good," he whispers, tangling his fingers in my hair.

His skin is soft and silky. I touch the sharp V of his obliques, chasing the shudder of his muscles with my fingertips. I want to touch him all over and eventually, I will. But for now, I'm concentrating here. Sucking my cheeks in, I bob slowly up and down, fondling his balls with one hand, still high off of my own orgasm. His long, smooth dick feels good in my mouth, makes me feel powerful. I pop off for a second, wiping my chin. "Show me what you like."

"I like watching you do this," he says, a sexy half-smile turning the corners of his mouth up.

Sucking him back into my mouth, I tongue his slit until his dick twitches, bringing a salty tang of cum. Closing my eyes, I love him the way he just did me, trying to relax when he grazes the back of my throat.

"Wren," he says, his hand a warning in my hair.

I ignore him, but he pulls me off and flips me onto my back, rubbing his very rigid dick over my entrance. Brushing his lips over my ear, he whispers, "I don't want to come like that."

Our eyes meet. "Okay," I breathe, nodding.

"Hold on," he says, pressing one more kiss against my mouth before getting up and going to his desk. There's a crinkle as he returns with a condom in hand. He rolls it on and then climbs back onto me as I gaze up at him, running my hands up and down the warm, smooth skin of his back. Our eyes lock. I thought I was ready for him, but nothing prepares me for the way he feels. It takes a moment for my body to adjust.

Pausing, he withdraws and then slides in again, this time fully seating himself. "You okay?" he whispers, kissing my jaw.

"Yeah," I whisper back, holding him close to me. "I..." I swallow, closing my eyes. "I love how you feel inside me."

"You have no idea how good it feels, Wren." Balancing on his forearms, staying close, he moves in and out of me in slow, measured thrusts. "So good."

I bring my legs up, and he grunts in satisfaction, gripping my thigh and hiking it higher so he can go deeper. "I'm not gonna last like this," he grits out after a moment, his face caught between pain and pleasure.

I tighten around him.

He exhales harshly, something between a laugh and a groan. "Hold on." Pulling out, he turns me onto my stomach and yanks my hips up. Entering me from behind, he holds my hip with one hand and slips the other beneath, stroking me.

The effect is mind blowing. Flashes of another orgasm threaten to overtake me, and I grasp the sheets, eyes clenched shut. "Luca..."

He groans, picking up the pace. He's so deep, we're so close.

I fall dizzily over the edge, crying out, and he follows, our skin slapping together every time his body hits mine. His fingers dig into my skin as he comes, and then he relaxes, pulling me down to his side. Wrung out, heartbeat struggling to slow, overwhelmed by how good the sex was, I look at him in the dim light. He presses his thumb to my cheek, angling my face

286

to his to kiss me once more.

"I need to go take care of this," he says, peeling himself away.

Boneless, I turn to my side and watch him walk to the bathroom. The faucet runs for a moment, and then the shower goes on. He comes back, running his hand down my spine and over my behind. "Come shower with me."

Luca

I'm not sure what wakes me up. The muted rumble of a silenced cellphone maybe, somewhere on the hardwood floor. Rubbing a hand over my face, I open one eye and peer at Wren, who lets out a soft snore before shifting onto her side.

The movement drags her part of the sheets down, revealing the smooth, lightly tanned skin of her back. The sweeping slope of her hip. Images of last night flit through my foggy morning brain...Wren, on her knees, pulling me back to bed...the way she took me, how warm she was from her mouth all the way down. Her eyes. God, her eyes. Even in the dark, I could see the way she looked at me. Trust. Lust. I run a fingertip down her spine, and she shifts again, sighing in her sleep. Her hair is tangled and wild, begging for my hands to get lost in it.

Palming my uncomfortably stiff dick, I slip out of bed and pad to the bathroom. Waking up with morning wood is nothing new but having Wren here beside me is. I'm caught between wanting another round with this pretty girl and letting her sleep peacefully at my side.

288

But she's up when I return, drinking from a glass of water I had on the nightstand. The blankets are back in place, pulled up to her chin.

I smile a little, unaccustomed to this tugging feeling in my chest. "Hey."

"Hey. What time is it?" She blinks against the pale light seeping in through the drapes, her voice husky and sweet.

"Just past nine."

"Mm." She gives me a tiny smile. "How'd you sleep?"

"I slept great." I give in to the urge to touch her, resting my hand on her sheet-covered hip. "You?"

"Great." She yawns, the apples of her cheeks pinkening. "Guess you wore me out."

Any self-control I may have had evaporates at her words. Reaching under the covers, I pull her onto my lap, grinning when she laughs and flails, her hands landing on my chest. Her eyes fly to mine when her lush nakedness meets the hard insistence of mine.

She looks just the way I knew she would, skin flushed from sleep and arousal, long, wavy hair tossed around her bare shoulders. She's got tan lines. My dick twitches. "You're so pretty." I reach up to push her hair over her shoulder, needing an unobstructed view of her tits. They're just as fucking sweet as I knew they'd be, small and full and perky, pink-brown nipples like ripe summer fruit. My mouth waters for another taste.

"Even now?" She laughs quietly, touching her hair. But she lets me look my fill, her eyes never leaving my face. "You're the pretty one, Luca."

"Yeah?" I settle my hands on her hips and stare at her. There's no denying that she's beautiful, but her inner beauty is what keeps me interested.

"First time I saw you, at the boardwalk. You were with the guys, and I thought you were so hot."

"Oh, yeah?"

She swallows. "You were my type."

"You were definitely mine."

"I know." She bites her lip, trying not to smile. "I could feel it between us."

I sit up, kissing her, but she squirms, turning her face. "Luca. I need to brush my teeth."

I lean over, getting the water. We share some of it, and then, gently gripping her chin with my hand, I sweep my tongue into her mouth.

She moans quietly, submitting, melting into me. Letting go of her face, I wrap my arms around her body and kiss her until my dick is throbbing. She's practically sitting on it; one move and I could be back inside of her warm, wet bliss.

I can't do that to her, though, no matter how tempting it is. Instead, I fit one of my hands between us, playing my fingers between the folds of her slippery little secret. She sucks in a surprised breath, her mouth going slack. It just makes me want her more. Keeping my thumb on her clit, I angle two of my fingers into her, fucking her with them until she's so wet she starts to drip.

It drives me insane.

Ripping my mouth from hers, I suck one of her nipples into my mouth. Her grip on me tightens and her breathing stutters. The steadily increasing rhythm she's got going falters, and suddenly she freezes, panting and pulling my hair as she comes. Slowly withdrawing my fingers, I fumble for the nightstand, knocking over the glass of water, which rolls to the floor with a thump and a splash.

I find another condom and ease Wren onto her back. She grabs me, wrapping her hands around my forearms as I move into her, gasping in relief. So hot. So slick. So good. So *essential*. I can't see anything but the green of her eyes, can't feel anything but the tight, hot, wet hold she's got on me. Everything else is peripheral.

It's different than it was last night. Sober. Intent. I drive into her, over and over, on a mission, fueled by the grip she has on me—everywhere—and her sounds, the little gasps and groans and cries.

"Don't stop," she pleads, knotting her fingers in my hair.

I kiss her as I fuck her, enjoying her taste, her feel. And when I come, my vision goes dark for a second, colors exploding behind my eyelids as pleasure rockets through my body. I feel like I come forever, finally collapsing against her. She runs her fingers through my hair, keeping her legs wrapped around me.

"Wow," she breathes after a time.

I kiss her and then, with great effort, separate myself from her and roll to her side. We lie still for a second, staring up at the ceiling. "I could wake up like that every day." I say this before giving much thought to what it sounds like, but once the words are out, I realize I mean them. In more ways than one.

"Me too." She doesn't blush like I'd expect her to.

Leaving a light kiss on her swollen lips, I take hold of the soggy condom and back off the bed. "Be right back."

But she follows me to the bathroom. "Let's take another shower."

* * *

I'd wanted to take Wren to breakfast before dropping her back to her place, but after hours of lying around and talking in bed, we ran out of time.

I speed all the way back to UCSC, hoping to circumvent the awkwardness of her dad seeing us arrive after a night obviously spent together. Maybe he has no real say in what she does, but that doesn't matter.

He's her *dad*. He matters to her, and I respect that.

Thankfully, we make it. Swinging into the empty parking place besides hers, I jump out and walk Wren to her front door. A group of girls walks by on the sidewalk, glancing at me, and then Wren.

She pauses at her door, keys in her hand as she looks up at me. "I had fun," she says, a faint pink staining her cheeks.

"Me, too." It's an understatement. I pull her closer by her hip, seeing her through the lens of our night and morning together. "Have fun with your dad today."

"I will."

Cupping her face, I bend to kiss her. She smells like my toothpaste, my shampoo. My stomach quivers. "Talk soon, all right? Call me. Text. Whatever."

She nods, swallowing hard. I think I might affect her as much as she affects me. I like that I can tell. Clearing her throat, she steps away and unlocks the door. "Bye, Luca."

I wait until she's inside before turning to go, smiling as the sunshine hits my face. It's hard not to smile after spending the night with someone like Wren, someone who inspires the purest kinds of feelings.

I'm not sure what my future holds, what I'm going to do after graduating, but right now, at this moment, I know one thing for sure. I'm happy.

As if he can smell that happiness, my father calls right as I pull into the Morgans' driveway. It's tempting to let it go to voicemail, but he'll just keep on trying until I answer.

"Olá, Pai."

"Olá, Luca. You have a minute?"

"Sure." I roll the windows down and put the car in park, cutting the engine. I might be here for a minute. "What's up?"

"Tomás and I are still putting together the team for the Mason-Ridley project…I wanted to know how you felt about writing code for our software architect. Renaldo—you remember him, I'm sure—is chief software architect, and Nathalia will be dealing with the structure and UML diagram. I think you'd work well with them." He pauses. Traffic horns blare in the background; he's probably on his daily lunch walk downtown. "This is a big deal, Luca. I need to know if you'll be joining us."

And just like that, I'm no longer in sunny Santa Cruz but somewhere in the busy beehive of my father's office building. Tomás Avila is the operations manager, one of Pai's originals from the very beginning. Not only is he Pai's number two, he still does much of the hands-on stuff with the firm's larger jobs. Nathalia Coval is a little newer and a lot younger, a thirty-something who was recruited straight out of college. She's diplomatic, efficient, and smart as a whip, making her the obvious choice as project manager. When I first started interning at Veritas, she was one of the employees that took me under her wing and trained me on the day-to-day functions.

It's a team I'd enjoy working with, and a project I'd be interested in. Mason-Ridley is a sustainable architecture firm based in Canada and Veritas has been brought on to overhaul the software they use on a daily basis. A few years ago, I would have already said yes, but these days there's an increasingly frequent ache in my stomach when I think about leaving again. It's not that the project isn't worthy—it is. It's not that it won't be successful—everything my father touches turns to gold.

It's that if I keep on doing this, keep on working for my father, I might never step out on my own. What's success if I realize, twenty years down the road, that I've been chasing the wrong person's dreams?

"Let me think about it," I say after a moment.

"Don't think too long. It's a good team and a very, very lucrative project. If this goes well, we might be able to get you a permanent position and who knows where that could lead?"

"Okay. I'll get back to you in a day or two."

"You do that. Talk soon." As is his custom, he promptly disconnects, off to conquer his little corner of the world.

My mind's still on our conversation as I walk around to the side of the house, where the savory, mouthwatering aroma of cooking meat mixes with the smell of weed. Shaking my head, I find Matty on the deck, doing bong rips while Saira and Kellan linger near the enormous grill. Matt's blonde is in the pool, drifting lazily on the pizza float.

I blink, surprised that Saira's still here. Guess they hit it off even better than we thought they would, judging by Kell's hand on her hip as she flips something with the tongs.

"Lucaaaaaa," croaks Matt, grinning through a cloud of smoke.

"Matty, what's good?" I knock his fist on my way to the grill.

Kellan arches his eyebrow when he sees me. "You by yourself, bro?"

"Yeah, Wren's going hiking with her dad. Hey, Saira."

"Hi, Luca." She smiles prettily, tucking her long, black hair behind her ear. "Hope you're hungry…we got a ton of stuff coming up."

"I can see that." I chuckle, eyeing a mountain of chicken and salmon that's waiting for its turn on the grill. "You having another party?"

"Nah." Kellan shakes his head. "But I mean, six people…if Wren's coming back."

Saira smirks, returning to her duties. "She'll be back."

Wren

On the Sunday before Arlo heads back to New York, Luca invites me to a family dinner up in Walnut Creek. His brothers will both be there, as well as his sister-in-law, nieces, and nephews. I'm a little nervous, but not really—his *Mãe* has been keen on meeting me for some time. The feeling is mutual. I've seen pictures of her, so I can see where he gets his eyes and that silky hair, but now it's time to meet the woman behind the smile.

We leave Santa Cruz behind for the Bay, playing a chill hip hop mix from the nineties; lots of Common, Mos Def and Tribe Called Quest. The sun is bright, the weather cool. Soft wisps of clouds pass by in a faded blue-jean sky. We stop at a Brazilian bakery in Oakland, a place Luca swears by.

"Mãe loves their *beijinho de coco*," he says, pointing to the little coconut truffles. "She has a wicked sweet tooth."

So does my mom. I buy her a few, making a mental note to bring macarons for Luca's family the next time we do this.

From there it's about forty minutes to the house where Luca grew up. The weather warms tangibly as we exit the tunnel, leaving behind the crisper microclimates of the Bay. I've only been to Walnut Creek a few times, but I remember how pleasant it is, with its wide, tree-lined streets and upper-middle class aesthetic against the backdrop of Mt. Diablo.

We pull up behind a minivan in the otherwise empty driveway of a large split-level. Luca had said his mother loved her garden, but now that we're here I see that might have been an understatement. The front yard is crowned with clover, Cirsium and yarrow. Pink, yellow, and orange California poppies line the walkway leading to the front door, where a tan welcome mat decorated with bananas proclaims *it's bananas in here!*

"Wow," I breathe, snapping a picture of the garden with my phone. "I have to show this to my mom...she goes nuts for stuff like this."

Luca chuckles, ringing the doorbell. "Mãe's all about *as flores*. You'll see."

Inside, a dog yips. Then another, along with the shrill laughter of a child. The door swings open, amplifying the noise and the smell of delicious cooking. I recognize Luca's mom right away, although she is taller than I expected. Perhaps that shouldn't be a surprise; Luca's very tall, too.

"There's my baby," she says with a happy sigh, scooping her boy into her arms as he bends to hug her.

"Hey, Mãe," he says, kissing each cheek before backing up. Resting his hand on the small of my back, he gives me a little push forward. "This is Wren."

"Wren," she says, beaming, bringing me in for the same treatment: hugs, kisses, genuine pleasure. "I have been after this boy to bring you up here forever, my goodness."

"Well, she's here now," Luca gripes, giving a good-natured eye roll.

I grin, glancing at Luca as I'm pulled into the house. "Thanks for having me. Luca talks about you all the time."

"I know he does," she says, winking at me as she slides her arm through mine. "And listen, before we even have to discuss it, none of this Misses stuff, okay? You call me Marissa like everyone else."

"Okay." I nod as we enter a bright, spacious kitchen where bossa nova coos from an unseen source. There's an enormous island in the middle, where three younger kids have their sleeves rolled up as they work on various meal prep tasks like chopping fruit and rolling out some kind of dough. The walls are pale yellow, a bright, mosaic-style backsplash behind the sink. The real showstopper, though, are the windows that comprise most of the far wall. Just beyond the glass are gentle slopes of wildflowers as far as the eye can see. It's so unexpected, so breathtaking, that I freeze, gasping.

"Oh. Yes, I know." Mãe's voice drops as she leads me over to the sink, where we can look out at the view. "When we first moved in, the window was much smaller, just around the sink here. And then the sliding doors, there." She inclines her head toward the glass doors at the other side of the kitchen. "But it was spring then, too, and the flowers…I wanted more. So, we hired contractors to replace most of the wall with this. It's the best."

"I love it. Really, it's incredible."

"I love it, too. If I'm gonna spend lots of time in here, I might as well love it." She gives a brisk nod and turns, clapping her hands. "Okay, Luca, get your lady something to drink. I need to make sure these three haven't made a mess of my mangos."

"We haven't," huffs the eldest, a doe-eyed girl of about nine. A long, sleek

298

black braid hangs down her back.

"Wren, these are Nico's kids. Delia." Luca squeezes the girl's shoulder before moving to the little boys. "Manny and Jay."

"Hi," I say, giving them a small wave.

Delia cocks her head and smiles. "You're way better than the last one."

"Delia Cardoso," snaps Mãe, but she's trying to hide a smile.

"What? She wore too much makeup." Delia shudders.

Kind of mortified, kind of pleased, I peek at Luca, but he just gives his niece's braid a sharp tug. "Yeah, no kidding."

* * *

Dinner with Luca's family is loud, crazy and fun. There's so much food, all of it delectable, that I eat until I can barely walk. Thankfully I had the foresight to wear a long, flowy maxi dress. Boho, cute and, most importantly, forgiving.

Dominic, Luca's stepdad, is handsome and suave, with his cologne-heavy hugs and sparkling, mischievous eyes. He and Nico—who looks like Luca but taller and skinnier, his dark hair cut more conservatively—obviously delight in having a guest at the table, making sure to tell all sorts of stories starring Luca throughout the years.

"Don't believe it," he jokes, squeezing my hand beneath the table. "They're full of shit."

"I know you did not just use that language at my table, *anjinho*," sings Mãe, flicking Luca's ear as she passes.

"Whaaaat?" Nico smirks. "Every word is true, Wren. Lu's trying to save face."

"Maybe they're not full-on lies, but you exaggerate," Luca says, balling up his napkin and tossing it across the table to his brother.

When all is said and done, and we're sent off with hugs and overflowing bags of leftovers, everyone crowds outside to see us off.

"Don't be a stranger, Wren," Mãe says, squeezing my hand. "Come back any time. I'll teach you how to make acarajé."

"I'd love that!" I laugh, nodding. I had more than my fair share of the tasty black bean patties tonight. "Thank you." Waving, I follow Luca to the car.

"So?" Luca asks, one hand on the steering wheel, the other on my seat as he looks at me. "What did you think?"

"I had a great time." I twist in my seat to look at him. "But you know that. You know they're awesome."

"They're crazy." He bites his lip, an affectionate smile warming his face. "But they mean well."

"Everyone's family is kinda crazy. I mean, look at my parents." I look at the dark road ahead, the green glow of road signs blurring past. "Anyway, you obviously have a solid support system."

"I do. Wasn't always so solid, though."

"Why?"

"I really went through it when my parents split up. I was pretty close to my dad back then, even though he worked twenty-four-seven, and it took me a while to get used to the fact that he was going to be gone and just…not home."

My heart tugs as I imagine a much younger Luca dealing with his parents' divorce. "I can't even imagine. There's only ever been me and my mom."

"It was rough. Nico and Dom hit it off right away. Me, not so much. I spent a lot of nights at Logan's when he moved in."

I pause, chewing my lip. "Do you ever miss Logan?"

He's quiet for a minute, navigating the twists and turns of the darkened road ahead. "Sometimes. He wasn't always easy to love, honestly, but he was one of my oldest friends."

Saira and I have been inseparable for as long as I can remember. It's hard for me to envision us going through a fallout of this magnitude.

"Well, you and Dominic seem tight now," I say, steering the topic back to safer waters.

"He's the best. He has always been there for us, always been there for *me*." Luca shakes his head. "He loves unconditionally."

"Even when you screwed up at that one summer job?" I tease.

He barks a sharp laugh, glancing at me in surprise. "I can't believe you remember that."

"I told you, I remember everything you said."

"Huh." He rests his hand on my thigh and squeezes, the way he often does while we're driving. I cover his hand with my own, and for a while, we're quiet.

"Arlo's leaving on Wednesday, right?" Luca asks.

"Yeah. I can't believe it's been nearly two weeks already."

"Was it everything you hoped it would be?"

"It's been better. I knew Arlo was accomplished and smart and talented and all that, but in the end, I just wanted him to be *nice*. I was so afraid he'd be...I don't know...hard to please."

"That's a valid fear," says Luca, returning his hand to the wheel as we merge into busier traffic.

"I know. But it was unfounded, thankfully."

Luca nods. "Yeah, he seems cool. Very down to earth."

"He is." An image of Arlo's face floats to mind, the smile he gets when we're digging in deep on some topic that lights one of us up. "He listens to me, like he's interested."

"I'm glad to hear that, but it doesn't surprise me. He did reach out to you first."

"Rationally, I know that. But I was still terrified." I take a deep breath, exhaling slowly. "Anyway, it's been good. We might try and meet up in New York this summer. I don't want to get my hopes up, because it might fall through depending on where his next assignment takes him, but I've got my fingers crossed. I haven't left Santa Cruz in forever!"

"I'll cross mine for you, too," he says with a grin.

"I promise I'll send postcards," I tease.

He chuckles. "You do that."

"I'll probably only be gone for a few weeks, though. You can still teach me to surf."

Luca shifts in his seat, running his hand over his hair. "Actually, there's a chance I might be leaving, too. My dad wants me back in São Paulo."

My heart sinks. "Again?"

"Nothing's certain yet...but his firm has a huge upcoming project, and they just offered me a pretty good position."

"I thought you were gonna look for stuff here, finally focus on architecture."

"I was. I still might. I don't know."

"Do you want to go?"

"Yes and no," he says, which is what he always says when this topic comes up.

"What're the pros?" I ask.

"The pay will be good. Really good. I'll be writing and checking code with a team of software architects, something guys with more seniority usually get…it'll look great on my resume."

"And you'd have more time with your father, I guess?"

He pauses. "Yeah."

"Cons?"

Luca doesn't say anything for a long time, but when he does, it feels like he's erupting, giving voice to things he's maybe always wanted to say. "The biggest con is that I want to just stay here. Relax. Find an architecture firm or something that'll hire me and figure out what I want to do for the rest of my life." He looks at me. "I want to teach you how to surf. I want to go to Mãe's for Sunday dinners."

My chest tightens. "Why don't you do all of that, then?"

"Because it'll disappoint him, so much," he says with a tired sigh. "He lives for these summers together, and he'll just wear me down until I do what he wants. He can't let go of the dream of us being in business together."

"I don't think those are good reasons to go." I'm quiet when I say it, and he doesn't respond, but I know he hears me. It feels like we're just getting started. The thought of him leaving now, after so many false starts, makes my stomach hurt.

I would wait for Luca, of course. I just don't want to have to.

Wren

Clutching an oversize cup of coffee, I pull up to my old apartment building and park. I'm here to steal Mom's trusty, old beach cooler. She hardly uses it these days, and Arlo leaves tomorrow, so today we're going on a picnic at one of my favorite beaches down the coast.

Yawning, I climb out of my car and head upstairs. It's a pretty morning, almost nine, the cheerfully blue sky packed with fat clouds. Luca and I spent most of last night outdoors, drinking beer and stargazing at Fremont Peak until we fell asleep on the hood of his car. We woke up at quarter to three, freezing, and spent the next half hour warming up in the backseat.

It was one of the best nights of my life.

I peer blearily across the lot, surprised to see the eyesore that's been parked in the corner has finally been towed. I never thought I'd see the day.

Sliding my key into the lock, I push open Mom's front door and kick my flip-flops off, leaving them behind on the welcome mat. I'm rooting quietly around the pantry in the kitchen, searching for the cooler, when it hits me. The apartment smells different today. Like patchouli, of course, but something else, too. Something like…cologne?

Still down on my haunches, I pause my search and glance around the kitchen, noticing for the first time the Chinese takeout containers and empty wine bottles littering the countertops.

"Wren?"

I whirl around at the croaky voice, falling back onto my ass. "Arlo?" I gasp.

My father gapes at me, shirtless, his phone in one hand and a broomstick in the other. His hair looks like he stuck his finger into an electrical socket and then left it there while he slept. Mom hovers behind him, clenching her teal kimono bathrobe shut. She's so red she looks like she might catch fire.

Oh, my God.

"Oh, my God!" Horrified, I spring up and squeeze past them. "Call me later, Arlo!" I snatch my shoes off the floor and escape out the door, past the men's Chelsea boots I somehow missed on my way in. Mom might be calling my name, but there's no way I'm going back there.

It's not until I'm in the car, squealing out of the parking lot with a pounding heart, that my shock turns to laughter…and then epic gross out. In all my years of life, I've never caught my mother the morning after with a date.

And I never, ever thought that when I did, it would be with my father.

* * *

306

Arlo sits across from me on the blanket, chewing on a carrot stick as he gazes out at the ocean. He brought the cooler. It sits between us, packed to the gills by my mother when she realized I wasn't coming back for it.

We don't have much planned besides sitting here and vegging out. It's a good way to spend Arlo's last day in Santa Cruz.

The wind whips my hair around as I close my eyes and turn my face to the sun. It feels good to be outside, even if I am still tired from last night's shenanigans. Arlo looks a little tired, himself. I swallow a giggle. This morning hasn't come up yet. I get the feeling he's waiting for me to say something. But what?

Hey, so you and Mom, huh? How long has that been going on? Impregnating her decades ago doesn't count, for obvious reasons...

"What are you smiling about?" he asks, amusement coloring his voice.

I open one eye and peer at him. "I think you know."

He chuckles. "If this is about this morning, we thought you were an intruder…"

"As funny as that was, it wasn't the most shocking detail of the day." Now I'm laughing, too. "I thought she didn't even like you, Arlo!"

"Well, to be fair, I don't think she did—"

"*Not* what it looked like a few hours ago."

"At first," he amends. "She didn't like me at first, but that's because she didn't know me."

"Let me guess—you seduced her with more macarons."

"No, I finally got around to visiting the studio...I even took a class."

I snort, shaking my head. "You did not."

"I did. It wasn't my first time doing yoga, you know."

"Yeah, I'll bet," I tease, rolling my eyes.

"Ah, there she is. The teenage daughter I never had," he teases, cocking his head.

"But I'm twenty..."

"My apologies. *Anyway*, Lily gave me a tour and then, before we knew it, it was time to close. So, we grabbed some takeout and headed back to the apartment. And you know what? We have more in common than you'd think."

"More in common besides me, you mean?" I smile sweetly.

"We're both independent, only children. We both like being in control, being our own bosses. We may have had different upbringings and lifestyles, but there's something kindred that I recognize in Lily."

He's so earnest that I can't even tease him anymore. I turn my attention to the churning sea, letting the lump that's begun forming in my throat dissolve.

"I'm sorry about this morning, that you found out like that," he says, his voice barely audible over the crush of waves. "It was inappropriate. But I want you to know that I don't regret what happened between your mother

308

and me."

"Were you guys going to tell me?" I ask, drawing my finger through the sand.

He pauses.

"You know she doesn't do relationships, right?" I say. "My mom's not…built for that."

"I think that's between her and me, Wren. And yes, we would have told you when the timing was better."

I wrinkle my nose. "When would've been a good time? You're leaving tomorrow."

I know I'm being a brat, but Arlo feels like he belongs to me, not my mom. Had all of this happened the way it does with regular families, they would've belonged to each other way before either of them belonged to me—but that's not how it happened. It's hard not to feel like the two of them went behind my back.

Although Mom did feel like I went behind her back when I first found Arlo, so maybe we're even now? I don't know. I wanted them to get along, but this might be a bit much.

Arlo just sighs. "I don't know, honey."

It's the first time he's called me that, and my heart thumps awkwardly. I grab a bag of chips, tearing it open. "Do you think you'll come back?"

"Of course, I'll be back." He looks at me askance. "I want to be a part of your life."

I blink at him, nodding. "Okay."

"You look like you think I'm full of it." He scoots closer. "Talk to me."

"It's just, you have a lot going on, so I wouldn't be offended or whatever if you…" I shrug.

He gazes at me warily. "If I what?"

"Look, one of the reasons I was surprised Mom and you"— I wave my hand, not sure what to call what Mom and Arlo were doing when I caught them— "is because she fully believes that men don't stick around. She's said it my entire life—I mean, half the time she leaves them before they can leave her."

Arlo nods slowly, listening.

"Getting that close to you just seems messy on her part—because of me."

"Do you believe that, too? That men don't stick around?" he asks, slipping his sunglasses up so I can see his eyes. "Seems like a pretty broad generalization."

I shake my head. "I don't know what I believe."

"Do you want us to have a relationship, Wren? Me and you?"

I force myself to look him. His eyes, so much like mine. "Yes."

"Good. Me, too."

"I just don't want things to go south if you and my mom get weird."

"Me and your mom have nothing to do with me and you." I raise my eyebrows, and he laughs, holding his hands up. "Let me rephrase that. I'm well aware that choosing to be intimate with Lily complicates things, but what happens, or doesn't happen, from here on out with your mom and me has no bearing on this relationship right here." He taps my hand. "Okay?"

"Okay." I dig through the cooler, discovering a treasure trove of mini chocolate bars. *Yum. Thanks, Mom.* "Can I ask you something?"

"Anything."

I pause, trying to figure out how to ask the question that's been on my mind since the first message Arlo ever sent me on Kith&Kin. "Okay, this might be awkward."

He grins wryly. "I think we've managed pretty well so far."

"I probably should've just asked you this in the very beginning—"

"Out with it."

"Okay, okay." I nod. "So…do you, like, have other kids? That you know of?"

He shakes his head. "Not that I know of. Honestly, I'm surprised I have you."

For some reason, I'm not expecting this. Straightening up, I pull my hand out of the cooler. "Why?"

"Because I only…donated…once."

"What?" I shake my head, trying to understand while trying not to think about him *donating*. "Why?"

For the first time since we've met, Arlo seems embarrassed. His cheeks flush, and a line forms between his eyebrows. "I was in college. Broke. I wasn't one of those kids who was able to graduate in four years, you know? It took me a while. I always had work study jobs along with my off-campus jobs, and sometimes that wasn't even enough." He clears his throat. "One month I couldn't quite make rent. I was living with a couple of buddies, and I just…couldn't do it. Someone suggested a place, a sperm bank in the city, so I went."

We're quiet for a long time. Down the shore, a man with a little kid and a dog runs around, throwing a frisbee.

"Did you ever think you'd have kids?" I ask. "Did you want any?"

"I never really thought about it. I've never been against it; my life just never went that way. When I did finally graduate and start working, I hustled so I'd never have to be broke again. My parents did their best while I was growing up, but things were lean. I was tired of that." He looks at me before glancing away again, and suddenly he seems so much younger. He really isn't that old; neither of my parents are. "But it's been a long time since I had to worry about money. I do what I do because I love it. I'm grateful it affords me the life I want. And that I can be here, with you."

"But you didn't even know I existed until—"

"Sometimes you don't realize what's missing until it shows up." He frowns, shaking his head. "I can't go back now, Wren. I don't want to."

"I think I know what you mean."

"Do you?" He stares intently at me.

"I never felt incomplete or anything, growing up. Curious, maybe, but I was

312

fine," I say, tucking my hair behind my ears. "But now…" I shrug, staring down at the blanket so he doesn't see my eyes welling up.

He scoots closer, taking my hand. "Maybe we were both wondering. We just didn't know it."

I nod, laughing a little.

"Come on." He ruffles my hair. "Let me get a couple of pictures of you while we're out here."

* * *

"You spent the night at his hotel, didn't you?" I ask, shouldering my phone as I scrub the shower stall that I share with Saira. We both hate the task, but it's my turn.

"No. Not that it's any of your business," Mom snips. She's at the studio, holed up in her office.

"I'm surprised you didn't offer to drive him to the airport."

"Is there something you'd like to say, Wren? Because Arlo told me the two of you talked it out plenty yesterday."

I snort, making a face at myself in the mirror. "Are you seriously giving me an attitude when you were the one treating him like a leper until last week? Excuse me for being confused!"

"I did not treat him like a leper!"

"Well, whatever. I'm glad you two hit it off so warmly. It'll make things way easier when he comes back."

We're silent for a beat. I move on to the counter, sweeping aside Saira's mind-boggling array of hair products.

Mom sighs. "I'm sorry."

I know her, so I'm not surprised she's apologizing. She only gets prickly with me when she feels guilty in the first place. "For what?"

"Arlo coming to Santa Cruz is all about you, not me. The last thing I ever wanted was to get in the way of that."

"You didn't get in the way of anything, Mom. We've hung out plenty, and we're going to keep on figuring out ways to get to know each other. I wanted you and him to get along! You're my parents, for God's sake."

She doesn't say anything, but I know she hears me.

"Be honest," I say. "Do you *like him,* like him?"

"We have good chemistry. Really good. It caught me off guard," she admits. "I would not have slept with him if I didn't like him, little bird."

"Thanks for the visual." I shudder, wishing I could bleach my brain as thoroughly as I just did the toilet.

She cackles at that.

"He's cute, though, huh?" I press.

"Very cute. He's intelligent, compassionate…a good storyteller and a good listener."

There's a catch in her voice. "But?"

"But Arlo's busy and so am I."

"So?"

"So, we had a nice time, but I don't expect anything."

It's her way of saying what she always says. Men don't stick around. But I remember what Arlo said to me on the beach, earlier.

"He'll be back," I say.

"Of course, he will," she agrees. "For you."

Arlo texts me when he lands at JFK later that afternoon. Well, it's afternoon here, evening there.

Arlo: Landed. It's hot and muggy.
  I already miss the weather over there.

It feels weird going back to typed messages with Arlo, as if we didn't just spend the past two weeks together. Getting up, I go to the window and snap a picture of the sky, a sunset gradient of orange, pink, and red.

Wren: It's pretty tonight.
  How was your flight?

Arlo: Probably fine, but I wouldn't know.
  I always sleep on planes.

We chat for a couple of minutes and then he logs off, eager to hit the hay so he can start recovering from jet lag.

Not that it matters much; he'll be in Sri Lanka by the end of the week.

Wren

"D"o you want to stay?"

He makes it so hard to say no. Luca is everything warm: his hand on my belly, his eyes burning into mine. His mouth on its way back to my nipple despite the fact we just went two rounds.

"Luca." I groan, clasping my hands around his head. "You know I can't. Not tonight."

"Okay." He doesn't stop, though, his fingers wiggling between my thighs to where I'm still wet. And sore. And still wanting him.

"I have to be up early," I whisper pathetically, my legs falling open.

"We should go, then." But his hair tickles my skin as he disappears between my thighs.

An hour later, we're in his car, hands clasped on his lap as we speed back to campus. It's been this way for weeks now, ever since the end of spring break, around when my dad left. Actually, maybe it was before that—since dinner at his mom's. We're together, all the time.

We meet between classes when we can, finding one another in the busy crush of people. Nights are for studying alone in his room, or at his kitchen table, surrounded by his friends. Saira comes along those nights. She and Kellan aren't dating or even sleeping together, but they hang out almost as much as we do. Which is interesting.

Weekends find us driving around with the windows down and the music up, the wind in our hair. We hike and hit up beaches, noshing at drive-throughs and taco trucks. Luca and Kellan try to teach me and Saira how to surf. She's way better at it than me so far.

We run errands. Grocery shopping is a lot more fun with Luca at my side.

I've never had this much sex in my life—Saira says we're in the honeymoon stage. Maybe we are. All I know is that we're addicted to each other, and I don't ever want to go to rehab. The last time I felt so caught up in a guy it was high school. Sean Bunker, my first love, first everything. I remember thinking, when we broke up at the end of junior year, that I couldn't imagine ever wanting someone so much again.

But I want Luca more than I ever wanted him.

The one thing we don't do is talk about the summer. I don't know if he's made any decisions regarding his dad's offer because I won't ask and he won't bring it up. In my heart of hearts, I suspect he'll go. According to what he's told me, it's what he always does.

Tonight, we slide into a space in front of my building. This is the part I hate, knowing that in a few minutes we'll be apart again. I try to tell myself it's just for a few hours, but my heart's having none of that.

"You got some studying to do, huh?" Luca slides his arm over my shoulder as we walk toward the door.

"Yeah." I nod. "I took good notes, so I'm not too worried, but this'll be the last one before finals. I need to do well."

A small group is coming out as we go in. They hold the door open for us and we slip inside, murmuring thanks. It's Sunday night, and the building's buzzing—all the people that headed out of town over the three-day weekend are settling back in.

Our door's wide open. Leighton's pawing through her desk as we walk inside. "Oh, hey y'all."

"What're you looking for?" I give her a quick hug.

She frowns, scratching her head. "My charger, dammit. Can I borrow yours?"

"Go ahead; you know where it is."

She disappears into the side of the room I share with Saira. Luca pulls me closer by the belt loop and I slide my arms around his waist. We stare at each other, and then I tip-toe to kiss him, closing my eyes as his lips warm mine.

"Happy studying," he says, squeezing me before letting go.

"You too. Are you going to the pool in the morning?"

He nods. "Around nine. I'll text you when I'm leaving."

My heart warms. "Okay."

His dark eyes shine. "Okay."

I lean in the doorway and watch him leave, my heart stuttering when he glances back with a wave.

Leighton watches from across the room with a little smile. "Y'all are really, really cute. I can't even lie."

Sighing, I shut the door and lock it.

"Any word on Brazil?" she asks, flopping down onto the couch.

I shake my head. Leighton and Saira know all about the situation. I had to tell them—it's all I can think about. When I'm with Luca, it's easy to forget. He kisses me, lays me down and does things to my body that leave me weak and brainless. He looks at me with those whiskey eyes, talks to me, teases me, and all I can do is savor the present moment. It's when he leaves that things get hard.

When he's not around to distract me with himself.

"I know I should just ask him," I say, sitting beside my friend. "It's been weeks since he brought it up. But I'm so afraid of what he'll say. At least this way I can pretend."

"Ignorance is bliss," agrees Leighton. "But it can't last forever. I think you should just bite the bullet."

In the morning, I head to my Art of Happiness class. It's my favorite class, the only one I break my nothing-before-nine a.m. rule for. The professor talks about the importance of keeping short accounts, of talking about issues before they can fester, and though Luca and I aren't having issues, it feels like confirmation.

Luca and I head to the beach early on a Friday morning, when the sky is still a little pink. He's been trying to get to the beach as much as possible these days, wanting to get some surfing in before summer responsibilities—like a job—kick in. My surf lessons have been sporadic, but that's okay. Sometimes I'd rather just watch him go for it while I lie on the beach and take pictures with my phone. Other days I stare at the clouds, letting the crash of waves lull me to daydreams.

But today is a lesson, which is why we chose this particular beach. Cowell Beach is a little gentler, better for beginners. We've been going for about an hour when Kellan and some guy I don't know show up. They goof off on the shore for a bit before swimming out on their boards, gracefully riding the waves I've been struggling with.

"My arms feel like jelly," I groan after a while, lying on my belly as a gentle swell lifts us. I can't lie, this is hard as hell. But I see why Luca loves it, and I think with time I might love it, too.

Luca splashes me. "Come on, newbie. Try again."

"I need a break…"

"I'll just drag you back if you get out," he warns, but I'm already paddling to shore.

After resting and gnawing on an apple I brought, I join the boys again. This time, I'm able to stand up for more than two seconds, and I cheer loudly, pumping my fist as I go crashing down.

It was great while it lasted.

Later, Luca and I stop by the boardwalk for tacos. To think, I used to have these every day and now it's been forever. I miss them.

"Logan stopped by last night," Luca says as we're finishing, wiping his mouth. "After I dropped you home."

"Wow. What was that like?"

He shrugs. "A little weird. He, uh, apologized. I guess he and Brooke are kind of dating now. I think he really likes her."

"Hm." Unsure of what to say about that, I sip my soda. "Interesting."

Luca snorts. "That's one way of putting it."

"So, he just stopped by to say sorry and tell you they're officially together?"

"I guess," he says. "I think we both know things will never be the way they were, but maybe they don't have to be so fucked, either."

"That makes sense. You can forgive someone without having them in your life, you know?"

He smiles a little, gathering our trash and tossing it in a nearby bin. "Yeah."

Standing up from our bench, I raise my arms over my head for a good stretch. "Are you okay?"

"About Logan? Yeah." He nods. "I'm glad he came over and owned up to that shit. It felt like closure."

I'll always find it sad that Luca lost one of his childhood friends that way, but people have to live with the choices they make. And, I guess, the choices other people make.

We stroll for a while down the uncharacteristically quiet main thoroughfare. It's slow right now; most people are still at work or school "Hey, there's something I want to talk about."

Luca slides his hand into the back pocket of my shorts and tugs me closer. "What's up?"

One launching platform of Sky Glider looms ahead, backlit by the sun. "Want to ride?" I ask Luca, tilting my head.

"Sure." He shrugs. "Let's grab tickets."

"We don't need tickets." I scoff. "I know everyone."

Sure enough, the bored looking kid on the platform yawns as we approach. "Hey, Wren. You getting on?"

"Hey, Jonah. If you don't mind."

Standing, he fastens Luca and me into the next car and we're off, drifting slowly into the sky. I grin, wiggling my toes in my flip flops.

"Don't drop 'em," Luca says, noticing.

"Never."

We gaze at each other. "I remember the first time we rode this thing," he says. "You were so nervous around me."

"How do you know I'm not still?"

He leans in, slanting his lips to mine. "What did you want to talk about?" he asks after a long, slow kiss, eyes serious as he pulls away.

I decide to go for it. "Summer. Are you gonna go to Brazil?"

He exhales, then nods. "I think so."

My heart falls to the boardwalk below. Maybe I've been in denial, but I'd hoped he'd say no. "When?"

"My flight's booked for the 16th."

Luca's graduation is June 12th. That leaves us barely any time. "You already have your ticket?" I shake my head, my stomach in knots. "Why didn't you tell me?"

"It was a pretty recent decision." He's quiet for a beat, finally bringing his eyes to mine. "I was going to tell you, but I knew you'd be upset, and I didn't feel like fucking up the mood."

Part of me likes that he considered my feelings. But most of me is just sad. Unsure of what I want to say, I stare at the empty car in front of us.

"See? You're upset." Luca's lips brush my temple. "Mãe's upset, too. I feel like I'm pissing off every woman in my life."

I smile a little, thinking of his mother. We've gotten to know each other better over the last month, mostly through Sunday dinners. It's easy to see she thinks Luca hangs the moon, so I'm not surprised she's upset at the thought of him leaving again.

"I'm not pissed off." I touch Luca's face, rubbing my thumb over the soft, smooth skin of his cheek. He's even more beautiful to me now than he was the first time we rode the Sky Glider together. "Just a little sad."

"I won't be gone forever," he jokes, but it falls flat. "Just the summer."

"How do you know, though?" I look out at the uncharacteristically calm expanse of water just beyond the beach. Two surfers float on their boards, killing time as they wait for a swell. "You keep going to Brazil; there has to be something about it that draws you in, right? And you're almost done with school, so it's not like you have to come back to Santa Cruz."

Luca drums his fingers over my knee. "School was never the only thing bringing me back, Wren. California's home. It'll always be home."

I nod. I can understand that.

"My dad's over there, but my family is here. My friends." He pauses, and I look up at him. The setting sun reflects in his eyes. "You're here."

Suddenly, the words my mother has spoken my entire life detonate in my brain like mental IEDs. *"Men don't stay...they never stick around, little bird...don't expect much."*

You don't need a man.

No, I don't need a man. But I want this one. His lips meet mine, soft and familiar, and I open to the warm, wet slide of his mouth, relishing the way his kiss touches my soul as much as my body. It scares me, because *this* man has become an integral part of my life.

Yeah, I'm here. I'll always be here.

But will he?

* * *

"How ya doing?" Arlo's voice is loud and echoey, like he's in a vast space somewhere.

"I'm okay." I grin, lying back on my unmade bed. "Getting ready for the end of the school year, exams, study groups…you know how it goes."

He chuckles. "I do. I doubt NYU in the nineties was anything like Santa Cruz nowadays, but some things don't change."

We chat for a moment about my grades, the classes I'm over and the ones I'll miss. "You'd love my Art of Happiness class, Arlo. It's my favorite. I'd take it again if I could."

"Dr. Sonia Torres, right?"

I laugh in surprise, trying to recall whether I'd mentioned my professor to Arlo. "Yeah! How'd you know that?"

"It's pretty well known—in fact, I listened to several of that podcast's episodes on my way to Rome last winter."

"That's crazy. I'll have to check out the podcast, too."

"You should," he says. "But it's fantastic you're taking the course live. You'll have to tell more about it when you visit this summer."

My heart leaps in excitement. "So, it's definite?"

"Of course, it's definite! I've already spoken to your mother about it. If it's okay with you, I'd like to keep you for the month of July."

"Hell yeah, it's okay with me!" Giddy at the news, I sit up straight. "I'll stay with you in New York?"

"For a week, and then we'll head out. Lily tells me you don't have a passport, so we'll have to rectify that situation immediately."

"Passport?" I echo dumbly.

"Yeah, they take forever sometimes. I have a few connections, luckily, so if we apply right now we should be in the clear."

My mind races. This can't be real. "Where are we going?"

"How much time ya got?" he teases.

"Plenty!" I sputter, gaping at myself in the mirror.

"Good!" Arlo chuckles. "I want to take you to Mexico City first, then make our way over to San Miguel de Allende. Lots of art. Great architecture. A protégé of mine from Tisch is going on a job there around then, so I figured we could travel together for a while. Amias—you'll love him," he says, picking up speed as he gets excited. "From there, I was thinking Belize; I have a couple of friends who own an ecotourism resort. It's beautiful. We'll finish up in Costa Rica. I want to show you the Cloud Forests near Monteverde."

"I don't know what to say." Swinging my legs to the side of the bed, I sit for a moment. "I've never even been outside of the country."

"I know," he says gently. "But there's so much to see. We're staying on this side of the world for now, but maybe we can hit up Europe next summer. Or maybe for the holidays—Christmas in Paris is pretty great. Maybe we can get your mom to come."

"Arlo!" I'm grinning so hard my cheeks hurt. "This is nuts!"

"I know, but you'll be in good hands. I travel for a living."

"I totally trust you!" I laugh. "This is like…the best news I've ever gotten."

"That's what I wanted to hear," he says. "We're going to have a great time."

I scratch my head, frowning. "Wait, so you said you spoke to my mom?"

"I talk to her all the time."

"What?" I'll have to talk to my mother about this, because her sneaky ass never mentioned it. "How did I not know this?"

"I have no idea." Arlo clears his throat, something I've noticed he does when he's uncomfortable. "Anyway, I've emailed Lily the details concerning your passport application, but I need you to jump on that too. It can take up to six weeks, and we don't want anything getting in the way of our trip."

Later, after I've completed an assignment for calculus, I shoot my mother a text.

Wren: Arlo says we gotta get me a passport

The three dots pop up. I wait and wait, wondering what the hell she could possibly be typing. In the end, all she says is

328

Mom: Yes! Exciting!

Wren: I didn't know you guys had been keeping in touch...ooh la la

Mom: Well, what can I say? We have a kid together.

Luca

Matty and I are halfway through a pint of beer each at one of our favorite dive bars when he wrinkles his nose like he just smelled something foul.

I pick my glass up and lean back in my chair. "What? Your beer off or something?"

"Your ex, bro. She just came in."

I take a long drag of beer, keeping my eyes on the darts game going on nearby. It's unfortunate that Brooke is here, but not entirely surprising. Everyone ends up at this place eventually, and now that we're slogging through finals, everyone's looking for a little reprieve.

"She's looking over here," Matty adds, funneling the last of his chips into his mouth.

"I really don't give a fuck," I mutter, balling my napkin up and tossing it aside. Two girls squeeze by, one of them tossing me a coy smile as she bumps Matty's seat. It's busy for Thursday.

"Where's Sweet Spot when you need her?" he murmurs.

"Sweet Spot's not twenty-one," I remind him.

"Never stopped me."

"And that's why you've been arrested. Twice."

"Hey, I was always let off." He scoffs, shifting to slide his phone from his pocket. "Anyway, you know I was only arrested for underaged drinking once. The other time was for fighting."

Amused, I finish my beer and rap my knuckles on the varnished, wooden table. "You down for one more before we head out?"

"I'm in no rush," he says, tapping out a text to God-knows-who.

Pushing back my chair, I thread my way through the close, crowded room. The bartender, a tall, slender girl with close-cropped hair and a nose ring, jerks her chin when our eyes meet. "Whaddya need?"

"Two Sierra Nevadas. Tap."

She nods, grabbing a couple of glasses from beneath the bar. The music shifts from old school alternative to old school hip hop, inspiring a group in the corner to yell along with the lyrics. Chuckling at the scene, I turn back to the bar and grab my wallet. Someone—female, by the softness—presses close, and then a familiar scent tickles my nose.

Brooke's hair is lighter than it was when we were dating, but other than that nothing's changed. Not the flirty smirk quirking her mouth, not the way she cocks her head as her eyes trail over my face. It's amazing how unattractive a beautiful girl can be when you know what ugly things she's done.

"Luca," she says slowly, biting her full bottom lip. "Hi."

"Hey, Brooke." I return my attention to the bartender, who's filled one glass and has moved on to the other.

"How've you been? I haven't seen you in a while."

Not entirely true. We've seen each other several times on campus; I've even spotted her with Logan. She still gives me the puppy eyes after all this time, but she knows not to talk to me. Until now, anyway.

"Really? You're not even going to talk to me?"

I don't know what she wants me to say. Glancing down at her, I catch a hint of the pout I used to think was sort of cute. Now it's nothing—not even annoying. Letting out a slow breath, I return my eyes to the bartender. "Classes going well for you?"

"Yeah. Can't believe we're about to graduate." She hesitates. "What about you? Are you doing okay?"

"Everything's great." I flash her a quick smile, wishing she'd take the hint. I wasn't enough for her when we were together, so why does she need this now? To assuage her guilt? Or is she still interested? I can't tell, but more importantly, I just don't care anymore. I wish she'd stop caring, too.

Silence falls between us, as much as it can in a place as loud as this. Another bartender passes by, briefly leaning in as she takes Brooke's order.

"Luca," she says, touching my arm long enough for me to look down at her. "I need you to know, for what it's worth, that I will always regret what I did. I messed up, and I'm sorry."

I study her for a moment. She's done a hell of a lot more than Logan ever did, apologizing like this. "I know you are. Apology accepted."

Flushing, she looks away. "You're different from other guys. I should've realized that."

I raise an eyebrow. It doesn't matter what kind of guy I am; no one deserves to be cheated on. "What difference does that make?"

"I just mean that I know what I had," she says. "You're a good guy."

The first bartender returns with my drinks. I hand over a twenty, telling her to keep the change.

"I've seen your new girlfriend," Brooke says as I turn to go. "She's cute."

"She is."

The bartender brings over Brooke's drink. "Are you going back to Brazil this summer?"

I hesitate, wondering what her angle is. "Yeah?"

She nods as she brushes past me, her words almost lost in the chatter around us. "I sure hope she weathers the separation better than I did."

* * *

Fucking Brooke, man. I shouldn't, but her words bounce around my brain for the rest of the day. It's just like her to get under my skin, although in a much different way than she used to.

I'd like to think she was being spiteful, trying to wound me with the suggestion that Wren might be unfaithful, but that wasn't the impression I got. She seemed honest, for once.

Maybe there was a tinge of spite in there, too.

At home, I take a quick shower and park it on the bed with my laptop, intending to get some studying in before calling it a night. I review my 3D modeling and linear programming notes for a while, trying in earnest to focus, but my mind keeps wandering.

Sighing, I switch over to my email account and pull up my father's latest message, which contains an overview of the Mason-Ridley project and the team I'll be working with at Veritas. Most of the names are familiar—I've shadowed several of Pai's senior software architects in the past.

This time things will be different. I'll be a real part of the team, testing segments of code some of the other guys are writing and checking for errors while writing code of my own. Pai's trusting me to pull my weight, and I will.

The next email in the queue is my travel itinerary. I read through the details, once again recalling the disappointment in Mãe's eyes when I told her I'd be leaving after all.

"But what about Wren?" she'd asked. That'd surprised me. I knew she liked Wren; I just hadn't realized how much.

"She'll be all right. She's spending the summer with her dad, too."

Mãe looked dubious. "The whole summer?"

I shrugged. "A good part of it. She's excited she's finally getting to leave the country."

And it's true—Wren can't wait to go. Shit, I can't wait for her to go—she's finally getting to see the world, and she gets to see it with her dad. No one deserves this more.

But now, sitting alone in my room, I know that this isn't just about her leaving; it's about me leaving, too. I'll be in Brazil long before she leaves for New York, and I won't be back until she's starting her junior year at UCSC. We'll be apart for a long time.

Putting my laptop aside, I reach over into the nightstand and feel around until I find what I'm looking for. The photo strip, the first one Wren and I took at the boardwalk. We barely knew each other then, but man we had chemistry. Just looking at us kissing has me wanting to call her now, get her over here so I can do a lot more to her.

I rub at the ache in my chest, acknowledging what I've been feeling for a while now...that I'm falling in deep with Wren. Every day, every night we spend together, I give myself to her more. Going in opposite directions this summer is going to be hard—for me, anyway. It'll probably be hard for her too; I know she's in this with me. But she's excited about this trip, more than I've ever seen her.

One of Arlo's photographer friends, some younger guy he mentored at NYU or Tisch or something, will be with them in Mexico for a minute. Apparently, he's got a magazine shoot Arlo and Wren can tag along on. He's kind of famous, and Wren's been all over his Instagram, gushing about how talented he is and how exciting it'll be. He's a good-looking guy, too, even if he is about ten years older than her.

Am I being weird about this? Is it fair to expect her to wait for me while we're apart? Wren's so fucking pretty. Guys check her out constantly, whether we're on the beach or at the grocery store. I don't cheat; it's never been my style, but maybe we should cool it for the summer so she can do her thing. Have fun. Be free. If our relationship is worth its salt, we should be able to pick up where we left off, right?

The thought of taking a break makes me queasy, but not as much as the thought of her hooking up with somebody else. Maybe this is the smartest choice.

After all, Wren can't cheat on me if we're not together.

Wren

Giving myself one last look in the mirror, I smooth the delicate blue fabric of my dress and grab the pair of espadrilles I bought for this occasion. The weather's cool now, so I grab a light jacket and stuff it into my bag. It'll most likely get hot as the fog burns off, but one can never be too careful.

"I'm heading over to the field now. You just about ready?" I ask Saira, pausing near the door to buckle the espadrilles. Normally we'd attend UCSC's commencement ceremony together to watch the guys walk, but she's doing something with Kellan and his family afterward while I'm going with Luca. "I heard it's already getting crazy crowded."

She glances up from painting her toenails, nodding. "Kellan's mom is saving me a seat."

For someone who constantly warned me about the pitfalls of a friends-with-benefits arrangement while I was hanging with Dallas, Saira sure has fallen into an interesting situation with the eldest Morgan brother. They're more friends than anything else—still no sex—but they hang out a lot. I've given up trying to figure them out. If she's happy, I'm happy.

"Oh, good. Hey, we'll probably be in Walnut Creek until pretty late, so I might stay with Luca tonight."

"Of course, you will." She grins cheekily, resuming the design she's painting on the nail of her big toe. "Have fun, be safe. Say hi to Luca for me if I don't see you guys."

Jumping into my car, I head over to the East Field's parking lot which is half full despite the fact I'm early. I wave to a girl I know and join the queue waiting for the shuttle that'll bring us over to the ceremony spot on the field.

It's tempting to text Luca, but he's got enough to think about without me bugging him, so I resist the urge. We went to bed early for once, going our separate ways after sharing an early dinner with friends on the beach as the sun set last night.

The next couple of days are going to be difficult. On one hand, I'm excited because it's summer—the summer I get to get away. By this time in two weeks, I'll be in New York City, a place I've always fantasized about. And then…everywhere else. It's hard to wrap my head around, despite the brand-new passport sitting on my desk and the tasteful luggage set the Mangal family gifted me to celebrate my trip.

But on the other hand, I'll be separated from Luca for the first time since we started dating. Even though the past few months have been a dream, there's a tiny part of me that worries things won't be the same when he gets back from Brazil—if he comes back. He'll be gone for such a long time, returning to a place where he has another life, whether he sees it that way or not. He has roots there, family, friends—a chance at a career, if he wants. And while I believe him when he says he doesn't want the career, I also think there's a connection to his dad and their country that keeps Luca going back.

I love him. I love him enough that I want his happiness no matter what he chooses, but also enough that being apart is going to hurt. A lot.

The shuttle lurches to a stop. Taking a deep breath, I stand up and follow everyone off, letting the collective buzz of anticipation take me to a happier headspace. And honestly, it's easy to let the excitement of the day and the beauty of UCSC's East Field distract me. Hundreds upon hundreds of people, looking somewhat like confetti in their colorful clothing, mill about the open space. Bright white tents are set up near the sand, but most people have wandered over to the field's edge, which overlooks Monterey Bay.

My heart squeezes as I walk over, and I pause, soaking in the view. Gramma Kate and I took lots of meandering walks around campus when I was little, many culminating in this very spot. It's as breathtaking today as it was back then. Most of the fog's gone, leaving the day so clear that I can see the tiny triangles of sailboats bobbing in the broad expanse of blue-green water. Directly across the bay, the Santa Lucia mountains float up from a gauzy swath of mist.

My phone rings from my bag, interrupting my reverie.

"Hello? Luca?"

"Hey! You here yet? Mãe's looking for you."

Warmed by the thought, I turn away from the bay and squint around the masses of people. "Yeah, I'm here. Just admiring the view. Where is she?"

"Oh—if you're over by the edge of the field, then stay put. I'll have her find you."

"Okay." I bite my lip, heart warm. "Thanks."

He's quiet for a moment, the ruckus of whatever is happening on his end filling the airwaves. "Hey. Sorry, it's crazy over here."

"I bet. Go ahead; I'll catch you after."

"Okay." He pauses. "Hey."

My heart skips at the grit in his voice. "Yeah?"

"Thanks for being here."

I wrinkle my nose, laughing. "Of course, I'm here! Where else would I be?"

"Just letting you know. All right, gotta go."

We disconnect, and I turn back around, snapping a few photos of the bay to send my mother. I would send them to Gramma Kate, too, but she's avidly against texting. I'll save these for our next visit.

Mãe—Marissa—and her husband Dominic emerge from the crowd.

"Hi, Wren," calls Marissa, waving wildly, a radiant grin stretching across her face. "We have been looking everywhere for you! Come on, come on!"

"Hi!" I laugh, allowing myself to be enveloped in a hug. "Sorry! I was admiring the view—"

"Oh, I know it's gorgeous, but come—Nico, Phoebe and the kids are saving our spot, but we have to hurry. You know how these people are. They..."

She rambles on, hurrying ahead as Dominic looks helplessly back at me.

"She's been like this all day," he says, slipping his hands into his pockets. "You don't want to see the kitchen."

"Is it a mess?" I giggle, falling into step with him.

"Oh no, no." His caterpillar eyebrows shoot up. "She cooked through the night and cleaned all morning. Had me hanging banners and balloons and all kind of—"

"And I will do the same for Daniel's graduation!" Marissa calls back, obviously having heard.

We join the rest of the family, where Nico's wife Phoebe pats the seat beside her and welcomes me with a hug. Delia slides over, touching the little bows keeping my straps up.

"This is so pretty," she says, biting her lip shyly. "You always have the prettiest dresses."

"Aw, thank you!" I touch the cap sleeve of her mint green dress, nodding. "But I love *your* dress. You look like a princess."

Her cheeks color. "That's what my dad said."

Before I can reply, a loud voice booms over my head. "Olá, Marissa! Como você esta? Dominic? How're you doing, man?"

Startled, I look up at a tall, broad-shouldered man standing behind our row of seats. He's dressed impeccably, in a gray suit, and handsome, with salt and pepper hair, a trim beard, and reddish-gold skin.

He looks just like Luca and Nico. Or rather, they look like him. This must be Carlos.

"Olá, Carlos," Marissa says, one hand on her hip as the two men shake hands. "I didn't think you were going to make it—you're late!"

"I'm not late!" Carlos protests, tapping his watch. His accent isn't as strong as I'd imagined. That makes sense, I suppose—he was born and raised in the States, after all. "The ceremony hasn't even started yet."

"You're fine," Dominic says calmly, obviously used to this. "We have a seat for you right up here."

"Excellent."

Luca did mention that his father would probably be attending the commencement ceremony, but as the days went by and we got caught up in the end of the year flurry of exams and graduation, I forgot.

But as I watch Carlos Cardoso interact with the people around him, I can see why Luca has a hard time refusing him. He's commanding and charismatic, and he has probably never heard the word no. I'd imagine it would be hard to resist, having someone like that believe in you. Luca told me once that Veritas was always meant to be a family affair.

It was probably always eventually meant to be Luca's.

* * *

Luca slides his arms around me, burying his nose in my neck as he hugs me from behind. Squealing in surprise, I spin around and hug him back, covering his laughing face in kisses. "Congrats, graduate!"

"Thank you, thank you." He squirms from my kisses, holding my face so he can plant a big one on my mouth before pulling me to his side.

"Could you hear us cheering?" I ask, leaning into him as we walk toward his family.

"Yeah, especially Nico's whistle." He snorts. "I bet Mãe loved that."

"I don't know; she was the loudest out of everybody."

"Have you met my father yet?" he asks, giving my waist a squeeze.

"Not officially, no. It's been a little crazy…" And, though I'd never admit it, I'm more nervous to meet Mr. Cardoso than I ever was to meet Luca's mom.

"Come on." He maneuvers us over to his parents, who appear to be bickering good naturedly in Portuguese as Dom looks on. Noticing our approach, Marissa breaks away and rushes over, eyes glistening with tears.

I let go of Luca as she rushes into his arms. "I am so damn proud of you, baby!"

"Thanks, Mãe. Feels good." Luca grins over her head, nodding as Carlos moves in, hands in his slacks. "Oi, Pai."

"Olá, filho." They embrace a long time, clapping one another on the back.

Not wanting to intrude, I step back and take in the bright, happy sea of jubilant families and their beaming graduates, hugging, laughing, snapping photos. One familiar face swims into focus—Luca's friend Matt. He does a double take when our eyes meet and blows me a kiss. I blow one back, chuckling.

"Wren," calls Luca.

I spin around, smiling expectantly. Carlos wipes gently at his wet, reddened eyes, obviously not ashamed to cry in public. It makes me like him a little more.

"Come, meet my dad." Luca's eyes soften, and he reaches for me, pulling me back to his side. "Pai, this is Wren…minha enamorada."

I bite my lip, feeling my cheeks go warm. Luca speaking Portuguese is always so sexy, but hearing that phrase, *minha enamorada*—grabs a hold of my heart. I've never heard him say it before, in English *or* Portuguese, but I know what it means. Girlfriend.

"Ela é bonita," murmurs Carlos, nodding. He grasps my hand, giving it a firm shake. "Hello, Wren. It is so nice to finally put a face to the name—this one talks about you like none other."

I wasn't expecting such a glowing review, but I try to take it in stride, nodding. "I'm so glad to meet you, too, sir. Luca speaks highly of you."

"Oh, I doubt that!" He laughs abruptly, giving my hand a pat as he lets go. "I'm always busting his chops. And call me Carlos, eh? Only my employees call me sir."

* * *

"So, how should we do this?" Luca asks. We're standing at the edge of the field, near the shuttle stop. "Do you want to drive up yourself or come with me?"

"You're coming back to Santa Cruz tonight, right?"

"Not sure yet." He smirks. "Depends on how much I drink."

I'd assumed I'd just ride with Luca, leaving my car at his place or something, but suddenly that seems selfish in light of his family. He should be spending time with them today, especially the ones that came in from out of town. "Then I'll drive. That way I can come home if I have to."

Luca stares off at the parking lot, absently rubbing at his chin. He shaved his stubble for today's event, giving him a much more clean-cut look than usual. Suddenly he focuses on me, the intensity in his eyes making my heart skip a beat. "You sure? There's space for you up there if you want to stay."

"Positive. Just message me the address so I can find it without you."

Nodding, he reaches for his phone and quickly types out a message. My phone pings seconds later, lighting up with his text. "I feel bad, making you do this drive solo."

"You're not making me do anything," I promise, leaving a kiss on his chin. The stubble is already on its way back, so it's rougher than it looks. I shiver, thinking of what it'll feel like on the inside of my thighs later.

He wraps his arms around me, kissing the top of my head. "I'll miss you," he says, so quietly I almost don't hear it.

I smile against his chest, dissolving into his embrace. "It'll just be a couple of hours."

"You look really pretty today, by the way." His hand sweeps the hem of my dress. "Like a real summer girl. Like the first time I saw you."

His sweet words, the nostalgia of what he says, tugs at my chest, put a lump in my throat. I wish I could stay here forever. I wish *we* could.

Back at my car, I text Mom to let her know I'm heading up the coast and then stop for gas. As much as I'd prefer riding with Luca, I don't mind the drive from Santa Cruz to the Bay. It's beautiful, the way it winds up the mountain, the road hugged by towering oaks of every kind: blue oak and canyon live oak, scrub oak and coast oak.

Still, by the time I enter Contra Costa county, I'm starving, and I have to pee. There are plenty of gas stations en route, but I'm anxious to get to Walnut Creek, so I continue on. The driveway and road in front of Dom and Marissa's house are packed, so I squeeze into a spot down the block.

Music blasts from inside the house. I knock loudly, but no one opens the door, so I let myself in. Marissa scurries by barefoot, balancing a tray of something—empanadas, maybe—as I come inside. "Wren, come baby! Were you ringing the doorbell? I couldn't hear—come, come—I need your help!"

The house is full of people, most of whom I've never seen before. Leaving my bag in a corner of the living room, I sneak off to freshen up a little before joining the party.

Luca meets me in the hallway as I emerge from the bathroom. His hair is loose, and he's in jeans and a button down that's rolled up to his elbows. "There you are. Mãe said she saw you, but when I looked for you, you were gone."

"Here I am," I tease, letting him tug me into his arms. Judging by the goofy grin on his face, he's started partying. "You're cute like this."

"Like what?"

"Drunk."

Scoffing, he presses me against the wall and cages me between his arms. "I'm not drunk. Yet."

I rise to my toes, pressing a kiss to his liquor-soaked mouth, and he deepens it with a soft groan, swirling his tongue into my mouth.

"Come have a shot of cachaças," he murmurs, biting the edge of my lip.

"What's—"

"You'll see." Smirking, he slides his hand into mine, he nods his head toward the back of the house. "Come on."

"I think your mom wanted me to help out," I protest, slowing as we pass the kitchen.

"You'll have plenty of time to help her later." He looks back as he pulls me along, his gaze running the length of me, pausing at all of his favorite places. "For now, I want you with me."

Luca

Wren laughs as I spin her, her long hair flying behind her like a flag fluttering in the wind. She's beautiful like this, barefoot in the grass, cheeks flushed with alcohol and happiness. She doesn't realize that half of my family is watching. They've never seen me like this with a girl before.

Mãe pauses at the corner of the group, chatting with Phoebe. She's looking at us, though, her eyes sparkling with joy. I can't deal with all that, so I tuck Wren close and dance her over to another spot, close to where the wildflowers start. The sun's setting over them now, casting the sky a ruddy gold.

The music changes, shifting from the rowdy samba Uncle Otavio was blasting to a lo-fi, low-key hip-hop track. Different vibe altogether, in a good way. I pull Wren closer, draping her arms over my shoulders as I wrap mine around her body. My cousin Bento winks at me as he joins the rest of our cousins and brothers, raising his bottle of beer to me in a salute. I return the gesture with my own bottle, giving him a warning glare when his eyes start to drift south to Wren's ass.

"I'm having so much fun," she says suddenly, her mouth at my ear. The sensation of her soft lips and warm breath goes straight to my dick. We've been dancing and hanging out with my family for hours, long enough for that little dress she's wearing to have inspired a couple of fantasies. "I love your family."

"I think they love you, too." I hug her tight, chuckling. "I'm glad you're having fun."

She sighs, leaning on me as we relax into a lazy sway. How the fuck am I supposed to ask her for a break when things between us feel like this? I don't even know how I'm going to leave for Brazil at this rate. Thankfully she'll be leaving, too. Otherwise I'd be having second thoughts about all of it.

My father knows this—he doesn't miss a thing. Wren was outside earlier, letting Mãe show her off to all my nosy aunts and cousins, when he ambushed me in the kitchen.

"Ela é bonita, Luca. Really beautiful," he said, leaning against the counter.

Cracking my beer open, I followed his gaze, out the big windows to the yard, to where my great aunt Linda was patting Wren's cheek. "You must think so, because you keep saying that."

"Beautiful women have a way of complicating things, you know?"

"That why you single?" I snarked, taking a long sip.

"Watch it, you little fucker." He chuckled, shaking his head. "I'm just reminding you not to lose sight of what's important. Set yourself up first, then focus on relationships. She'll be around if she's the right one."

Someone bumps into me and Wren, pulling me back. I blink, looking around. Bento's music switch didn't last long; we're deep into the bossa nova now, and the yard is full of dancing couples.

"You wanna take a break?" I ask Wren, mood dampened by thoughts of Pai's words.

She nods, pushing her hair back. "I could use some water."

We weave through the crowd, stopped every few minutes by increasingly drunk well-wishers, and into the house, which isn't much quieter. Grabbing bottles of water from the fridge, I lead Wren to my old bedroom. It's a guest room these days.

I lock the door and sit on the edge of the bed, watching Wren wander around, looking at the paintings on the walls. The house is filled with art; Mãe's been collecting it for years. Some she bought at art galleries, others she found discarded on curbsides.

But Wren's ass in that dress is the real work of art. I pull her to stand between my thighs as she passes by, kissing the soft skin between her breasts. "Finally."

She laughs quietly, setting her bottle of water down so she can bury her hands in my hair. "It's been a long day, right?"

"It has been, but there are a few things left on my to-do list." I slide my hands up her thighs and under her dress, squeezing. She releases a shaky breath, her nails scratching lazily at my scalp, and I know she wants this as much as I do.

"I might have to head out soon, you know," she says quietly. "I don't want to be out on the road too late."

350

"Too late? What are you, eighty?" I tease, pressing another kiss to her chest.

She snorts, flicking my ear. "You're in a feisty mood."

"Stay here with me. We'll head back down in the morning...I'll follow you."

"I don't know how I feel about staying in your mother's house with you, Luca." She pauses. "Don't you have family staying here?"

"They're all staying in hotels. Mãe couldn't let some stay and not others—you know that would cause drama." I can feel Wren's eyes on me, so I look up into them. The soft, yellow lamplight glows behind her head, giving her a halo. Wren *Angelos*, indeed. "Just stay. Don't worry about my mom; she'll understand. She knows we only have a couple days left before I go."

Wren runs her hand down my cheek before curving over to kiss me. "Don't remind me."

Wrapping my arms around her waist, I gently pull her down onto the bed and kiss her the way I've wanted to all damn day, filling her mouth with my tongue, filling my mouth with her taste. She moans as I roll on to her, wrapping her legs around me. The sound goes right to my dick. I want her.

It goes to my heart, though, too, because I love her.

I pull back, looking down at her. "I'll miss you."

"I'll miss you, too," she echoes, eyes wet. And then she closes them, pulls my face back to hers, and kisses me over and over. "So much."

I sweep my tongue through that sweet mouth, knowing I've never felt like this about anyone. I can't explain it. But whatever it is, I need it now. All of it. All of her. I push into the cradle of her hips, high off the way she makes me feel. Her hands in my hair, her nails tickling down the back of my neck. Everything fades: the music, the voices from outside.

She runs her hands up and down the bare skin of my back, edging my shirt up. Pulling away, I sit up and unbutton it, my eyes never leaving her. "Take off your dress."

Smiling a little, she does, yanking it up over her head and tossing it aside. She's in white underneath: skimpy, white panties and a soft, sheer bra I can see right through. I've barely gotten it off before one nipple is in my mouth and the other is in my hand.

Moaning, she arches beneath me. I slide over to the breast I've been fondling, sucking it into my mouth. Reaching down, I push her panties aside and slip my fingers inside, finding her hot and wet. And that's it. There's no more rational thought. Just feeling. The rest of our clothing comes off and then there's nothing but warm skin. Wet skin. My hard to her soft.

Her hands wrapping around me, my fingers exploring her.

She cries out, her eyes wild and then closed and then burning into me as she pulls me closer, pulling me into her.

"Is this okay?" I half-beg, wanting inside so badly it feels like I might actually die if she says no.

"Yes," she pleads, her legs tightening around me, closing in so that there's nowhere else for me to go but inside.

"Are you sure?"

"Yes—"

And it's heaven. Pure heaven. Wren and I have been sleeping together for months now, but we've never gone bare like this. We've talked about it, but nothing prepared me for how good it actually is.

Warm waves of pleasure ripple through me. It's almost unbearable. *"Fuck."*

She's so beautiful. Inside and out. Literally. Figuratively. I'm lost in how good she feels, how good she looks beneath me. Fuck, I love her. I should tell her, but somewhere in the recesses of my more logical brain I know I shouldn't tell her while we're having sex.

She whispers my name, tightening around me, and damn.

"You're gonna make me come." I laugh, shivering as she scratches at my back.

Her lips part, and she smiles this sexy little smile. "Don't hold back."

I do, though. I ease up a little. I want this to last, but it's hard when she keeps digging her heels into my ass like she wants me to slam into her.

"I mean it…don't hold back," she whispers, bucking her hips. "I'm so close, Luca…"

That's it. I can't resist. Flattening my body over hers, I rock my hips in sharp little circles, knowing what I need to do to push her over the edge. It's so much more intense like this, with nothing between us. I thrust into her over and over until she gasps and cries out so loudly that I kiss her to quiet her.

She clenches rhythmically around me, pulling me along with her as she falls.

* * *

Mãe raises an eyebrow when we rejoin the family out in the yard. It's only been an hour or so, and most of them are too drunk to notice, but that woman doesn't miss a thing.

I would have been happy to stay in bed wrapped around Wren, but it would've been rude. Some of these people flew in from other states to celebrate my graduation. Still, it's late, and before long, the aunts and uncles and cousins begin to peel off and head out for their hotels and Airbnbs, loaded down with tin-foiled plates of food and slices of Tia Sophia's Brigadeiro cake.

My father, Nico and Phoebe stick around to help clean up. I'm saying goodbye to my father when Wren wanders outside. She's got my hoodie on. It's so big it nearly covers her dress.

"Ah, there she is. Goodbye, Wren. Hopefully this isn't the last time we meet," Pai says.

She smiles, coming closer, hands clasped. "Maybe I'll come out to São Paulo one day. You can show me around."

He gives her one of his charm-infused grins and takes her hands in his. "I would love nothing more; it's a spectacular city. Perhaps Luca could have you visit."

"What time's your flight, Pai?" I ask, hoping he doesn't kiss her hand or anything equally over-the-top.

Thankfully, he doesn't. "Noon. I'm dropping the rental off right at the airport."

Nodding, I clap his back. "Okay. I'll see you soon, then."

He gives me a quick hug. "Have a wonderful night, Wren. It was a pleasure to meet you."

"Your dad is…nicer than I thought he'd be," Wren admits as we walk back inside through the garage.

"He has a soft spot for women," I say. "But that's about it."

"He loves you," she says softly.

I wonder what she'd say if she knew what he'd said about putting her behind my career. But I'm tired, and I don't want to think about that. All I want is to crawl into bed with Wren and fall asleep with her next to me.

"I know he does."

* * *

I come back to the room with two forks and an enormous hunk of cake.

"Oh, my God." Wren sits up with a giggle. "That cake was crazy good."

"The best." I kick the door shut, pausing to lock it. The last thing I need

355

is Daniel strolling in while we're messing around. "You haven't been to a Brazilian birthday party till you've had this."

"Chocolate cake?"

"Brigadeiro cake." I slide into bed with her, balancing the plate as she takes a fork. We eat in appreciative silence for a while.

"So, you did it," says Wren, placing her fork down. She licks a crumb from her lip. "You graduated. You never have to go back to school again, unless you want to."

Nodding, I put the plate aside and lie back. "I know. It's surreal. You were probably right when you said it would be different this time, going to Brazil."

"How so?"

"It'll be more like a job, less like an internship." I clasp my hands behind my head, staring at the ceiling. "It feels more...real."

When Wren doesn't say anything, I look at her. She pulls at the blanket, kneading the thick fabric between her fingertips. "It is real."

"Hey." I wrap my fingers around her wrist, shaking her a little. "Just a few months, right? You know I'll be back. I have a return ticket, Wren. I'm not staying over there."

She nods, smiling a little. "I know."

"But I have been thinking a lot about something. About us."

"What about us?"

My stomach turns over. Gorging myself on all that cake right before having this discussion wasn't the best idea. "You're gonna be gone with your dad, traveling all over the world. And I'll be in São Paulo, working like a dog. Pai doesn't fuck around."

She nods, her eyes intent on mine.

"I think maybe we should take it easy while we're apart."

Wren stares at me. "What do you mean?"

Taking a deep breath, I grab her hand. "You've wanted to travel for your whole life. I want you to do it, do it all, and have fun without having to worry about me."

"Why would I worry? You have some gorgeous Brazilian girl waiting for you over there?" She laughs, but it's forced. I wonder if she's thought about that, if what I'm saying to her plays into some fear she's had.

"Only girl for me is right here." I chuff softly, tapping her knee. "I'm just saying, let's take it easy. Have fun. Things can get complicated when they go long-distance, trust me, so let's make it easier on ourselves."

But she shakes her head. "I don't want easy. I want you."

"Wren…" I sit up. "Things get crazy on the road. What if you, I don't know, meet someone else?"

She blanches. "Is that what you think I'm about? I'm traveling with my dad, Luca!"

It won't just be her dad, but my stomach turns at the stricken look on her face. Deep down I knew she'd be upset. I wish I could make her understand that I'm doing this for us, to make things easier. Simplified. No attachments. No pressure. "I'm just saying I know what it's like trying to maintain a relationship across the miles. It's easier said than done."

"Hey, if you want to be free of this," she says, a small tremble in her voice as she tips my face toward hers, "then just tell me now. But don't act like it's for me."

I shake my head, touching her cheek. "I don't want to be free of you at all. But I know what happens when people spend a lot of time apart. This, right here? This feeling? It becomes hard to remember. It was even hard for my parents."

"What the fuck, Luca?" Her eyes fill with tears. "Why does it sound like you're breaking up with me?"

"I'm not." I pull her onto me, holding her body close to mine. "I just want you to be free to have fun and do whatever you want this summer. Send me postcards and then—"

"What, we can reevaluate how we feel when you get home?"

"Look, the last time I had a girlfriend, I left her too long and she cheated on me. I'm not going to let that happen again, okay? What we have now is too good. Too pure."

"I'm not Brooke."

"I know you're not." I rub my hand over my face. "I just don't want anyone to get hurt."

"I'd never hurt you," she says, even as her face tells me that I'm hurting her.

When she starts to cry, I kiss her. I kiss her until she kisses me back, her nails digging into me like she won't ever let me go. It's hard to put into words how I feel about this girl, how I love her so much that I *will* let her go. She lets me love her again, hard and fast like we're trying to climb into each other. It's not supposed to feel like goodbye, but maybe it is, because when I wake up in the morning, she's already gone.

Wren

Summer

Luca: *You're really not going to say goodbye to me?*

I set my phone down, blinking back tears. It's the third text I've gotten from Luca in the past hour. I don't know what to say to him.

"Is that him again?" Mom pauses, a slice of vegan pizza midway between her mouth and the plate.

Nodding, I push my leftover cauliflower crust aside and sink into the couch.

She wraps her hair into a knot, then lets it fall loose again. "I don't get that boy."

"Me, neither."

My stomach hurts. From Luca, not the pizza. He's never seemed like the type to play with my feelings, but this is confusing. If he doesn't want us to be committed to each other while we're traveling, why bother being together now? I just don't understand him.

Maybe my mother was right, after all. Maybe men really are flaky and rarely stick around. The only time Luca ever actually called me his girlfriend was in another language, so maybe that's a sign.

She presses play and our movie resumes. Two seconds later, my phone rings.

"Go talk to him. Now," she commands, pointing the remote. "He's obviously desperate."

Sighing, I peel myself off the couch and take the phone to my old bedroom. I'm back at Mom's apartment now that it's summer. Back in the time warp.

"Hi," I answer, catching the call before it goes to voicemail.

"Hey." Luca clears his throat. "I thought you weren't gonna pick up."

I toe the open suitcase sprawled on the floor, half-filled with new summer clothes. "I thought about it."

"Can you come outside?"

My heart leaps, but not in the carefree way it used to. It feels more like it leapt to its death. "You're here? Luca, why?"

"Because you left the other day without saying anything and you won't text me back. I'm leaving tomorrow, and I won't see you for almost three months."

That's not my fault, but I'd be lying if I said I didn't want to see him. My stupid heart's been crying for him for days. I catch a glimpse of myself in Mom's gilded mirror as I pass it on my way out. Messy ponytail, old t-shirt, older jeans. I look like shit.

Luca's downstairs, leaning against his car like an 80's movie heartthrob. He looks like shit too, which is somewhat gratifying.

I hesitate in front of him, arms folded, but he reaches out and pulls me close. We stare at each other for a moment and then he kisses me, sliding his hands into my hair. I grab his wrists, but I don't pull away. I feel like an alcoholic who's been dry for days being given a drink.

"It doesn't have to be like this," he murmurs, tucking my head beneath his chin.

"No, it doesn't. We could just stay together."

"What's the point of being together if we're not in the same place?"

"What's the point of breaking up if we're just going to get back together?" I frown at him, shaking my head. "I feel like I'm paying for someone else's sins, Luca."

"Maybe you are." Pain glimmers in his eyes. "And maybe it's not fair to ask you to wait for me while I get my shit together. But I can't be in Brazil for three months wondering what you're doing and who you're with."

"You know who I'll be with," I say flatly. "My dad."

"And that photographer guy..."

"Amias Jon?" My mouth drops open. "Are you for real? He's old, Luca!"

362

"Not that old."

Disgusted, I try to shove away from him, but he won't let go of me. "You're crazier than I thought if you think anything would ever happen with him."

He closes his eyes for a long time before opening them again. "I just want you to have fun, okay? Can you do that for me? Do all the things you dreamed about doing. And maybe, when I get back, you can tell me about it."

"You know, Luca, it doesn't matter to me that we'll be miles apart because having you transcends that." I push on him, and this time he lets me go. I can't touch him anymore. It hurts too much. "If you do this, if you want to pretend that we're just friends or whatever, I can't promise you how I'll feel when I get back. But I know how I feel now. I love you. I've loved you for a while, and I love you enough to stay faithful to you. And if that's not enough for you, then I have nothing else."

I walk away, my eyes burning as the wind blows tears across my cheeks. I can't keep arguing with someone who's convinced they're doing the right thing.

To her credit, my mother doesn't offer any of her usual man-hating advice. She lets me cry alone in my room, bringing me tea when it starts to get late.

When I wake up around three a.m. to use the bathroom, I hear her in the living room, speaking in hushed tones on the phone. Interestingly, this isn't the first time. Curiosity piqued despite my half-awake state, I lean against the wall separating the hall from the living room and listen in. Does she have a new man or something?

But then she says something about me. And New York. And when I hear her whisper Arlo's name, something in me calms. My mom's talking to my dad.

* * *

"You don't have to come in," I say, chewing nervously at my thumbnail as we approach San Jose International. "Parking's expensive."

"Screw the parking, little bird. You'll be gone a while," Mom says. "Let me at least help you get your bags checked."

I nod, secretly glad. I've never been on a plane. Shoot, the only time I've ever been out of state was when we went to Las Vegas with Gramma Kate and her best friend Maureen. I was ten.

"You have your passport, right?" Mom asks, for about the thirtieth time. Sometimes the item in question varies: passport, toothbrush, debit card, phone charger.

"Yup." I pat my purse. "Got it all." But I check again, just in case. Arlo and I will be in Manhattan for about four days before we fly down to Mexico, so I suppose Mom could overnight my passport if I did forget it. But no, it's right where it should be, nestled securely between my insurance card and a wad of cash Mom gave me on our way to the airport.

"Plastic's good, but paper's essential," she'd said, pressing the crisp stack of ATM twenties into my hand.

We park in the deck and make our way into the busy terminal. My stomach's full of butterflies, which I both love and hate. Mom steers me over to the

364

ticketing counter, where we get in line. After the couple ahead of us goes, it's my turn.

"Go ahead," Mom says, pushing me a little. "You'll figure it out."

Swallowing, heart bumping along, I drag my suitcases to the counter and smile at the immaculately coiffed blonde. "Hi."

Once I've bumbled my way through that, and my bags are safely—I hope—on their way to the plane, I return to Mom with my boarding pass.

She smiles, lower lip trembling. "Well, this is it. I can't go with you…they stopped all that after 9/11."

"Stopped what?"

"You used to be able to go to the gate and wait with people."

"Oh." I nod. I guess I'll see what she means when I get there. "Okay. Well, bye. I love you, Mom."

"I love you, too. So much. I'm so glad you're doing this." She squeezes me in a hug, briskly rubbing my back. "You're gonna have a ball. You and Arlo."

I grin, keeping their late-night phone calls to myself. I like that they have a thing. A secret thing. Or whatever. "Yeah. We will."

"I want you to have fun. Don't worry about…" She falters, probably tripping over Luca's name. "Anything. This is about you and your dad. You deserve this in so many ways, baby. I'm so proud of you."

"For what?" I giggle at her emotional display. "For accepting the trip of a lifetime?"

"For being brave and putting yourself out there. For finding your dad and letting him find you. And for telling that silly boy how you felt even if he can't find his ass from his elbow. Things don't always work out the way we want them to, but don't let that stop you from trying, Wren. Ever. When you were little, you were so much like me. You even copied the way I spoke. But you've changed as you've gotten older. You think with your heart, and that's powerful. Don't lose that."

She's rambling, but I think I understand. This is her way of telling me not to be so emotionally closed off. Like her.

Now I hug her, kissing her cheek. "Thanks, Mom."

"Now, go on. Be careful. Keep your bag close! Don't leave it anywhere…"

"All right, all right."

"Love you, little bird!"

I glance back over my shoulder to wave one last time. "Love you, too!"

Locating the sign directing me to my gate, I join the river of people pouring through security and then the rest of the terminal, going deeper and deeper inside until I find my gate. I have about forty minutes until my flight takes off, so I grab a granola bar from my backpack and have a seat.

My butt vibrates; I'm sitting on my phone. Wrestling it from my pocket, I find a notification from Venmo. I stare in disbelief. Marissa—Luca's mom—just sent me $200 for my travels. I'm not even sure how she got my Venmo details. From Luca, probably.

A lump forms in my throat. I don't know what to think. I'm grateful, obviously, and touched that she would do this, but I'm trying not to think about Luca or his family too much right now. I adore them, but that's part of the problem. The part of me that was raised to always write thank you notes wants to respond immediately, thanking Marissa, but I don't have her contact info and I can't bring myself to ask Luca for it. We haven't spoken in nearly a week, since the night before he left for São Paulo.

He texted me that night, late, asking me not to give up on him. To try to understand. I asked him to give me some space because he was confusing me.

I love him. I'm *in love* with him. I don't know how to be his friend.

I catch a flash from the corner of my eye and look up in time to see a plane as it soars into the sky, the sun glinting off its sleek, metallic body. It seems impossible that flying even exists, but in about a half an hour, that'll be me.

* * *

Arlo's waiting for me in baggage claim with a smile and a sign that says *Wren Angelos*.

I practically run toward him, relieved.

"Welcome to New York, little bird," he says, hugging me. My mother really is rubbing off on him.

New York City is even more grand than in the movies. I gape at everything as we pass by in our Uber: the frenetic crowds, the glowing lights, the jaw-droppingly tall skyscrapers. I've heard that you can always tell who the tourists are in NYC because they're the ones staring up. Well, that's me.

Arlo talks a mile a minute—I swear to God, his accent is even stronger here. We stop at his apartment in the West Village so I can drop off my luggage, where I'm met by the exuberant barking of Melvin, Arlo's little black and white rescue mutt. Pamplemousse, a regal marmalade cat, watches the spectacle from the windowsill.

"Are you in the mood for some real New York pizza or would you prefer Thai food? Two of my favorite joints are within a block of here," he offers as we jog down the steps.

"Pizza, for sure."

And, of course, we stop at a bakery for macarons after.

"We'll come back for chocolate croissants in the morning," he promises as we hurry across a crosswalk. "They make 'em fresh every day."

By the time I collapse that night on a pull-out in the living room, I'm so exhausted I can barely move. My mind whirs with memories of the day—taking off for the first time, watching the ground below us drop away, turbulence in clouds, landing, Arlo. Bridges and people and lights and traffic and Arlo's nonstop narration of the city he loves.

He pauses beside the bed before sitting on the edge of it, his hand resting on my back. "Are you comfortable? I can move her, if you want."

He means Pamplemousse, who's curled and purring against me. We've been cuddling since I lay down, like she knows I need it. "S'perfect," I mumble, smiling sleepily. "Thanks."

"Good." He smiles, nodding. "So, ah, Lily told me you and Luca are taking a break or something?"

The unexpected mention brings a hot round of tears. I close my eyes, shrugging. "I don't know."

"I know it's kinda late now, but if you wanna talk about it, I'm all ears. Anytime. Okay?" he says. "I know how guys think."

"Okay." I give him a little smile. "Thanks."

"Sure thing." He ruffles my hair and stands, stretching. "Get some sleep."

Luca

ooo

Shutting my laptop, I rise from my desk and glance over at Nathalia. "I'm heading out for lunch."

"Hold on, I'll come with you," she says, distracted by whatever's on her screen. She's got seniority, so her desk is right by the window.

Sighing inwardly, I slide my wallet into my pocket. I shouldn't have said anything. In the past, I always enjoyed taking lunch with my coworkers, but lately I've preferred going solo. I'm always around people these days—I share an office, albeit a big one—and sometimes I just need time to think.

Wren and I haven't spoken since she landed in New York last week. She messaged me the night she got in, asking for Mãe's number.

So I can thank her, she'd said.

Mãe had wanted to send "a little something" to celebrate Wren's first time going overseas. She didn't say anything, but I could tell she was beyond disappointed by my decision to cool things off with Wren for the summer. In retrospect, that was probably one of the first indications I'd fucked up—Mãe's silence. She never, ever passes up on an opportunity to share her opinion, so it's a little ominous she held back this time.

Anyway, I gave Wren the number, then told her I missed her. Which was painfully true. Still, I don't know why I said it, other than I was a few drinks in, and it was late, and my filter had evaporated in the vulnerability of being alone in a foreign country.

It's not like I have to be alone here. My coworkers, many of whom I've come to know well over the years, always invite me out for drinks or dinner. Former classmates from my time at UFSC are scattered all over Brazil—I could spend next weekend at my friend Martim's villa down in Florianópolis if I really wanted to.

But I meant it when I told Wren that São Paulo would be a cycle of work, eat, sleep, and repeat. I'm not here for fun this time.

Which is good, because I'm definitely not having fun.

Wren said she missed me too, and then quickly typed that she had to go, cutting the conversation short. I don't know that I would've continued it, anyway. She said, before I left, that she needed space so I'm trying to give it to her.

After all, by telling her I didn't want to be in a relationship over the summer, wasn't I telling her I wanted space too? Thing is, I don't want space. I want to keep the relationship on ice: perfectly preserved. No infidelity or long-distance drama to push it past its expiration date.

"Ready?" Nathalia asks in her husky voice, smiling over at me.

"Sure." Giving her a brief smile, I nod for her to go on ahead of me. With her bronze skin, long, dark hair and full mouth, she's a real Brazilian beauty. The first time I met her, years ago, she was engaged, and I had a little crush on her. I was fresh out of high school, and she was this super-hot, very unattainable older woman.

She's single these days, but we're just friends. Even if I was still attracted to her, which I'm not, Wren's all I can think about.

Heading down the elegant, dark-paneled halls of Veritas we pass several other offices before arriving at the front desk, where Agueda, the secretary, is busily jotting notes while on the phone. Nathalia and I take the elevator down to the lobby and leave the air-conditioned tranquility for the midday bustle of Paulista Avenue. Veritas couldn't be in a more exclusive location—Avenida Paulista is the economic, financial, and cultural heart of São Paulo.

"You okay?" Nathalia slicks on a coat of deep red lipstick, never breaking stride. I don't see the point of this, as we're about to eat. Brooke used to do that, too. "You look tired."

"I'm fine."

"No, I don't think so." She chuckles. "I think you are either hungover or maybe *coração partido*." *Heartbroken*. When I don't reply, she glances at me, eyebrows raised. "Maybe both."

"Maybe," I agree, stopping at the crosswalk. There's a Japanese restaurant I like another block up. It feels good to be outside, walking the tree-lined sidewalks. I spend too much time indoors these days.

Another indicator I could never live this life long-term.

"Who is she?" Nathalia presses as we begin walking again. "Come on, Luca. I've never seen you so…what's the word…dramatic before. So sad."

Now I chuckle, pushing a stray lock of hair back. Pai requested I cut it for the summer, but I wouldn't, so it stays back in a bun. "Dramatic and sad, huh?"

She smacks my arm. "Stop it; you know what I mean."

"I didn't really want to come this summer—"

"Luca, you never want to be here. You're great at what you do, but you are so miserable doing it…I don't know why you do this to yourself!" She huffs and charges ahead, black high heels clicking loudly on the sidewalk.

I blink at her in surprise. I've always kept it professional during my internships and jobs here, whether working at Veritas or the offices of my father's colleagues. I thought I'd hidden my feelings well, but perhaps I've fooled only myself. Makes me wonder if my father senses my discontent, too.

Nathalia reaches the restaurant ahead of me, so I hurry to open the door for her. Inside, the hostess smiles and seats us at the bar along with dozens of other professionals schmoozing over lunch.

"Her name's Wren," I admit, when it seems as though Nathalia has decided to wait me out by staying quiet.

Her bright red lips quirk into a knowing smile. "I knew it. Did she leave you?"

"No." I shake my head. "I sort of left her."

Nathalia's smile falls, and she frowns. "What do you mean, 'sort of'? Please don't tell me you're one of these fuckboy types, Luca. That would break my heart."

I laugh at the disgusted way she says *fuckboy*, rubbing my hands over my face. "I'm not. It's kind of a long story."

"Well then give it to me fast," she says crisply as the bartender comes to take our order. "Your father doesn't like it when we're late."

So, I do. I offer up the cliff notes version of how Wren and I met, dated, and ultimately split before going our separate ways this summer. Nathalia listens intently, eating her sushi with gusto, until I get to the end.

"Typical," she says with a sigh, dabbing at her mouth with a napkin.

"What?" I ask warily, chewing.

"Every time men get hurt, they carry it around for the rest of their lives, like a wound that won't stop bleeding. I mean, come on, Luca. Your ex-girlfriend cheated on you—so what? Men cheat too, you know. Your father, my ex…" She scoffs. "It sounds like you have a good thing with this new girl, but you are not being fair to her. If you can't trust her while the two of you are apart, then you can't trust her when you're together."

It's a different version of what Wren said to me on my last night in Santa Cruz, and while I know in my heart that it's true, it's a hard pill to swallow.

"If she doesn't want to get back together with you when you go home, I don't blame her," she continues.

"Okay, okay, Nathalia. Way to kick a man when he's down." I glance at my watch. We have to be back at Veritas in ten minutes. Polishing off the rest

374

of my sashimi, I slap my card onto the counter and wait for the bartender to pass by again. "Lunch is on me."

"Oh no. My advice is free." She puts her own card beside mine, and the bartender snatches the two of them up at the same time.

"You didn't tell me anything I don't already know," I mutter.

Nathalia slicks on some more lipstick. "Then it's worse than I thought."

"What?"

"You're gorgeous, but stupid."

"Are you always this verbally abusive?"

"Only with people I care about." She cups my cheek. "What's that saying? Stupid is as stupid does? Luca, mas tens de perceber que merdá é esta." *You've got to figure this shit out.*

Nathalia chats about our work project on the way back to the office, but my mind is on Wren. If splitting up with her was the right thing to do, I wouldn't feel stuck. But I am stuck, my brain circling the situation like a problem that needs solving. It's so obvious now: if I can't trust her just because we're apart, then I can't trust her at all.

But that's the thing. I do trust her.

I pause outside our building, motioning for Nathalia to go up without me. I have a couple of calls to make.

Wren

❧

Mexico City is first. It's one of Arlo's favorite places on earth because of the architecture.

He's been here a million times, but I've seen nothing like it, except for maybe in movies. He brought two extra cameras from New York—one that takes real film and a DSLR for me to use. This is a big deal—besides my phone, I've never had a camera of my own.

It's fun being mentored by someone as passionate as Arlo Janvier.

We start with the Zócalo—a big main square also known as the Plaza de la Constitución—and explore the Templo Mayor, a famous 13th-century Aztec temple. We take turns posing in front of Diego Rivera's murals at the Palacio Nacional and we eat our weight in tacos sudados and tamales and chicharrónes. I develop a cavity-inducing craving for the decadently sweet frutas en tacha, sweet potatoes in a brown sugar syrup.

Amias Jon meets us on our third day. He's handsome all right, a moody character with guyliner around his dark eyes and messy black hair. He's more sarcastic than I anticipated, and maybe a little conceited. But his respect and admiration for Arlo are obvious, and the two of them regale me with stories of past trips and photoshoots they've worked on over the years. I can see my dad's proud of him. We have dinner at a posh spot in the city that night, and the next morning Arlo and I tag along while Amias works his magic at a fancy fashion photo shoot at Chapultepec Castle.

I keep thinking about how Luca was afraid I'd be seduced by this guy, and I don't know whether I want to laugh or cry about it.

Next is San Miguel de Allende, another architectural hotspot for Arlo. It's like stepping back in time, with its cobblestoned streets and dramatic, towering churches.

"Luca would like it here," I muse once, listening to Arlo monologue dreamily about the particulars of Parroquia de San Miguel Arcángel, a neo-Gothic church famous for its pink towers. "He's really into architecture, too."

Arlo pauses, cocking his head. "Have you spoken to him lately?"

I shake my head.

"You should send him a postcard or two," he suggests thoughtfully. "That's your thing, isn't it? Postcards?" He wanders off to photograph a lizard perched on a nearby wall.

I can't believe he remembers that.

I squint at the church's towers, bringing my camera up to snatch a couple of shots. My confusion and anger at Luca melted into something softer and sadder now. I think about him all the time, which seems ironic seeing that he wanted me to focus on my travels and *not* him.

He thought about me when he was traveling a few summers ago, didn't he? We weren't together then, hardly even knew each other, but he'd remembered our conversation and bought me postcards.

I find a tiny souvenir shop and buy a postcard of the church for Luca.

Arlo settles beside me on a bench, resting his hands on his knees. "Are you ready to talk about it?"

"He didn't want me to cheat on him, so he broke up with me before I could."

He frowns. "What?"

"Luca's been traveling to Brazil every summer for years to work at his dad's software company."

"Right." Arlo nods. "I think I remember him talking about that."

"He was with this girl for a year or two, and it turned out that she was cheating on him, especially when he left town," I say. "With his best friend."

"Oof. That's nasty."

I bring the camera to my eye, focusing on a man across the courtyard pushing a cart with an enormous bouquet of balloons. "He made it sound like he wanted me to just enjoy my time with you, no worries, nothing and no one to worry about, but that's bull. I mean, maybe that's a tiny part of it…a tiny, misguided part, but mostly he just doesn't trust me. And that makes me not trust him. Gramma Kate always says that suspicion haunts the guilty mind."

Arlo chuckles quietly. "Interestingly, my grand-mère used to say, 'mieux vaut prévenir que guérir.'"

"What does that mean?"

"Something to the effect of, 'an ounce of prevention is worth a pound of cure'. Like it's better to take precautions against something than have to deal with the damage afterward."

My heart sinks. "So, you think Luca's right?"

"No." He shakes his head. "I'm just pointing out that there's a saying for literally every situation and grandmothers seem to know them all."

Snorting, I smack his knee.

He grins, folding his arms as he sits back. "Did I ever tell you that Luca and I kind of kept in touch after my visit to Santa Cruz?"

Surprised, I shake my head. Luca never mentioned it, either. "No."

"Just on Instagram. He likes my photos...I like his surfing."

Something warm trickles into my hurting heart. "That's cute."

"What's cute were the pictures of him teaching you how to surf."

"We only went out on the waves a couple times, but Kellan was there one day. He took those pictures." My eyes blur with tears at the memory, and I wipe them on the back of my hand. "I never really learned. I still suck."

"It takes a while," Arlo says. "You just have to keep putting yourself out there."

We're quiet for a while. Sniffling, I look up at him. "Why do I feel like that was a metaphor?"

"Because it was. Luca got hurt and he's using that to stay where he is instead of moving forward. But I don't want that for you. Regardless of what he does, I want you to keep going. Okay? Promise me that. He doesn't define you. Whether he stays or goes doesn't define you."

Didn't Mom say something similar before I got on the plane? My face warms, and the tears I thought I'd kept at bay brim over. Arlo puts his arm around my shoulder and pulls me close.

"Your mom was partly right. Not all men stay," he says, squeezing me. "But the right ones do."

* * *

After spending four days in Belize at Arlo's friend's ecotourism resort, we hop a plane to our last destination, Costa Rica. I'm getting used to this flying thing. I have about a dozen pictures of clouds and water and landscapes, all taken from the sky.

"I know we've been roughing it with buses and taxis, but I'm going to rent a car here," Arlo says as we walk through the San Jose terminal. I find it funny that I'm once again in an airport with this name, but thousands of miles away.

"Sounds good," I say through a yawn. I'm exhausted. We spent all of yesterday sunning and snorkeling on Glover's Reef, an island in Southwest Caye, which is a coral atoll in Belize.

I'm just dozing off when Arlo lowers the volume on the radio. The reception is crackly anyway. "Are you awake?"

"Mm?" I peek at him with one eye.

"I've been wanting to get your take on something." He drums his fingers on the steering wheel.

"Okay…"

"I'm considering renting a place in Santa Cruz."

Now I'm awake. I sit up a bit, twisting in my seat so I'm facing him. "My Santa Cruz?"

He nods.

"Part-time?"

"Full-time."

"But you love New York!"

"New York's not going anywhere," he says, shrugging one shoulder. "I travel all the time, anyway. I can go back whenever I feel like it." He glances at me. "I just think I should be closer to you."

"And my mom." I waggle my eyebrows.

He cracks a grin. "And your mom. But mostly you."

"We could pet-sit whenever you go out of town," I say, warming to the idea. "Pamplemousse and Melvin wouldn't have to go to the boarders anymore."

"That's true." He nods, smiling. "And I'm sure Melvin will love the beach. I think it'll be a good thing. I've needed a change for a while."

"Mom would say the universe has brought all of this together in your favor, then." I narrow my eyes. "You guys have been discussing this, haven't you? I know you two like your late-night phone calls."

Arlo snorts. "We may have talked about it once or twice."

We spend two days in Monteverde, exploring and, of course, photographing the magical cloud forests. The Cloud Forest Reserve is actually a rainforest, but the constant mist makes it feel like we're in the clouds. I can see why it was on Arlo's must-see list for me. I probably take five photos for his every one, and he takes a lot.

And then we're back on the coast, in a cute little village called Samara.

After staying the night at a hotel that's literally on the beach, we grab breakfast and eat on the sand, watching little kids play on the shore. Kind of like home, especially when a couple of surfers jog past with boards beneath their arms. I watch them, my heart aching at who they remind me of.

"So, what's the story with this place?" I ask, tucking into my bowl of gallo pinto. It's a delicious mishmash of rice and beans, plantains, eggs, and meat.

Arlo takes a sip of water. "What do you mean?"

"Well, every place you've chosen has had some sort of significance to you so far."

"Ah." He nods, picking up his own bowl. "I've actually never been to Samara before, but it was one of the closer beaches, coming out of Monteverde. And there's a surf school here. I thought we could practice a little…waves are small. Good for beginners."

I glance back at the beach shack I noticed as we walked in earlier, colorful rows of surfboards lined up against it. "That sounds really fun."

"I thought so, too." He winks, and I grin out at the ocean, where sunlight sparkles off the waves.

After cleaning up our breakfast mess, we take a dip in the warm water. I take a few pictures with my phone and send them back to Mom and Saira, both of whom have been following our journey from across the miles. Which reminds me...

"I should probably send those postcards," I say, brushing sand from our blanket. "I need stamps."

Arlo gets to his feet, thumbs flying across his phone as he texts someone. "I'm sure the gift shop has some," he says, distracted. "I'm going to go check in at the surf school, see if anyone's available to help us out. Be right back."

I drop onto my towel and lie back, enjoying the warmth of the sun. The distant call of birds, kids laughing, and the constant push and pull of water at the shore are such familiar sounds. While this beach is nothing like the ones I grew up on, it makes me the tiniest bit homesick.

I'm glad. It's nice to know I'm going back to a place I love, a place I want to be. After so many years of feeling stuck in Santa Cruz, I've finally gotten the chance to miss it.

The sun beats down on me. Droplets of sweat form between my breasts, running down as I sit up. Shading my eyes with my hand, I peer over at the beach shack. There are a couple of people chatting near it, but no Arlo.

And then a tall, built guy in board shorts makes his way across the sand, a yellow surfboard tucked beneath each arm. My heart skips a beat. He reminds me so much of Luca.

Wait. It *is* Luca.

I freeze, gaping in disbelief as he stops in front of me. Putting the boards down, he sits beside me on the blanket with a tentative smile. "Hey, Wren."

I shake my head. "What are you doing here? Did…did Arlo put you up to this?"

"Actually, it was the other way around." He looks out at the water, sheepish. "I asked him if I could come. Begged."

I stare at his profile, hope and frustration warring within me. Luca always looks even better than I remembered. Today he's darker than he's ever been, his skin a rich golden brown that makes his eyes seem even lighter. His hair, loose today, looks lighter as well, like he's been spending a lot of time in the sun. God, he's beautiful. He was mine once. Maybe he still is.

"I fucked up, Wren." He brings his worried gaze back to me, making my heart dip crazily as our eyes meet. "I was scared and stupid, and I let all that bullshit from my past mess with me when I should've just listened to you."

"Yeah," I whisper, looking at my hands.

"I think about you all the time," he continues. "I'm so sorry. I'm sorry I hurt you, and I'm sorry I didn't trust you. That was my problem, not yours."

"You came all the way to Costa Rica to tell me that?" I exhale. "Why didn't you just text me? Or call?"

His eyes search mine. "Because I love you, and you deserve to hear it in person. And because...I didn't want to be away from you anymore."

Luca's never been loose with his words, so his declaration is the last thing I expected to hear. I swallow thickly, looking away. "You and Arlo are sneaky. I'm surprised he told you where we were."

"It wouldn't have been hard to figure out. He's been posting about your adventures on Instagram even more than you have."

A chuckle escapes me. "That's funny...he did mention that you two followed each other."

We're quiet for a moment, the breeze ruffling our hair.

"Did I fuck this up beyond repair?" he asks, his pinky touching mine on the towel between us.

Having Luca next to me again, knowing he loves me, settles me in a way I didn't know I needed. I want to push against it, rail against the notion of needing anything from him, but my heart wants what it wants. And it wants him.

"We're not beyond repair, Luca," I whisper. "It was brave of you to come."

"You're the brave one," he says. "I'm trying to catch up."

I touch his chin, thumbing the new blond on his beard. "I missed you."

"I missed you, too. Every day."

"I have postcards. In my backpack."

His eyes soften. "For me?"

I nod, and he takes my hand, lacing our fingers together. I stare at them, dazed at how something so small can feel so good. "What about your dad? The project? Are you taking a break, or something?"

"No, I'm done. I left. I told Pai I could either work remotely or he could pass on my role to someone else." He shrugs. "He was pissed, but he told me I could work remotely until this job's done."

"I can't believe you did it...you actually left!"

"Me, neither." He shakes his head, smirking. "I thought he was gonna kill me. We talked for a long time, though and I think he understands now...Veritas will never mean to me what it does to him. I love him, and I'm proud of what he's built, but it's not my dream."

"Well, *I'm* proud of *you*. It took a lot to finally stand up for yourself."

Luca leans closer, and my heart begins hammering in my chest, like when we were brand new. "So, you forgive me for being an idiot, then?"

"Do you trust me?"

"Yeah. I really do."

"Then I forgive you. Just, no more making decisions for the both of us, okay?"

He glances down at my mouth. "Okay."

We lean toward each other, meeting in a gentle kiss. The past month has been a whirlwind, the most fun I've ever had, but nothing compares to the feeling of his lips on mine. I've missed this so much.

Arlo waves from down the beach, a beer of some sort in his hand. "Guess he found you, huh?" he calls.

Shaking my head, I get to my feet. "I can't believe you two plotted this."

"It was all this kid," he says, holding his hand up. "He wouldn't let up. I just let him know where we were going to be."

Luca stands by my side, offering his hand to Arlo once he's close enough. "Thanks for letting me shoot my shot."

"What can I say? I'm a sucker for second chances." They shake, and Arlo claps his back affectionately. "Now, are you gonna teach my girl to surf, or what?"

Luca cuts me a smile, his hand sliding into mine. "If that's what she wants."

I nudge a board with my toe. "It is what I want."

"Then come on." He grabs a board, motioning for me to take the other. "Vamos, meu anjo."

Wren

One Year Later

Kellan pulls up to the curb at San Jose International airport, braking so hard we all jerk forward.

"Jeez!" yells Saira, bracing herself against the Jeep's dashboard. "You trying to kill us?"

"Gotta get these kids on their flight," he says, turning to look at Luca and me. "You need help with your bags?"

"No, we're good," Luca says, giving him a fist bump. "Five stars, Uber Driver."

I stretch forward, kissing Saira's cheek before opening my door. "Bye! I'll text you once we're there."

"You better!" She pokes her head out the window. "I want postcards, too!"

Luca's already got my stuff when I meet him outside. Giving our friends one last wave goodbye, we hurry into the airport. There's no time to waste; we have a flight to catch, and we're running behind schedule. Thankfully, neither of us is checking a bag, so we go straight to security.

It occurs to me, as I slip off my shoes and put them in a grey bin, that this is now normal for me. The first time I went to see Arlo in Manhattan, the TSA people practically had to hold my hand as I fumbled through the essentials.

Luca grins over his shoulder as he empties his pockets. That's the other thing: I might be a seasoned traveler now, but this is my first time going on a trip with Luca. He's met Arlo and me abroad a couple times—Costa Rica one summer, Paris another—but this time we're flying to Brazil together.

Because Carlos, Luca's father, is getting married.

* * *

Thanks to a couple of layovers, it takes us nearly twenty-one hours to get to São Paulo. I usually can't sleep on planes, but Luca and I both knock out during the night thanks to the edibles Kellan gave us. I get a bleary-eyed impression of the city the next morning as our taxi takes us from São Paulo-Guarulhos International Airport to the Cardosos' apartment downtown.

"Wow," I say through a yawn, gazing at the leafy, hilly streets of the famous Jardins district. "This is so pretty."

"You should see Pai's new house," Luca murmurs, leaning close as we take in the sights. "He's been sending pictures. It's a few blocks away, and it's just ridiculous."

"So, why doesn't he live in the apartment anymore?"

"Mariana wanted a pool." Luca smirks. "She likes to entertain."

Mariana is Carlos' fiancée. Apparently, the two met at a fundraiser last year and really hit it off—she's a hotshot in the corporate world, too. They've already gone ahead to Rio de Janeiro to prepare for the wedding, which takes place next week, but Luca wanted to show me around his city first.

The taxi pulls up to a classy residential building on a sun-dappled, tree-lined street. The driver jumps out to retrieve our bags from the trunk, and Luca tips him as I dawdle nearby, gawking at how nice the building is. Luca waves to the doorman, who lets us inside with a grin. "Bem vindo de volta, Sr. Cardoso."

"Obrigado, Sr. Luís," Luca says, giving him a handshake as we pass by.

I give Luís a cheesy grin and a "oi!" as I follow my boyfriend into the lobby. "These are like, luxury condos," I whisper accusingly. "You said it was an apartment!"

"Same thing," says Luca, shrugging as we wait for the elevator.

"No, an apartment is what Mom has in Santa Cruz."

"Semantics, bebê." He kisses my nose as the elevator doors open with a ding. "Come on, let's go."

Carlos' apartment/condo is fancy but also lived in, full of family photos and comfy furniture. It's also pretty spacious, with an open floor plan and large windows letting in soft beams of sunlight.

"I don't know about you, but I'm starving," Luca says, dropping his bags on the floor.

"Me too. Should we order something?"

"Nah, Pai always makes sure the fridge is full when I come. He probably had the housekeeper stop by."

Sure enough, there's enough food to feed a small village. After a breakfast of fresh papaya and pao de queijo—cheese bread—we take showers and fall into bed.

"Just a quick nap," I mumble into the pillow as Luca rains kisses over my neck and shoulder. "Then I'll be good to go."

* * *

Despite his romantic overtures before I passed out, Luca's still asleep when I wake up hours later. I'd be dismayed that we slept for so long, but it couldn't be helped. We were beyond exhausted. Stretching, I roll out of bed and pad over to the bedroom window, which looks out over a canopy of thick, green trees and terracotta-colored roofs. Winter in Brazil is warm and sunny, and a balmy breeze ruffles the leaves outside.

I've just finished making coffee in the kitchen when Luca emerges, yawning. "I came to help you, but I see you know what you're doing," he says, eyeing the two steaming cups.

"Pretty much. My grandmother has a French press, so she taught me how to use one when I was younger."

"You want milk? We usually drink it without here."

"Just sugar, then."

Luca gets sugar from the cabinet and fixes our coffee up before coming to stand beside me at the counter. "We slept the day away, but we can still go out on the town. There are a lot of great bars right in the neighborhood."

"I'd love that," I say, although I'd also love continuing what he tried to start earlier. Turning from Luca's yummy bare chest, I poke around the fridge. "Is there any more of that cheese bread?"

"Pao de queijo." Luca corrects me, smacking my butt. "You're in Brazil now, querida."

"You're right." My cheeks warm, more from his pet name than anything, and I close the fridge. "I use Google translate sometimes…I should use it more."

"Or just use me," he says, hoisting me up onto the counter.

I wrap my legs around his hips and my arms around his neck. He cut his hair right before our trip, and it's shorter than I've ever seen it, falling just below his ears. Leaning closer, I press a kiss to those ears, gratified when he shivers a little. "How do you say, 'you're so beautiful'?"

I feel, rather than see, him smile. "If you're saying it to me, it's você é tão bonito."

"Você é tão bonito," I echo slowly, pulling back so I can look at him when I say it.

Luca's eyes search mine for a moment, and then he kisses me. We make out for a while, long, lingering kisses that go on and on as the afternoon light folds in around us.

"This is surreal," he says, lifting my tank top up over my head. He kisses my chest, brushing his lips over the tips of my breasts. "I thought about you all the time the last time I was here."

Now I'm the one shivering, threading my fingers through his silky, dark hair. "What did you think about, exactly?"

He smiles, naughty. "I'm sure you can guess."

"Tell me." We kiss again, pressing our chests together, skin to skin. I run my hands over his bare back, feeling his goosebumps raise beneath my fingertips. Luca tugs on my sleep shorts as I lift my hips off the counter, and then my panties too. My heart skips a beat as he gently pushes me down so that I'm lying flat on the counter.

He kisses my stomach and each of my hipbones before opening me with his hands and licking me so deeply that I arch up. Startled, I giggle, my hands pressed over my mouth. But then he does it again and again, and any urge to laugh dissolves with the need to come. When I do, he yanks me off of the counter and turns me around, bending me over it. "I thought about this," he says quietly, dipping his fingers into me. Widening my stance, he enters me with one deep thrust.

I gasp, tightening around him, my pussy still fluttering from my orgasm. *Wow.*

"Fuck," he whispers, gripping my hips, and that's just what he does.

When he comes inside me minutes later, he leans over, sweeping my hair aside and kissing the back of my neck. His heart races against my back. "Eu quero estar com você para sempre."

"What does that mean?"

He bites my ear. "Use Google translate."

Luca

~⚬ЭꙖꙎ⚬~

The next few days are a whirlwind as I try to show Wren all of my favorite places: Skye, a stunning rooftop bar and restaurant that overlooks the city, Ibirapuera Park, Jardim Bôtanico de Sâo Paulo, and Sé—an exquisite neo-Gothic cathedral that I love for its architecture.

Sâo Paulo is filled with art, and thankfully Wren likes that kind of stuff as much as I do. We check out the murals at Beco de Batman (Batman Alley) one day and several art museums another. On our last day, I take her down Avenida Paulista so we can people-watch, explore the shops and cafes. Pai's company, Veritas, is closed for the wedding, but I have the keys, so I let us in to show her around.

Friday afternoon finds us back at the airport, where we catch a quick flight to Rio de Janeiro.

We take a taxi to the Belmond Copacabana Palace, an iconic five-star hotel near the beach. Wren wiggles next to me, her excitement plain.

"Okay, I've seen some nice hotels with Arlo, but this one really takes the cake!"

"Pai loves to be extravagant," I say with a laugh. "Nothing but the best, especially for his wedding."

"Lucaaaa!"

I turn toward the familiar voice, grinning at my brother as he makes his way across the lobby. "Nicoooo!"

Grinning, he catches up to us, hugging me and kissing Wren's cheek. "You guys just get here?"

"Yeah…haven't even checked in yet. Where's the fam?"

"Phoebe took Delia to the spa. Manny and Jay are with the cousins."

I look at Wren. "The cousins could mean five kids, or it could mean thirty-five."

Nico snorts, nodding. "He's not joking, Wren. Pai has two brothers and three sisters, and they all have a ton of kids."

Wren beams, eyes shining. "I can't wait to meet everybody! I'm telling you now, though, I'm horrible with names—"

"*We* don't even know half their names," says Nico, following us to the front desk. "Anyway, I was just on my way down to the bar to meet Pai and some of the guys for drinks. You in?"

I shake my head. As much as I love my family, we'll have plenty of time for that. "Maybe later. We just got here, Nic."

"Yeah, yeah, sorry." His eyes glitter with mischief. "Sorry, Wren. I'll let you have him a little longer."

He wanders off, leaving us to check in. Our room is on the third floor, a spacious, well-appointed suite with city views. There are rooms with ocean views, as well, but when Pai asked what we'd prefer I told him we saw the ocean all the time. I wanted something different, and there's no place like Rio.

"I sound like a broken record," Wren says with a sigh, flopping back onto our enormous, white bed. "But...this is amazing."

"It is," I agree, gazing out the window at the buildings and streets. "What do you want to do first?"

"Are you sure you don't want to go see your dad? I don't mind hanging out here," she says. "Maybe I'll go down onto the beach."

I pause, considering. I'm not sure I want Wren wandering the promenade and the beach by herself.

"I think it's great that Nico seems so relaxed, by the way," she adds.

Wren knows all about Nico's complicated feelings about Pai. Things have changed a lot over the past year, though. In many ways, my leaving Veritas for good was the wake-up call our father needed. He began reaching out to us more, trying to rebuild the bridges he'd all but burned over the years, and Nico's responded well. It's been a long time coming.

"Me too. It'll feel good, being together again."

She rolls onto her side, propping herself up on her elbow. "How long has it been, you think?"

"Since we were all in the same place? My graduation."

"I think you should go meet them at the bar, Luca. What better gift for your father than to have his two boys with him?"

"When you put it like that…" I sit beside her on the bed. "Fine. I'll go. And save the beach for tomorrow—I want to go with you."

She narrows her eyes. "What would you have me do in the meantime, then?"

"How about the spa? I hear it's world-renowned."

"Really?" She perks up, nodding. "I'm gonna get a massage. And maybe a facial."

* * *

Wren was right. Being here, with Pai, Nico, and a host of uncles and cousins gives me a warm feeling in my chest. It's rowdy and affectionate, with plenty of reminiscing, toasts, and calls of *saude!*

We linger into the evening, long enough for me to get buzzed. By the time Nico pulls me aside to let me know that Phoebe and Wren are tanked in his room, it's nearly nine o'clock. I wince, looking around. Only a few of us are left.

I walk back to my father, who's still holding court at the table we've been sitting at. "It's getting late. I'm gonna head upstairs."

"Missing your pretty girl, eh?" He squeezes my shoulder, cheeks ruddy with drink. "She's a good one, Luca. Don't fuck it up."

Tio Rafael chortles, lifting his glass in approval.

"Tchau, Luca," Pai says, all drunk and affectionate. "Te amo."

"Te amo, Pai."

My brother says his goodbyes and then we're heading upstairs, both a little unsteady after all that cachaça.

"Shhh! The kids are sleeping!" Phoebe says the second we enter their suite, where she and Wren are plowing through their own bottle of cachaça and an assortment of room service goodies.

"Sorry, sorry," Nico says in a stage-whisper, smirking at me.

"Oi, my love," Wren coos as I pull her off the couch. She's flushed and more than a little handsy, caressing my cheek. "Quão bonito!"

Phoebe cracks up, smacking her thigh. "You better watch out, Luca, she's been waiting for you!"

"Now who's being loud?" Nico teases, easing his shoes off.

"I think I can handle it," I say to Phoebe, wrapping my arm around Wren's waist. I'm not exactly sober, but my girl's a bit of a lightweight. "We'll see you guys tomorrow."

"Yeah, we're going to the beach," Wren says, pointing at Phoebe. "Right?"

"Yes! Text me," Phoebe cries, holding up her phone as Nico shushes her.

Wren and I walk out into the hallway, where she sighs and leans into me. "You really are bonito, Luca."

Chuckling, I kiss her cheek and tuck her a little closer. "Not as pretty as you."

"Mm, I think we should christen that bed," she says, squeezing my ass.

My dick twitches, even as I catch her hand and put it back on my waist. "Sounds like a plan."

But by the time we reach our suite, one floor up, Wren can't stop yawning. "Man, I'm sleepy."

"Day drinking will do that to you," I say, catching her yawn.

"I really love your family, Luca," she says suddenly, wrapping her arms around me as I shut the door. "Everybody is so warm and loving and I just…love them."

Gratitude, and that warm feeling from earlier, wash over me as I hug her back. I have such a good life, filled with people I cherish. If I died right now, I'd be completely happy. "They are pretty great." I hold her tight. "And they love you, too. I'm glad you're here with me."

"Pfft, wouldn't have missed this for the world." She yawns again. "You're stuck with me, I'm afraid."

"Good. Eu quero estar com você para sempre."

She frowns, looking up at me. "You've said that to me before. What does it mean?"

"Come, take a shower with me."

Now she's pouting. "Luca…"

Laughing, I pull her toward the bathroom. She'll figure it out eventually.

Wren

⚜

Carlos and Mariana get married two days later. They have an intimate ceremony on the beach, about as intimate as you can get with fifty of your closest friends and family, and then we celebrate in the hotel, in a room filled with flowers.

The whole thing is so romantic, so achingly beautiful, that I'm on the brink of tears for most of the day.

"Would you like a glass of champagne?" asks a server, offering her tray.

I shake my head, giving her a small smile. "I'm fine, thanks though."

Smiling back, she moves on. I love champagne, but I've been going light on the alcohol. My shenanigans with Phoebe our first night in town have been a cautionary tale against too much imbibing—my hangover the next day was intense. Thankfully, Phoebe was in the same boat, so we hung out on the beach with Luca, Nico, and the kids until we felt human. No regrets, though.

Beside me, Luca's chatting with one of his cousins. His fingers are linked with mine on his lap, and every once in a while, his thumb brushes over my hand. He turns to me suddenly, standing. "You want to get out of here for a while? Go for a walk?"

I nod, grabbing my purse. "Sure."

Outside, there's a light breeze on the beach. We walk along the shore, barefoot, admiring the view. Christ the Redeemer glows in the distance, arms spread wide as if to beckon me closer. "I still can't believe I'm really here, looking at it."

"I know." Luca glances at me. "We'll go tomorrow, rain or shine. I think it's supposed to be sunny, though."

"I'm not worried. I know we'll get there." I let go of his hand so I can slide my arm through his. "Thank you for bringing me, Luca. You know how much that statue means to me."

"I'm sure Arlo would've gotten you here if I didn't," he jokes.

"Yeah, but I'm glad I came with you." I pull him to a stop. "Brazil's a part of you."

He nods, gazing down at me, the hotel lights glimmering in his eyes. "Wanting to see Christ the Redeemer was one of the first things you told me about yourself."

My heart squeezes as I remember those early days. Our night on the Sky Glider, sharing our lives, our dreams. "I love you, Luca."

"I love you too, meu anjo," he says, tucking my hair behind my ear. The waves crash nearby, a soothing, familiar sound. "Eu quero estar com você para sempre."

"Sempre means *always*. Or forever? I heard that at the wedding today." I grin, tiptoeing so I can link my hands behind Luca's neck. "And I know that quero means *I want*."

"Yeah." A smile flickers across his face. "I want to be with you forever."

Made in the USA
Monee, IL
05 February 2023

27117373R00246